IT'S JUST A DRILL

"Sergeant, really, it's worse than that." Real fear was audible in the underlying tones of Tavana's voice. "Maybe we do have atmosphere reserves, but right now I'm not even sure the environmentals are working right. Dumping our atmosphere and bringing it back? I don't think we can. And there's some alert on the medical systems..."

He hadn't even *thought* to check the medical systems; aside from the freefall and tumbling nausea, it seemed obvious everyone was physically fine. He switched channels, tapped into the internal alerts.

Holy mother of God. I've never seen a radiation pulse like that. For a moment, despite his lifelong training to never put off looking at bad news, he couldn't quite force himself to look. He hadn't been prepared for a literal lifeboat situation when he did this drill—stupid of him, but after twenty or thirty drills you did start treating them like routine.

When he checked, he finally was able to relax a bit. The dosages were high, but he had the military combat parameters for internal nano treatment of radiation damage; he could transmit that to the kids, and Pearce would already have—

He froze. Pearce...Pearce was *outside the hull.*

CASTAWAY ODYSSEY

ERIC FLINT
RYK E. SPOOR

CASTAWAY ODYSSEY

This is a work of fiction. All the characters and events portrayed in this book are fictional, and any resemblance to real people or incidents is purely coincidental.

A Baen Books Original

Baen Publishing Enterprises
P.O. Box 1403
Riverdale, NY 10471
www.baen.com

ISBN: 978-1-4814-8293-6

Cover art by Bob Eggleton

First Baen Mass Market printing, October 2017

Distributed by Simon & Schuster
1230 Avenue of the Americas
New York, NY 10020

Pages by Joy Freeman (www.pagesbyjoy.com)
Printed in the United States of America

ACKNOWLEDGMENTS

No book is written in isolation. For her continuing support despite all the demands of life in other directions, I gratefully acknowledge my wife Kathleen. And for their constant support and invaluable advice and comments, my beta-readers on rykspoor_beta.livejournal.com.

DEDICATION

This book is dedicated to the memory of two other authors.

First, to Robert A. Heinlein, whose series of "juvenile"-targeted science fiction novels was one of our greatest writing inspirations for both the Castaway series and for *Boundary* itself.

And

To Armstrong Sperry, whose *Call it Courage* remains one of the great stories of personal bravery in a strange world; despite its age, it can still capture the imagination of children and adults alike, and was directly inspirational in the writing of *Castaway Odyssey* ... and the creation of the character of Tavana Arronax.

CASTAWAY ODYSSEY

PART I

ADRIFT

Chapter 1

"Franky, get strapped in *now!*" Xander Bird said.

"You're not my mama!" the red-haired little boy snapped back in a frightened tone. "You can't tell me what to do! And I'm not Franky! I'm Francisco Alejandro Coronel!"

Xander closed his eyes for a moment, ignoring the lifeboat drill alerts, and took a deep breath, running his fingers through his slightly-too-long curly hair before opening his eyes again. "I'm sorry, Francisco. But you know the rules; your parents—and ours and Tavana's, too—were at that dinner party on the other side of the hab ring, and so they had to go to a different lifeboat. You've *got* to strap in. Your mama would want you to be a good boy, right?"

At his apologetic tone, Francisco stopped glaring, and finally nodded unwillingly and sat back into his assigned seat in *LS-88*, their lifeboat and landing shuttle for the starship *Outward Initiative*, currently bound for the colony world of Tantalus. Under Xander's watchful eye, the eight-year-old carefully pulled the multi-point restraint harness on and locked it in place. "There."

3

"Thank you, Francisco. Hopefully the drill will be over in a few minutes, unless they go to Phase II." Xander looked over to the Polynesian boy in the next seat. "You okay, Tav?"

"I'm not a baby, of course I'm okay," Tavana Arronax said. The sixteen-year-old's voice wasn't so much angry or defensive as abstracted; Xander could see that Tav's eyes had the distant look of someone viewing data in their retinal implant displays. He was reading or maybe playing a game.

"I'm strapped in and secure!" announced Maddox Bird. "Can I play Jewelbug with Tav while we wait?"

"That's up to Tav if he wants to," Xander said, "but I don't have a problem with it if you guys keep it down to a dull roar."

"Okay! Tav? Tav, you wanna—"

Tavana sighed, something which was very visible in someone that wide-bodied, but smiled. "Okay, okay. Seventh Gate Adventure, yes? We were about halfway through that one."

"Yeah!"

Good, that would keep them occupied. Xander checked on Francisco again to make sure that he didn't feel left out, but it looked like whatever book their youngest shipmate had chosen was holding his full attention for now. There was no guarantee that'd last long, but for the moment it was good enough.

Xander looked up front at the vacant navigator's station. He had to admit that made him a little nervous. The lifeboats were completely automated, with their own capable if limited AI systems that would handle even complex situations well; but still, it would be nice to have someone up front. Unfortunately, that someone was supposed to be Ariel Coronel, Francisco's mother, and she, her husband, and Tavana's parents were—

His thought broke off as another form dropped perfectly down through the hatchway and landed with practiced ease.

The man straightened to his full intimidating one hundred ninety-eight centimeters—eight centimeters taller than Xander himself—and his hard brown eyes, the color of dark, polished oak, surveyed the whole cabin in an instant.

As he was already strapped down, Xander couldn't salute, but he had an impulse to anyway. "Master Sergeant Campbell!"

"Relax, Xander, sorry to intrude. This boat's the closest to my position, so you're stuck with me for this drill." Campbell's voice was dry, mildly humorous, but his size and the smooth, pantherish stride still reminded Xander that this was a man who'd spent two decades in military service across the settled worlds. His age showed some—there was a sprinkling of gray through his black hair, his weathered, deep-brown skin showed lines of time and strain, and one scar stretching from his chin almost to his right ear but he moved like someone not much older than Xander's nineteen rather than someone in his early forties.

"Parents stuck somewhere else?" he asked, glancing at Francisco and Tavana.

"Captain's Table party," Maddox said.

Sergeant Campbell nodded. "Then if you don't mind, I'll take the hotseat."

"Please, sir. It'd be an honor."

"Leave out the 'sirs.' I'm enlisted, I *work* for a goddamn living. I wasn't ever 'sir.'"

"Yes, sir."

"Wiseass." Campbell took his place at the pilot's console and strapped in; Xander saw him touch the panel and the manual controls extruded, just as the manual required. *"Outward Initiative,"* he said, "this is Samuel Morgan Campbell, Chief Master Sergeant, Colonial Security. Put me down as present in *LS-88*, which was closest to my position when the alarm went."

"Acknowledged," replied the AI running the immense colony ship. A chime echoed through the shuttle. "Proceed to Phase II of drill."

Campbell leaned back in the seat. "All right then, people; as I'm the qualified pilot, I'm your acting captain on this tub, so we're going to do this by the numbers. Samuel Campbell present and secured. Sound off, the rest of you—in order of age, oldest first!"

"Xander Bird, present and secured," Xander said promptly, checking his harness reflexively; it was tight enough but not too tight.

There was a pause. Sergeant Campbell's eyes narrowed, and Xander sent an interrupt *ping* to the Jewelbug server. *Tav, Maddox, we're doing countoff and Sergeant Campbell's here! Your turn, Tav!*

Tav's eyes snapped wide open and he immediately half-sat up in his urgency. "T . . . Tavana Arronax, present and secured!"

"Maddox Bird, present and secured!"

Xander held his breath, but relaxed as he heard a slightly accented voice say "Francisco Alejandro Coronel, present and secured!"

"Well all right then. I'd do the assigned station check-in, but Pilot Station—mine—is the only one currently manned, and everything's green across the board. The rest of you can just relax; this'll be over once they've done the random inspections and all the boats have checked in."

"We know that, Sergeant," Maddox said. "We've been through a lot of these before."

A chuckle from up front. "I suppose you have, at that."

"Inspection!" sang out a voice from the hatchway. A small woman in full protective suit gear, helmet back to reveal her short-cut, brilliant-red hair and green eyes in a slightly-freckled, tanned face, dropped into the shuttle.

Random inspections my butt, Maddox sent him over their private omni link. *That's the sergeant's girlfriend!*

That was an exaggeration, Xander thought. So far as he'd been able to determine, the relationship between Pearce Haley and Sam Campbell was a professional one. She was an officer in the regular military of the United Nations and Campbell was a noncom in Colonial Security—technically speaking, a private security contractor working for the Colonial Initiative Corporation, a semi-public/semi-private company somewhat akin to a public utility. But there wasn't much doubt in his mind that the two people were very attracted to each other.

"Why, hello, Lieutenant Haley," said Sergeant Campbell with a quick grin. "Fancy seeing you here."

"Just checking in." She quickly examined each person's harness, made Tav's tighten a slight bit more, and then smiled at the sergeant before turning away. "Lieutenant Pearce Haley reporting," she said into the microphone in her suit. Her English accent was perhaps a bit more pronounced than it normally was when she was speaking informally. "*LS-88*, all secure."

She started up the ladder, glanced back. "See you after the drill, Sam?"

"Look forward to it, PG," Campbell answered.

Just as Lieutenant Haley disappeared through the hatch, alarm klaxons ripped the air; the sound of the hatchway closing was as abrupt and fatal-sounding as a guillotine. At the same time, the forward display suddenly switched to a view of the velvet-black of Trapdoor space with the exterior-lit *Outward Initiative* and its hab ring.

There was a chunk missing from the ring; even as they watched, another piece...*faded*, and then was gone, leaving a ragged gap.

"Trapdoor Field instability," *Outward Initiative* reported calmly.

"*Merde!*" Tavana said in a panicked voice that echoed Xander's own shock and disbelief. "Instability? How? Who's messing with the Field? That should—"

Poison-green light flared from the screen; there was a ripping crash and Xander heard himself yelling incoherently as *LS-88* spun crazily, tumbling as it plummeted into the infinite darkness of space. Lights flickered, went out, came back on.

The spinning and whirling continued, on and on, and Xander felt himself starting to get ill. "Medical options, *on*," he said quickly. The omni display appeared, asking him for instructions. "Motion sickness, counter. Activate for Maddox, too." He didn't know what to do for Tav and Francisco; he had no authority for their omnis, let alone their medical nanos.

Sergeant Campbell showed he was already thinking ahead on that. "Francisco, Tavana, give me omni access to you both *now*."

Neither of the two argued with Campbell—not that almost anyone would. Once the anti-vertigo started to work, Xander felt some better—though he was still shaky, shocked, and honestly terrified. *But at least I'm not going to puke in a free-falling, spinning shuttle.* "S . . . Sergeant? What—"

"Don't know yet. All of you stay quiet for a minute." He did something at his board, but nothing seemed to change.

Lighting's . . . off, too. Thought I saw a flicker.

"Attitude jets won't fire," the sergeant said after a minute. "Automated systems completely out, but that shouldn't be stopping the manuals. Telltales claim they're still locked down."

"Manual lockdown, Sergeant?" Tavana asked hesitantly.

"Looks like it. Almost as though we were still docked."

Tavana nodded. "Maybe . . . maybe when we . . . broke free, sir, some pieces of the dock got stuck, so they're still registering."

"Maybe." Sergeant Campbell shook his head. "I don't like the rest of what I'm seeing here. No AI response. Integrated controls out; can't access the other cameras yet, just getting the forward view. Hard to get an overall picture. Xander, you finished the freefall maneuvering course, right?"

"Yes, Sergeant."

"All right." He hesitated, then sighed. "Unstrap *carefully* and go check the hatch. See if you can see anything out there that looks like it's still stuck to us. Take your time and *do not* make the mistake of thinking this is ordinary freefall. This thing's spinning like a tumbling pigeon in a hurricane, and you'll get all sorts of tugs and pulls on you as you move through the cabin. Last thing we need is someone slipping and bouncing through the cabin."

"Yes, Sergeant." Xander first unlocked the cable at the waist of his suit and hooked it to the eyelet on his chair; he saw the sergeant's approving nod. Then Xander carefully unsnapped his harness.

As soon as he started to rise, cautiously, he could feel what the sergeant meant; moving shifted the forces on him. As Xander began to slowly, cautiously make his way through the cabin of *LS-88*, he had to take exquisite pains to keep from being shoved or pulled from the chairs and handholds. In the chaotic whirl of the tumbling lifeboat, the journey from his assigned seat to the ladder of the hatch was like climbing a tree in a storm; he had to stop, remove his anchor cable from one point and attach it to another, and then move forward a meter or so before repeating the maneuver.

Finally he was at the ladder, so he hooked to the highest rung and then climbed up carefully to the point that he could get his head up to look through the hatch window.

To find himself looking across the tiny sealed airlock straight into the frightened, wide green eyes of Lieutenant Pearce Greene Haley.

Chapter 2

"Sergeant!" came a half-panicked call from above, and Samuel Campbell turned from the mostly-unresponsive board.

"You see something, Xander?"

"It's . . . It's Pearce Haley, Sergeant!"

"*What?*" Of all the answers he'd expected, that hadn't been one. Given the timing, a part of him had thought that Pearce might have been killed at the interface, but the idea that she was just outside . . . "Is she alive? Her suit intact?"

"Yes, sir."

Alive? And outside? "What the hell's she standing on?"

"Looks like the whole entrance tube," Xander replied, his voice still incredulous. "The far end's open though, so she's definitely in vacuum."

Samuel switched to the private channel. "Pearce? Pearce, you copy me?"

There was no response. "Tavana, you're a comm whiz, aren't you?"

The French Polynesian boy straightened a bit in

11

his seat. "I'm pretty good at them, yes, Mister...
Sergeant Campbell."

"I can't get through to Pearce on my own comm.
Are all comms out?"

"Permission to unstrap so I can see the board,
Sergeant?"

"Permission granted. Just make damn sure you hook
on securely with every step."

He watched the broad form of Tavana Arronax
make his careful way across the cabin, and nodded
approval. The kid might be mostly an egghead, but
he knew when to be careful and follow instructions.
Campbell had had lots of worse recruits. As Tavana got
close, the sergeant locked himself to the console and
unstrapped from the seat. "I'll move back one seat, let
you get a look. Actually, while you do that—Xander,
you come back down and strap back in. I'm going up."

By the time he managed to get up the ladder,
he heard Tavana grunt. "Yeah...sorry, Sergeant, all
comms except the interior relays and personal nano-
based and omni networks are out. And I've got a lot
of other bad news coming up."

"Wonderful." He lifted himself the last half-meter
and looked into green eyes that immediately looked
slightly less worried. *She's not looking sick; that's
good. Must've thought of activating her nanos right
away. Good soldier.* He gave her a smile and a wink,
and mouthed "We're working on it" through the glass.

"She's only a couple meters or so away from me;
why can't I hear her personal net?"

"I don't..." Tavana paused, forehead wrinkled in
obvious thought. "Windows and the airlock include
a lot of shielding. No transmissions directly through

them. They're supposed to be relayed through the antenna layers cross-connected with the interior. But with even the backup software down, there's nothing to tune the antennas to our personal frequencies, which you really need to do with the low power our personal nanos and most omnis can generate."

"Got it. So . . . can you tell me the natural frequencies for these antennas?"

"What?" Tavana's face suddenly lit up. "Oh, of course. We can adjust our own transmit frequencies. Let me see, I think that's in my internal manuals . . . yeah! It's a three-layer antenna design . . . two of the main resonant frequencies are too low for us to reach, but you should be able to get through the airlock with a transmission on four point two gigahertz."

Samuel checked his omni controls. "Yeah, I can transmit on that band. Hold on." He triggered his omni's external display and had it display "4.2 GHz," then pressed his wrist up to the window.

Pearce grinned broadly and nodded. A moment later, he heard a warm contralto voice: "Sam, can you hear me?"

"Loud and clear, PG," he said, feeling cool relief spreading through his chest at that simple exchange. "You okay?"

"Well . . . for now. The airlock won't open from the outside. Can you exhaust it? Once pressures equalize it should open."

"Tavana?"

"Sorry, Sergeant. That's part of the bad news. If you hadn't deployed the physical controls we'd have nothing at all, but whatever happened . . . I'm not sure I understand all of what I'm reading, but it's taken all the AIs offline, most of the instrumentation, the drive systems are reading yellow at best and none of that will work unless we can get the external locks to release . . . I think we'll have to just wait until *Outward Initiative* gets back—"

The boy's words made Samuel wince. The kid had trusted his technology all his life and never been in a situation where it had failed like this.

He took a breath, let it out, and then shook his head. "Sorry, but we can't plan that way. What if that instability didn't end when we dropped off? We saw at least two other bites taken out of the ring. If *Outward Initiative* isn't completely wrecked already, they'll be diverting to the nearest colony."

Francisco's head snapped up. "No! My mama wouldn't leave without me!" The panicked exclamation was actually spoken in Spanish, but that was one of several languages Samuel's omni would automatically translate.

Blast it. Tavana reset everyone's comms. I hadn't wanted to get into this *conversation yet.* "Xander, I hate to drop this on you, but try to explain to Francisco why his momma's not going to override the captain and the regulations. And that it doesn't mean his family wants to desert him."

He tried to tune out the tearful discussion that followed—one that got Maddox crying also—and focus on the problem at hand. "Do we have atmosphere reserves? If we could all button up suits and blow our own atmosphere—"

"Sergeant, really, it's worse than that." Real fear was audible in the underlying tones of Tavana's voice. "Maybe we do have atmosphere reserves, but right now I'm not even sure the environmentals are working right. Dumping our atmosphere and bringing it back? I don't think we can. And there's some alert on the medical systems..."

He hadn't even *thought* to check the medical systems; aside from the freefall and tumbling nausea, it seemed obvious everyone was physically fine. He switched channels, tapped into the internal alerts.

Holy mother of God. I've never seen a radiation pulse like that. For a moment, despite his lifelong training to never put off looking at bad news, he couldn't quite force himself to look. He hadn't been prepared for a literal lifeboat situation when he did this drill—stupid of him, but after twenty or thirty drills you did start treating them like routine.

When he checked, he finally was able to relax a bit. The dosages were high, but he had the military combat parameters for internal nano treatment of radiation damage; he could transmit that to the kids, and Pearce would already have—

He froze. *Pearce... Pearce was* outside *the hull.* He turned his head back to look at her questioning face.

This time he set it to private communication and spoke quietly enough that no one else could hear him—not that anyone was likely to, with Francisco crying and the others talking. "PG... Lieutenant, can you check your medicals, especially—"

Her smile faded. "Already did, Sam." Her voice was apologetic, as it always was when giving someone bad news.

"The tube—"

"—probably shielded me some, but... the burst seemed to happen along the interface, and that meant it had a straight line on me from the end that got cut. Sorry, Sam . . . Sergeant Campbell, I'm walking dead. I'd just hoped . . ."

. . . hoped to be able to die comfortably inside, not in a vacuum suit in the middle of space. "Yeah, I know. Is it really that bad? Internal nanos—"

"—got partly fried themselves, Sam," she said quietly. "If my omni wasn't a top-flight military model, it'd be dead too. Even if they hadn't gotten toasted . . . I had some surgical tech training, I know what I'm looking at. I've got a little while before it hits, but only a really, *really* heavy infusion of top-flight medical nanos—within a few hours—would give me a chance."

His mind cast about, desperately trying to figure some angle, a way to keep this from happening. He'd lost soldiers before—after over twenty years in the business, you couldn't help it—but he'd never failed to save someone who hadn't been killed outright. "I don't know the whole cargo of this boat, there might even—"

"*Sam!*" Her tone was sharp, and her green gaze caught his with anger and sympathy. Then she smiled and shook her head. "I heard that boy's report. You can't even stabilize *LS-88* right now. It will be many, many hours before you could get to the cargo, if there's anything there for me at all. You can't help me, Sam. I'm sorry. But maybe I can help you."

He swallowed, feeling the rough, acid tightness that came from suppressing tears. "Help *us*?"

"This piece of junk I'm standing in is what's keeping your remaining systems from running, if I understand what Tavana's saying correctly. Well, there's a manual disengage mechanism out here, meant for being able to launch a lifeboat in the event of power failure."

Samuel closed his eyes, then sighed and nodded. "That should do it. It would sever the connections and let the manual interlocks register that the lifeboat was free, so we could work the attitude jets and drives, at least."

"Then I've got a job to do, Sergeant."

"Wait!" He took another breath, thinking. "Look... you're right. But... give me access to your nanos and omni?"

"I... guess? All right, Sergeant."

He linked up and surveyed the display. *Yeah, as bad as she says. Maybe four, five hours before she starts really feeling it. But there's enough nanos still up for something else...*

He checked his own systems, assembled the code he'd used a few times before on badly-injured comrades. "Here. Program this in. Once you... once you cut us loose, make sure you're locked well down and then start this program running."

"I don't read nano code; what's that for?"

"Either a comfortable way to die, or a real, *real* longshot at living. It's called field suspension—suspended animation using your nanos and your suit environmentals. You never got deployed to active combat duty or you'd probably already have it; me, I've had it, and watched it get upgraded, for more'n twenty years. This'll give you weeks, maybe a couple months, before the damage can't be fixed... and..." he heard his voice almost break, got it under control, "... and it'll put you to sleep once you activate it. So if you don't get rescued..."

She smiled wanly. "... at least I don't die puking my guts out inside my suit. Thanks, Sam."

"If there's any chance... we'll come back for you."

"I know you will." She stiffened her spine, held by her boots so she could stand ramrod-straight, and saluted. "Sergeant Campbell."

He saluted as best he could. "Lieutenant Haley. Do what you have to. Give me a few minutes to get to the controls; this bird's going to shift a lot when you blow the tube."

"Yes, Sergeant. And . . . goodbye and good luck, Sam. Take care of those boys."

"I will, PG. I promise."

Samuel turned and immediately, methodically, began making his way back down the ladder, shoving all the grief and anger away. "Tavana, move back. I gotta get to the controls."

Tavana nodded. "Okay, Sergeant. But nothing's working."

"It will be in a minute. Lieutenant Haley's going to use the manual launch controls to disengage from *LS-88*. That should at least give us back attitude jets, and maybe other systems will come online once the mechanical linkages confirm complete isolation."

"That's good," Tavana said, a little relief in his voice.

Xander Bird, however, had already recognized the flaw in the plan. "But sir—Sergeant—if she does that, she'll—"

"—be flying away with the boarding tube, and we might have a long, long time before we can catch her, yes. But my responsibility—and hers—is to keep you, the passengers, safe."

Xander looked horrified. *Too much imagination, that boy; he can figure out what drifting through space alone in a spacesuit would be like.* "But Sergeant—"

"She *has* to do this, Xander. We'll save her if we

can, but she reminded *me* what my job is, and that's to keep you four alive. Now be quiet and let me do that job . . . and let her do hers."

Xander bit his lip but said nothing more.

"Lieutenant, I'm at the controls. You may proceed when ready."

"Roger that, Sergeant. I am now unlocking the manual controls." A pause. "I have grasped the release wheel. Beginning to turn. Please be braced."

"Everyone—*Francisco*, I mean you!—sit straight. Make sure your harnesses are on correctly. This could be rough."

A few minutes went by, silently, with the faintest sound of exertion being transmitted from Lieutenant Haley's suit.

"Manual clamps disengaged; go for CAD actuation?"

CAD; short for *Cartridge Actuated Device*, and a military euphemism for "controlled explosion." For this, that meant detonating explosive bolts that finalized the separation. "Lieutenant, we are all prepared. We are go for CAD actuation."

Almost instantly, a sharp, loud *BANG!* echoed through the cabin of *LS-88*, and the tumbling of the forward view twitched, shifted, now slower and along a different line. Across one edge of the view he could see, for a moment each revolution, a metal tube, trailing ragged lines of severed pipes and wires, spinning with slow deliberation away into space.

"Separation achieved. Good job, Lieutenant."

"Thank you, Sergeant. Activating suspension protocol." There was already heavy reduction in signal from Pearce Haley; it would not take long for them to be out of range entirely.

"Good luck and godspeed, PG," he said.

"You too, Sam. And..."

The signal faded to nothing, and he closed his eyes. *Later,* he told himself, but for a few seconds it was all he could do to *not* cry, to *not* break down, and a part of him realized with surprise just how very much he had cared about Pearce Greene Haley.

But then he shook himself, put his hands on the board, and—not without a prayer—touched the controls.

The attitude jets rumbled to life.

Chapter 3

Tavana stared at the screen, where Lieutenant Haley and the severed boarding tube from *Outward Initiative* were dwindling out of sight, and felt cold horror spreading through him. He'd seen the readouts, known how bad *LS-88* was damaged, but this—a living person, now cast away into the endless void so that they could get *some* systems back online—hammered home the terrible situation in a way that no words could have.

He found himself shaking and gripped the arms of the seat so hard he saw his knuckles whitening. He was barely aware of the fact that the tumbling of the shuttle was slowing, then stopped, and the distant, somersaulting tube was steady in the middle of the screen.

There was the sound of a harness unsnapping. Sergeant Campbell rose slowly, and then brought his hand up in salute, gaze focused resolutely on the receding wreckage, far enough now that it was almost impossible to make out the figure of Lieutenant Haley.

Tavana heard another harness release, and Xander was rising, taking the same stance. Tavana followed suit; he knew this wouldn't change anything, but somehow the gesture, the effort *meant* something. As he stood there, rigid, his boots keeping him firmly attached to the deck, he saw Maddox and finally even little Francisco do the same, sniffling and clearly not really sure of what the gesture meant, but that it was something important.

They stood immobile together for long moments, until the tube had become a near-dot and there was no way, in the feeble starlight, to see any details. Then Sergeant Campbell slowly lowered his arm and turned.

Tavana saw surprise and a moment's gratification on the usually controlled face . . . and also saw water sparkling in the sergeant's too-full eyes.

"Thank you, all. Now we have to make sure her courage doesn't get wasted, understand?"

Tavana swallowed hard. "Yessir." The others echoed the agreement. He tried to shove the thought of the lieutenant out of his head. It wasn't easy. "Sir . . . if we get things running . . . will we be able to find her?"

Campbell nodded. "We know exactly at what speed, and on what vector, her piece of wreckage separated from us. In space, that'll stay constant. Plus here in interstellar space? She's going to be the only thing within millions of miles bigger than my thumb, and even on the absolute lowest power setting she'll still be radiating heat we can spot. So if we can get things running, we'll find her." He made it sound like an order. "We good now?"

He nodded, feeling a tiny bit better. "Yes, sir!"

"Right, then. Tavana, get back here and talk to me. I need to know what our condition is."

Without the shuttle tumbling it was easy to switch seats. He slid into the pilot's seat and locked in, noticing how much the straps had to pull up to secure him. *Sergeant's a big man.*

There were some more green lights, and some of the reds had turned amber, but still . . . *merde.* "Do you want the good news or the bad news first, sir?"

"Stop calling me . . . ahhh, never mind." The sergeant shook his head and grinned, something Tavana found astounding given the situation. "Give me the bad first, son; I like to know how deep it is before I take an inventory of the shovels I have."

"All right, sir." *Que Dieu nous aide,* he thought. There was so *much* bad news he might have to summarize, because doing it in detail would take a long time. "Well . . . the worst news is that right now we're running on stored power. The reactor's dead. Even if we had power, the Trapdoor Drive is completely down. I'm going to have to do more diagnostics before I know what's really wrong. Nebula Drive basics show green, but dispensers won't respond and I'm getting yellow status from the smart dust for the dusty-plasma; why, I'll need more time to do diagnostics. In fact, whenever I say I don't know the details, just repeat that. Um . . . environmentals are borderline; I *think* what I'll need to do is figure out something to kick the air exchangers into activity every so often, because usually it's controlled by the onboard AIs."

"AIs still down?"

"All of them that were in the main ship and operating, anyway—which means all of the *LS-88's* system AIs. My guess is that the Trapdoor Pulse disrupted the systems. Worse, it took out the advanced interlocks— not AI systems but using some of the same core technology—between the automated and the manual systems. Without those, a lot of systems won't work at all until we figure out how to force the switchover to manual. Sensors . . . I think most of the cameras and other sensors got fried by the pulse. Certainly the ones on the belly and sides. Communications are totally down; even the emergency distress beacon's dead, which isn't even supposed to be *possible* if the beacon wasn't just crushed or something." He paused; the litany of things gone wrong was even worse when he listed it out loud. *I haven't seen a sign of a sun anywhere on the screen, and if we're between stars with no Trapdoor Drive . . .*

"Good news?"

"Ummm . . . well, the front camera's still working, and that one's actually got a lot of sensing and control capability, so we're not totally blind. The reactor . . . I'm not seeing anything that says the reactor's *damaged*, and controlling its operation doesn't require an AI—or at least not one any more capable than that of a standard omni, and we're all wearing one of those, so I *think* we'll be okay there if we can just switch control and safety over. Storage coils were fully charged, so we've got . . . um, weeks, at least, before power runs out."

The sergeant scratched his head. "What's the reactor for this thing?"

"This model's got a Toshiba-IEM FP-300M," Tavana answered, the data sheet shimmering in his internal display.

"Really? Well now, I helped maintain a 300M back some years on Piper Colony. You tell me what needs doing, I think some of that might come back."

"Dieu merci!" The relief was astounding. "I've never actually—"

"Not a surprise, son. You're still studying. No one's going to want you playing with neutrons this early in your career, no matter how good your medical nanos are. Still, you've got most of your propulsion degree, right?"

"Er...yes, sir. Most of it. I think I can figure this out, especially with some help."

"No rush, we got time. What's our cargo like? I'm especially interested in food, water, medical supplies, things like that."

"I *think* I can get the manifest—"

"Got it!" Maddox Bird said, his voice still a little thick from crying, but now wearing a smile. At Tavana's startled glance, Maddox said, "I was already looking for it before the sergeant asked."

"Well, don't keep us in suspense, then," Sergeant Campbell said. "What's our cargo?"

"There's the standard emergency rations for a lifeboat..." Maddox was squinting at the invisible listing in his retinal display, even though squinting wouldn't help. "Um...oh, there's a bunch more in the cargo! Two pallets. Water...don't see anything, sorry. But...there are emergency medical kits, quantity...two hundred."

Tavana noticed the sergeant stiffen a bit. "Those kits, they have medical nano injections as part of the standard supply?"

"Yessir. They're military issue, too—new as of our departure."

Campbell murmured something Tavana couldn't catch, but it sounded hopeful. "Good news. What else? Together that stuff wouldn't take up much space."

"Well...looks like power equipment, digging, construction type stuff. Plus some finished materials that're hard to produce on new colonies, a bunch of other things, but nothing I think's helpful right now."

"We'll go over that list in detail later, though." The sergeant nodded. "Tavana, I think the first order of business is to figure out the environmentals. Don't matter how much equipment or food or medical supplies we got if the air goes bad. Can you handle that?"

Tavana looked at the board. The readings were suddenly intimidating. He knew what his answer would be if this were just some test, but this was *real*. If he screwed up *this* answer . . .

"Tavana?"

With a start, the French-Polynesian realized he'd been just staring at the lights and indicators for a minute without moving. "S . . . sorry." He shook himself. "I . . . sir, I've never actually *done* this kind of work . . ."

"I know. But we're kinda short on professionals, so you, me, Xander, and maybe Maddox for a couple things is pretty much all we got. Francisco's a good kid, but he's not quite ready for the job. Can you do it?"

"I . . . I'll try."

"All any of us can do, as long as it's our *best* try. Now get to it. Francisco, why don't you come with me and we'll see what's in the rations we can reach?"

Francisco nodded reluctantly and followed Sergeant Campbell.

I'm not sure how much Francisco *understands of what's going on yet, but he's already figured out that he's not seeing his parents for a long time.*

Neither am I. Or any of us. The truth tried to sink in, and Tavana gritted his teeth, shoved it aside. *I can't afford panic now.*

Mouth dry, Tavana turned to the board and adjusted

the controls to accept direct I/O from his omni. *My brain's already trying to tell me the air's getting stale. Stupid! The cabin's big enough for more than twice this number of people, and the environmentals aren't actually completely down.*

At the same time, they *were* down. While the main system showed that it was operational, there was no indication that the recycling system had done anything since the disaster, and it really should have.

Okay. Think of it like a test. "Given this situation, consider what element or elements of the system could fail to produce this situation. Remember to apply Occam's Razor."

That meant to choose the simplest explanation first. Okay, simplest explanation was a power failure. That wasn't the case here, though; board showed that the environmentals were getting power from the storage coils, and connectivity was good. So that wasn't it. Next...the relay? But those relays were pretty much foolproof, and showed green anyway. As long as they weren't physically damaged, they should activate whenever the sensors—

The sensors. That made sense. The air-quality sensor suite was actually a distributed network of sensors all interconnected for comparison in a way that *could* have received enough energy from the pulse to be damaged.

Tavana got up and carefully moved to the rear of the cabin; his retinal display highlighted the service panel he was looking for. "Sergeant Campbell, can you authorize me to open service panels?"

"Done."

The panel popped open, showing several of the

control relays, including the environmental control relay. *If I can force it to trigger...*

Examining the panel's design showed him that there were, as he hoped, subtle but definite holes meant for test points during manufacture and installation. *Which I don't have the probes for. But...*

He called up data on test procedures from his omni—given that this was one of the vehicles he'd expected to be maintaining on Tantalus Colony, he had the complete maintenance handbook. It didn't take long to get data on the test probes.

Tavana felt a cautious trickle of optimism. The test points had been designed for relatively crude methods of interface, since they might be maintained in far less than optimal conditions. He had a pocket TestTool— similar to the typical pocket Shapetool, except designed for electrical testing and engineering work, so it had several elements of different composition to work with. He *thought* the TestTool might barely be able to make test probes small enough to fit the holes.

After a few minutes, though, he was tempted to curse in Tahitian, something he didn't do unless he was *really* mad. Instead, he settled for *"Merde!"* again.

"Problem?" Xander asked from nearby.

Tavana grimaced. "This TestTool *me fait chier*, as my mother would say. I need probes half a millimeter wide and it stops at one millimeter."

Xander pulled out his own TestTool and checked. "Sorry, mine's not even as good as yours; then again, we structural engineers don't need your fancy gadgets."

"But then *how* am I going to get to these circuits?"

"Hold on, don't get all frustrated again. Let's ask Maddox."

"*Maddox*? He's mechanical all the way. And," he lowered his voice, "still a kid."

"Don't sell my brother short, Tav. Hey, Maddox! Tav's TestTool's not testing."

Maddox bounced up—and immediately bounced into the ceiling with a grunted *oof!*

With scarcely a pause in his examination of the rations stored in the *LS-88*'s cabin, Sergeant Campbell snagged Maddox and dragged him back down until the boy's boots touched the deck.

"*Watch* yourselves!" he snapped. "You do that kind of damn fool trick too often, someone's going to get killed. And I'm not joking, Maddox; that little stunt you pulled, I've seen rookies in training do it and hit a little harder and break their goddamn necks! You understand me? Zero-g maneuvers are no joke, and if you don't take them seriously I'm going to lock you in your seat for as long as it takes us to get to a planet! You understand?"

"Yessir! Sorry, sir! I won't do it again, Sergeant!"

"All right, then. Carry on."

Maddox made the remainder of the little trek without incident. "What's wrong with your TestTool?"

"I don't know if anything's *wrong* with it, I just may have hit its limits, that's all."

Xander explained the problem to Maddox, who nodded and asked if he could access the TestTool; Tavana allowed it, and didn't let any of his doubts show in his voice. No point in making Maddox feel bad.

After a few minutes, Maddox grinned and then handed him the TestTool; two glittering probes were visible, seeming barely wider than hairs in the cabin light.

Tavana couldn't conceal his surprise. "Are you

serious? No, wait, hold that thought. Let me see if this works."

According to the manual, if he put a pulse of 3VDC through *those* test points, it should...

There was no sound—the relay wasn't a physical switch—but he could immediately detect a shift in the flow of current. More importantly, an instant later a gentle breeze began flowing through the cabin—a breeze noticeably cooler and fresher than the now-obviously-stale cabin air. "*Yes!*"

"Good work. Breathing easier means we *can* breathe easier. Can you automate that, or does someone have to kick it every so often?"

"Um...When I don't need it, I can leave the Test-Tool to do that every couple hours, sure."

"Good. Do that whenever you're not using the thing, then."

Tavana turned back to Maddox, who was still grinning. "Okay, I admit it, I didn't think your brother had a clue when he called you over. How'd you do that?"

"I love tools. I have a collection of TestTools, Shapetools, and a lot of old-fashioned regular tools..." His face fell. "Well, I *had* a collection. They were on *Outward Initiative*. Anyway, I'm not into software or use design in most things but I really dug into the controls for the tools. Link up and I'll show you."

Tavana connected his omni with Maddox's and suddenly saw the interface for the TestTool—with layers visible he hadn't known were there. "What—"

"Yeah, see that? What you ran into is over here— see that?"

"It's a *handholding* limit," Tavana said slowly, hearing the disgust in his own voice.

"Well . . . it's a limit to keep the user from damaging the tool, yeah. Below a millimeter thickness it gets real easy to do damage to the controlled conductive alloy that's hard to repair, so it normally doesn't let any component go below that thickness. But here's the override; you can pretty much tweak *anything* in here."

Tavana grinned as he realized how much he *hadn't* known about his own TestTool . . . and how much more he could now do with it, precisely when he was going to need it more than ever. "*C'est genial!* Awesome! Thank you very much, Maddox!" He nodded to Xander. "And you—for insisting we call him over. I would've started trying to rip things apart for tiny wires next."

"Word of caution," came Sergeant Campbell's dry voice. "No ripping *anything* apart without my permission. No matter how much you think it might be necessary."

"Sorry, sir."

"No problem. And now that we've got our air for sure, me and Francisco have our next problem covered." He gave an exaggerated bow and indicated a small stack of ration packs. "Dinner is served."

Chapter 4

"What next, Sergeant?" Xander asked as they put the wrappers from the ration packs into the disposal.

"Yeah, that's the question, isn't it?" Sergeant Campbell glanced around the shuttle's cabin. "What do *you* think?"

"I think you're probably better qualified to answer."

"Damned right I am, but in this situation we all need to *learn* to be qualified. We're in an emergency like none of us ever expected to deal with, and something could happen to me any time, or to any of you. So I ask you, what do *you* think is next?"

Xander understood now. *He doesn't want us just letting him boss us around; he wants us doing the thinking with him.* "I think there are at least two things we could work on right now. Technically... even if all the other systems were working, the vital ones—the drives—need reliable power. That means the first thing we have to do there is get the reactor back online."

Samuel Campbell nodded slowly. "Sounds reasonable to me. What's the other thing?"

"Find out where we are—if there's an inhabited

star anywhere near us. If we *get* the drives working, we'll need somewhere to go."

"Spot-on, son."

The approval in the older man's voice warmed Xander, and he saw Maddox grin. "But . . . where's access to the reactor?"

Tavana gestured to the back. "Through the main cargo hold and down. So first we have to get the cargo hold door unlocked."

"We can do that together," Maddox said confidently. "Right, Sergeant?"

"Sounds good to me," the sergeant said.

"Which is good," Xander said slowly, "because I think you're probably the only one of us who might be able to tell us where we are. You're not just a pilot, you're trained as a navigator, right?"

"Spot-on. I've done a lot of things in my time, but yes indeed, flying things both fast and slow, that's what I do best. I've got the star maps stored in my omni; I think I can get us at least a reasonable guess, since I know where we *should* have been when we were dumped off."

"Okay, then, Sergeant, I say you work on finding our position, Maddox and Tavana work on getting the cargo door open, and me and Frank—Francisco—will check out the other systems that I can access and see if we can get some more details on what *LS-88* has for us."

"As the old-timers sometimes say, make it so," the sergeant said, and moved over to the pilot's seat.

Francisco came to join Xander. The startlingly red-headed, dark-skinned Mexican boy looked up at him with a worried expression. "You're just pretending I can help," he said bluntly.

Xander remembered similar situations with Maddox and how he'd handled them—or not. *Try to learn from the right and wrong I did with him.* He grinned down at Francisco. "Well, not *pretending*, no. I know what you're good at is more the artistic stuff. But like the sergeant says, we've all got to learn, and I know you can learn whatever you need to. So we're going to check out all the systems that *I* know anything about while they do the top priority work."

"Do...do you think we'll ever get home?"

The little boy's tone sounded even more lonely and scared in the original Spanish, which Xander could hear under the running translation from his omni. He reached out and hugged the boy to him. "I won't lie and say I know we will. But I know we'll do our best, and Sergeant Campbell's best is damn scary good."

Francisco managed a giggle. "He's a scary man."

"But a good one. Look, Francisco, I'm almost as much a fish out of water as you are here. I'm a mechanical engineer, and honestly, if we had major mechanical problems on *LS-88*, we'd be screwed. So we're *both* just doing some makework right now while the others get stuff done. But that's better than doing nothing."

"Okay."

He moved over near the pilot's console, which with its deployed manual controls and displays was the only one with useful data. Careful not to get in the sergeant's way, he studied the indicators he could. "Okay, let's go look at the airlock," he said to Francisco. "If anyone has to go in or out, we'll need that working."

"Sounds good to me," the sergeant said. "Be warned, everyone; I'm going to tumble this bird—slowly—a few times over the next hour or so. I'll warn you with each burn, of course. I'm doing this to get a good look at the stars in all directions."

"Understood, Sergeant. C'mon, Francisco."

The little boy made his way over to the airlock panel. "How's it supposed to work?"

Xander made sure they were both clipped on. "Pretty simple, really. The thing that keeps that door closed tight is the pressure inside here compared to the pressure outside. If we could flood that room—the airlock—with air of the same pressure, we could open this door, and go into the airlock. With the door closed, you pump the air out again. Then you can open the second door and be outside in space."

"Hold on," came the sergeant's voice. "Rotation burn in three, two, one . . . now!"

The two of them gripped and held, but the rotation was very slow; with their anti-vertigo settings still active in their nanos, it didn't bother anyone.

"Air pressure?" Francisco said, puzzled. "The air doesn't push on me when it's still."

"Actually, it does, so evenly across every square centimeter of your body that you don't feel it; your body's pushing out with exactly the same force—about a hundred kilopascals, roughly, or a little less here—so your body doesn't squish in or out. But on the other side of that door, there's basically *nothing*, so there's literally *tons* of pressure holding that door shut. You could get a crowbar and have all of us try to pry that door open and all we'd do is bend the crowbar. But equalize the pressure and it'd open just as easy as anything."

"So why wouldn't it work before?"

"The radiation pulse disrupted the circuits that control most of our systems. Plus the tube being connected made some of the sensors think we were still docked, which cut in other safety interlocks."

"So the only way to open the airlock is if the circuits are working?"

"Well, no, there's a set of manual controls." He indicated a couple of buttons and a wheel set into the wall. They both held on as the sergeant tumbled *LS-88* again. He pushed the green—which was the "flood" control actuator—but it felt flat and inactive. "But they're not active and I don't know why, at least not yet."

The little boy floated up and looked into the airlock. "That's a small room."

"Smaller the better for getting in and out. You can't recover a hundred percent of the air you put in, so you're always losing some, so the smaller the room, the less you lose."

Xander studied the controls, wishing he had been an electrical engineer instead. "Hey, Tavana, how're you guys coming?"

"This door is not as easy to trick as the air circulation," Tavana answered. "Everyone has reason to want to keep the environmentals running, but not everyone is supposed to go to the cargo."

"I got a kinda stupid idea here and I wanted to run it by you."

"Okay, let me hear it while I think about how to get the cargo door open."

"Electronic controls are the default even for the airlock, right?"

"*Oui.* We have manual backups, but the electronics and photonics run everything normally."

"Well, we never really lost power, even though the reactor went down, and the sensing and analysis circuits got kinda fried, right, which is why I can't just toggle the manual on and off?"

"Right. What are you asking?"

"I guess . . . look, is there a way I could cut the power to the airlock? Make it think the whole ship lost power? Maybe that would trigger the interlocks and let me use the manual controls?"

Tavana paused for a minute, during which Sergeant Campbell sent *LS-88* on another leisurely spin. Then Xander heard a chuckle. "The brute force approach, eh? It might work. Hey, Maddox, see if you can get my TechTool to extrude the control contacts for these parts here while I look at the circuits to the airlock?"

"Sure!"

A few minutes later, Xander saw areas of the wall highlighted in red in his omni display. "See that, Xander?"

"Yeah!"

"See if you can get any of those three panels unlocked and open."

Xander sent Francisco to work on the closest indicated area while he moved to the other two. In a minute, Francisco gave a triumphant yell as he got the recessed panel to slide open.

"Good work, Franky!" Xander said.

Francisco was so proud of his success that he didn't object to the use of the nickname. "So what do we do in here?" Xander asked.

"See those cables? I'm highlighting one. If you pull that cable out of its connectors, you should cut power to the airlock controls. If your idea works, it'll unlock the manuals. It's a SSJ standard connector."

"SSJ?"

Tavana audibly restrained a sigh. "Secure Super-conducting Junction connector. Like old-style BNC, it's a push and twist to unlock."

"Got it." Xander looked at Francisco. "Wanna be the one to try?"

"Can I?"

"Just be careful. Grab that part, push it toward the other part as hard as you can, and then turn it towards you like unscrewing a jar top."

Francisco reached in and managed, with difficulty, to grasp the connector. His fingers weren't quite strong enough to manipulate the cable end himself, so Xander ended up helping him a bit.

Even from where they were, Xander heard a sharp *clack!* from near the airlock. Tense but hopeful, he floated himself up to the manual controls and pushed in the green button; this time the button sank in and *clicked* satisfyingly, engaging a physical relay. Feeling hope rising, he turned the wheel slowly.

Air flooding the compartment became swiftly audible. "Yes!"

"Great. Can you reverse it?" asked the sergeant.

"Umm . . . I don't think so. The manual system assumes that you've got minimal power, so it's not trying for recovery; it'll dump the flooded atmosphere out through the valves."

"You didn't let it flood *all* the way, did you?"

"No, sir."

"Good for now. I think we can reasonably assume it'll work now. No point in wasting the air we put into it. Leave it that way, in case we have to use it. Later we'll see if we can get the powered systems working so it's not going to waste our atmosphere.

Tavana, when you got the environmentals tripped, did you get a look at our reserves?"

"We're good, sir. None of them got released in the accident, and we were fully supplied, so we've got months of air, even if the recyclers don't do so well."

"Good."

"How about you, Sergeant? Any luck?"

"Wouldn't say it's so much *luck* as good preparation, son, but yes, I know where we are. And I've got myself quite a puzzle, too."

The others turned to look at Campbell. "What sort of puzzle, sir?"

"Take a look here."

A starfield shimmered into view in front of them, scattered pinpoints of brilliance dusted across the blackness of space. "See, that's the projected perspective view for the area of space I thought we were in, taken from the files I've got onboard."

"Doesn't it fit?"

"Fits perfectly...with one little exception."

The starfield blinked, and a brilliant point of light blazed out in the middle of the darkness The point faded, then reappeared. "I'm toggling back and forth between the projection and what I actually got from scanning the starfield."

"There's...another star there."

"Which shouldn't be there at all, yes. And judging by the brightness and all, I'd guess it's the closest star to us. Not in the catalogs, and there shouldn't be *anything* this close to Earth that isn't in the catalogs. Last I knew they were done even with the brown dwarfs and well into categorizing the rogue planets in the region."

"How close do you think it is?"

Sergeant Campbell shrugged, running a hand through his graying hair. "Hard to say for certain. I don't know what the spectral type is, and that makes a huge difference. But if I had to guess, it's less than a light-year off. If I get the color right, it's possibly a G-type star. Nearest colony, though, is Orado—and that's about ten light-years off."

Xander nodded. "Well, that's not *too* bad, if we can get the Trapdoor running. That'd be, what, about two months, maybe?"

Samuel Campbell's face looked a lot more grim all of a sudden, and Xander felt a chill. "Not quite. That'd be true for *Outward Initiative*, probably a bit less than two months, but these lifeboats can't keep the Trapdoor running all-out constantly. I figure it's about a third the speed of a regular Trapdoor, on average, so we're looking more at six months. *If* everything works perfectly, and honestly, I'm not sure it will. But that'll be more on Tavana and me later on, once we get power up and running."

Six months. That *was* a long time to live in this little shuttle . . . and it was six months added on to the time it would take to repair things. "But we can't just go to some other star, sir?"

Sergeant Campbell grunted. "Not unless we have no choice, no. We don't know there's anything livable there, even if it *is* a G-type star. But I'll tell you, it's a mystery . . . and mysteries make me uncomfortable until I get answers to them."

Maddox was looking at the sergeant wide-eyed. "Sergeant . . . you don't think . . . something from that star *caused* our accident?"

Campbell stared at Maddox a moment, and then burst out laughing. After a moment, he got himself under control. "Sorry, Maddox. No, no, I don't think that. Sorry if I sounded too melodramatic there. I think what happened to *Outward Initiative* was just an accident, field instability that rippled around the outside of the hab ring. I doubt that star had anything to do with it. I'm just saying that stars don't just *appear* out of nothing. I really, *really* want to know how this one managed that trick."

He looked back at the front screen. "But that'll be a question for someone else to answer, I'm afraid. We have to get ourselves somewhere safe first. *Outward Initiative* will probably already have gotten there, since it's the closest colony, and I'll bet the answer will already be obvious." He leaned back. "But no point in even worrying about it until we get the reactor back, eh?"

"Yes, Sergeant," Tavana said. "And I think I'm going to need your help just to get through this door. What was your clearance on *Outward Initiative*?"

"Full security clearance, secondary command clearance. You need my biometrics?"

"Yes, sir. I *hope* it's still got all the data loaded in the onboard memory, so it'll recognize you. Maddox and I, we've got the TechTool configured to act as a simple security gateway, but we can't fake the door out."

"No, they definitely did *not* want the average Joe being able to walk into the cargo holds. Lot of stuff in there that's very valuable . . . and some of it's real delicate." Campbell levered himself out of the pilot seat and pushed off to come to a quick rest near the rear door. "All right, let's give it a try."

"Hold it *here*—careful, the probes are very thin, do not break or bend them! Then look directly into the flat surface there."

The TechTool blinked swiftly, projecting a faint laser beam against Sergeant Campbell's face.

Abruptly the door swung outward.

"YES!"

"Well, now, good work there, all of you!" Campbell was grinning like the rest of them. "Now we can get to the cargo . . . and find the access to the reactor. Let's get a move on!"

Chapter 5

"You sure it's safe there, Sergeant?"

"Sure I'm sure," he answered, focusing again at the indicator in his retinal display. "The 300M's got real good shielding. Barely above background levels outside the shell, even when operating. Right now she's down, so the only way it'd be dangerous is if I cracked the shell open and she was still hot inside. I only see about twenty-five service hours indicated on the system, so the lining's probably still safe enough to use as dinnerware. Stop worrying."

He was, of course, exaggerating a tad. After twenty-five hours of operating fusion under the Cavan-Ares design—derived from the original units found on Ceres, way back when—the interior of the fusion reactor was not going to be something you wanted to spend much time with, even with supposedly-aneutronic fusion going on. But the exterior was, indeed, just about stone-cold dead.

Tavana's head appeared in the hatch above him. "You've got data from the system?"

"Don't get excited yet, Tav. The exterior indicators and tracking recorders are about as dead simple as anything gets. It's the complex stuff we need to worry about."

"And the simple things like the harvest-fusion loops."

"And those, yeah, but I'm pretty hopeful they're okay."

He managed to keep from muttering "they'd better be," but he was thinking it. The keys to the modern fusion reactor were the resonant magnetic loops. They generated a fusion reaction that triggered a powerful magnetic surge that could be harvested as power— power sufficient to maintain the reaction and provide external energy.

It was in a vague way analogous to the way an old diesel engine worked—mechanical movement compressing an air-fuel mixture to explosive levels, causing the same mechanical components to move along constrained paths which allowed part of that mechanical energy to be sent off to do more useful work while the rest of it was devoted to triggering another explosion. Except that it was a lot more complicated than that, of course, and involved magnetic fields, electromagnetic power generation, and a hell of a lot of energy with very specific timing and conditions required.

Still, he was pretty sure the coils themselves would be okay. They were made to carry *massive* energies, so even the rad pulse shouldn't have caused significant EMP from their point of view, and the shielding around the reactor should have minimized any chance for radiation of significant levels to reach the more delicate interior components.

That left the exterior control components. Sergeant Campbell inverted his body and managed, just barely, to squeeze in past a narrow-clearance bulkhead. The space beyond was none too large, but at least he could turn around in it. Set at the base of the large, steel-gray fluted sphere was a small, solid console. "Tavana, I'm at the built-in calibration and test panel."

"Good. Any lights?"

"All red or dead black."

"*Merde*." That seemed to be the boy's favorite curse; he figured there could be worse.

"Don't get discouraged yet. Lemme think a minute." He went back through his memories to his prior work on the 300M. "Right, as I recall, this thing's going to be pretty much dark unless it's getting control signals from the outside, or unless I override it; this panel's not supposed to be operational when the reactor's installed."

"So there's a gap in the control signals from the main console or central computer to here?"

"Given that we haven't managed to get the main systems back up yet, I'd say there's a gap. But that means that this thing's having something like the problem the airlock had; something didn't shut down like normal, so the local panel still thinks it's under shuttle control."

"How are the reserve restart coils, Sergeant?" Xander asked from somewhere up above.

"Can't check that yet."

"Without them we're screwed." Tavana's voice was grim.

"Don't go borrowing trouble from the future, son; it'll get here on its own. Tavana, how the heck do I disconnect this bad boy? This thing's linkages don't look *anything* like the ones they used for the colony 300M I maintained."

Tavana projected an animation of the disassembly. *Oh, that's gonna be fun. Here we are sailing the stars, and engineers still gotta put connectors where they're gonna bash my knuckles trying to turn them.* "How's the inventory check going?" he asked as he got his Shapetool to configure into the right wrench design.

"Pretty good, Sergeant. The heavy equipment isn't very exciting for us, but we've got a couple cases of field rations in assorted types, spare power packs in about five standard sizes, crates of hand tools—mostly for field work, not electronics or anything like that, though—those medical supplies that were part of Dr. Kimei's shipment, hunting supplies, some camping or survival gear of assorted types, and three *big* crates that I don't recognize—they're stamped ICS-GIS-S-C-178."

Campbell managed to get the first connector turning, then grinned. "Well, a lot of stuff Tantalus is going to miss if we don't get there, that's for sure. Don't know how much of it's that useful for us sitting here in interstellar space. Those three crates— *ow!* Blasted stupid f—" he cut himself off before he started swearing, "freaking idiot designers. As I was saying, those three crates are comm satellites for idiots, so to speak. Basically just kick 'em out the door and they do the rest, work with almost all omnis on the ground. Low orbit stuff, but still good. I'm most interested in the food and medical supplies. That's what makes me happy."

Xander pinged him privately. "Thinking of the lieutenant, sir?"

He saw no reason to deny it. "I told her we'd pick her up if we could. Of course, first we gotta get this tub moving again."

One off. Four more to go. The name "Kimei" reminded him of his youngest pupil; he wondered if Sakura was all right. He hoped so, but he remembered the flashes of light as the field instability had chewed up *Outward Initiative*'s hab ring. The first loss might have been awfully close to *LS-5*, the Kimeis' assigned boat. *God help them if they're in the same fix we are.* "Any electronics or optronics components?"

"None in the cargo, sir," Maddox said cheerfully, "at least nothing marked that way. But I *did* get the rear service closet open and there's a bunch of spare modules for various systems in there."

"Excellent. Maybe we'll be able to get through this after all." It was going easier now that he'd figured out the technique; fasteners two and three were loose. "I'm almost set with this interface. What's the deal with the actual power junctions?"

"Standard, Sergeant," Tav answered. "You're not touching any major power stuff there, it's all going out from the top or bottom of the main casing."

"Good. While I'm doing these last couple, I want you and Franky"—a sound of protest from above—"Fran*cisco* to go pull every breaker unit you can. If we get a restart, we don't know how the systems are going to react, and the *last* thing we need is something screwing up because it wasn't ready for the power."

"On it, Sergeant!"

Good kids. He could've gotten stuck with far worse, he mused, as he managed to finally get the last fastener to let go. He checked the diagram again, undid the latches, and pulled.

The short cable slid out of its slot and away from

the base of the console. Instantly, Samuel Campbell saw several lights turn green. "That's got it!"

"Can you restart?" Tavana's voice was tense, and he could sense the others hanging on his words.

"Hold your horses, kids. First I want confirmation you've pulled all the breakers."

"Almost done. The one for the pilot's panel was hard to reach, but we're . . . all right, that one's up and locked."

"Is everyone clear? I don't expect any stupid Hollywood spark effects or anything, but I want you all clear of those areas anyway."

"Hold on . . . come *on*, Francisco, over here . . . Yes, we're all clear."

He looked down at the panel. Under the circumstances, there wasn't much to do. The bottom green light showed that the integrity of the restart coils was good and they were still holding the charge; to continue the shaky analogy, that meant that the starter motor was still there and hooked to the battery. The second green light showed that the fuel supply—purified boron-11 and pure hydrogen—was intact and ready.

The third light indicated readiness for start; all of the internal circuitry, then, was okay—or *thought* it was okay. Given the way things had happened, he wasn't sure he trusted that cheerful green glow, but what choice did he have? None of the heavy equipment stored in the hold was going to be running on a reactor—almost certainly all of it was on superconductor storage batteries—and there weren't any other alternative power sources.

"All right, everyone . . . cross everything you've got two of. I'm about to initiate restart."

He unlocked the manual start control, poised his finger over it, and said a little prayer to whoever might be listening. Then his finger stabbed down.

Almost instantly a throbbing hum came from the casing—faint, almost subliminal, but definitely *there*— and the panel's lights all came on. Two showed red— the external control connection and the disconnection through the breakers of all external systems—but everything else was a wonderful, wonderful green. "Restart successful! We have power, kids!"

The cheer that followed sounded like a lot more than just four boys, and he joined in. "Now no one touch the breakers yet. I want to do that in order. Tav, what do you think would happen if I hooked up the control harness now?"

Tav was silent for several minutes, but Campbell was patient. There was no reason to pressure anyone here and now.

"After looking at the manuals, I think the worst that would happen is that the reactor would think it still wasn't connected—if none of the systems outside make contact. The control linkages don't carry dangerous voltages so there shouldn't be any major consequences even if the whole set of linkages is messed up."

"All right, then, I'm going to hook that up first. If we can establish control or—if we're lucky—trigger a restart in the core systems, we'll be in a *lot* better condition."

After a few minutes jockeying it back into its tight position, the control harness linkage slid suddenly into place and locked. "Okay, Tav, throw the connecting breaker for the controls up there at the pilot's position. Let's see what we've got."

Lights suddenly appeared, not on the console, but in the air, projected by his omni through his retinal display. They weren't all green—far, far from it—but they were status lights showing that the controls weren't all dead. "We're on!" he heard Francisco shout excitedly.

"Looks like we are, at that." He put away his Shapetool. "Okay, kids, I'm getting out of this box and stretching for a few minutes. Then we'll see if we can't get everything else running and start heading for home!"

Chapter 6

Xander blinked himself awake and stretched, letting the tensing of his muscles start the blood pumping. The interior of *LS-88* was quiet except for the faint hum of various pieces of equipment and the murmur of the environmental systems.

It should also have been pretty dark, but there was a glow from the pilot's seat. That was probably what woke him up. He glanced around. To his surprise, not only were Francisco and Maddox asleep, but the sergeant hadn't awakened either. Well, he'd been doing an awful lot of work before they all turned in.

That plus the nearby empty seat/couch told him who was at the controls.

"What's up, Tav?" he asked quietly, once he'd gotten close.

Tavana twitched but didn't jump—not that his restraints would have let him jump far anyway. "Don't *do* that."

"I tried not to startle you."

"Sorry." As Tavana turned to face him, Xander suddenly realized how worried the other boy looked.

51

There were dark circles under the eyes; the usually smiling mouth was drawn tight. "What's wrong?"

Tavana muttered something in a language that wasn't in Xander's translation protocols; probably Tahitian, given Tav's ancestry. Then the younger boy sighed. "The drives . . . they're not in good shape."

That was not something Xander had wanted to hear. "What do you mean by that?"

"What do you *think*? I mean that neither the Trapdoor or the Nebula Drive are working, and I am thinking that it's going to take a long time to get them working."

A *long time* . . . Xander couldn't help but glance back at the cargo area. There was food there, but it wouldn't last forever. And if any other systems were damaged . . .

"Do you think we *can* get them working?"

Tav gave an elaborate shrug that was partly restrained by his harness. "I am trying to figure that out now. Maybe."

Then his fist clenched and he shook his head. "No. Not maybe. Yes. Because we *have* to. The sergeant . . . he told us that we have to rescue ourselves."

Xander grinned. "That's the way to talk!" Inside, he wasn't fooling himself; all their dedication wouldn't make a difference if the ship was too damaged. But thinking positively was better than getting discouraged right away. "So . . . can you tell what's wrong?"

"Well . . ." Tavana rubbed his broad chin and paused for a moment. "What do you know about the Trap-door Drive?"

"Not much, really. It lets us go up to about seventy times light-speed, it still has a lot of physicists arguing about it, and when it's running we're in some kind of warpspace, right?"

To his credit, Tav kept himself from sneering or rolling his eyes, though Xander could tell that he'd nearly done both. Instead, the French Polynesian simply shook his head. "Not really. A 'warpspace,' if we actually could make such a thing, would be a distortion, a bubble in our own spacetime. The Trapdoor Drive drops us into a sort of parallel space to our own where we effectively travel much faster. That's why the old Bemmies called it the Trapdoor Drive—you'd open a sort of door and drop out of sight."

Xander nodded. "Okay, that makes sense. You're saying it's sort of like dropping to a lower floor and running along until you decide to go back upstairs, except that somehow you run faster on the lower floor?"

Tavana nodded. "Though my professors would *hate* that analogy. Or those words, really. They didn't like the word 'faster' used that way because velocity's still supposed to be relative. Anyway, the mechanism that *does* this, the Trapdoor Drive, it has to be very precisely balanced and tuned to the vessel, sort of the way a good resonant antenna has to be properly tuned."

"And something's screwed up the tuning?"

"Worse than that." Tavana gestured, linking their omnis. "See that? That's a scan image of one of the main Trapdoor Field coils."

The strange-shaped coil at first looked reasonably all right to Xander, but as he studied the rotating image, he noticed what looked like small spots, asymmetries on the delicately wound wire. "There. Those."

"Right." Tavana stared at the image as though *willing* it to change. "See, the field coils have to be located in niches outside the hull. I think the rad pulse generated enough fluctuating current that parts of the coils *melted*."

While mechanical engineering was his specialty, Xander didn't need any explanation for that. If elements of a coil melted, that amounted to multiple short circuits in the actual material of the coil. "So they won't work."

"Not unless I can fix them."

"But you can't just cut out the defective parts. That would leave cuts—"

"I *know*," Tav said, cutting him off. "I think . . . if we don't have spares, I think we'll have to *re-wind* the coils."

Xander swallowed, looking at the gleaming shape with the multiplicity of faint lines across its surface. "That . . . that could take a long time."

"Like I said. Yeah. Especially since you gotta do it *right*. The coil geometry's crucial. You can do *some* compensating in software, but only so much."

"What about the Nebula Drive?"

"Well . . . first off, even if it was running, it'd be useless for us right now. We're in interstellar space. Theoretically the dusty-plasma sail could eventually get up near light-speed, but out here there's pretty much not enough light to push us. Even if there was, we'd take years getting anywhere, and I'm pretty sure our supplies won't last years."

"No, I don't think so."

"Anyway . . . I think the main problem there is the dust dispensers. They're on the outside too, so the pulse probably fried them. Those *should* be easier to fix, though."

"But that won't matter if we can't get the Trapdoor running again."

Tavana nodded. "Yeah."

"Did it fry *all* the coils?"

"No. Two seem untouched. But you need all five running to close the field. Believe me when I say you do *not* want an incomplete field. On *Outward Initiative*, they had twenty-five, and we still saw instability, did we not?"

Xander didn't even want to contemplate what would happen if they turned the Trapdoor on without everything working right. They'd all seen what happened when the Trapdoor Field intersected matter. "We did, and I understand. So we should go see if we have the stuff to replace the wire with, right?"

"I . . . yes, of course. I hadn't thought that far yet. But I guess it wouldn't hurt to find out if we've got stuff we can use first."

"Exactly right," said a rough voice from behind Xander.

"Sergeant! When did you wake up?"

"Few seconds ago; combination of light and you talking. No," Sergeant Campbell raised his hand, "don't go apologizing. You were quiet. I just spent a lotta years in places where you wake up and check every sound you didn't expect. Now," he looked at Tavana, "what kinda wire do we need?"

"Two kinds, really. RTSC-B7 in gauge one-two-five, preferably, plus E-M structured alloy in the same gauge."

"A little under old-style 36-gauge. Pretty skinny stuff to work with by hand, but if that's what we gotta do, that's what we do. But we might be in luck. I'm *sure* some of the smaller motors in the equipment back in storage use thin RTSC, and I wouldn't be surprised if it's B-7." He gestured. "Since you're both up, why don't we just take a look now?"

Tavana unstrapped, looking a lot less unhappy than he had a few minutes ago. "Lead on, Sergeant."

Xander followed them both, and felt some of his tension turn to hope.

Chapter 7

Campbell activated the shaped pad inside his suit; the sweat on his forehead and eyebrows was quickly wiped away. "All right, Tavana. I'm out."

He stood on the dimly-visible hull of *LS-88*, the innumerable stars of the galaxy sprinkled across the utter darkness like frozen sparks embedded in obsidian. Down and towards the rear of the landing shuttle, he could see the enigmatic nearby star—one he was pretty sure was less than a light-year off—gleaming steadily. He still wondered where in the name of God that star *came* from. It wasn't possible for stars to materialize out of nothing.

"All right, Sergeant. The first broken Trapdoor coil is...three meters forward from your current position and, um, two point two meters clockwise around from that point—clockwise from your point of view facing the front of the ship."

He made his way cautiously across the shining surface of the shuttle. You couldn't rely on magnetic boots when so much of a modern vehicle was nonferrous, nonmagnetic material; you had to walk carefully and make sure you were always clipped onto a

safety eyelet. In a few minutes he was floating at the
described location. "I see a dark indentation. Is that
the right target?"

"Umm...yes, sir. That should be the only depression near you."

*People need to work on these. Where are the hand-
rail and lockdowns?*

He muttered to his omni, which shifted spectra
slightly and enhanced the view. "Ah, *there* we go."

Clipping onto the now-easily-visible handrails, Campbell was now secured near the Trapdoor Field coil.
"Right, now display me the release sequence."

Unlocking and removing the field coil from its
proper place in the hull was a five-step process that
had to be followed in precise order. Naturally the
first step involved getting a specialized tool into the
least-accessible spot just under the forward portion of
the coil. Even with a modern flexible carbonan suit,
that took some bending. "I am getting too *old* for
this s...er, crap."

"Are you sure you wouldn't like one of us to do
that, Sergeant?" asked Xander in a concerned voice.

"Absolutely not." With the tension of a spacewalk
and the situation weighing on him, that came out
sharper and louder than he intended. "Sorry, son. I
appreciate the offer. But my job's to keep you kids
safe, and I've spent more time in spacesuits than
Francisco's been alive. I know what I'm doing here."

*Which of course is the signal for me to screw up
big-time with some rookie mistake. Dammit, Campbell,
you know better than to wave a red flag at Murphy
that way!*

"It's okay, Sergeant," answered Tavana. "It's just . . . we worry about you too, scary man."

He couldn't keep from chuckling. "Well, thank you for that, anyway. And I'll try to be a little less scary, okay, Francisco?"

"O . . . okay." The youngest of his impromptu crew sounded like he wasn't sure whether he could laugh, but wanted to.

He felt the first locking clamp move. "Got that part. Moving on."

It took about fifteen more minutes to finish removing the coil, following the procedure carefully, by the numbers, one step at a time, followed by rigorous double-checking. Finally he opened the case at his waist and very carefully stowed the coil inside. "One down," he said, and heard a subdued cheer over the comms. "How's Operation Unwind going?"

"It is actually doing well!" Tavana's voice held both surprise and pride. "Two motors' windings are now unwound and we're working on the next one."

"What I see of this coil . . . it looks pretty fancy. Can we adapt something to wind it?"

"We think so," Maddox said cheerfully. "Tav found the winding patterns in his reference books. If we can salvage the armatures in the originals, we'll have the right core configuration already." A note of concern crept into his voice. "But boy, between the motors we're taking the wire from and the ones we're using to make the winding machine . . . there's not going to be much left in the cargo."

"Don't exaggerate, Maddox," his older brother admonished. "You mean there won't be many *small* motors left. The main motors and drives on the machinery, we haven't touched those."

"That package of additional TechTools sure helped," Tavana noted.

"Sounds great. You boys keep at it while I finish this work."

He moved to the next location with Xander verifying his movements, then settled down to remove the second coil. *Good kids. I know this is wearing on them, but they're keeping it together so far.*

The success at a coil-winding (well, currently *un*winding) machine was gratifying. Unlike the others, he'd seen failures of jury-rigged repairs in the field, and they couldn't afford failure here. The Trapdoor coils depended on some pretty demanding precision—way beyond what he thought hand-winding could ever accomplish, and even if it could, the thought of winding hundreds, maybe thousands, of turns of wire by hand onto a complex armature, and then doing it twice more? His hands ached just at the *thought* of it.

But modern controllable motors, programmable omnis, simple actuators—Tavana, Xander, and even Maddox had figured out how they could be combined and mounted on one of the excavator machine's supports to make a winding device.

The second coil was out. He rested for a moment, watching the unmoving stars. "Hopefully we can make 'em move soon enough," he muttered to himself, and then went to remove the third coil. "Last one, then I can get back inside."

He mentally kicked himself again. What the heck was wrong with him? Never, *ever* start looking forward to the end, or you start rushing! Campbell made himself go over the steps extra-carefully on the third one. He was *not* going to make a mistake on this last coil.

He didn't. Finally he was done, and made his way—with exquisite caution—to the airlock. He didn't let himself relax until he entered the main cabin and swung the lock door shut.

"Whew!" he said, letting his helmet retract. "That was a long bit of work."

"You got them all, Sergeant?"

"All three, Tav. Guess we'll have to cut away the old wire, then you'll be ready to wind again?"

"Well, soon, yes. First we must finish the unwinding of all the motor wires, you know."

"I'll leave it to you. I've got just one more thing to do today before I take a break." He moved to the pilot's console and strapped in.

Xander looked puzzled. "What are you going to do, sir?"

"We've got a friend to pick up. Now that we're working on what we hope is the last repair we need in order to get somewhere, it's time we started heading towards her."

"But . . . how can we find her out *there*?" Francisco sounded a little scared as he gestured towards the starspattered endless dark. Campbell couldn't blame him.

He gestured for Francisco to come join him. Once the little boy reached him, Campbell pulled Francisco gently over to sit in his lap and strapped him down. "Here, lemme show you. You know that in space, if you were to throw something, it'd just keep on going forever. Right?"

Francisco nodded. "*Si*. I mean yes, I know that, Sergeant."

"But it's more than that. If you throw something on Earth, or any planet, gravity accelerates it, changes its direction. Air can slow it down. Other things that it hits will change direction. But that's not true in space. There's no gravity to speak of out this far, a light-year or more from any star; there's nothing to hit for millions, billions of kilometers, more—practically forever. Space is *big*. And there's no air."

He looked at Francisco expectantly.

The boy wrinkled his forehead, obviously thinking hard. Campbell knew Francisco wasn't a tech-head like the others—more an artist, from what he'd heard—but he wasn't stupid. "So . . . the lieutenant, she will keep going and going just like she was?"

"Exactly like she was. More, we know exactly how fast—and in what direction, from our point of view— she went. We were all watching, and the *cameras* were watching. I've had my omni keep the numbers current; if I'm right, she's about fifteen thousand kilometers *that* way," he made his omni generate an arrow in Francisco's field of view. "Been drifting that direction at about eight meters per second ever since we separated."

"That's a long way away."

He couldn't keep from laughing. "Sorry—but for a spaceship, that's like a baby step. If we had all our sensors running, we could still probably detect her on radar. Not like there's anything else out here to look for. So right now, I'm going to start us back towards her. We've got reaction jets—the basic rockets work fine. They won't get us home, or even let us cruise fast around a solar system, but for landing—or a slow chase—they're just fine."

Francisco sat still in his lap as Samuel reached for the controls. "Now, I have to turn us *just* like this—so we're centered on her vector." He triggered another program and routed it to the boy's omni. "Watch that green dot and blue circle on your retinal display, Francisco. You see 'em?"

Francisco gave a quick nod. "Yes, Sergeant!"

"Now, you let me know when the dot's getting close to the circle." He could see the same display of course—and a lot more detail—but Francisco had been feeling left out, and he needed things to do.

"Okay, Sergeant!"

Campbell slowly started adjusting *LS-88*'s orientation.

"Getting closer, Sergeant ... closer ... it's heading high. Should it be doing that?"

"No, it shouldn't. Good catch." The boy did have a good eye, and he recognized when things didn't look right. "That better?"

"Much better. Do we want the green dot right in the middle of the circle?"

"We do indeed."

"It's *really* near the circle now ... touching ... a little low ... it's gone past the middle!"

He slowly reversed the rotation the tiniest bit.

"Right in the middle!"

He was actually surprised. The kid's eyes were *good*. His own instruments couldn't find significant error. "Very good, Francisco! Thank you!"

"Now what?"

"Now we go catch her, that's what. She's going away from us at about eight meters a second, and it's going to take a while for us to take apart the coils and rewind 'em and put 'em back, so ... I'd like to start closing with her a little faster than we separated. Say, start getting closer to her at about ten meters a second."

"So we need to accelerate by ten ..." The boy hesitated. "No, we're going *away* right now, right?"

"Right."

His face lit up. "So we need to stop, and then accelerate by ten meters a second!"

He chuckled. "It's all the same acceleration, but yes. So about eighteen meters per second all told." He looked back. "You boys lock down everything for a few seconds—including yourselves. I'm going to start us after Lieutenant Haley."

"Yes, sir! Hold on, I'll let you know when we're secure." After a few moments, Xander said, "I think it's all secure here. Tavana?"

"Secure, check. Maddox?"

"Let me look . . . yep, I check you! All secure back here!"

Campbell nodded. Good procedure, there; they hadn't relied on one person to make sure nothing was loose. "All right, then, come up and strap in. This won't be much of a burn, but still, best to be safe."

Once they were all strapped in, he continued, "I'm just going to run her for nine seconds at a two-meters-per-second-squared burn. That'll still feel pretty massive to you, after all this time in microgravity, so be warned."

If it weren't for modern medical nanos, he'd be really worried about the effects of microgravity on their health, but that should be okay, at least for now. He hoped.

True to his warning, the sudden force of acceleration came like a ton of lead weights dropped across his chest. He had to verify the thrust twice before he relaxed. After exactly nine seconds, it cut off.

Pearce, we're on our way. And just maybe with the stuff you need. But in any case . . . you're not going to drift away alone.

Chapter 8

Xander watched the installation of the precious coil in his VRD, one of the gloved hands gripping the coil and the other tightening part of a not-quite visible fixture.

"There, that's got it!" the sergeant said. "Check the connectivity, would you?"

"Connection shows good, sir!" Tavana answered from the pilot's seat. "We just had the Trapdoor status light go green!"

"Well, now, that's a relief and a half."

A tiny glint in another part of his VRD caused Xander to straighten. He murmured and gestured directions, and the remaining camera on *LS-88* shifted its focus and resolution to maximum in the indicated area. Something was there, ahead and (in a relative sense) above them, tumbling slowly, showing a reflection of dim, dim starlight on something shiny.

"Sergeant, I think I've just spotted the lieutenant's piece of the wreck."

"You have? How far off?"

"If it *is* her ... three to five kilometers, I think, ahead, starboard one and a half degrees, azimuth two point oh-five degrees."

"I'm on my way in, then. Get everyone strapped in, we'll be doing some maneuvering to match up with her."

"Yes, sir!" Xander raised his voice. "Okay, everyone, strap in again. Francisco, you can play one of your games if you want while we're maneuvering. Maddox—"

Francisco suddenly let loose with a torrent of Spanish which, roughly translated, said how much he hated the little cabin of the shuttle, he wanted to go home, Mommy should be here, he didn't want to play any games, and he wasn't going to be strapped in, no!

As the tantrum gained momentum, Xander looked helplessly at Maddox and Tavana. The little boy's voice was cracking as he spoke faster and faster, tears starting to form and pool in his eyes, clinging to his cheeks in tiny shivering waves without the pull of gravity.

Maddox launched himself slowly towards Francisco. "Hey, Francisco, it's okay. None of us are happy about—"

"No!" Francisco's flailing arm took Maddox by surprise, sending the older boy spinning end-over-end in one direction and shoving an also-spinning Francisco into the back of one of the chairs face-first. The impact was a dull *thud* that Xander could hear several feet away, even as he sprang to intercept the stunned but still-crying boy. "Francisco! Are you okay?"

The red-haired boy had one hand clamped over his mouth, the other now gripping Xander, keeping Francisco from floating away again. The tears looked like they were also tears of pain now, and with a pang somewhere near his own heart Xander found himself reminded of Maddox, looking up at him with the same expression of pain and loss after a similar tantrum.

He reached out a little farther, hugged Francisco to him. "I'm sorry, Francisco. I really am. If we could wave our hands and fix everything, believe me, we would. Can I see your face, please? Come on, let me take a look."

Francisco swallowed audibly, then nodded and slowly took his other hand down.

Blood dotted the boy's hand and his lip. "Okay, Francisco, I need to take a closer look at your lip. Hold still, okay?"

"O-okay." He winced as Xander gently pulled the lip out and examined it. Xander relaxed slightly.

"You'll be all right," he said, and gave the smaller boy a hug. "You know... Maddox had almost the same thing happen to him when he was a kid."

"Oh, Xander, you're not gonna—" Maddox caught himself, then nodded. "Y-yeah. I did. We were left on Earth with our uncle, and then Unc got sick..."

"And he threw a tantrum about pretty much everything. He tried to run away, slipped, and smacked his face on the stairs," finished Xander. "Scared me half to death when he got up crying with blood all down his face. Worse than yours; his front teeth almost went through his upper lip. He had to get stitches. You've just got a little cut. It'll hurt for a while—Maddox, can you see if you can get us a cold pack to get the swelling down until his nanos can get to it?"

"Sure."

Francisco was silent for a moment, then said. "I'm sorry."

"It's okay. We all feel the same way."

"But you didn't act all stupid and cry and yell like a baby," Francisco said, now angry with himself.

"That," said the sergeant, coming in from the air-lock, "is because we had plenty of years to have all our tantrums before you ever met us. Once Maddox gets that pack on, Francisco, can you get strapped in?"

Francisco nodded. "Yes, sir."

"Good man." Xander gave their smallest crewmember one more hug and let Maddox take over. *I'm lucky I've got a brother like him.*

As he helped the sergeant get the gear stowed back in place, Campbell murmured, "Good work, Xander. You handled that just right—probably better than my reflexes would have."

"Oh, they'll listen to you a lot better than me."

"Maybe, but partly because they're scared of the old guy with the scars. You, it's because you understand how to talk with them. Just wanted you to know I appreciate it. It's a good thing you were on board."

"Hey, it was our shuttle. It was a good thing *you* were on board."

"Okay, good thing both of us were. Now, you get yourself strapped in; we've got one more castaway to bring home."

By now, the glint was visible through the forward port without any assistance. "Getting close now. Everyone strapped in?"

Securing his last strap, Xander reported, "Xander, all secure."

"Tavana, all secure, Sergeant."

"Maddox, all secure."

"Francisco, all secure."

"All right, then. Here we go!"

Xander tied into the navigation systems so he could really watch what the chief master sergeant did; he could tell that Tavana was doing the same thing. Maddox and Francisco just watched the forward port.

Two quick hissing rumbles echoed through *LS-88*, and the little ship rotated slightly. Suddenly the tumbling, glinting object was centered in the viewport, perfectly centered and unmoving, merely growing larger. Xander was startled. The sergeant wasn't calculating anything; he had just adjusted their vector and alignment on the fly and made it so they were heading directly towards the wreckage.

Now he could see clearly that it was, in fact, the broken boarding tube that they'd left the lieutenant in, somersaulting lazily through the endless black, growing swiftly larger in the port. The forward rockets fired once. The approach was slow, leisurely, down from a speedy bicycle to a casual walk, the tube a hundred meters away . . . fifty . . . twenty-five . . .

A rippling flash of thrusters activated in a sequence too fast to follow. Abruptly the tube seemed frozen in space, neither approaching nor receding, simply rotating slowly like a model in a 3-D projection.

"*C'est magnifique,*" Tavana murmured. "Sergeant, you can *fly.*"

Campbell leaned back, a pleased grin on his face. "Guess I haven't lost my touch *quite* yet. All right, I've got one more spacewalk to do now. For this, I *do* need someone else. Xander, you're coming with me. I'm gonna have to float myself over there, unsecure her from whatever she locked herself onto, and come back. It'll be easiest if you can haul us in at my direction."

"Yes, sir."

"That means that while we're both out there, Tavana's in charge. You two younger ones got that?"

"Yes, Sergeant!" said Maddox.

"Yes, Sergeant," agreed Francisco.

"Okay."

Xander felt his heart beating faster. *I took all the classes, but I've never actually done a spacewalk on the outside of a ship.*

Suiting up and preparing was quick enough. Old-style suits and EVA approaches, in the dawn of the space age, used to take a lot of time because the suits would run at much lower pressure for ease of physical motion and other issues, but modern skintight EVA suits maintained full pressure while allowing full range of motion, and were far more resilient than old-fashioned spacesuits. That suited Xander just fine; waiting *hours* slowly decompressing just to go outside would have driven him nuts.

The external door opened. Xander looked out into pure darkness with scattered gems of unwinking light. Sergeant Campbell was ahead of him, blocking most of the view. "Now listen carefully, son. You will follow me out. You will lock onto each and every holdfast, guardrail, or anything else that I do, and you will do it in the *exact* same sequence I do. If I tell you to stop, you will stop *immediately*. If I tell you to go back, you will do so in order, as carefully as we came out."

"Yes, sir."

"All right. When we get to the right position, I'll tell you how we'll handle the retrieval."

The sergeant clipped onto a guardrail just at the edge of the airlock. He swung himself carefully out, keeping a grip on the rail, and lowered his boots to the surface. Once the older man had moved out of the way, Xander locked his suit onto the same guardrail and tried to maneuver himself out of the airlock with the same ease and grace. Instead, he ended up failing to stand, twisting his hand free, and bouncing off the hull and outward. Fortunately, the resilient energy absorption of his tether slowed and stopped him, so he could pull himself back down with care.

"Not as easy as it looks, is it, son?"

"Not *nearly* as easy as you make it look, sir."

"You've learned your first lesson on real spacewalks, then: don't try to pretend you're the guy who's done it all when you haven't done any of it."

"Yes, sir."

Xander looked up and around. "Wow."

He'd seen thousands of views of the stars—through ports, simulations, and the night sky on Earth. But there was nothing to compare with this.

The pure, unadulterated darkness that surrounded them made the darkest black he had ever seen look gray. Yet at the same time there was no sense of the dark that one had on Earth, because there were *stars* everywhere—not the blurred, dimmed, washed-out wavering pinpricks of light seen on Earth, but an innumerable set of intense, blazing points set against darkness. Shining brightly out within a glowing band of light and dark that he could see—really *see*—was a section of the Milky Way Galaxy itself, mottled with black banding of gas and dust, glowing with the light of not hundreds but hundreds of millions, billions of stars. Thousands of suns illuminated the darkness all around him, not dispelling it, or even reducing its absolute pitch-blackness in the least, but instead making it not an oppressive, threatening presence, but a backdrop of beauty.

"Yeah, I have the same reaction every time I come out. Doesn't ever get old. Especially here, between the stars." Sergeant Campbell was silent a moment, letting him admire the view. "All right, son, let's move along. Follow my every move, right?"

"Right."

They made it to the forward portion of *LS-88* easily enough; the sergeant had been out twice before, so he already knew where everything was and could make sure that Xander took the right path the first time.

"Okay, listen up, son," he said. "This part of the ship we're standing on, it's magnetic. Stay here. There's nothing better than having more than one thing keeping you in place.

"Now, this here is going to be tricky. We don't have any attitude jets to adjust the spin of that piece of junk out there. She's only rotating at about one and a half RPM, luckily, or it'd be even tougher. If she was spinning at say five or ten RPM, we'd *have* to figure out a way to slow her down, and I honestly haven't a clue as to how we'd manage that without risking *LS-88*. But at forty seconds per rev, we can pull this off without having to do that."

Xander stared . . . up? Out? Directions were odd when there was no gravity. He decided on "up" since they were on the top surface of *LS-88*. He stared up at the slowly-turning tube. Inside, he could make out a shape that had to be Pearce Haley's suit. "So what do we do, Sergeant?"

"Mostly what do *I* do, son. You're here to back me up. I'm going to jump across, timing it so I end up inside and stop myself around the middle. Problem is that with it rotating, I can't have a tether on me.

It would snap right off as it rotated, or drag me out. Another problem is that these suits don't have real maneuver jets on them, just some dinky anti-spin thrusters with real, *real* limited delta-V, so if I make a bad mistake, I might be haring off into the black without a way to turn around."

"But, Sergeant." He swallowed. "Sergeant, I hate to say it, but shouldn't we..."

Campbell waited.

Xander felt his grip on the nearby rail tighten, but forced himself to finish. "...shouldn't we think about, well...whether we can *afford* to rescue her?" When Campbell didn't immediately answer, he felt a spurt of shame. "I'm sorry, Sergeant, I—"

"Don't apologize, son. You asked the hardest question there is, and it's the *right* question. The question she'd want us to ask." Campbell looked up. "Is it worth risking me—when I'm arguably invaluable for you boys' chances of getting home—to bring her in when she might already be a goner?" He turned back to Xander, and Xander's retinals showed Campbell's serious expression inside the helmet. "What do *you* think?"

"*Me*? Sergeant, I—"

"Don't back out on me now, son. You asked the question, now answer it."

Xander felt shaky just contemplating the idea of turning away, but he made himself think about it. "Well...Sergeant, given what you see up there, and what you know about your own skills...what's the chance that you *won't* have something happen that's so bad we can't get you back?"

A soft chuckle. "I'd say about ninety-five percent. I'd have to screw up pretty damn bad for us to get to the point that either I couldn't rescue myself or you couldn't manage to catch up with me somehow. I've done zero-G work a *lot* over the years. I ain't saying this one isn't one hell of a tricky maneuver, but no *part* of it's really ridiculous for someone with experience. It's just not gonna be following the best practices manual."

"And . . . again, from what you know . . . what are our chances of getting back home *without* you?"

"That's a harder question, Xander . . . but we're close to finishing the coil replacement. If that doesn't work, none of us are getting home anyway. So let's say it works. If it does . . . I'd say even without me you boys have at least an eighty-five percent chance of getting home *now*, since you've got power and ship's key systems up. With the Trapdoor at this distance, you can *see* the star you're going towards, and you have to drop out of Trapdoor periodically anyways, so if you just keep heading towards *that* star," he indicated the star that Xander already knew was the one for Orado, "you'll get there. And you're pretty levelheaded; I think you'd keep 'em together until you got there."

Xander felt a huge sense of relief. "Then I say we don't leave anyone behind, Sergeant!"

"That's the way to talk, son! But you asked the right questions. Now let's cross our fingers that we stay just a *little* lucky today."

"So after you get across, Sergeant, then what?"

"Then I go and unsnap Lieutenant Haley from where she's locked herself down. Once I've got her hooked to me securely, then I move to one end of the thing and use my omni to time my jump back so I head back here at reasonable speed. *You* throw me a lifeline as soon as I get clear; I'll *probably* be headed close enough to reach some part of *LS-88*, but a lifeline locked down to the hull will really help make sure."

"Got it, Sergeant."

"You understand how to throw one of these lifelines?"

"We did study that, yes, Sergeant. Throw underhanded, not too fast, and use your fingers to slow it gradually down. If you do it perfectly, the line will stop and not bounce back."

"That's the *classroom* method, but it's like how we teach kids to do multiplication longhand when they'll pretty much never be without an omni in real life. There's a *lot* better way to do it if you know how those lines work. See, they're wrapped in a jacket of electrorigid polymer; zap it with electricity and it stiffens, like a hose with water running through it. So what you do is throw it out in the general direction you want, and then stiffen it up so you can *point* it at your target. Once you've got it set where you want it, you turn off the juice."

Xander looked at the shiny, looped cable. "Really? That's a *lot* easier. But how do I get the electricity through it?"

"Check the settings for your gloves. The menu will give you an *active* option. Set the glove holding the lifeline to *active* and that'll do the trick. Electrify the part of it extending away from you, as long as the other end's clipped to your suit. It's low voltage so there's no danger."

Xander drew about a meter of the line out and activated the gloves; the line swiftly straightened itself out, feeling something like a very flexible fishing rod. "Got it!"

"All right, then." Sergeant Campbell unsnapped his short tether and wrapped it safely around him, locking it securely to his suit. "Here goes nothing."

With a single jump, Campbell broke his connection with *LS-88* and floated away, directly for the remains of the boarding tube. At first Xander thought he'd badly mistimed the jump, because the entrance to the tube wasn't even visible; but as Campbell gradually approached the rotating wreckage, the tube opening appeared and Campbell travelled straight into the ten-meter-long piece of boarding tube. "Bull's-eye!" he heard Campbell announce cheerily. "All right, I am now clipping myself to a holdfast and making my way up to Pearce. She's about two meters from me now."

A short time later, Xander could see Campbell next to Pearce's suit. "I have reached her and . . . secured. Checking Lieutenant Haley now."

A few more minutes elapsed, and then his cheerful voice returned. "She's in full suspension, suit systems maintaining her at minimum temperature. Everything looks good. She's locked down at two holdfasts. Clipping myself to her now." A pause. "All right, releasing first holdfast. Releasing second holdfast. Verifying secure to carry. I am secure to carry. Now heading for the end of the tube. Xander, verify you have the lifeline ready."

"Ready, Sergeant."

"Good. Watch the rotating end. Get a feel for where its maximum silhouette is against the stars. That's probably where I let go. I probably don't even have to jump; the rotation will allow it to pitch me straight at *LS-88* at less than a meter per second. So *before* I jump, see if you can get that lifeline out there."

Xander nodded. "Got it, Sergeant."

He took the lightly weighted line in his fingers, remembering the simulations he'd gone through. *The peak of it seems to pass* just *underneath those two stars, so I'll aim there.*

The throw was a little off, but as he'd thrown the line gently he had plenty of time to wait and very carefully slow it down with his fingers. When it seemed almost stopped, he activated the gloves.

The line straightened out, feeling almost like a skinny snake lazily trying to wriggle out of his grasp. He stood as still as he could, waiting for the rippling movements to fade away. Then he very, very slowly moved it to point straight at the rotating cylinder, where he could now see the sergeant, with Lieutenant Haley in his arms, waiting. "All right, Sergeant. I've got it set, I think."

"Looks good from here, son. Now just let it go inactive; unless you pull on it, it should stay right where it is, and I want it real flexible for me to catch."

"It's inactive." Xander could feel the line go the tiniest bit loose in his hand, but kept stock-still.

"All right, I have moved to a nonmagnetic part of the tube. Letting my omni time my release . . . count-down to release in three, two, one, *release!*"

As the rotating part reached its apex, the sergeant let go and was flung slowly outward like a ball released by a pitcher. Xander could immediately see that the sergeant's timing must have been not *quite* perfect because he started drifting very slowly to one side. However, he was very near to the end of the lifeline, and managed to snag it with his left hand. "Clipped to lifeline," he announced as he slowly approached.

Xander noticed the line stiffening and relaxing several times in succession; the stress in the line as it curved seemed to pull just enough on the sergeant to reduce his drift.

"On my way in, son. Just step back and give me a little room. Remember, no magnetics back behind you there."

"Understood."

He edged back, watching the incoming suits. Leaving the magnetic area caused him to bobble slightly, but he kept himself mostly under control and didn't say anything.

Moments later, Sergeant Campbell rotated himself and came to a perfect landing on the magnetic section of the nose of *LS-88*. Xander could see Pearce Haley's face now through the helmet, looking as though she were sleeping peacefully.

"Retrieval accomplished. Good work, Xander. Now let's keep focused for a few more minutes. By the numbers, back to the airlock, and then we can breathe a little easier!"

Xander allowed himself to relax—just a little bit—as they made their way back. *Now we just have to get home!*

Chapter 9

"Do you think we have enough, sir?"

Sergeant Campbell didn't answer at once; Tavana could see he was still carefully transferring the contents of injector after injector into a treatment pack. Finally he looked up. Tavana was startled to see the lines on the sergeant's face; they seemed far more pronounced now than they'd been when they were first marooned. "I wish to God I knew. To be dead honest with you . . . if it were just me and her, I'd use 'em all. But I can't do that. There are four more to worry about, and I'm responsible for all of you. I have to leave some in case something else happens."

"Sir, if it'll help, you can use any you're saving for me."

"Not one chance in hell, Arronax." The gentle smile took the sting from the sharp words. "I appreciate the gesture, but I am not reducing your safety margin— or honestly, even mine. I have to assume I have as much chance to get hurt or sick as any of you, and if I'm responsible . . . I have to be ready and willing to treat myself."

"So," Maddox said quietly, floating over Tavana's shoulder, "how many *are* you using?"

"Half of our supply. One hundred treatment injections' worth."

"A hundred injections?" Xander looked at Campbell with his eyebrow raised. "I would think that's enough to almost raise the dead."

Campbell didn't smile. "That's about the size of it. The dose she got? It's already killed her. Her body just hasn't admitted it yet. The nanos are going to have to work through her body and fix stuff before it collapses, and *damnation* I don't know if it can. This stuff's customized for trauma treatment, though it has anti-rad properties too. But hell, I'm no doctor. If I was I could customize this stuff, program it specifically to fix radiation damage. Then I'd be pretty sure she'd survive. Right now . . . I just don't know."

Francisco, who was sitting next to Pearce, suddenly stiffened. "Sergeant! She opened her eyes!"

All of them immediately floated themselves to the other spacesuit, currently locked down to one of the conformal seats. The sergeant's grin was broad and reassuring. "Hey there, Lieutenant."

"Chief Master Sergeant," she said, with a slow, surprised grin. Her voice was sluggish, sleepy. "You came back for me."

"Promised I would. Now, you're not better yet, Pearce. Think you can help us get you outta that suit for treatment?"

"Sure."

Lieutenant Haley's suit seam unlocked and split open, and she sat up. "Oh, ouch ouch ouch *ouch!!*"

The sergeant looked torn between anger and laughter. "Dammit, Haley! You've been a popsicle for a couple of months now! You can't just sit up like that."

Her face was pale and sweat beaded on her forehead. Tavana realized that what she'd felt must go *way* beyond "ouch."

"Yeah," she said in a whisper. "Kinda figured that out."

"Okay, then, just let me get your back . . ." Tavana watched the sergeant ease his arms around to support her in position. "We'll have to try to move you as little as possible. Tav, unlock her suit from the seat. I'll hold her. You and Maddox should be able to slide the suit off."

Tavana nodded and released the seat restraints. Maddox followed him to the lieutenant's feet. Each of them took one of the boots. "Now, Sergeant?"

"Hold on. Give her a few minutes to recover." Haley was still pale as a ghost.

"Okay." Tavana looked to the rear door, where he could vaguely hear sounds of Xander and Francisco moving around, digging into the last sections of cargo they hadn't touched, performing a current inventory. They'd been in *LS-88* for long enough that the sergeant had said it was time to reassess their situation. Tavana, having noted the glances between Campbell and Xander, guessed that Campbell wanted Francisco well out of the way when they were tending to Lieutenant Haley, just in case.

"I'm okay now," Haley said after a moment. There was some slight color back in her cheeks, so Tavana figured she wasn't entirely lying.

"No, you aren't, but you're better than you were. Right, then, kids, remember to brace yourselves properly. Pull steady and slow. I don't want you flying off and bouncing into the walls if the suit comes off all of a sudden. Got it?"

"Yes, sir," Tavana said. Maddox nodded, taking a

firmer grip on the lieutenant's right boot and settling his feet against the base of the seat. Tavana did the same.

"All right, I got her. Together now . . . three . . . two . . . one . . . *pull!*"

The suit, already instructed by Haley to be in release mode, slid free with startling ease; even with the sergeant's warning, the two boys found themselves drifting backwards with the suit and bumping gently into one of the other seats. An unpleasant odor filled the cabin.

"Ugh," said Haley. "Sorry, Sergeant."

"Don't worry, we'll take a few minutes to get you cleaned up before we have to put you back under, Pearce."

She looked around, not moving her neck or body much. That sudden movement sure gave her a warning. "You said a couple of months. No rescue, huh?"

The sergeant looked grim. "None, Pearce. Not likely to be, either." He cradled her and started towards the tiny free-fall shower. "I'll fill you in while we get you clean. Tavana, you and Maddox have got a not very fun job: clean out her suit. That means empty all the reservoirs and make sure they're one hundred percent clean. Then restock everything."

Tavana winced, but nodded. "Yes, sir."

Maddox wrinkled his nose. "He means—"

"Yeah, everything. Even in suspension she must've made some waste, and maybe she did when the disaster hit." *I would have wet myself at least if I was standing in a boarding tunnel and it was suddenly chopped off and I was spinning through space. Maybe Lieutenant Haley didn't, though. She's tough.*

But not so tough that he couldn't hear cries of pain, and an occasional sob. Tavana tried to ignore it, but he could see Maddox's shoulders tighten. "Tav... why does she *hurt* so much? Is it...the radiation?"

Tav tried to grin, couldn't quite manage it, and settled for a tiny smile. "No, no. She was in suspension, yes?"

Maddox nodded, wiping out part of the interior of the suit. "Yes. And?"

"Then you know she was not moving for months. Even with nanotech maintaining you, things get stiff. Have you ever sat in one position for too long, then tried to get up and found it was stiff or sore? Now imagine that after two months, without moving even the tiniest bit. Plus she was more than asleep. She was almost dead. Shut down. So it's like when your foot falls asleep. Slowly feeling comes back, but it tingles and hurts sometimes. Make that a thousand times worse."

Maddox's eyes were wide, looking back at the tiny enclosure. "She's...really tough, then."

"*Oui.*"

A little while later the sergeant came over to them and inspected the suit. "Good work. We'll get her back into it as soon as we give her the nano doses."

"Um...Sergeant, sir?" Maddox said hesitantly.

"Oh, for the love of...Maddox, you can call me Sergeant, or if you boys insist you can call me 'sir,' but in the name of all that's holy don't do *both!*"

For the first time that day, Tav found himself giggling. Maddox said in a slightly panicky voice, "Sorry, Sir...Sergeant...I mean..."

Campbell cracked a smile too. "Oh, never mind. What is it, son?"

"Well, I know that Lieutenant Haley's ... well, *dying*, like you said, even though she looks okay. So why didn't you just give her the treatment and leave her under?"

"Now *that* is an excellent question, Maddox. Good thinking. Two reasons, really. First is purely personal. Last we left off, she was drifting by herself, alone in space. Some of the eggheads think that once you go all the way into suspension you don't dream, don't think at all, but I don't believe that. I wasn't going to leave Pearce thinking she might just be going to her death in the black, maybe dreaming a slow dream about it for months as she died." The older man's face was somber as he said that; Tavana realized how far ahead someone like Campbell must think, and it made him wonder if maybe he shouldn't start doing that too. "As for the other reason ... why don't the two of you think about it while I go get her dressed and bring her back out?"

It took a few minutes, so Tavana did. Why *would* the sergeant risk taking her out of suspension and speed up the deterioration of Lieutenant Haley's body rather than leave her in the suspension that would keep her alive as long as possible and give her the treatment that way?

After a few minutes, he thought he understood, and looked over to Maddox, whose frown of concentration had suddenly smoothed out in an expression of surprise. "You got it?"

"Yeah ... yeah, I think so. Sergeant?"

"Hold on, hold on ... here we come."

Lieutenant Pearce Greene Haley looked a lot better, as the sergeant carried her back. There was some color back in her face, the sweat was gone, and there were fewer lines of pain on her face. She was even moving slightly without wincing much, and was dressed in one of the one-piece coveralls that they'd found a small stash of in the cargo. The coveralls were big enough for most adults and could be adjusted to just about Tavana's size, but they'd had to do some clumsy cut-down work to get one to fit Francisco. Still, it had given them some extra clothes. Tavana suspected that the sergeant had used the free-fall shower to also clean and dry the lieutenant's underclothes. There weren't any of those in storage; not that they'd found yet, anyway.

"So," Sergeant Campbell said as he deposited Haley on the seat and they strapped her in, "you got an answer for me, Maddox?"

"I think we do, sir. You're going to inject all those nanos into her as quickly as you can, right?"

"Quick as possible, yes."

"Well, if she's awake, her blood's circulating faster. Her whole body's going to help with transport better, right? So you'll be able to inject it faster safely, and it'll be distributed through her whole body a lot more efficiently." Maddox looked up questioningly at Campbell, who glanced at Tavana.

Tavana gave an emphatic nod. "That's my guess, Sergeant."

"One hundred percent right," Lieutenant Haley said with a wan smile. "Sam thought all that out before he even put me under, I bet. It's what I would do, too."

"You're a surgical tech, aren't you, Pearce? Don't suppose you know how to reprogram these nanos to be pure anti-rad repair units?"

She shook her head reluctantly. "Not really. If you've made sure the standard options are all active, that's about all I could do, at least without a full medical setup, which we don't have."

"Worth asking. Okay, hold out your arm."

The infusion of even that many nanos didn't take very long; ten minutes later, the sergeant withdrew the injector and replaced it in the kit. "Okay, Pearce... that's all I can do. I'm going to have to put you back to sleep now. You okay with that?"

"Better now than I was. At least let me get back into my suit."

"You *sure*? I don't want you to—"

"For goodness' sake, Sam, I'm not a china doll. I may be dying, but I'm not shattered. Let me do *something* before I have to go back to being a human freeze-pop." She unfastened herself slowly and drifted over to the newly-cleaned suit. With stiff, cautious motions, she donned the suit, sealed it, and checked the telltales. "Good work, boys. Everything checks out. And boy, does it smell better in here."

Sergeant Campbell smiled, though Tavana could see a glitter at the corner of his eyes that said he might rather be crying. "Yeah, well, it'll be back to stinking by the time we open it again."

"Sergeant? Does she have to be in the suit?"

"You mean couldn't I just have the nanos suspend her right here in the cabin? Sure I could, but the suit can keep her temperature as low as possible—down to around ten Celsius—which keeps the degeneration as slow as possible. The nanos can continue operating more efficiently even at that temperature than her cells can, so it's a net gain for them, even though some will have to spend their time preventing the damage of extreme hypothermia. Like thrombosis. Plus, if and when we land anywhere, she'd damn well better be in a suit."

Sergeant Campbell helped the now-suited Haley to the seat he'd chosen for her. "Okay, Pearce. Time to go back to sleep." He gave her a quick hug, which she returned. "See you later."

Her smile was bright through the filmy helmet. "Later, Sam."

Her eyes closed. A few moments later she looked almost dead, just as she had when they first brought her in. Tavana shivered; it was an eerie thing to see, even knowing that it was just a trick of modern technology. Campbell stood immobile, holding her hand, staring down at her until the last trace of consciousness had departed. Then he put her hand down gently, bent and locked all the restraints in place, and stood again.

"All right, Tav," he said. "It's time we got everyone home."

Chapter 10

Samuel Campbell went into the cargo hold once he was sure that Tavana and Maddox were securing themselves. He still felt shaky inside; the relief that—once more—the suspension procedure had worked warred with his worry that Pearce still might not make it. It wasn't a good place for his head to be in, but he accepted that it would take a bit to drive the personal turmoil out. *These aren't the best circumstances for keeping my distance, either.*

"Hey, Xander. How's it going?"

"Just about done, Sergeant," the older Bird answered. "There are a few more boxes we have to unseal and sort, but I don't think they have rations or anything like that in them."

"Never mind, then. Francisco, go up front and strap in. We're getting ready to start moving."

"Yes, sir!" Francisco looked excited as he bounced towards the front of the shuttle. *Kid still probably doesn't grasp that even once we start moving, it's going to be a long time before we get to civilization.*

That did, however, leave him alone with Xander, which was what he'd intended. "So . . . what's the final word?"

Xander looked serious, then suddenly broke into a broad smile. "It'll be a little tight, sir . . . but we've got enough to last us the full six months, maybe a little more if we tighten our belts."

Campbell felt a huge knot loosening in his gut. He'd been even more worried than he'd realized that the long time spent rigging repairs to the little ship would have taken their chance to live long enough to reach Orado, the only colony within any reasonable range—ten light-years off. "Well, now, that's just great. Let's get up to the front and strap in. I'm going to get us set for the long trip right away, then."

Once Xander was in place, Campbell strapped into the pilot's chair and spun to face the little group. *Kids all of them, except Pearce, who's out and not waking up.* "All right, crew. We've finished our repairs, we've retrieved our castaway. Now we've got one more long trek to make—so we can go home."

There was a ragged cheer.

"Thank you, but thank yourselves. I couldn't have done this alone. All of you should be proud of the work we've done." He waited a moment, then said, "and now let's get going!"

He spun back to the main console and locked the chair in position. *Everything by the numbers.* He checked every system, calling them off, the reds, the yellows, and the now far-more-numerous greens— enough green and yellow to get them home, anyway. "Destination, Orado Colony. Distance, best as I can guess it, ten point zero five light-years. That'll be a haul—about six months—but we've got what we need to make it there. Air purifiers and oxygen reclaiming facilities show green. Water reclamation, green. We've got enough food. We have power. Setting course and maximum jump sequence."

LS-88 reoriented itself, pointing now in the direction of the moderately bright K-class star that was Orado's primary. With even the reduced velocity of their Trapdoor Drive, the motion of stars was effectively zero over human timescales, so he just needed to point and drive, adjusting some when they got closer, but if he could see and line up on his target, they'd get there.

"Trapdoor Drive . . . engaging!"

The stars wavered and vanished, the perfect blackness of the Trapdoor space replacing them, and Campbell found himself joining in the near-deafening cheer that erupted from behind. "It *works!*" he heard Tavana shout gleefully. "*Mon Dieu*, it *works!*"

"It does indeed," Campbell said, "And another round of applause to Xander, Tavana, and Maddox, who figured out how to rewind the darn coils." He unstrapped. "We'll be doing about four-hour jumps before the coils need to be recharged, which will take about eight hours. In the meantime . . . it's almost dinnertime. In honor of our successful jump back to violating the speed of light, I've got a little surprise."

"A surprise?"

"When I was digging around back in storage, I found a little box. It looks to me like it was a special present for someone at our destination, probably one of Tantalus' top admins. Turns out it's a box of Buckleys."

"Buckleys?" Xander blinked, then suddenly his eyes lit up. "You mean, Buckley's Space Gourmet Dinners?"

"The very same, yes."

"Wow," Francisco breathed. "I've had those; they're even better than what they served at Captain's Table."

"That's why Buckley retired richer than anyone else in the Europa crew, 'cept for Baker," Campbell agreed. "And we've got enough for a few special feasts. Figure this is the right time, especially since we've spent a couple months eating regular rations."

The others enthusiastically agreed. Campbell went into the cargo area and extracted five dinners from the box he'd hidden inside one of the construction machines' casings. He shared them out and the group let the dinners' built-in superconductor batteries warm the meals to the proper temperature.

As he was taking his third bite of buttered garlic asparagus, there was a loud *ping!* from the front console, and the starfield appeared again.

He barely restrained himself from swearing; instead, he locked his dinner down and started checking the board.

"What's wrong?" Xander asked tensely.

"Don't know. Tav, you're the closest we've got to an expert. What's going on?"

Tavana gestured for him to move out of the control seat, which he did. He continued eating, but the Buckley Dinner didn't seem nearly as good as it had been a few minutes ago.

A few moments later, he heard a phrase in Tahitian which he was pretty sure was not something said in polite company. "What is it, Tav?"

"It's the windings, Sergeant." Tavana's voice was rough, filled with anger and at the same time on the edge of tears. "They're not perfect, we knew that, but I thought it might be good enough...but..."

"But what? Are they ruined again?" It was hard to ask. Assuming they had enough wire to re-wind the coils, the amount of time needed would be almost fatal. It *would* be fatal if they had to do it more than once.

"No, not ruined; the failsafes cut in. The field resonance through the coils that aren't perfectly aligned makes them heat up slowly. Eventually they get too close to the transition temperature."

The transition temperature, of course, was the point at which a superconductor stopped being a superconductor. When *that* happened, all the energy stored in the superconductor was liberated pretty much instantly—an explosion, in other words. Thus, any superconductor that carried or stored significant power was monitored for temperature. "Does that mean that when it cools down, we can start it up again?"

Tavana looked a little less angry. "Well, yes, sir. But..."

"I can guess. That takes a while."

"The coils are sealed up in enclosed, insulated spaces. Normally they don't heat up appreciably. But now they have to radiate the energy away, and there's no good way to do that. We can't take the covers off; they're designed as part of the field resonation circuits. So... I guess I'll have to model it and see what the optimum duty cycle is. I know it'll take a *lot* longer to radiate this away than it did to build up, and it was only twenty minutes to build up."

"Get to it, then."

The cabin was deathly quiet as Tavana worked. Campbell wished he could think of some way to break the tension, but in all honesty, there wasn't any way he could imagine. This was a potential death sentence, and Tavana was going to tell them when the execution would occur.

Finally, after what felt like forever, Tavana turned

slowly to face them. From his expression, Campbell knew it was bad.

"Sir..."

"We're all here. Give it to us straight."

Tavana swallowed, and then sat up. "Best case, modeling heat buildup and...well, never mind. We can run them for about five minutes every two hours."

The words hit him like a blow. "That's one part in twenty-four, Tavana. You sure?"

Tavana looked down, miserable. "Yes, sir. Other scenarios take longer for various reasons. It's going to be almost ten hours before we want to start that cycle. We want the coils to drop to as low a temperature as we can get them, and they're hot right now." He looked up with a slightly less miserable expression. "On the positive side...we will have plenty of time to recharge, so we gain that time back. Recharging won't heat the superconductor, so it won't hurt us."

Campbell gritted his teeth and tried to relax. "Still, If I get you right...that means it'll take *eight times* as long to get anywhere as we thought before."

Tavana nodded.

From two weeks per light-year, they'd now gone to four *months*. Forty months to Orado. Even starvation rations would never get them that far.

For a moment he was overwhelmed with a sad, sick fury. *No. It's not fair, it's just not* acceptable *that we could have done so much, come this far, and just end up crippled in space. These kids have worked so hard, hardly complained—shoot, I've had squads of recruits who were more of a pain in the ass.*

But he got a grip on himself. *There has to be an answer. I won't* let *there be no answer to this.*

Even as he thought it, he suddenly knew the only possible way out.

"All right. Then we've only got one choice left."

He took the controls and spun *LS-88* slowly around. He then steadied the little ship, now pointing at a brilliantly blazing point of light.

"That's the only star near enough. Just comparing its position in the sky with our little jump, I can tell it's less than a light-year off—a lot less, maybe a little more than a quarter light-year. It's also probably a G-class star. It might just be a barren system, nothing there for us.

"But maybe...just maybe...there's a planet we can live on there. It's a damn sight better chance than drifting here praying for a miracle. So what do you say?"

Xander stared at the star. "That's the star that shouldn't be there."

"Right, son."

Tavana nodded. "Like it was waiting for us."

"I'm scared," Francisco announced suddenly.

"So am I," Campbell said quietly. "So am I. But I'm not giving up yet, and that looks like our last throw of the dice to me. If you're sure the coils will last that long. Tav?"

Tavana bit his lip, straightened, and nodded. "If we don't push them...yes, Sergeant. They'll last that long."

"Then set up the program, Tavana. Like it or not, we're about to become explorers."

He looked at the enigmatic point of light, blazing in the dark. *You damn well better have something for us when we get there, because I'll be damned if I'm leading these kids to their deaths.*

Chapter 11

"Sergeant?" Xander whispered.

He saw the sergeant's eyes snap open, look around, registering where he was, the person speaking to him, the fact that everything else seemed normal, in the time it took a normal person to blink. *He's always ready for everything.*

"Sorry to wake you, sir."

Campbell sat up slowly. "I figure you must have something you want to say that the others shouldn't hear. If I agree with you, then there's no problem. Go on, son."

"The chances of finding a habitable planet...what are they?"

Campbell pursed his lips. "Well...understand that odds make no real difference here. But anyway... I'm pretty damn sure that's a G-type star. I was able to do a little trigonometry from our first little jump and the way the star shifted. That tells me the star's distance, which isn't far away at all. The apparent brightness combined with distance really helps nail that down. So, that said...G-type stars in this neighborhood tend to have planets, but only one in ten's got an Earth-type planet in the habitable zone. Of those, only one in two's compatible with our kind of life. So . . . one in twenty."

"And if this doesn't work out . . . we're dead, right?"

Campbell looked as though he wanted to argue that, then bowed his head. "Yeah, that's about the size of it. It's why I said we've got no other options. We have to make a go of it here, because there's nowhere else *to* go."

"Then . . . look, the main reason we can't go where we want to, to Orado, is that the supplies won't hold out, right?"

"Right. Though from what Tavana said, I'm not sure I'd bet on those cobbled-together coils holding out for a ten-light-year journey. He had to think about it making what turns out to be about a fortieth of that."

"Still, why can't you just put all or most of us under, like the lieutenant? If only one of us—you—is up, or maybe not even you most of the time, we won't need much food or water."

The sergeant was shaking his head even before Xander finished. "It's a good idea, but I already thought of it. Fact is, I only know how to do that using military nano setups. Civilian nanos, like yours? Different setup, different protocols for operation. I don't have authority to modify them the same way I did for Lieutenant Haley, and none of us know how to reprogram nanos for that kind of stuff. I could dump the procedure to hers easy, but yours? That'd take a nanoprogrammer with a medical bent, or a doctor with the right programming experience, like Dr. Kimei. *She'd* be able to do that, no problem."

"You knew her, sir? I didn't interact with them

much." He remembered Dr. Kimei well—an attractive blonde woman, friendly and competent . . . but she usually wasn't alone, because she tended both species on the ship.

His expression must have given him away, because the sergeant gave a wry grin. "Not comfortable around Bemmies, eh?" Sergeant Campbell made a face. "I don't have anything against 'em, myself, but for a colony? They're experiments, a few generations old. Some were unstable, mentally. They *say* that's all cleared up, but dammit, you don't want to rely on someone's well-meaning experiment on a colony world." He sighed. "Anyway, yeah, I know her. Or knew her, if she got killed in that mess. Nice lady. Her girl Sakura's a born pilot."

Xander felt a tiny grin on his face. "I heard Tav mention Sakura a couple of times. Think he likes her."

"Lot to like about the girl. Little late for that now; if she's still alive, she and her family are on Orado by now, maybe getting on another colony ship for Tantalus."

Xander looked out the port as the pitch-black of the Trapdoor space transitioned to the star-scattered darkness of normal space, the mysterious star now blazing brilliantly directly before them. "One chance in twenty. Sergeant . . . what do we do if . . . ?"

"Honestly . . . I don't want to think about that. But . . . I'll want to do what I can to make the end easy. We'll live as long as we can, though. Always a chance someone will find us, no matter how slim. And then, well . . ." He shrugged. "You understand?"

The thought of having to "make the end easy" made Xander shudder inside. But at the same time, he knew the sergeant was right. Death by slow starvation or suffocation was something he wanted to spare Maddox, Tavana, and Francisco. "Yes, sir."

"But let's keep our fingers crossed. I've beaten worse odds more'n once in my life, Xander. Hell, I think we beat odds at least that bad surviving that disaster; that field instability could've just cut straight through *LS-88*. We're still alive, we've fixed all the problems we ran into, and we're moving. Don't think I'd have given odds on us doing *that* well if someone asked me before the fact."

Xander thought about it. What would have happened if Sergeant Campbell hadn't happened to be on board? What if Lieutenant Haley hadn't been caught in the boarding tunnel and able to release them? What if they hadn't had enough food on board, or no heavy equipment with the right kind of wiring? "You're right, Sergeant. We've been beating odds all along."

"Damn straight we have. I'm betting we're going to beat them once more."

"So do I, Sergeant," he said. "After all, it's the only bet left worth taking."

"Good man. Now," the sergeant said, letting the straps pull him gently back into his chair, "let me get some more shuteye."

Xander grinned and nodded. His mind more at ease than it had been before, he found it wasn't long before sleep came for him.

Chapter 12

Tavana gazed at the brilliant disc of the star—filtered, of course—that was the center of their hopes. "Program concluded, Sergeant. We made it. I think we must be, um, what, something like a hundred eighty million kilometers from the star right now. What now?"

"*Now* we have to look for a planet we can land on," Campbell said easily. Tavana knew he was putting up a front, mostly for Maddox and Francisco. There was no guarantee of a planet at all, let alone one worth landing on. "Tav, what I'd like to do is use the Trapdoor to make really short jumps around the system, do a survey. I can pilot like that—I did a stint with a survey team some years back. But I know that takes some tricks with the coils to let you do that any shorter than four hundred million miles, and precision's not the Trapdoor's strong point."

Tav found himself rubbing his chin. "I hadn't thought about that, sir. Too busy just hoping they didn't give out on the way here."

"Well, we're here, so I'm not so worried. You boys figured out the solution for the Nebula Drive, right?"

Xander laughed. "Brute-force solution, yes, sir. We'll

manually operate the dispensers. The autodispensers got fried pretty completely, according to Tav, so we just made some we can control from inside the cabin. The control field extensions for the Nebula Drive seemed okay."

"So," the sergeant said, "that means that worst comes to worst and the Trapdoor coils go down, we just use the Nebula Drive. Right?"

"Right," agreed Tav. There wasn't much point in disagreeing because the sergeant was basically right, though the Nebula Drive—or "dusty-plasma containment sail," as his professors preferred—was a lot slower.

"Then what about it? Can you give me short-jump capability, or not?"

"Um . . . let me check some things."

"Take your time. Don't do it fast, do it right."

"Yes, sir."

Tavana accessed his notes and references. He hadn't gotten to the classes that covered short-jump approaches, but he *had* actually read ahead; that was an interesting part of the Trapdoor engineering, pushing its limits, and he'd had some discussions with his teachers on it. The keys were synchronization, field control, and dissipation.

One nice thing was that all those jumps from where they'd been marooned to here had given him a lot of data on the regular coils and the ones they had to rewind. He could can nail down their resonances and quirks pretty well. If his omni could crunch all that data . . .

It turned out that the omni could crunch that data pretty well. Looking at the plots, it was easy to see the hand-wound ones; they had a lot of anomalies. But none of them seemed fatal to Sergeant Campbell's idea. There was one limitation, though . . .

"Sergeant, I think we could. But it would need you

to go out and add a couple of components to each drive coil circuit. We *have* the components, and they're not hard to install, I don't think. But to control the timing and dissipation of the field well enough, we need to install these networked synchronizers."

"In each bay? So about a day, a day and a half of work to save us weeks of cruising? Let me suit up while you get the components together."

It actually only took Campbell most of a day to do the work. Tavana guided him through the first couple, then just watched as the sergeant carefully and precisely installed the components, verified function with Tavana, and then moved to the next.

The next ship-morning (Tav doubted they were still synchronized with any clock in the Galaxy, but still, they needed some kind of schedule), Campbell had them strap back in. He settled back and gripped the controls. "So I should be able to do a short-jump now?"

"Should, yes, Sergeant. I'm not an expert, though, so—"

"Tavana, it's all right. I'm not an expert in most of the things we need. You did your best and that's all I'm ever going to ask of you." The sergeant strapped in. "Let's test this bad boy. All set, Francisco?"

"Yes, sir, Sergeant!" Francisco had been showing extreme mood swings during the journey here, but right now he sounded cheerful.

Well, we've gotten where we were going and we're talking about finding a planet. He's feeling hopeful.

"Then let's go!"

Sergeant Campbell first tumbled the ship carefully on two axes; Tavana knew that this gave a full view of the entire sky around them. "Okay, here goes nothing."

The port went black and then stars flashed out, after a pause that Tavana thought was no more than ten seconds. *It worked!*

"Nice jump, Sergeant."

"Thank you kindly, son."

"So where did you jump us to?"

"Didn't really matter; not towards the star, not away from it really, just a sort of lateral line. That should give us a chance to locate planets, by checking any parallax from the motion. Let me tumble her again, and then we can start looking."

"I think I've got an automatic comparison set up in my omni," Maddox said. "Not too hard, right?"

"Shouldn't be," Tav agreed.

The stars spun by once more, and Tavana looked over at Maddox. For a moment everything was quiet, and then Maddox shouted, "Yes...*yes*! There are planets, sir! And maybe...um, a couple other things?"

"A couple other 'things'? What kind of things? Let me see what you've got."

Maddox broadcast the detected targets—objects that had changed their relative position due to the microjump. Ignoring the central star, there were no fewer than nine targets.

"Well, now, I see what you mean. We've got a couple comets, good-sized ones. And that's a Jupiter-type gas giant. Maybe another one there. Rocky planet, way too close in, you can tell that by relative position..."

A few more minutes went by; Tavana did some calculations on some of the targets that had a questionable relative position, but his spirits were falling. *None of them are in the right location.*

He looked at the older man, at Xander, and saw the grim reflection of his own fears. "Sergeant—"

"We aren't giving up yet!" Campbell said quickly. "See, from these measurements, it turned out we were actually pretty close to the ecliptic before we jumped. There's a whole swath of the sky over here that we couldn't see clearly enough to get a match on. What we're looking for could be right there."

Tavana didn't argue, but the "swath" wasn't very large; it was just the relatively tiny angle where the central star's glare had made it impossible to resolve—basically little more than the star's apparent diameter at their prior distance. "Doing another microjump, sir?"

"You got it. Everyone locked in?"

Assured that they were, Campbell triggered another short-jump; this one lasted about the same length of time, and the stars shimmered back into existence. After the obligatory tumble, Maddox ran his comparison again.

"Sir, there's one new target!"

"What's the location, Tavana?"

Tavana triangulated from the two observations and compared it with the prior results. A trickle of hope started, a painful trickle because there were so many things that could dash that hope. "It's at . . . about one hundred twenty million kilometers from the primary, maybe just a little less. That's well inside the Goldilocks Zone!"

"Well, now, that's looking up. Can we get a good look at it from here?"

"If you can point us directly at it."

"I will most surely do that, then."

A few moments passed. Tav finally got the newly-discovered planet centered, then triggered the telescopic function of the viewport camera.

The enigmatic dot of light brightened and expanded, becoming a tiny but distinct crescent of brilliant green and white.

"Looks like atmosphere. And something else, but I'm damned if I can tell what," the sergeant said after a pause. "But if it's got an atmosphere, our odds just shot way up. Strap in, I'm getting us closer."

"But, sir," Tav said, "it's not at the right distance for a microjump."

"No, but if you're really good at feeling these things out, just about everything's at the right distance for *two* microjumps."

Tavana thought for a moment, and then wanted to smack himself. "Triangulation!"

"Exactly right, son. Once you get close enough, find the direction and distance that *will* put you a minimum jump away, and then jump to *that* point. Hold on, we're doing it now."

Another ten seconds of blackness, a moment of the ship turning, realigning, and then another few seconds.

The screen cleared. Before them was a small globe, but still far larger than the magnified image they'd seen before. Tavana triggered the telescopic magnification again, and the new world swelled hugely. From their new vantage point, slightly to starward of the planet, the surface was more complex; swirls of white cloud contrasted with brilliant green and darker green and brown and buff-colored areas. *Seas and continents!*

"Sure does look promising. Shame I haven't got a

spectrometer, but it looks good. Except that green color's funky."

"Algae bloom?"

"Over the whole planet? Well, if so, that'd be good news for us; that looks like chlorophyll green to me. Let's check out her vitals, shall we?"

The view from the other microjumps helped refine the size of the new planet—slightly larger than Earth— and Tavana spotted a couple small satellites of the planet which helped pin down the gravity and mass of the target. "It's a little bigger than Earth, but surface gravity's going to be just a little less."

"Is it . . . is it going to be safe?" Francisco asked. "I mean . . . will we be able to go there? It looks very pretty!"

"Does, doesn't it? Sure a lot better than just black space and stars, I gotta say. But the only way we'll really know if it's safe is to go there. All the survey software that might've been on this tub is gone, and all I've got to go on is my gut."

"What does your gut say, Sergeant?"

Campbell got up and stretched. "It says that tomorrow's another day. We've been busy today and I'm not going to *think* about doing a landing until I've gotten some rest."

"We should name the planet first!" Francisco was emphatic.

"I am tempted to call it 'Hope,'" Tavana admitted.

"Too obvious. Xander?"

"Looks like it has a lot of water, and it looks sort of tropical. Lagoon?"

"Hm. I could live with that, I suppose. Maddox?"

"It looks like a gem to me. We could call it Gem?"

"I say we call it *Esmeralda*—Emerald, to you."

The sergeant chuckled. "You know, I think the kid's got it. Emerald it is."

Francisco beamed, overjoyed at being the one to name the planet they had found. Tavana wanted to object, but he suddenly realized that the sergeant probably would have approved *any* suggestion by Francisco. The boy needed things to make him feel better, and Tavana was old enough not to need that kind of help, right?

So he shoved the petty disappointment back and clapped; the others joined in. "To Emerald, then—tomorrow!"

"Tomorrow," Sergeant Campbell said. "By this time tomorrow, we'll be landing!"

Tavana knew that landing wouldn't mean anything if it turned out that Emerald's atmosphere was toxic, the green color caused by something lethal and alien... but in his heart, he didn't believe that the universe *would* be that cruel. Looking at the brilliant green sphere, he closed his eyes and said a silent prayer. *Please...be a place that we can live.*

Please.

PART II

EMERALD

Chapter 13

"Listen up, people. We are about to attempt a landing on a planet no one has ever landed on before. That means we're going in cold, no survey, no beacons, nothing. With the way we lost most of our instruments, we can't even do much of a once-over from orbit. We'll basically just get a glimpse of the land that's not cloud-covered and pick the best-looking landing spots."

The huge curve of Emerald cut across the forward port, softened by the presence of atmosphere, white and green and brown. "Tavana, is the Nebula Drive retracting?"

The French-Polynesian boy nodded. "The dust is going into the containers we set up for it, yes. The gas, however—we will lose most of it."

"No biggie. It's done its job."

It had taken a day or two to deploy the Nebula Drive dusty-plasma sail, and several more days to use the controlled nebula to get them into orbit around Emerald. Other than being slow, however, the Drive had performed flawlessly, something that had made the trip a mini-vacation. They weren't worrying about improvised coils or wondering where they were going. Emerald had always been there, reassuring them that they weren't just drifting through empty space anymore.

Getting the dust—programmable nanotech motes descended from the original designs by the European Union for the famous *Odin*—was important. There was no telling when they might need a bunch of nanodust, even simple stuff like that. And they sure weren't making it themselves.

"Right. Francisco, Maddox, I want you two to go through the cargo area, all the way from the back to the front, and secure anything that might be loose. If you find anything, like a big piece of machinery, that you don't think you can secure right, mark it in your omnis."

He pushed himself over to where he'd hung his EVA suit. "I've got one more job, but it's a quickie."

"What is it, sir?" asked Xander.

"You can help, actually. While I'm getting suited up and checking out all telltales, go get me those SC-178s, would you?"

"SC-178s?"

Campbell snorted at himself. *You think these kids live and breathe acronyms and designations?* "Those things I called 'commsats for idiots.' In the crate marked ICS-GIS-S-C-178. Crate that size probably holds ten of them. Just drag the crate up. Remember that—"

"I know, Sergeant, it's still just as massy even if it's weightless, and don't crush myself or anyone else by getting cocky with it."

"That's *sounding* almost cocky, kid. Just be careful."

By the time he was satisfied that the suit was operating perfectly, Xander had arrived with the crate. "Now what, sir?"

"Now I basically dump these things out the airlock. Once they go into vacuum they wake right up. I can give 'em the update on the diameter of the planet and things like that from my omni. They'll use their built-in micro-ion drives to work their way into a reasonable-coverage set of orbits over time, and deploy their solar recharge sails, which they can also use for a little boost. Once on-station, the sails reconfigure to standard power-gathering panels. Guaranteed to last at least seventy-five years on-station."

"What will we get out of them, with what we don't have in infrastructure?"

"Don't sell these things short. They've got a lot of standard commo packages, software update services, and more importantly great GIS/GPS capability. That will come in handy if we end up having to navigate around this globe. Good remote storage servers, and—not least—they can use their power to send distress pings out regularly. Not very often, but there are ten of them."

"Distress pings?" Xander looked skeptical. Campbell couldn't blame him. "That's a ten-year delay on reception, Sergeant, if we're looking at Orado."

"If it's Orado, yeah," Campbell agreed, opening the lock and cramming the crate inside; he would just barely be able to fit in with it. "But no one on Orado would notice it, unless they had a radio telescope pointed in this direction for no particular reason. This is just in case anyone comes looking. It wouldn't take much brainpower to say, 'Hey, here's a star right near where the disaster happened, maybe survivors went there.' And if we have constant distress beacons, they might be readable from billions of miles away by a search vessel."

He clambered in and made sure his body was clear of the hatch. "All right, close her up and put us in vacuum."

Pressure dropped swiftly. Once it hit less than one millibar—less than a thousandth of Earth-normal atmospheric pressure—he saw activation signals coming up on his omni. "There you are," he muttered. Opening the crate, he could see each of the SC-178s with its two indicator lights—one for drives, one for electronics—glowing a comforting green. "What do you know, ten for ten. Will miracles never cease?"

A few minutes sufficed to update the satellites with their meager store of information, and then—as he'd told Xander he would—he simply opened the outer hatch and started throwing the soccer-ball sized spheres with their strangely seamed sides out the airlock. Once clear, the greenish-painted satellites opened two small hatches and began preparing for orbital modification.

Campbell couldn't help but grin faintly. Every time he saw an SC-178 deploy, it looked like they'd suddenly grown little circular wings or flappy round ears, at least before the solar panels started to deploy. The lines and indicator LEDs gave the rest of the sphere a vaguely cheerful face between those ears. He shook his head, closed the exterior door, and waited for the airlock to repressurize.

"Mostly secure, Sergeant!" Maddox said as he re-entered the cabin. "We marked a few things that we couldn't be sure of."

"Outstanding. Xander, you come with me. Tavana, make sure all ten of our little satellites get clear of our position. Francisco, Maddox—use the head, and then get yourselves strapped in." He accessed Maddox's and

Francisco's omnis; there were five questionable areas marked, all of them—as he had expected—associated with the larger pieces of machinery. He and Xander got all of those tended to.

"So now I guess I'd better strap in too?" Xander asked.

"Not yet," said the sergeant. "Now the two of us go front-to-back, inch by inch, and make damn sure there isn't a single loose object, not so much as a bolt. We're about to do re-entry at orbital velocity, and anything not strapped down could kill someone."

Xander nodded, and the two men began a careful survey of the large cargo hold. Sure enough, they found several loose objects that had been hidden behind or under others, including one TechTool that Samuel Campbell had been sure would turn up in exactly this situation. "Tav, found your missing tool. Locking it into a crate back here for now."

"*Merci*, Sergeant! I was worried about it not being found."

"No more than I was. How're those satellites doing?"

"All have cleared our immediate vicinity; there is nothing within several kilometers now."

"Good. Then get to your own couch and strap in; we're just about ready to go."

Campbell settled himself behind the controls and made sure the restraining harness was secure. Then he checked telemetry on all the others. "Tav, you're a little loose. So are you, Francisco. Strap in. This isn't going to be a picnic. When we land at first we'll think we're in hell, because we aren't used to weight anymore. But we're going to land, at last, on solid ground."

All four of his passengers gave a cheer at that, and

he grinned back before turning his attention to the controls. "All right, now. You can read, or play your Jewelbug, or whatever, but keep it quiet and do *not* distract me. I have to do this on manual, and that's dangerous as hell."

That was something of an exaggeration, he admitted to himself, but he really didn't want to be disturbed. He'd done quite a few hands-on de-orbits in his time. Every one was a little different, and even after a couple centuries of space travel, the friction of re-entry was still one of the things that could kill a spaceship faster than you could say *oops*.

And, of course, every other time he'd either had an expert, or at least a serious survey, to help him out. This time, it was all seat-of-the-pants and gut instinct.

First he tested the manual reconfiguration. With the automatics out, they'd had to use two of the five omnis to provide processing power to direct the metamaterial that made up a large portion of the shuttle's exterior. The hookups still worked, fortunately, otherwise he didn't know how he'd be able to land this thing. Its default shape wasn't all that different from the "brick airplane" first made famous by the American Space Shuttle back in the 20th century, which meant that it was great for re-entry and absolutely abominable for anything else, like actually *flying*, let alone landing on anything that wasn't a gargantuan salt flat or immense tailored runway.

But the reconfiguration *did* work. It was slower than the original systems would have been, but it did the job, and he was pretty sure he could handle the rough moments while it was between modes. "All configurations check out. Starting first de-orbit burn."

He did a series of burns to slowly lower the altitude

until he started getting evidence of atmosphere. He wasn't sure of the scale height for Emerald. Even if he was, their altitude wasn't absolutely precisely known. Just how high or low he'd have to be before noticeable drag set in would also depend on a lot of other factors, ranging from just how much atmosphere Emerald had to how active Emerald's sun had been lately.

It was after the third burn that he felt an infinitesimal quiver. *That's got it*. "We are about to start re-entry," he announced. "Stay calm; this *will* be rough."

There was no way to avoid some battering, at pretty nasty levels, on a re-entry. And here, he was having to wing it. On the positive side, if he got the angle wrong, they wouldn't have too much time to worry about it because they'd be dead right quick.

The vibration grew, became a faint singing hum, getting louder, louder, dropping in pitch while rising in volume. *LS-88* was starting to shake slightly now. "We are in the soup. Starting to see heating. Boys, we are about to do a good job at emulating a meteor." Or of *being* a meteor—but he didn't say that out loud.

The shuttle was shuddering now, violent shakes as pressure of deceleration mounted inexorably, crushing down onto Campbell like a load of wet sand slithering out of a dump truck. He heard Francisco whimper. "Only . . . about four G's," Campbell managed to say, trying to make it sound casual. "Just a few seconds, kids. Keep calm . . . breathe slow and deep."

The forward viewport was black, closed against the heat, but Campbell could see the telltales, temperature climbing. There was one spot that heat was going up faster than anywhere else. He stared at that indication, *willing* it to slow down, to hold out.

Then the rise *did* slow down. He glanced at the others, saw that a similar slowdown was starting. Slowly, the massive weight lifted from him, and the temperature telltales began to drop. *Made it! God-damn but we made it through the re-entry!*

The forward port showed a gleam and then lit up as the Thermal Protection System retracted, showing blue-black sky above and fluffy clouds far below, green ocean dotted with islands. "Reconfiguring for supersonic flight in three...two...one..."

The manual transition was a pain in the rear. For a few seconds he almost bobbled it, the *LS-88* swaying dangerously through the air like a drunk trying to drive home on icy roads. But he finally got it under control, and now the much more streamlined aircraft screamed its way through the sky with nuclear jets driving it forward.

"All right, people, we are now flying, not falling, and not drifting in space. That heaviness you feel is real honest gravity, and we'll have to get used to it again. But believe me, I'm damn glad to feel it."

"This world has worse gravity than Earth!" Tavana said. "Will it be dangerous?"

While his limbs were trying to present the same argument as Francisco, his trained reflexes told him something else. "Hate to tell you, but if anything it's a little lighter on the gravity here. I've been to a dozen worlds, maybe more; believe me, I know what high gravity feels like."

"Where are we going to land, sir?"

"Spotted a couple of candidates on our orbits, and figured our re-entry to...yep, that should be it ahead."

A large island was coming into view; it took several

minutes at their supersonic speed to draw near enough to appreciate its size. "An island?" Maddox asked. "Why not a continent?"

"We can always move somewhere else if we want. An island tends to have a more limited population, especially of hostile predators, since any predator has to rely only on what's on the island. It can't trot off to the mainland and get himself food like we'd order takeout, after all. And this island's plenty big enough for four people."

He was puzzled by the lack of real mountains; from orbit he had seen things that looked like mountain ranges, but now that he was closer he didn't think any of the peaks he had seen topped three hundred meters. That was really rare. *No plate tectonics? Something wearing them down fast?*

Still, everything was reasonably promising. The way *LS-88* was responding, the atmosphere was similar to Earth's in density at this altitude. It was a shame there wasn't any atmospheric sensor functioning so he could tell if the chemistry was like Earth's. If *LS-88*'s jets had been powered by chemical fuel, like old-style airplanes, he'd have had his answer already; without oxygen they'd have stalled instantly. But this craft used nuclear jets, driving the turbines through sheer nuclear heat. No answers there.

One thing at a time, he reminded himself. First they had to get down.

He triggered the second transition, slowing to subsonic speed, watching flight conditions narrowly. There was no rain; the skies were clear and the winds weren't terribly strong. It was hard to tell direction. But when they got closer, the trees and such would give him an indication, as would wave movement.

LS-88 swept in over the shore, and he began a leisurely survey of his selected target. The island was about seventy kilometers long by thirty-five wide, a ridge of low hills or tiny mountains running down the center from each end and meeting in the middle. The middle ridge extended to the shoreline on each side and bowed outward in the center of the island, where clear water showed.

He took *LS-88* on a high inspection. *A circular area in the center, a lot of water in a ring around a central island. Caldera or impact crater, I'm guessing.* But that was only a guess. If a couple centuries of space exploration had taught the human race anything, it was that alien worlds were full of surprises, even the ones without anything living on them. Any assumptions you made might get shattered at any moment.

Still, the important thing was that it looked big enough to support them. There was a larger landmass, maybe a continent, not all that far away if they wanted to move. The question now was, where to land?

"Okay, crew, I'm thinking we want to be pretty close to the shore; fishing and such will be a good way of catching food."

"Sounds reasonable to me, Sergeant," Xander said.

"Look for a river," Francisco said unexpectedly. When they glanced at him, he smiled—a pained smile still, with the pressure of gravity weighing on him, but a smile. "My mama was reading a book to me about old civilizations and said all of them started near rivers."

A genuine contribution. Not that I wasn't thinking along those lines myself, but it'll be good for Francisco to know he was right. "Very good. We'll want fresh water to drink, and streams are good for fishing too. If it's big enough, might even be useful for moving stuff."

From the high vantage point, it wasn't hard to spot streams. One looked particularly prominent, gathering several tributary creeks into a respectable flow. The difference in elevation wasn't very large, so they weren't going to get too many whitewater rapids or anything of that nature. Without a discontinuity like a small cascade, though, tides might make it brackish quite a ways up. Solar tides only—the moons weren't big enough; they'd get about half the tides they'd see on Earth. He didn't know what the slightly different gravity would mean for that.

The large stream also had a somewhat clear region near it, standing out from the surrounding forest. It surrounded a small lake maybe half a kilometer across; the stream went into the lake and went out the other side to the sea.

"Got our landing spot picked out, boys." He flashed it onto their retinas. "Look good?"

There was a chorus of enthusiastic *yesses*; of course, a lot of that was just the excitement of actually landing. They'd probably have agreed to anything that looked halfway decent.

"All right, descending to five hundred meters. Hold on; I'm about to convert us to VTOL."

"VTOL?" repeated Francisco.

"Vertical Takeoff and Landing. That means we can land and take off straight up and down, which lets me put her down on any space she'll fit, instead of needing a runway. Now pipe down, everyone, this is going to be tricky."

It *was* tricky. The slower-than-design conversion

induced turbulence and threw off the aerodynamics drastically. *LS-88* almost tumbled, spinning once completely around the ship's central axis as Campbell fought to regain control. He heard a frightened curse from Tavana, a gasp from Xander, and a squeak of fear from Francisco. Maddox was silent, but his hands gripped the armrests so tightly that his knuckles were white.

In a few moments the ship steadied, and Campbell began to breathe easier. "We're okay now, kids. Just hold on a few more minutes."

He dipped the nose once more, circled his chosen landing spot. He could see *something* flying away from the area. *Well, now I know there's life beyond plants here. Probably a good thing. And the air looks clear. The green color's from the seawater, somehow. Maybe, just maybe, this is a livable place.*

Now came the trickiest part of all. He had no operating radar, no spotters, just 3-D images he'd recorded that his omni was now overlaying on what he could see through the forward port, showing its best calculation of his current height above the target ground. He let the ship drop to what he guessed was thirty meters, and then reduced his descent to the most exquisitely slow progress he could manage, measured in centimeters per second. Slowly, very slowly, the trees rose up, the horizon began to vanish, and the waving grasses gradually became visible at the lower edge of the forward port.

LS-88 vibrated slightly in an unexpected wind, but he didn't let her sway more than a few centimeters. Now he could see dust and debris flying. He knew he had to be close. *Keep it slow, keep it steady, no need to hurry. Slow as you can get it—*

The *thud* of the forward strut striking something transmitted itself throughout the cabin. It was followed almost instantly by smaller thumps from the side struts landing. Tense, Sergeant Campbell started stepping the power down. This was the moment of truth, when he'd find out if what he landed on was solid and stable, or if he'd chosen a pile of quicksand.

As the vibrations of the engines diminished, *LS-88* remained immobile, steady as solid stone. Finally the whine of the turbines faded to nothing. A wide smile spreading across his face, Campbell spun his chair to face the others.

"Gentlemen, we have landed."

Chapter 14

Tavana let out a whoop and for a few moments everyone was cheering except for the sergeant, who was just grinning from ear to ear and leaning back in his seat with obvious relief.

Finally the noise died down and the sergeant stood up. "Whoo. Feels real funny standing now, but also seems my medical nanos didn't let me get *too* weak. Still, everybody be a little careful moving around 'til you get used to walking again."

He looked around the little group. "Now, we've got one question left: can we breathe the air? If we can, odds are a hundred to one in our favor that Emerald's a Terran-type world, and we can live here."

Tavana thought, and suddenly a chill went down his spine. "Sergeant . . . we don't have any chemical sensors, do we?"

"Not without ripping them out of *LS-88*'s air system, and ripping the air system apart—even a little bit—before we know exactly what the air outside is like sounds a little bass-ackwards to me."

Maddox pursed his lips. "If I had my collection, some of those would have sensors on them."

122

Xander shook his head. "Sergeant, there's got to be something in the cargo with a sensor that could be adapted."

Campbell looked at him. "If you've got a suggestion, I'm all ears."

"It's oxygen we need to check for, right, Sergeant?" asked Francisco.

"That's right. The chemistry that supports an oxygen-rich atmosphere is the one we depend on. We've only found one exception."

"Well...then can't we just put something in the airlock that's on fire, and if it stays on fire *after* we open the airlock, then we know there's oxygen?"

For a minute Campbell just stared, and then threw back his head and laughed loudly. Xander snickered and started to laugh, and then Tavana joined in. "*Dieu*, how we miss the obvious!" he exclaimed.

Francisco looked embarrassed and angry; but before Tavana could call the sergeant's attention to it, Campbell stopped on his own and knelt down next to Francisco. "Hey, we weren't laughing at you. Laughing at myself, really. Here we were looking for some fancy high-tech way to find out if we could breathe the air, and damned if the youngest kid in the crew sees the answer that was right in front of us! Good work, Francisco! *Great* work!"

The uncertain face suddenly broke into a brilliant smile. "*De veras?* You mean it?"

"I sure do! And let me tell you I'm relieved as all h...heck, because without *some* trick to tell us if there's enough oxygen out there, the only way we'd have known is to have someone step outside and find out."

Tavana shuddered inwardly. Of course if the air

outside *wasn't* breathable ... He shoved that thought as far away as he could.

Francisco blushed visibly. "It wasn't just my idea, though, sir. I remembered something in one of the old books my mama read to me; one of the people in it said, 'Where a light can't live, I know I can't,' so ..."

"Memory or your own idea, you were the one who came up with it for us."

Campbell went into the cargo, and came out with a plastic bottle of clear liquid. "Alcohol. All-around good disinfectant, useful for a lot of things. And perfectly flammable. Now, let's see ... sure, I can use a cooking pan to hold it."

"Can I do it, sir?" Tavana asked.

"Why not? You've got the idea, I'm sure."

"Go into the lock, put alcohol in the pan, set it on fire, and then go out, close the door, and let it equalize with exterior air."

"Simple and straightforward. But here," he handed Tavana a wad of packing material, "add that. Pure alcohol flames can be tough to see; adding something else fixes that problem."

"I wanna light it!" Francisco said.

"Your idea, your right to help out. Okay, you two."

Tavana walked to the lock—slowly, feeling as though his pants were made of lead, and his shirt too—and opened the inner door. Placing the pan on the floor, he poured it half-full of alcohol and dropped in the packing material. It swiftly absorbed a lot of the liquid and sank in a sodden mass to the bottom. "All right, Francisco. Careful! Don't get too close, there'll be fumes."

But Francisco obviously knew how to light a fire—his

pocket TechTool actually had a firestarter mode, which Tavana's didn't. The little multitool extended into a slender wand that allowed a hot, bright spark to be generated quite a distance from the user's hand.

With a gentle *whoomph!* the alcohol ignited. The vapors around it making a momentary, ghost-blue fireball; the alcohol-soaked packing material began burning briskly with orange and blue flame.

"Okay, let's get out!"

Tavana felt his gut tensing sourly as the airlock door swung shut and the cycle began. He turned to watch, but Campbell was standing in front of the door, looking through the port already. "Excuse me, sir."

"Eh? Sorry. Here, everyone crowd around." He lifted Francisco up so he could look through the port and the others managed to stand and peek through one way or another.

The little pan of fire burned, but the air exchange was still going on. It flickered and guttered momentarily. Tavana felt sick. *Is it going to go out?*

But whatever air current had wafted its way around the room faded. The fire rose slightly higher in blue-tinged orange.

Then the outer door opened, admitting brilliant sunshine and the pure air of Emerald.

The dazzling sunlight dimmed the flames . . . but they were still there.

The fire was still burning!

"Sergeant—"

"It's burning. By *GOD* it's still burning! Boys . . ." His voice broke and he sank to his knees. "I think we're going to be okay. I finally think we're okay."

Tavana felt a burning in his throat and eyes, tears

answering those pouring down the sergeant's dark, lined face; he realized how terrible the strain must have been on the seemingly invincible Sergeant Campbell. *He said it himself, he was responsible for all of us. And no matter what he could do, he couldn't change whether Emerald was livable. He knew how thin the chances were before we even started for this system.*

"Sergeant?" he said, seeing the others as dumbfounded as he was by Campbell's sudden breakdown. "Sergeant, it's all right. You did it. You got us all here safe. It's okay."

"Yeah . . . yeah, I know. Sorry, kids. Just finally had it all catch up to me, you know? Started as a god-damn milk run, and then suddenly we were stranded in space. Couldn't take time to panic." He stood up. "Sometimes it gets you like that, when you finally *aren't* in a crisis. The relief, you know." He grinned at them and wiped the tears away. "Felt good, actually. Released all that tension I had."

He looked at the door. "Well, this isn't going to be a picnic, either, but if we're smart and careful, I'll bet on us living here. So we're going to get us some proper equipment for a little expedition, and then we are going to be the first people to step foot on this planet!"

Chapter 15

"No, Maddox, Tav, no one but me and the sergeant gets armed."

"But *Xaaaaaander*—"

"No *but Xander*, Maddox. You don't even know how to handle a gun yet, and I don't think that Tav or Francisco do either."

The other boys glared at him and Campbell. Finally the glares turned to pouts. "Well . . . okay. You're right."

"Good listening, kids," Campbell said. "Guns are not toys. We've got several from the cargo, so *if and when* I think you boys are ready, all of us can, and will, be armed when we go out. For now, Xander's the only one who's convinced me I can trust him with something that might put a hole in me if he plays with it wrong."

"But we *all* want to go out!" Francisco said.

Xander shook his head. "Francisco, I know you do. But we haven't got a clue as to what might be waiting out there, and until we do, we're not taking anyone else out. Now, you guys *can* do something, and that's digging out that temporary shelter and making sure it's in good condition before we bring it outside and set it up."

Maddox looked at him with just a bit of resentment

and then shrugged it off. "Okay, bro. We'll do that. Anything else?"

"Check inventory on food," Campbell said, "and then start checking readiness on the construction equipment we brought with us. I know we chose the motors we did to minimize damage to the cargo, but I want you boys to make sure we didn't do any real damage to them before we actually try to make use of them."

"Got it, Sergeant," Tavana said.

"All right. Let's take a look at our new home, then."

The sergeant went first, stepping into the airlock and opening the outer door; that was no surprise. Xander hadn't even tried to argue otherwise—it would make no sense for the less-experienced mechanical engineer to stick his head out on an unknown world rather than the soldier with a couple of decades of knocking around colony worlds and dealing with whatever they could throw at him.

That didn't stop Xander from feeling a little jealous.

Sergeant Campbell stepped down and mostly out of sight, then gestured for Xander to follow. Xander opened the inner lock and stepped in, closing the door behind him.

It was the smell that struck Xander first. There was a lingering smell of burning packing fluff and alcohol, but dominating everything was a sharp, sweet *freshness*, something that he couldn't describe precisely, but that shouted *outdoors!* in an unmistakable, joyous way. Faint hints of other smells—heated metal from the *LS-88* as she cooled down, spicy scents of flowers or their analogues, and a grassy smell that he thought must be from whatever they'd landed on. He stepped to the outer lock and took a deep breath.

"Yeah, that's something you wait for after every trip," Campbell said from just below him. "First breath of real air. Especially after you've been in a tin can like this one."

For a few moments, Xander couldn't answer. He was taking in the panorama before him. He'd seen the landing site from the air, but that had been a quick glance through a camera's eye. Now they were down on the ground, and he was seeing everything *himself*.

They sat in a small clearing—scarcely two or three times as wide as *LS-88* was long—bordered by towering growths crowned with what looked like delicate green sprays of fine hair, but were probably tough, slender strands. Interspersed with these were other treelike things with spiral green sheets that were definitely leaves, and huge columns rearing dozens of meters into the air. He could hear faint noises in the distance—piercing calls, chiming, answering chimes or screeches—and saw brightly-colored somethings darting in and out of the forest canopy. Nearer, tall growths with banded joints grew side by side with swaying grass-like things that almost *had* to be plants, and sparkling-winged somethings dancing among them. The sound of running water chuckled somewhere on the other side of *LS-88*.

Campbell's chuckle broke into his reverie. "It sure is pretty, I'll say that for it."

The sergeant stood on the last rung of the ladder; he had not yet stepped down. Campbell grinned up at him. "You want to take the first step?"

A huge rush of gratitude roared through him, and he felt an incredibly stupid grin spreading across his face. But..."I...of course I would, sir, but shouldn't you . . . ?" It was hard to say, but it was the *right* thing to say. Without Campbell, they'd never have gotten here.

Campbell shook his head, but returned the grin. "Can't say it's not a major temptation, Xander; even with all the exploring we've done, you could get all the people who've been the first to step foot on another world into one auditorium, and it wouldn't be all that full even after two hundred years. But," his grin broadened, "I'd already be in that auditorium, and you wouldn't."

Xander felt a momentary sting of tears. "I don't think I can say *thank you* enough, sir."

"The way you're smiling says it all, Xander. Now take that first step."

He climbed partway down, then measured the way his legs felt. "I think it might be more like a jump and fall."

"Be careful. We've flattened stuff nearby, but any farther and who knows what you'll hit."

Xander gave a tiny jump and let go, passing the sergeant by inches. The impact felt like he was landing with a couple other people on his back, after all that time weightless. Somehow he stayed on his two feet, not falling, and slowly rose. "And that's one tiny leap for mankind," he said. "Welcome to Emerald!"

"Well, nothing's leapt out of the grass to kill us yet. Good sign."

"Did you expect something to?"

"Nah, not really. Something more than thirty meters long made of metal drops screaming out of the air and lands in your field? Anything halfway sane's running as far as it can go until it's sure nothing more's going to happen. Predators don't survive by attacking things they don't know. The main danger on planets like this for newbies like us? Dangers that look harmless until we touch them, kick them, sniff them, or eat them. Or walk past 'em—had a trooper get killed once when we walked past what looked like just any other hole in the rock and something jumped out and whacked him."

Xander looked around with more caution and suspicion at the waving grass, brush, or whatever-it-was, and realized that stuff that grew almost a meter tall could hide a *lot* of things.

Campbell nodded. "*That* is the look you need. Until we're familiar with this place, we haven't got the faintest idea of what could kill us. There are risks we really can't avoid—if the equivalent of the grass is lethal, we're pretty much hosed. But I wouldn't yank up a stalk and stick it in my mouth to whistle with until we're damn sure it's not filled with strychnine or something."

"What now, Sergeant?"

Campbell surveyed the area. "I want to walk a perimeter around the *LS-88*. If everything looks kosher, we'll get out one of the excavators."

"Why—oh. You want to make a *real* perimeter."

"You got it. First rule of safety: clear out any possible threats and establish a secure camp. Sure, we can stay inside *LS-88*; that's pretty much a damn fortress. But we really need to get used to staying here. That's not happening if we use the ship as an excuse to keep from acting like colonists. You were all going to be colonists, well, here's your chance."

Xander followed Campbell, who was proceeding

up towards the nose of *LS-88* with careful, measured steps, surveying everything as he went along. "Yeah, but we were planning on arriving at an already established colony."

"Can't give you one of those." Campbell stopped, touched a point underneath *LS-88*'s front cabin. "Hmm. There's the problem child."

Xander saw a blackened streak. "What is it?"

"Don't know for sure. Some small flaw, probably minor damage from the accident. It affected the TPS deployment just a tiny bit and almost led to burn-through. I wouldn't want to try another landing with her." Campbell grinned and patted the lander. "But she did her job long enough."

Xander repressed a shudder. He hadn't realized they'd come *that* close to being a flaming wreck. "Why didn't you say anything?"

"Would you?"

That stopped him. He considered a moment. "I guess not. No point in it."

"Exactly. If it'd holed-through, we'd all have been dead in seconds. No point in worrying anyone with it." They rounded the nose. "Well, now, isn't that a pretty sight?"

Stretching away from them, starting perhaps fifteen meters from *LS-88*, was a sparkling sheet of pristine blue water, rippling slightly from wind and the tumbling waters of the stream feeding the little lake. "Do you think that's fresh water?"

"I'd bet on it, though the lake itself might be brackish. The stream's almost certainly fresh water."

Without warning, something leapt from the water, far out in the lake, and came down with a splash;

CASTAWAY ODYSSEY   133

Xander had a momentary impression of a slender body trailing more fins than he might have expected. "Wow!"

"Wow indeed. That beast was more than a meter long, easy. Maybe twice that. Hard to tell at this distance. Looks like we can expect to do some fishing if we're lucky."

"If we can eat it."

"That *will* be the question, yes. But we know from Earth and other planets that there are some basic rules we can follow that make it safer. Like not eating the innards of animals until we've had a chance to test 'em." Campbell surveyed the area. "Let's keep going, but right now I'm inclined to stay right here. Looks about as good a spot as we could hope for."

"We don't need an excavator to clear an area for the shelter, do we?"

"Technically . . . no. Practically speaking, I would *strongly* recommend it. What if the local grasses can poke holes in your shelter?"

"Well, we did clear out some areas right around the jets when you landed."

"So we did. I also avoid camping right underneath nuclear jets, on basic principle alone."

Xander laughed, but he had to agree that there was something unsettling about the idea of sitting directly beneath a high-powered jet engine. He squatted down and looked carefully at the soil. Near the edges, he could see some shield-shaped things scuttling about. "I see beetles or something."

"Careful." With practiced ease, Campbell bent over and impaled one on a needle-fine spike from his Shapetool. "Hm. Not exactly anything we know—no surprise. Crustacean of some sort, exoskeleton and all.

Mandibles look like they could nip through flesh, don't know about cloth. Might be plant-eaters, though. Don't show any response to one of their fellows' deaths—not that I expected them to, or we'd have seen swarms all over the place after the landing." He scraped the thing off against *LS-88*, then wiped off the Shape-tool. "But where there's one thing like that, there are probably ten thousand species ranging from harmless to very nasty. And—whoops! Will you look at that?"

That was one of the plant-things, which had been exhibiting what Xander had thought were brilliant red flowers composed of many hairlike petals, like asters. But as they approached and the sergeant's boot landed near—or perhaps touching—the stem, the "flowers" suddenly withdrew into a bulge on the stem. "What is it?"

"Could be a plant, still—I've seen some on various planets that move. Mimosa's one on Earth—touch it and it folds up fast. But it *looked* more like an animal movement to me. Interesting."

They had reached the tail section. They looked up the stream to where it disappeared into the forest; low hills were visible in the distance. He saw Campbell frown and shake his head.

"What is it?"

"Those hills. I know we haven't seen but a fraction of the planet yet, but near as I can tell there isn't a mountain on this planet worthy of the name. Most of 'em wouldn't even qualify as hills. I think the highest peak I saw might just barely clear three hundred meters. Most habitable worlds have pretty active tectonics, so you get plenty of mountains *somewhere* on the planet. Never seen a habitable world without decent mountain ranges. It's a puzzle."

Then he shook himself. "Well, anyway, the cargo bay door's here, and clear. Looks like we can get to work! Get inside and let's get started!"

Xander glanced at the hills; he didn't really understand what was bothering the sergeant. But first things first. "Coming in, Maddox, Tav," he said, seeing that his omni had switched to the proper channels. "We're going to get one of the excavators working!"

Chapter 16

"This," Campbell said, "is a JD-CAT Model 450 Universal Excavator."

The boys watched attentively, even Francisco. Heavy machinery still held a fascination for most children, and these—thank goodness—were no exception.

Campbell walked around the big machine and smacked the wide, thick bar that was held up by the manipulator frame. "Excavation is just part of what the 450 can do, though. This is a fully controllable advanced SMA—Shape Memory Alloy—universal blade component, similar to the main control surface units on *LS-88*. It can be a bulldozer blade, a backhoe scoop, a snowplow—pretty much any kind of tool you need to clear an area, dig a hole, smooth the ground, and so on. The rear 'ripper' attachments are also SMA units, and can be configured for hole digging and other operations."

"Cool," Maddox said with a broad grin.

"It is that," he agreed. "We have four of these beasts, each one massing fifteen metric tons, and believe me, Tantalus Colony's going to be *real* unhappy they don't have them. These were designed specifically for new colony setup."

Campbell grabbed the door, opened it, and swung up into the small cabin. "C'mon up, take a look. Manual controls are built in and parallel to the automatics."

"So they can be automated?" Tavana asked. "That will be useful!"

"You better believe it. We'll start out doing things by manual. With the AIs knocked out by that Trapdoor Pulse, we can't count on them to make the right evaluations and decisions. But once our satellite network gets established, we'll have an Emerald-centric GPS system to guide everything they do."

Xander checked the drive systems along with Tavana. "Superconductor loop batteries, right?"

"Right. No fuel, minimal maintenance—moving components sealed as much as possible, with near zero-wear bearing materials. We just plug her into the shuttle mains and recharge every so often."

Francisco looked at the machine longingly. "I wish I could drive it, but I'm too small."

"Maybe not," said Tavana.

Campbell looked at him with a raised eyebrow. "How you figure, Tav? His feet won't even reach the pedal pads."

Tavana grinned, holding up his omni. "Manual can still be via remote, yes? And I know Francisco; he is quite good with delicate control in the games."

Yeah, but still, that's fifteen tons of machinery with a lot of power behind it. He caught Tavana's meaningful stare, and knew what the kid was up to. *Francisco's an artist and a kid; he's not like the rest of these boys, an engineer or on the way to being one. He wants to contribute, and Tavana wants to show him a way he can.*

Campbell had to admit, it couldn't hurt to have someone with an artist's as well as an engineer's eye in on the work. If they were going to be stuck here, letting Francisco try to add aesthetic touches would be a good thing.

"That's . . . not a bad point at all, Tav," he said after a momentary pause. "Tell you what: I'll start teaching Xander and Maddox how to run it, but you can hook into the controls in parallel and we'll see if you can figure out a good interface that Francisco can use. I'm not giving any remote control, though, until I'm sure whoever's doing it knows exactly what they're doing. This thing can do a *lot* of damage real fast."

The others nodded. Xander said, "So what's our plan, sir?"

"I want to clear a perimeter all the way around us," Campbell said, gesturing in an arc around them. "Clear the ground, make sure there's no surprises waiting for us in our base camp. Take everything down, out to about fifty meters in all directions from LS-88, down to the water's edge in the direction of our little lake there."

Maddox frowned. "We're just going to wipe out *everything* around us? That's pretty mean! What about the animals and things that already live here?"

Campbell sighed. "If this was a proper survey and colonization setup, you'd probably be right. Modern approach to colonization is to try to find a way to fit in. But honestly, Maddox, even there, once we decide that we're setting up a colony in a given area? Every-thing has to go that might be dangerous."

He pointed out at the towering spiral-leaved trees, the distant columns that he couldn't quite figure out, the shadows under the trees. "We don't know *anything* about what lives here. We don't know if we're sitting on top of, oh, a nest of *chojago* like they ran into on Porlumma, sort of super-fire-ants, and we sure don't want to find out the hard way. It may not be the proper environmental approach, but for survival this is the way we have to do it. Everything for a certain radius around this ship goes. Got it?"

Maddox bit his lip, but then nodded. "Yes, Sergeant."

"Good."

The controls of the Model 450 were fairly simple; manual control of a bulldozer, backhoe, and similar machinery really hadn't changed in centuries. There were handgrips, called "joysticks," to steer, and hand and foot controls for moving forward and backward, for raising and lowering the blade or bucket, and so on. He configured the universal blade to a standard "scraper" blade shape, lowered it, and—after making sure all the kids were well clear—started forward.

Unlike the old-fashioned internal-combustion designs, the 450 didn't roar and rumble, but it did move forward with massive authority. The sound of earth and stone and plants being torn and scraped was loud and emphatic.

He noticed movement to the rear. "Hey! Boys, don't follow me! You can keep monitoring and watching, but you stay right there at the ship!"

"I thought I'd just look at what you were uncovering, Sergeant," Xander said, slightly defensively.

"You gotta start thinking more paranoid, son. What if there *was* a nest of something, like I mentioned?

What do you think the reaction's going to be? You boys have to stay away from the machine in case something here takes violent exception to our trying to clear everything up."

There were no arguments to that, and he was pleased to see the boys simply went and watched from the main ramp. His occasional glimpses showed that Francisco was paying close attention to whatever Tavana was doing, so maybe the boy *would* learn how to run one by remote.

He took the 450 out the full fifty meters and a little more, then turned at right angles and started carving out a wide, flat perimeter border.

Ha! Saw something there, long and pretty nasty looking, wiggled out of a hole ahead of me and ran off into the forest. There are animals on land and some of them probably dangerous. With the cabin door closed, he wasn't worried for himself here. Even if a swarm of this world's equivalent of bees came after the 450, they'd never get in to bother him. But he was now more sure than ever that they needed this perimeter.

After a couple of hours, he'd managed to cut a swath all around the grounded *LS-88*, a double-wide pathway of scraped earth showing white, dusty streaks where he'd been digging into rock running a total of several hundred meters. The debris from the scraping ran in a bulwark all around the encampment. "There we go. You got it now, Xander?"

"I think so. Can I try it?"

"I'll bring her back in and you can. Now, what I want us to do is work from the inside out. We'll end up with quite a wall, nice earthworks that'll discourage casual intruders, and a smooth place for us to set up camp inside those walls."

"I heard something running away from you," Tavana said. "I guess there are some animals here for sure."

"And probably a lot more farther in. Like I said, when we landed we probably made most things run far, far away. The few things still here were in burrows—exactly the kind of thing I wanted to make sure we got rid of." He finished running the excavator back in to near *LS-88*. "Once we have the area cleared, we'll have to pack it down, steamroller it, as they used to say, and we can start really getting set up."

Maddox was looking at the small lake. "Sergeant, do you think we might be able to do some fishing? We saw something jumping out there..."

"I'm sure we will. While your brother gets the hang of clearing our field here, you're welcome to see if you can figure out some good fishing gear."

"Should we get out a second excavator?" Tavana asked. "I could start prep on that now."

Campbell considered, while keeping an eye on Xander's first hesitant attempts with the 450. "Not right now. Maybe we'll want two of them, but keeping them charged will be a bit of a chore. It's not like we're going to be building miles of highway. Keep working with Francisco; if he gets the hang of running one of these things by remote, that'll free the rest of us to do other work."

Tavana nodded and sat down next to Francisco.

The older Bird seemed to be getting the 450 under control; the movements were smoothing out, and the scraping noise becoming smoother, more constant. Campbell leaned back with a grin. *Positive mental attitude, first aid, shelter, fire, signaling, water, and food. That's survival in a nutshell. Attitude, well, the kids are doing pretty well on it. We're not hurt. LS-88's a dandy shelter, even if I really look forward to getting into something bigger. We've got all the fire we need. The SC-178s are the best we can do for signaling. Water's not a problem, as long as the whole planet isn't a deathtrap, and we've got food for a bit.*

He sat down and let himself relax against the hard, strong alloy of one of the landing struts. *Not bad, Campbell. Give yourself a pat on the back and five minutes of peace.*

"Yeah," he muttered to himself. He could probably afford five minutes. But not much more, because if his years in the Service had taught him anything, it had been this:

Planets hold surprises.

Chapter 17

Tavana sagged back into the shelter's narrow bed and let out an explosive sigh. He hurt in places he didn't remember he *had*.

The temporary shelter was made of the lightest, strongest materials available. But it was also designed to house up to ten people, which meant that even *with* the lightest and strongest materials it was very heavy, very bulky, and unfortunately required some manual work to unpack and set up. The automated anchors had failed. They were meant for use on soil surfaces, and after the whole perimeter had been scraped down, there was nothing but stone. Tavana, Maddox, and Xander had been forced to use a hammer—a real, actual *hammer*, a piece of reinforced composite with a big chunk of heavy metal at the end—to pound the sharp carbonan and steel spikes into the ground.

Fortunately the rock in question was pretty soft, but it had still taken hours to get everything fastened down to the sergeant's satisfaction. "You can't cut corners with this stuff, kids," he'd said after forcing them to pull out three spikes, pull the shelter tighter, and start hammering again. "This shelter's going to be our home until we can figure out something better and more permanent. That means she's gotta be locked down damn near perfect."

But it wasn't all bad. After all that work, letting himself slowly sink into the softness of the bed felt that much wonderfully better.

"Tavana!" came the sergeant's voice. "Bringing your stuff inside doesn't mean stopping for a nap! Come on, sunshine, we've got work to do!"

"Merde." He said the curse quietly, then levered himself upright. His muscles protested this unwise course of action, but he knew he had no choice. "I thought we were done for the day, Sergeant," he said as he came out.

"Not yet." Campbell was looking around the wide, clean perimeter. "I've got one more job of cleanup I need to do, and you're going to come with me."

Tavana opened his mouth to ask "Why me?" but caught himself at the last moment. Arguing with the sergeant would be stupid. After a pause, though, he figured he could ask the question without the whining overtone he knew would have been in it a minute ago. "All right, Sergeant, but why me instead of Xander?"

"I want at least one armed person with any group, which means in practice that at most we've got two groups. Xander, Maddox, and Francisco are down at the lake trying their hand at fishing, since there turned out to be line and rods we could combine with the TechTools to make a decent fishing rod. Got them some gloves, gave Xander serious instructions on how I want him to do this, and made damn sure the other kids know that Xander's in charge. So that leaves me and you to do this little chore."

Tavana followed the sergeant across the scraped rock. "What exactly are we looking for?"

Campbell's sharp dark gaze flicked around the landscape, then he reached out an arm and pointed. "Over there."

Tavana looked, but he just saw more scraped earth and stone. Even as they got closer, he really didn't see anything notable. "Sorry, sir, I don't get it."

"Hm. Well, maybe you need a little observational training. Don't you notice anything different a little ways ahead of us?"

Tavana frowned. Campbell wouldn't be joking about stuff like this, so there had to be something special about the area ahead. But all he saw was the streaky white of the scraped bedrock, interspersed with some dark brown (occasionally with white streaks) that was dirt stuck in a ripple of the landscape. "Wait. That patch looks pretty circular."

"Now you're catching on—but tell me why."

He thought a moment. "Hole. There has to be a hole there, a round hole."

"And a hole, Tavana, could be a burrow. I saw some nasty-looking things wiggling away from the excavator, but there's no guarantee all of them got away." He looked back at the shelter. "I made sure there were none of them under the place we set up the shelter, but there are going to be quite a few out here, I'm afraid. If I had my way and unlimited resources, I'd *glass* this whole area over, but there's no way for us to do that. Suppose I could try to hover across the whole place with the jets on, but that wouldn't get far down. Which means we have a less safe job to do."

"What's the plan?"

"Operation 'Poke It With a Stick,'" Campbell said with a wry grin. "I've got a nice long piece of thick carbonan rod here from one of the storage areas. You will poke that rod into these round areas when I tell you to, and try to annoy anything that might be under there into coming out. I wish I had a better way, but not with what we have available now."

Tavana looked doubtfully at the long, white, slender pole. "And if something *does* come out?"

"I will—in all likelihood—gun it down," Campbell replied, hefting a pistol with a muzzle that looked like a cannon. "Depends on my instinct when I see it. Can't say ahead of time—those decisions are split-second and not always conscious. But I'd bet on shooting first and second-guessing myself later; since we can't take chances." His gaze dropped to Tavana's legs, and nodded. "Those coveralls are tough enough to protect you some, and you *are* wearing the boots we got out of storage, right?"

"Yes, sir. Come almost up to my knees."

"Good man. Those are Pathfinders, not top of the line, but solid boots for colonials or military alike." He looked wistful for a moment. "Wish I had mine. Best damn boots in the universe, practically a toolkit in themselves. Unfortunately they're still sitting in my cabin on *Outward Initiative*, unless they've already cleaned it out. If they did, hope someone saved the damn things; they cost me a month's salary."

Tavana blinked. A pair of *boots* cost someone like the sergeant a month's salary? "At that price, sir, they should be doing the walking *for* you."

"Damn near could, too." He sighed. "Anyway, these are solid boots for us both. Wearing ship's shoes would be an invitation to getting bit, or worse. Here, take these."

Tavana accepted the pair of padded gray gloves and pulled them on; he was glad to take any protection offered. The work gloves fit well enough, and had gripping surfaces that made the smooth carbonan pole easy to hold. "Guess I'm ready."

"All right." Tavana saw Sergeant Campbell get the distant look of someone activating their omni, looking at things others couldn't see. "Xander, you hear me?"

"Yes, Sergeant," Xander's voice answered; apparently either Campbell had cut Tavana into the conversation, or Xander had. "What's up?"

"I'm going to be checking out potential burrows here with Tavana. If you hear gunshots, don't panic; I'll check in within a few minutes. If you *don't* hear me check in within, say, five minutes of a shot, give me a holler. Otherwise, just keep fishing. Any luck?"

"We got our first lines out after finishing making the hooks out of the steel wire Maddox dug out of the one crate. That stuff's *tough*—took two of us to bend it into shape. But that means it's going to be a good hook, I think. Anyway, we've baited one with a couple of those shield-like bug things, and I put some of the jerky out of one of the rations on another."

"Sounds good. You boys enjoy a day fishing but keep your eyes out for anything dangerous. And if you see *anything* that makes you nervous, you just get out of there and make for the shelter—or *LS-88*, if you feel you need to. Don't worry about being too cautious. Got it?"

"Yes sir."

"All right. Have fun. Campbell out." His eyes refocused and he nodded. "Okay, Tavana, it's our turn to have fun."

Tavana felt his heart starting to beat faster. "*Oui*, fun. I am hoping, Sergeant, that this will be a very boring job."

"Me too. You're half-joking, but believe me, that's no joke. Nothing I'd like more than to have a real boring time out here, finding empty holes."

Tavana approached the circular region of dirt cautiously, with the pole in front of him. "Where should I stand?"

"Wherever you like. I'll stand just a little ahead of you and to the side, so there's no chance I shoot you instead of whatever's in the hole. I've got my omni tied in to my retinals; military targeting link. Later, we'll have to figure out a way to program something like that for you boys. Faster shooting and a lot safer, done right."

"I might be able to do that. I do games programming and interfaces, some a lot more complicated than Jewelbug."

"We'll look into it. You ready?"

Tavana swallowed and gripped the pole tighter. "I . . . think so."

Campbell grinned. "No, you aren't. Here. Relax that grip a hair. Hold it like *this*." He repositioned Tavana's hands. "See? You can push or pull better that way, and you can let go easier, if things go bad. Don't hold onto it with a death-grip; not only does that give you a lot of control problems, it'll wear out your muscles fast. Then you'll have to stop sooner and rest."

"Okay." He forced his hands to relax the tiniest bit. "Ready now, sir?"

"Guess we are." The sergeant raised his pistol. "Go to it."

Tavana put the tip of the pole in the middle of the circular patch of dirt and pushed. The pole sank slowly into the dirt, which stubbornly contested the way but yielded nonetheless. He was five centimeters in, ten, fifteen, twenty, twenty-five—

The pole abruptly slid down half a meter.

"Whoa, there. You've gone through. Definitely a hole."

"Definitely. I don't feel anything under the pole except empty air."

"Push it down until you hit something, or until you've gone a full meter and a half."

At just over a meter he hit something hard. "Rock, I think."

"Hole probably curves away. Wiggle and scrape it on the bottom a bit. If there's something in there, it'll either try to run away if there's another exit, or try to drive us out."

Tavana followed the instructions. He was not exactly happy at the idea of the pole he was using being attacked by some unknown creature that might decide to dig up after whoever was holding the intruding pole, although he was comforted by Campbell's confident posture.

But after several minutes, nothing seemed to be happening. "Enough, sir?"

Campbell pursed his lips, and then nodded. "Yeah, that's all we can do for now. Onward."

They walked a careful spiral, following the same general path as the excavator. The holes weren't spaced terribly closely, but the size of the clearing they'd made still meant there'd be quite a few. He spotted the next one when he was about ten meters away, which made the sergeant nod in appreciation. "Good eyes, son. You'll get the hang of this soon."

Tavana used the same procedure. This hole seemed pretty much like the last: twenty, twenty-five centimeters of pretty hard-packed dirt as a cap on top of a hole that was a meter or so deep. Once more he banged and rattled the pole and nothing happened. "That dirt sticks together pretty well."

"Noticed that, eh? Yes sir, it's not just sandy junk. Got some substance to it. Not surprising, of course, with all this water and all these things growing in it, but still, that's got me thinking there might be clay around."

"Is that important?"

The sergeant chuckled, shaking his head. "Right now, no. But if we're really stuck here for the long haul..."

A chill went down his back and crept down his arms, despite the warmth of Emerald's sun. "Do...do you think we *are* here for...well, for a long time?" He pulled up the pole, moved on.

The sergeant was silent for a while, long enough for them to approach the next hole. "Honestly, Tavana? Probably."

"Won't they send a rescue party?" Tavana's voice rose unsteadily. *I...I thought we would be rescued once we got here. Stupid, but...*

"I wouldn't bet on one." The craggy face looked grim. "See, there's no way that *Outward Initiative* would just go on about its business. If the ship survived—and I hope it did—it was pretty badly damaged. Maybe took some of that radiation pulse we got. So they'd have to get her back in flying shape."

Tavana nodded. "I know that, yes. The Trapdoor coils, they would have to be re-tuned for the changed shape of the ship."

"Right. So that's a week, two weeks, at least. Then they have to get somewhere they can get fixed. That pretty much *has* to be Orado. That's about ten light-years from where we dropped off, so figure it took them a couple months to get there."

"So they will have been there a while now, yes?"

"Problem is . . . at best, they're going to have a *guess* as to where we are in space, because out between the stars there aren't any road markers. Any rescuers would be searching a volume probably larger than our solar system back on Earth. That's . . . a long, long time searching for something the size of our lifeboat. Years, maybe less if they have a lot of searching vessels—but they won't have a lot, because Orado's not going to have a bunch of starships on hand for the job. And honestly? They'll know that anyone in an *intact* lifeboat will be heading for Orado on their own, taking a lot longer to get there, but if they're well supplied, they'll make it. If they don't detect a distress beacon in the right general area, they'll assume we've either headed for Orado, or our ship didn't survive. They might set up some automated search drones, sort of like unmanned lifeboats . . . but they'd be looking just for closure, not rescue."

"But the star! Emerald's sun, they will see it, yes?" Tavana poked a bit more forcefully at the next dirt-covered hole.

Campbell shrugged. "If someone does a starfield comparison, yes. They'll notice it. And if someone does that, they might possibly think that survivors could

look to that system as a refuge—but only if they think
of the possibility that we *couldn't* head for Orado."

The pole sank again. Once more Tavana shook and
scraped the end around.

Campbell continued, "But Tav . . . that's a really long
shot. You'd have to be either crazy or desperate—like
we were—to head for an unknown system, even one
close by, rather than tighten your belt and make the
trip to the inhabited system you *know* about. Maybe
someone will come here. I sure hope so. Just the fact it's
a star not on the charts will make people puzzled. But
indulging curiosity with a starship, that's an expensive
whim. More likely they'll just get someone to take a
good look at the system with a telescopic array. They'll
be able to see the planet all right . . . even make out the
continents and larger islands . . . but not us."

Tavana pulled the pole out, started walking again.
His steps dragged leadenly—a sensation that was not
just from gravity, annoying though that was. "So we
are stuck here forever."

Campbell spread his hands. "Maybe not. We can
hope for the best, but we damned well better plan
for the worst."

Tavana squinted ahead, slowed down. *Something's
different . . .*

The sergeant followed his gaze. "What is it?"

"I don't know. Just . . . this one isn't like the others."

A brilliant smile. "You *have* got some of the instincts.
Wish you'd spent more time working them, but this
is good. Look again. Tell me what's different about
this one than the others."

Tavana stood still, looking, thinking. Finally, he
nodded. "The others, they were all flat. Really smooth.

Hard-looking. This one . . . it has sunk a little in the center, and part of it looks softer."

The sergeant nodded; Tavana saw him draw his weapon and check it carefully, and the gun did not return to its holster. "You got it. Looks to me like something might have been digging underneath. Maybe was doing it when we were walking up, and stopped because it sensed our vibrations."

"Vibration sense? Is that common?"

"Very, especially in subsurface creatures." Campbell studied the terrain carefully. "All right, let's do this. Be ready, though. I would not be surprised if this doesn't go nearly as smoothly as the others."

Tavana nodded, and his heart was back to hammering against his ribs. *Something* is *there, I can feel it.*

The pole sank into the top layer much more easily than it had in the prior holes, then slowed down, encountering earth of a heavier sort. Tavana pushed—

And something suddenly seized the pole, yanking on it so hard that it was almost ripped out of Tavana's hands.

But Tavana Arronax was not letting go. As it gave another yank, Tavana braced himself and started pulling.

"You got something?"

"*Oui.* And it wants a tug-of-war? It will have one!"

Tavana found himself grinning, despite the fact that the sudden grab-and-pull had scared him so much he felt his pulse racing and a giddiness in his head. Tug of war was the one thing he'd been *good* at when his school had phys-ed classes. He couldn't run fast, he couldn't duck and weave, and he didn't like punching and wrestling, but with his low, squat build, he could brace and pull better than anyone.

He gripped the pole, tucked it under his arm like a rope, and dug in his heels. The pole stopped, and then slid backwards. Tavana braced again, pulled once more. Another step back, and now he could feel a vibration, something scrabbling for a hold, fighting the pull and losing. Then it was harder, but something was still holding on, wriggling as Tavana dragged it through the dirt capping the hole.

With an abrupt rush, most of the pole slid free of the dirt, bringing with it a sinuous, segmented, multi-legged shape. It released the pole, making Tav stagger back. It started a lunge—

Three flat, sharp reports shattered the stillness. The creature was shoved sideways, red-purple blood splashing in the air as it rolled over and then contorted in writhing agony, needle-tipped mandibles slashing empty air.

Campbell studied the thing as its convulsions juddered to a halt, then nodded, sheathing his weapon. "That's definitely not something we wanted inside the perimeter."

The two moved a little closer. The creature was serpentine, a long body well over two meters long and almost twenty centimeters thick, equipped with multiple pairs of legs, two on each body section. Tavana noticed that the frontmost legs shifted from being narrow to broader and contoured. *Digging tools, almost certainly.* The mouth was mostly closed now, but he could make out what looked like blue-black fangs in the four-sectioned mouth.

"Good shooting, Sergeant," he said. "That was not a happy animal when it came out."

"Very *un*happy, I think. Thanks. Lemme contact Xander, let him know what's up."

As the sergeant gazed into the invisible distance, Tavana stepped a little closer. This was the first alien lifeform he'd really gotten a good look at, aside from the preserved specimens back home. It looked like a cross between a centipede, a worm, and a lamprey. *Terrifiant*; creepy, as Maddox would probably say.

The way it was lying, he couldn't get a good look, but it seemed to have eyes spaced such that there were *four* of them. And there were four ridges on the thing's body. *Four-sided symmetry?* He stretched out his boot and tried to roll the creature over, so he could get a look—

"Tavana, *NO!*"

The limp body suddenly convulsed at the touch of Tavana's boot. The head whipped around, hissing, fangs extended. In the same instant, Sergeant Campbell slammed into him, sending Tavana sprawling, out of the path of the thing's reflexive strike.

But that left Sergeant Campbell directly in its path.

Wide-stretched mandibles found Campbell's boot and clamped down. Three of the savage hooked teeth skidded on the Pathfinder boot, getting no purchase, but the fourth slid upward...

...and over the top of the boot, plunging directly into Campbell's leg, just below the knee.

Chapter 18

It wasn't a conscious decision, but a reflexive action, almost as instinctive as the not quite-dead-enough creature's strike. Campbell had seen Tavana move forward, watched his leg lift, and he knew *exactly* what Tavana was going to do. Having seen this scenario on half a dozen worlds, he knew how it might go wrong.

But that was the conscious thought. It lagged far behind the reaction, which was to shout a warning and lunge, as fast as he could, to shove Tavana out of harm's way.

For an instant—just an instant—he thought he could relax, because he saw Tavana falling far to the side, clear, definitely clear of the thing's striking range.

And then a red-hot nail drove deep into his upper calf.

Campbell used language he'd promised he wouldn't around the kids.

A quick glance—and the increasing pressure with the pain—showed him the reflexive bite also included a clamping reflex. On the positive side, that gave him a chance to reach down and grab the thing just behind the head. The glove would probably keep any spines or such from penetrating ... but maybe not. What the hell were its teeth made of? There was carbonan weave in these pants!

"Oh, my God. Sergeant!"

"Calm down, Tav. Panic won't do us any good." He gripped the creature's head tightly, started levering against the one fang that had penetrated. "Gotta get this thing out. Call Xander. Let him know what's happening."

An alert went red in his retinal's field of vision— reality overlay from his omni and medical nanos. *Oh, sweet mother of ... poisoned.* The damn thing was venomous. He gritted his teeth. This wasn't going to be any picnic, but he didn't have much of a choice. He pulled hard.

The pain was shocking, even for him. As the fang tore free and he hurled the body away, he could see tatters of his own flesh caught in serrated barbs. *Extended out when it hit? Damn. That's going to be a bad one.*

He'd managed to keep from screaming, but there'd been a definite pained grunt. Tavana was staring at the blood now flowing freely from the wound, looking noticeably paler—pretty bad, when one considered his Polynesian deep-brown complexion. "Tavana! Stick with me! Don't lose it now."

"Sergeant ... it's my fault, I was—"

"Stop with the blame. Talk about that later. Right now I need you to *focus*. That thing's bite was venomous." His head was starting to feel like it was floating, and at the same time he noted an ominous tightening of his chest. *Damn medical nanos, what the hell are they doing? Get on the job!*

Tavana shook himself, still looking sick. "What . . . what can I do?"

"Call Xander, like I said. But while you do that, run, don't walk, to the lander and get me one of those medical nano injectors. Fast."

"Fast." Tavana blinked, and then seemed to finally snap back to the present. "Right! Fast!" The sixteen-year-old sprinted towards *LS-88*, shouting "Xander! *Xander*! The sergeant's hurt!"

Campbell's mouth felt dry. That could be his imagination, but the data his military nanos were conveying was not comforting. *Neurotoxin. Powerful one, too, mixed with a necrotic. Fantastic.* The nanos were, of course, trying to counter it, but countering an unknown venom without medical backup wasn't easy even for those top-of-the-line micromachines. He could hear his breathing becoming labored.

Pounding footsteps approached, and Tavana was there, looking oddly distant even when he knelt beside Campbell. "I have the injector, Sergeant. Do I use it?"

The words were hard to assemble into meaning. Campbell had to focus hard to force them into a coherent thought. That wasn't good—not good at all. The toxin, whatever it was, must be able to leak across the blood-brain barrier. "Yes," he said, slowly, hearing his voice, tense and awkward. "Inject . . . above wound site."

The pinprick and warm tingling told him the injector was working. Instantly telltales on his retinals showed the medical nanos communicating with his resident nanorepair systems. *Better get working fast.* "Xander?" he managed to say.

"Here!" Xander's face swam into view, blurred and indistinct.

Here? Didn't notice him arrive. Can't focus eyes. Not good. "Another... injector. Need..." *What the hell was the word? Stuff you breathe... hard to breathe. Hard to concentrate.* "... need oxygen."

"I have it right here," Tavana said.

A distant part of him realized that meant that even half-panicked, Tavana had thought ahead and brought just the right equipment. *Good kid.*

He could barely feel it as Tavana clumsily put the mask on and started the oxygen concentrator running. *Descendant of old OBOGS units*, his brain said, completely out of the blue. It was true—the same concept of a selective sorbent that trapped the inert nitrogen of the air and let oxygen through was at the heart of the device—but that little tidbit wasn't very useful or even relevant right now. *Dammit, brain! Think useful things!*

The fog lifted a tiny bit as the concentrator hit its stride. He was having trouble breathing and his muscles were close to paralyzed. The nanos were overriding where they could, forcing action. Trying to clean out the poison.

What were the kids going to do if he died?

The gray fog was still there. He could barely make out the others at all. "X... Xander," he managed.

"Yes, Sergeant?" The older boy's voice sounded as though it came from half a mile away. It was shaking.

Concentrate. Got to finish. "Open... omni interface..."

A moment later he heard a distant *ping* and could make out, with great effort, the fact that Xander Bird's omni was open.

The fog and detachment were deepening. But Chief

Master Sergeant Samuel Morgan Campbell had never left anything undone, and he wasn't going to let that happen now. With supreme effort, he managed to gather his scattered thoughts and activated the right protocols to dump the data that had to be sent.

The fog darkened, and Campbell slid down into blackness.

Chapter 19

Xander Bird sensed the information dump hit. It streamed through him and into his omni. He saw the sergeant slump down. It felt as though the bottom was dropping out of his world as it did.

The other three boys stared at him and the unconscious sergeant, eyes wide. Tears trickled down Francisco's terrified face. His own terror clawed at his mind. The thought of facing a world filled with things like that monster without Sergeant Campbell loomed up like a monster before him.

Xander straightened up, forcing back the tears. "Sergeant's unconscious," he said. "But he's not dead." He could immediately see some of the incipient panic... not fade, but draw back, waiting. But that was better than real panic. "Tav, run back and check the medical supplies; I'm pretty sure we had some folding stretchers—"

"Yes, there were! Sorry! I should have—"

"You're doing great, you remembered the oxygen. Just go get it now."

"Can...can I do anything?" Maddox asked, voice unsteady but mostly controlled.

Give him something to do. "Go prep the sergeant's

161

bed in the main shelter. Put down one of the self-cleaning sheets at the foot, in case he bleeds more." The nanos seemed—for the moment—to be winning the battle against blood loss, but he couldn't tell what was going on inside. "Francisco, you stay with the sergeant. It's important to have someone watching him."

The smallest boy nodded and hunkered down next to Sergeant Campbell.

Now that I have a few seconds . . . He turned his attention inward. *What the heck did the sergeant send me?*

As soon as he thought the question, his omni responded, displaying the data and annotations on his internal retinal display.

What he saw sent chills through him, because it told him how worried the sergeant was. Campbell had given Xander full authorization over everything—his medical nanos, the secure ship procedures, weapons locks, everything. The sergeant hadn't taken any chances that he might die and leave something unavailable to the rest of them.

As far as the ship systems—and even medical nanos and other related systems—were concerned, he, Xander Bird, *was* Chief Master Sergeant Samuel M. Campbell. The authorization was revocable—if the sergeant woke up, he had a code to do so—but as long as the sergeant was out, the authority remained.

Tavana came running up, a small package in his hand. "Here!"

Xander took the folding stretcher, found the release, and pulled. The little package swiftly unfolded into a full-size stretcher, including hollow but nicely broad handholds for the bearers. It would easily support someone twice the sergeant's weight, or even more, due to being composed of carbonan weave. "Great!" He checked the sergeant's vital signs—not that he knew a great deal about them—and was reassured to see none of them had changed too much in the last few minutes. "He doesn't have any injuries other than the leg wound, so we don't have to worry about how to get him onto the stretcher too much."

This was a good thing, since the sergeant was a very big man. Xander was tall, but the sergeant topped his 191 centimeters by at least seven centimeters and probably had at least twenty kilos on Xander, too. But Tavana was startlingly strong for a kid who was honest about his preference for working by sitting down, so together he and Tavana got Campbell onto the stretcher pretty quickly. Carrying the stretcher with the unconscious man on it wasn't easy, but with a couple of pauses to rest, they finally got Campbell into the shelter and onto his bed.

"Do you think he'll be okay?" Maddox asked finally.

Xander hesitated. "I don't know, Maddox. But... check the medical kit. Maybe there's a diagnostic and treatment database somewhere. If *I* were sending medical kits to pioneer colonies or putting them on lifeboats, I'd sure want to add in reference material for amateurs."

"That almost makes too much sense," Tavana said, trying to sound casual and funny. "But we can hope."

A few minutes later Maddox gave a shout of triumph. "Yes! There is one! It just wasn't automatically online; it was actually on a *chip*, if you can believe that!"

"Can your omni—"

"Already loading it, Xander! Everyone should take a copy, just in case!"

That made sense to Xander. "Just a warning—and I'll bet there's a warning like this in the database—we're amateurs. The best database, even a smart linking one, won't make us into real doctors." The local omni network, linked through *LS-88*, quickly transferred the data.

Now let's see if I can make sense out of what's happening with the sergeant. He pulled up the data feeds from the sergeant's medical nanos and fed them to the active database.

The database responded instantly. *Envenomation. Two primary components with additional supporting elements; one neuroactive venom and one necrotic.*

Xander didn't know what "necrotic" meant exactly but it didn't sound good. A query told him that it was in fact worse than he thought: a venom that triggered extensive cell death in a self-destructive cascade. *Based on patient data and current status, what is the treatment and prognosis?*

The answer came in a set of weighted probabilities, with the database obviously basing its evaluations on known similar venoms, doses, and nano capability. *Provide IV fluids and nutrient solution END-5W for support. If subject remains unconscious longer than six hours, support for excretory functions will be needed.*

Ugh. Catheters and stuff. He hoped it wouldn't come to that. But now that he thought about it, didn't their spacesuits come with that capability? If so, he could probably get that part taken care of automatically just by putting the sergeant into his suit.

Internal nanosupport appears (85% confidence level) to have neutralized 65% of the necrotic activity and is progressing swiftly. 82% of the delivered dose of neurotoxin has been neutralized, and other nanos are attempting to undo the binding on specific active sites. Recommended treatment: two additional nanosupport injections. Maintain oxygen support until the patient becomes conscious. Repair of the wound will require significant time due to necrotic damage. Full analysis of other venom components and interactions are uncertain, but generally positive. Overall prognosis is 79% for a full recovery in between one and five weeks, 9% for a full recovery in between five and nine weeks, 10% for significant recovery with minor remaining damage, 1% for loss of limb due to necrosis, and 1% for worse outcomes.

It required a moment to take that in, but Xander felt a huge surge of relief. *He's going to make it.* Oh, there was that one percent unknown, but much more important was the almost ninety percent chance of full recovery in a couple of months or less. "Everyone, the sergeant is almost certainly going to be all right!"

"Dieu Merci!" Tavana said in his Polynesian-accented French. Francisco just gave a cheer and clapped.

Maddox sighed and sat down shakily. "So what next, bro?"

"Well..." *Can't stop working just because one of us is down. He's going to be okay, probably.* "First I'm going to get an IV going. Maddox, you get two more of the nanosupport injectors and administer them. Tav..." A thought occurred to him. "Tav, get one of the brush machetes out of storage. I want you to go and cut the head off that thing."

Tavana raised an eyebrow. "I guess I can, yes. But why?"

"Because we're stuck here for at least a while, right?"

"Right . . ." Tavana agreed, face still clearly puzzled.

"Well, I want to find out if we can eat things that live here. And before we try fillet of monster, I want its head off."

Tavana's face cleared. "*Oui!* That I can do!" He headed out of the shelter.

Francisco made a face. "That thing? But it's poisonous!"

Xander held the injector for the IV over the sergeant's arm; after a moment it pinged and latched on. Relieved, he hung the IV bag on a hook above the bed. "No, it's *venomous*. There's a difference. Venom's a weapon, something the animal injects into you. Poison's stuff that kills you if you eat it. Of course I'll bet most venoms are poisonous, but they're not through the whole body. I remember reading about people eating rattlesnakes, and they're venomous."

"Oh," Francisco said. "So it isn't dangerous to eat?"

"That's what we have to find out," Xander said.

Maddox looked up from finishing his injections. "How? We don't have chemical analysis stuff."

"Well, actually, we *do*. Just not labeled as that." He tapped the medikit.

Maddox's eyes narrowed. "But *that* only works if it's in a living body for diagnosis."

Xander shrugged, trying to look more casual than he felt. "Well, yes. But I'll only eat a tiny bit at first."

"No!" Xander was surprised to see that both Maddox and Francisco had spoken. Maddox continued, "You're the captain now, right? Now that the sergeant's out?"

"Yes, I think so."

Maddox nodded, folding his arms in the way that he usually did when he'd made up his mind on something and was ready to fight about it. "Then *you* can't be the guinea pig. We can't take a risk on *you* ending up down too!"

Xander opened his mouth to argue, then realized that Maddox was right. He was the only other person qualified with firearms. He was the oldest, the best trained, the biggest, and probably the toughest. The others would be in a lot of trouble without him.

Maddox read the expression on his face—as Maddox often did. "You know I'm right."

"Yeah," Xander said after a moment. "Yeah, Maddox. You are, a lot of the time."

His brother's hazel eyes lit up for a moment with the compliment, then looked serious. "Okay. So that means that *I* will be the test—"

"No!"

This time it was Xander and Francisco; he glanced at the younger boy, who was looking at both of them fiercely.

"No," repeated Francisco, holding himself straight and jaw set. "It will be *me*."

Xander stared at the smallest of their crew, startled; he could see, out of the corner of his eye, that Maddox's expression mirrored his own. "Francisco, no, we can't—"

"Yes you can!" Francisco stamped his foot. "You think I am a baby, but I'm eight years old, and I am a *Coronel*! I am not a coward, and I'm not stupid either!"

"Franky... Francisco, no one thinks you're a coward or stupid, but you *are* a kid. Not a baby, but you're someone we're supposed to take care of."

Francisco looked down, and then back up. His face

was scared, but still as determined as it had been. "The sergeant told us the ship is not coming back. Maybe not ever, right?"

He wasn't going to deny the obvious. "Right."

"So we all need to do what we can."

Xander wanted to hesitate, but he couldn't argue that, either. "Right, Francisco, but—"

"*¡Cállate!*" shouted the eight-year-old; he was obviously fighting off a crying fit, despite the tears on his face that were bright in the light against his dark skin. "I am not an engineer. I do not shoot or fight. I am not even big and strong like you and Tavana. I just draw pictures and things." He drew himself up to his full one hundred thirty-five centimeters and jabbed his thumb at his chest. "But I *eat* like everyone else, so I can try food for you, and if it makes me sick, everyone else is not sick and can help me better and help everyone else better!"

Xander found himself unable to speak. He really wanted to. He *really* wanted to argue against this.

But in cold, hard fact, Francisco Alejandro Coronel was dead right. In their current situation, the eight-year-old couldn't contribute very much yet to their survival. But this way he could.

And with the medical nanos, and very small bites, it *shouldn't* be a terrible risk. But still...

Finally, after a long pause, he knelt down in front of Francisco, whose teary gaze was still locked defiantly on Xander. He reached out and put his hands on the little boy's shoulders, like the sergeant sometimes did. "Francisco...you're right. You're one of the bravest people I've met, and you are one hundred percent right."

Francisco's deep brown eyes widened. "I . . . I am?"

"You are. We can take care of you better than you can take care of us, and you haven't had time to learn other things that you can help us with. I know you *will* . . . but for now, you're right that this might just be the best thing you could do. It shouldn't be *too* dangerous . . . but it will be, at least some."

Francisco swallowed so hard that Xander could hear it. "I . . . I'll do it anyway."

"Your parents will kill me if they ever find out," Xander said after a moment. "But . . . they'll also be incredibly proud of you."

Francisco did burst out crying then, but there was a tremulous smile on his face.

Chapter 20

"You have to eat *something*, Tav."

Tavana jumped slightly at the unexpected voice. He was sitting on the steps of the lander's ladder, looking up at a comet whose slowly-fading tail covered thirty degrees of the now-dark sky. "Not hungry."

"Bullcrap," Xander said, and held out a plate.

He was about to refuse again when his nose caught the scent. "A *Buckley*? *Merde*, Xander, we were supposed to be saving those for special occasions!" Even though his anger and depression were trying to keep his stomach in a knot, his mouth was arguing strenuously that he really should take the plate.

"This *is* a special occasion. Sergeant's hurt but going to be okay, we've survived our first attack by local wildlife, and it's my first day as captain. Maybe not a happy day, but really, we needed *something* good to make up for all of that."

"To make up for my screwup, you mean." Tavana dropped down from the ladder heavily, falling to his hands and knees, and then stood and tried to stalk away. "For me almost getting the sergeant killed."

He heard a quiet, sharp *tap* as the plate was put

170

down on the ladder, and then one of Xander's hands came down on his shoulder. "How much time did you spend outdoors back home, Tav?"

He was puzzled by the question, and it almost annoyed him. He was ready for someone to argue that it wasn't his fault, and this wasn't something he'd prepared for. "Um ... not much. I mean, I wandered outside and looked at the stars, things like that, but I didn't do much fishing, or boating, or anything of that sort. Reading, studying, sim games like Canister Seven or Jewelbug, those were my things."

Xander's head was a shadow limned with faint silver from the stars and comet-light above, but Tavana could make out the nod. "Right. And you're a propulsion and power engineer type, not a bio major. Never did much hiking, and even if you had, you were on one of the Polynesian islands, right?"

"Right." He couldn't figure out what the point of this was, but he knew Xander; the older Bird brother *would* have a point.

"So you've never seen a dangerous land animal before in your life," Xander said. "Except maybe human beings. No snakes or crocodiles or even, if I remember right, poisonous spiders."

He pulled away. "Well ... once in a while there was a poisonous centipede. So what?"

"You know that the sergeant gave me full authorization just before he blacked out?"

"No—really?" He'd known the sergeant was trying to tell Xander something, but this ...

"Yep. So I reviewed the playback for the whole thing, straight from the sergeant's omni. The only thing you did wrong was something you couldn't have known was wrong. Sure, *I* would have known it was a bad idea to poke something like that even when you think it's dead. I've seen a rattler take a bite at someone's boot in pure dead reflex, just like that thing. But you hadn't. The sergeant shot it three times, and killed it sure—it *was* dead. You didn't know, and the sergeant should have told you to stay clear. It's as much his fault as yours."

"No it's—"

"Yes it is!" Xander snapped. "And when he wakes up, I'll bet you anything that he will say so himself. Maybe you should've guessed that you should be more careful, but that's not worth beating yourself up this much. Learn from it. And don't starve yourself. That's a Buckley dinner that's going cold over there."

Tavana stared up at the comet again, then bit his lip and looked over at the shadow of Xander near him. Without saying anything, he turned, walked back to the lander, and picked up the plate. *Southwestern Taco Supreme Meal.* "How'd you know this was my favorite?"

"Remember when we first broke out the Buckleys, way out in the middle of interstellar space? We all talked about our favorite meals." Xander's brilliant smile flashed visibly in the dark. "I knew it'd get your attention."

"You are sneaky."

"I had to raise Maddox for four years. You learn a lot of tricks that way."

Tavana wasn't sure he liked being compared to a thirteen-year-old...but then, Maddox was awfully bright. He guessed he could live with it. And the first bite of the taco, powerful with cumin, chipotle and ancho peppers, and other spices, helped push away the feelings that had been darker than the night around him. "So I'm not all to blame."

"No. Maybe you'd have made a different decision on a different day. Who knows? But the sergeant should have known—*did* know, or he wouldn't have reacted that fast. And he achieved what he was after, protecting *you*. He's going to be okay, I think. No long-term harm done, as long as nothing really bad happens in the next few weeks. We'll just have to be about a dozen times more careful until then."

Tavana heard Xander take a bite of something, realized the older boy had probably been carrying part of his own meal all along. "So how did the fishing go?"

"Got a couple of bites, I think, before the disaster, but we didn't pull in anything. I'm sure we will soon."

The silence wasn't complete. There were vague buzzing, whispering noises from whatever the equivalent of insects were, and some distant shufflings and other noises from the forest outside the perimeter. A *plop* signaled something that had jumped from the water and fallen back. "How's Francisco?"

"Fine. Nanos didn't pick up any toxins immediately, and he even liked the taste of the thing. If the nanos still say all clear tomorrow, I think we've found our first edible native food on Emerald. Keep your fingers crossed."

Tavana knew that expression, anyway. "Everything I've got two of, as my grandfather used to say." He looked up at the stars again. "This place has *long* days."

"And nights. I think the sergeant said about a thirty-six hour rotation. That'll take a little getting used to."

A shuffling sound. "Xander, back home, there were

animals—like sharks—that did a lot more hunting at night than in the day."

He saw the older boy stiffen. "I hadn't thought of that. Maybe we'd better stay inside at nights."

"Right now? *Oui*, that is probably a good idea. We should be able to use a few omnis or other sensors to give us a perimeter monitor. Maybe we can work on that for a while."

Xander nodded. "Probably for the best. We don't know whether that . . . worm-snake is the worst that Emerald has for us."

From far off came an eerie, booming noise, a cry of something huge that feared nothing in the dark.

Tavana stood back up, holding his plate. "No, and we had best act as though there's a lot worse waiting out there for us."

Xander followed him inside. All the way in, Tavana felt the prickle of tension. He wondered what alien eyes might be watching them.

But once in the shelter, with the bright light and the tough, layered-carbonan weave walls, he felt his spirits finally lifting. *Maybe it* wasn't *all my fault.* "All right," he said, "we will plan out a perimeter monitor, and a defensive perimeter too, if the sergeant approves when he gets up. They can make all the noise they want out there. We," he finished, seeing Xander smiling and Maddox looking up hopefully, "will be getting ready for them in here."

Chapter 21

The pistol bucked three times in Xander's hand, almost without him willing it. A screech and convulsive writhing showed that he'd hit the sinuous creature just as the targeting app had said he would. The centisnake, as Maddox had named the thing, shuddered to a slow halt. Once it was still, Tavana stepped forward and brought the machete down hard, taking the head from the body and causing another powerful, but this time harmless, sequence of thrashings.

The younger but broader boy wiped his forehead and face with a cloth he carried at his belt. "That is the last of them, I think."

"Hope so. We'll have to do another full walk-around of the entire area, though."

There had been a total of four of the ambush predators lurking under the cleared area around *LS-88*. Xander's priority was to finish the job the sergeant had started. There was no way he was taking a chance of something like that hiding in a hole where it could jump out and grab Francisco or Maddox. He was puzzled by the presence of that many of the things. Must've been a nest or colony of them here, even though ambush predators didn't usually hunt in packs. They were fairly large animals, too. Predators that size couldn't usually be very concentrated because they needed enough non-predators around to support them.

He reminded himself of what one of his teachers had once called Exobiology Rule Number One: "Don't assume that alien life forms will be analogous to anything terrestrial." He said this could be simplified to *aliens can get really weird*.

"You did good, Tav. I know you were scared—"

"I was not..." Tavana trailed off, then rolled his eyes and grinned sheepishly. "*Oui*, I was scared half to death coming back out here."

"I know you were," Xander repeated. "I saw your hands shaking at first. But you did everything just the right way, and we've got probably a safe perimeter and definitely more to eat, now that we know the centisnake's meat is good."

He made sure the hole was at the center of his field of view, and then said "Mark hole finished." Immediately a red blotch, looking for all the world as though someone had spray-painted the hole, appeared in his retinals—and on Tavana's, he knew, since the two were linked. "*This* was a great idea."

"One that I am proud of," agreed Tavana. "I was thinking how hard it was to be sure which holes we had checked, and realized it would be simple to tell the omnis to mark them. Took only a few minutes to instruct."

"Well, it'll make re-checking the grounds a lot easier. If there are any holes we've missed, they won't be marked."

They started the second patrol, beginning right at

the edge of the berm of scraped earth that surrounded the camp. "What's after this?"

"Hold on. Maddox!"

His brother's voice responded almost instantly through his omni. "Yeah, bro, what's up?"

"We've got three more centisnakes. Sorry to put this on you two, but come pick them up, and then clean and fillet them. We need to get the meat into storage."

"All right," Maddox sighed. "*Francisco!*"

Fortunately Francisco didn't argue, and so the two younger members of their little crew were soon on their way to pick up the catch of the day. Xander turned back to Tavana. "After this? We should start getting that perimeter monitor set up that we were working on during the, what, the dark of the day?"

"Dark-day? Heh. I like it. We will have to deal with dark-days a lot. We are near the equator, yes? So daylight and night-time are about eighteen hours." Tavana nodded. "Hm. So we have to start taking apart one of the excavators for sensor systems."

"I think so. There are only five omnis between us—six, if we count Lieutenant Haley's, I guess—and we'll want those for ground comm, tool support, all sorts of stuff. I really don't want to sacrifice an omni if we don't have to. Unless we've got a case of them in storage somewhere?"

Tavana shook his head. "That would have been nice, but no, I did not see any such things. So then yes, we will have to strip the situational awareness sensors from one of the excavators."

"Will one excavator give us enough? I know we have four of them."

"I think so. They need full panoramic awareness,

and the design uses dedicated sensors for all sides, not a single sensor on a mast like some cheaper designs. Though it does have a mast-mounted scanning LIDAR. I will probably leave that installed."

Xander looked around. "That perimeter's going to be huge, though. Compared to the machine, anyway. Will they still have the range? And for that matter, can they operate by themselves?"

Tavana pointed to a suspicious circle of dirt that they had somehow missed. The two began the "poke it with a stick" protocol. "If we put a solar pack on them, I think they will operate fine alone; even very stupid sensors these days are more than able to function independent of central systems. Range, that will not be a problem; sometimes they use their sensors to coordinate operations with other devices a long way off. I can tie the sensor data to our omnis—or better, I will tie them to *LS-88's* main computers and they will be able to do a target evaluation."

"Sounds good." There simply weren't enough of them—even if the sergeant were up and about, which he wasn't—to maintain a good watch using people. But if the sounds they'd heard out there in the dark were any indication, there were definitely things on Emerald bigger and more dangerous than the centisnakes.

There was no reaction from this hole, so they marked it clear and continued. "We . . . or maybe just I . . . will have another little task that has to be done soon," he said after a few moments.

"I think there are many tasks we will have to do soon. What is this one?"

"Lieutenant Haley. The sergeant won't be able to tend to her for a while, and we know what happens if she's just left in the suit for too long. She needs to be . . . um, cleaned off, and the suit needs to be washed out."

Tavana nodded. "If it's embarrassing for you, maybe it would help to wait for the sergeant to wake up. He's in his suit now, yes?"

"Yes." It worried Xander, but there wasn't much he could do about it. The medical database was helpful, but it wasn't a full-blown AI, and couldn't fully understand or model the devil's brew of toxins the centisnake had injected. The necrosis appeared to have been halted, but some of the other effects were apparently harder to reverse.

"So wait for him to wake up. If he directs you, there will be much less for you to worry about." Tavana's smile seemed patronizing.

"What are you grinning about?"

"You North Americans, you are so shy about things. You'd worry about having chaperones even for the doctors and nurses, I think."

Xander couldn't think of an appropriate retort. Tavana was probably right. This was a nursing situation; they had to take care of their patient, and there wasn't anything inappropriate in that. But waiting a day or two for the sergeant to be awake enough to direct it wouldn't hurt.

By the time they finished the second sweep of the camp grounds a few hours later, Maddox and Francisco had completed the cleaning of the centisnakes. "What do we do with the, um, remains?"

"Good question." They did not want to start leaving a garbage dump to attract whatever the equivalent of flies and rats might be.

"Let's pick out some organs that might be useful

for fishing. The rest . . . I think we should probably burn it for now. When the sergeant's up, we'll all talk about how we want to handle that for the long run. How much meat have we got?"

"A lot!" Francisco answered. "We've almost filled the shelter freezer!"

That *was* a fair amount. "I was hoping for something more like an actual weight."

"Well," Maddox said, "Umm . . . here, we've got the pressure sensors at the doors to open and close them, right? If we tie our omnis into that—"

"We could just put the meat on a plastic sheet on the doorstep and find out. Good thinking, Maddox!"

After a few minutes work, Xander nodded. "Not bad. A little more than twenty kilos."

Tavana frowned. "That seems awfully small. Just one of those things must have been over thirty kilos!"

"Closer to forty," Xander said. "But they're long and skinny. You're not going to get a huge yield out of them. Even fish like sea bass don't generally give you more than about a third of their mass in really usable food, so this is actually really good. Great job, Maddox, Francisco!"

Francisco made a face. "It is *messy*. And *smelly*."

Maddox and Xander laughed. "Oh, it sure is. Cleaning what you kill is always the part everyone likes least. The stalking and the hunting, that's fun. Cooking, that can be fun too. Eating, that's fun. Gutting and cleaning, not so much."

"So we're going to eat some of this tonight, right, Xander?" asked Francisco excitedly. "I cut this one!" He held up a fillet that was obviously more ragged than others. "Can we eat it?"

This time none of the smiles were forced. "Of course we can. I'll fry it up for everyone."

As Xander got out the cooking utensils and the limited seasonings that were part of the shelter's equipment, he wondered what he could do for the future. They couldn't just live on meat. On Earth, some traditional cultures like the Inuit were almost entirely carnivorous, but they got the vitamins they needed by eating the internal organs of animals. Xander was reluctant to try that experiment. Internal organs were also where toxic substances got concentrated. The Inuit had had millennia to learn what to avoid. They didn't.

At the very least, that would be a last resort. They needed to find other things to eat. And stuff like seasonings, salt, to make it fun to cook. They were incredibly lucky that they'd landed with all their resources, but they'd run out eventually—and some would run out pretty fast. He didn't think they had dietary supplements anywhere on board, either. Not many, for sure.

It was starting to dawn on him just how *complicated* this was going to be. Going to Tantalus Colony was a completely different situation; there, they would be the second wave, with the first part of the colony set up. Things like *what can we eat?* and *what will kill us?* would be questions answered long before. The issues of nutrition would not only have been figured out, but the ship they arrived on would also have had everything they needed to stay alive.

He cut the meat into pan-sized sections, dusted it with a bit of salt and pepper, and started frying. Not having analytical equipment was really going to make this dangerous. Francisco made sense as a taste-tester, but as Xander remembered from his camping days, animal-borne toxins weren't nearly as bad as those that plants might be carrying. They'd just have to be very careful. If he remembered right, there were plants on Earth that could kill people with as little as one seed. In fact, there were some things on Earth that you didn't even want to *touch*—certain toads in the Amazon rain forest, for instance. Maybe they'd find an animal they could keep or observe as a test subject.

Xander *really* didn't like that last thought. Not only would it be hard to keep any animal they didn't understand to begin with, but also it was just not a nice thing to do— imprison some animal so it could eat things and maybe die for your protection. But something like that might be necessary if he was going to keep everyone alive.

The sizzling meat smelled appetizing; Francisco had enjoyed the little bit he'd eaten a couple days ago. *Well, let's see what it's like!*

"C'mon, everyone, dinner's ready!" Xander called. He served everyone straight from the pan onto their plates, and then sat down.

His omni gave a loud *ping* that he'd been praying for. He stood up so suddenly he almost tipped over the little table.

"What is it, Xander?" asked Maddox, concern on his face.

"It's the sergeant," Xander answered, heading to the side room where the older man was lying. "He's waking up!"

Chapter 22

Campbell blinked his eyes blearily, forced them to focus. *What . . . Oh. I'm inside my suit. Was I on EVA? Fixing something? What happened?*

When he tried to sit up, he felt the tremendous lethargy and pain of having been still for many hours, even days. His leg gave a dull throb despite what his nanos reported as "significant pain reduction."

That cleared his head. He knew exactly why he was here.

"Sergeant? Sergeant, do you hear me?"

He managed to force his lips into a grin, though that hurt too. "Loud and clear, Captain Xander."

The other boys crowded around, all looking relieved. "How long have I been out?"

"Longer than we expected. Earth-time, about a day and a half?"

"Damn. That *is* a long time. Hold on." He consulted his nanos and winced. *That venom was a nasty cocktail, that's for sure.* "I'm conscious, but a long way from running a marathon. Damn thing's venom ate a hole in me that goes to the bone. You could fit two, three fingers into it right now."

Tavana made a face. Francisco shuddered. Xander nodded. "Yeah, I saw that. Took it a while to get all the necrotic under control; there were some kind of other elements to the poison that didn't count as venom themselves, but helped it work. Same for the neurotoxin."

Campbell reviewed the data. "I see that. It neutralized most of it fairly quickly, then there was a second wave of activity. Wish I was a biochemist, I might know exactly how that worked. Anyway, looks like I'm on the mend, just slowly. Good thinking, by the way, putting me into the suit. A lot easier than bedpans and such." He noticed that one arm was out of the suit, so that the IV could be used.

He smelled an unidentifiable but still savory scent, and his stomach growled. "Now that smells good, whatever it is. I'm starving. No surprise there."

"That's what bit you," Tavana said. "And I'm sorry—"

"Not your fault. Mine," Campbell said instantly. "You didn't know what to watch for. I damn well did, and didn't brief you. I earned that bite. Let's just learn the lesson it taught us."

Tavana glanced at Xander and the two grinned. "You were right, Xander."

"Told you."

Campbell raised an eyebrow. "You boys obviously had a talk or two. Anyway, before we go around eating the native food, how do you know it's safe?"

Xander hesitated; to Campbell's astonishment, Francisco stepped forward. "I tried some first, and my nanos decided it was all safe. I was watched for a whole day afterward."

"*Francisco*? How'd that happen?" demanded Campbell.

Xander, looking nervous, related the entire conversation that had led to the decision that Francisco
would test native food.

Campbell could see the others becoming increasingly
nervous. Finally, with an effort, he forced himself up
to a semi-sitting position. "Francisco, that was damned
brave of you," he said finally. He saw the boy's chin
come up proudly. "In principle, you boys were correct.
Right now, Francisco's the one we can risk most, no
matter how much that sounds bass-ackwards."

"But in practice?" Xander said, clearly braced for
a major dressing-down.

"Relax, Xander. In practice, you boys just don't
know how to do this. You already realized there are
probably poisons out there that even a small nibble
of could kill, right?"

Xander nodded.

"There's a procedure for this kind of thing that
avoids most of the danger. From now on we use it.
We're not in danger of starving; we have time. We'll
work out details later, but basically you first do a
contact poison test—touch it to part of the skin, like
inside the arm or the wrist. Wait a while and see if
you have a reaction—the nanos would be able to tell
if it's an allergy or a toxin. Then you take a tiny bit,
chew, and spit out—don't swallow *anything*. Rinse out
your mouth. That will catch really virulent poisons
that are mobile through the mucous membranes. *Then*
you try a little nibble.

"For animals, internal organs are 'be *real* careful'
things. Might have a lot of nutrients, or might have
heavy-duty toxins." He had to pause then. *Damn, this
lying around poisoned sure takes it out of you. Good*

thing the nanos are keeping me more functional than I might be otherwise. "But really, you did good, both of you. Anything else to report?"

Tavana summarized the other work they had done, including finishing the job that had gotten the sergeant laid up.

"Got back on that horse, did you?"

Tavana nodded. "Xander said we had to. I . . . I'm glad he did."

"So am I." He let the two of them—with occasional interruptions and additions from Maddox and Francisco—finish their briefing.

When they were finished, he opened a private channel to Xander. *You've done well. Kept things going, prevented any panic, and moved our little colony forward—quite a ways in the little time I was out.*

Thank you, sir.

No, thank you. *I had to dump the whole load on you in the middle of an emergency. I've seen trained recruits that would've dropped that ball, but you took it and ran the whole length of the field.*

Campbell spoke aloud. "You all did a great job. It's good to know that even if I'm out of commission, you'll still get things done."

All four of them straightened, looking proud and happy. In Campbell's view, they damned well ought to.

"Now," he said, "can I get some of that, what did you call it? Centisnake? Let's see what the native food's got to offer?"

"Yes, Sergeant!" Francisco said eagerly, and ran to the other room. Both Maddox and Tavana followed to make sure he remembered things like plates and utensils.

In the momentary quiet, Xander nodded to him. "I guess you can send that revocation code now."

"I could, but I'm not." At Xander's startled, gratified look, Campbell grinned, and then went serious. "First off, I'm a long way from being in any shape to run things. The boss of this expedition's got to be able to cover the ground—run his ass off, really. Best guess I see here is that it's going to be at least a week or so before I can get on my feet, and a couple months before I'm going to be close to my old self."

"That long?"

"Necrotic damage is *nasty*, Xander. And regenerating lost muscle tissue . . . well, if these weren't military grade, it might not be happening at all. That's another reason I didn't hesitate to take the hit for Tavana—I can afford that kind of injury more than any of you." He shook his head. "So while I'll be giving you all the advice and support I can, for the next few weeks, you're still the captain of this crew."

He took a breath, but at that point the others came back in, bearing a length of well-browned meat on a plate. The smell was extremely tempting; however, knowing how long it had been since he'd eaten and how much he was still adjusting to consciousness, he controlled his initial ravenous impulses and cut a small piece. He chewed thoughtfully and carefully. "Well, now. That's not bad at all." He took another bite. "I've eaten gators that tasted worse. This could be a pretty good staple, if there are enough of them."

A ping from a private channel—Xander, of course. *And after you're better?*

Still not revoking your access, he replied silently. *Might tweak it so that I can still override you, but honestly? We can't take the risk that we will lose access to key capabilities here just because one of us—even me—gets killed. Truth be told, we should probably make sure that Tavana has the codes and they go active if we get taken out.*

Makes sense. Thank you again, Sergeant.

You're welcome. And thank you again.

"Well, there were four of them here, at least," Tavana said in response to his last audible comment. "But probably harder to hunt them when you have not plowed their holes down to rock!"

"We should see if we can find out what they eat," Campbell said. "Carnivores are usually a lot rarer than their prey. But we won't be doing much exploration for a bit."

He took another bite, feeling better already. He was now sure that, even without him, these kids would make it. *Oh, Emerald's got more surprises. I know it. I can smell 'em out there. But Xander's got sense, Tavana's got more guts than he knows, and the other two aren't lacking, either.*

The only thing left to mar his mood was the knowledge that Pearce Haley was still in deathly sleep a dozen meters away. *But we have months to work on that, too. Maybe, just maybe, we can save her, too.*

And now . . . now I know we have those months.

Chapter 23

"*Whoa!*"

Tavana lunged reflexively, catching Maddox before he was dragged headlong into the water. The carbonan fishing pole was bent in a sharp curve, vibrating furiously even while Tavana managed to get the smaller Bird brother back on his feet.

"Got something, Tav, we *got* something!"

"*Vraiment*, that we do! Can you hold it?"

Maddox's face was set in lines of determination. "If...you can...keep me from falling on my face..."

Tavana grinned, slid both arms just under Maddox's arms, and braced himself. "That I can do!"

He raised his voice a bit to activate his omni. "Xander! We have a bite, a big one!"

"You do? We'll be right there!"

"Give me a video feed, Tavana," came the sergeant's voice. "If I can't be there, I darn well want to watch!"

Whatever was on the other end of the carbonan-reinforced line was strong, Tavana had to give it that. Maddox's muscles stood out on his arms like slender bundles of cord as he pulled back, trying to force his prize to turn towards him. But there was no way he

189

could keep doing it all himself—the drag on the pole was set to a third of his own weight!

"Let me take it, Maddox," Tavana said.

"No!"

"You can't hold it in one hand if it yanks like that again, and how are you going to reel it in without letting go at least for an instant?"

Maddox grunted as another powerful yank pulled him forward. "Okay, okay . . . you turn the reel. Hold me with one arm?"

"Works." He didn't want to deprive Maddox of the first catch on a new planet. Sure, he really would have liked to be the one to do it, but it hadn't been his turn, it had been Maddox's. The smaller boy hung on grimly.

None of them had expected their first real hit on the line to be this big!

He got hold of the reel, which had been made from the take-up reel of the coil-winder they'd cobbled together months ago, and started cranking back hard. The fish, or whatever it was, had suddenly turned towards them and the line was threatening to go slack.

Maddox immediately pulled up and tried to back-pedal; Tavana did his best to go along with him. *Gain as much on this thing as we can—*

The rod whipped down again and the line screamed out at astonishing speed. *Mon Dieu*, it was strong!

Xander and Francisco appeared around the side of *LS-88*, the oldest boy wiping grease from his hands. "Holy crap, that thing must be a monster!"

"Be damned careful, boys," the sergeant admonished from inside the lander. "If that's the local equivalent of a shark, it'll be hell on wheels even when you beach it. Stay sharp, stay clear, and don't get stupid; Xander, when and if you get a clear shot, take it. We're not sport-fishing here, we're doing survival. Got it?"

"Yes, sir, Sergeant," Xander said. Out of the corner of his eye, Tavana saw him give a sideways smile. "Is it fun ordering a captain around?"

The sergeant's laugh was loud and cheerful. "Only when they're young punks! But you're right, Captain, I should be *advising* you."

"And it's good advice. Francisco, get *back*. I want you up against the landing strut there. WOW!"

The creature reached the surface and breached spectacularly, like an Earthly marlin, except no marlin had spiky, segmented armor, or four rows of paired fins, or that edged, flowering nightmare of a mouth. "No joke, Sergeant, that's a top predator for sure!"

Maddox swore. "That thing's huge!"

"Big enough—I guess it at four, five meters, boys," the sergeant said. His voice was now serious. "Might not be a *top* predator, but I'll tell you, seeing that makes me damn nervous. Xander, you've done this before?"

"Yes, sir. This is going to be a long fight, if that thing's anything like a shark. Maddox, I'm sorry, but we'll need to take turns."

Sweat trickled down Maddox's neck; his hair was matted and he was breathing heavily. Tavana could feel his arms shaking. Reluctantly, Maddox nodded. "O . . . okay. Tav, can you take it for a bit?"

"Right." Tavana reached out, clamped his left hand firmly on the rod just above Maddox's, and then grabbed the bottom of the rod. "Got it."

Maddox let go and ducked out, just as the monstrous fish-thing gave another mighty yank. But Tavana had been braced, and he had no trouble keeping a grip on it. It felt like twenty kilos or so—quite a tug, but nothing outrageous. The line streamed off the reel again. "I can do this for a while."

"You'll have to." Xander sat down next to him. Maddox had flopped down onto the dirt, exhausted. "Unless this thing tires a lot faster, we might be fighting it for *hours.*"

"*Oui*, I am aware. I only did a little fishing, but I remember the people saying how long it took to land the big ones. You know that Maddox and I, we will be landing it, yes?"

Xander looked out at the water, where the thing was visible by the bulge it was making on the surface as it streaked away again. "Honestly? I'm seriously thinking of cutting the line."

Maddox sat bolt upright. "What? *No!* Why?"

Tavana had the same impulse as Maddox, but his brain caught up to Xander's. "Maddox, your brother, he has a point. It will not be safe, landing this monster. We do not even know if it will be something edible."

Xander nodded slowly. "Basically, yes. That's what's got you nervous, right, Sergeant?"

There was a moment of silence, then a grunt from Campbell. "Partly. More than that, though, but nothing to concern you right now."

"So you think I should do it? Cut the line?" Xander carefully looked away from his brother's outraged face.

"Son, right now, you're the captain. You're going to have to make that call."

"I am asking the old laid-up soldier for *advice*, Sergeant."

That got a chuckle, one that even Maddox joined in on. "Well, now, that's fine. Advice? I think we can argue it either way, assuming it doesn't somehow get off the hook. This is the first bite we've gotten. It's going to be our first look at what lives in these waters, and something that big will have a *lot* to tell us—not just from itself, but from what it's eaten lately, too. Edible or not, we might find it's got other useful aspects—those armor plates might come in handy, for instance.

"And of course there's no guarantee the next thing you hook will be any safer." He paused. "Now, if you *do* bring it in, I want you all to remember what we've learned so far. That thing might be venomous, from its teeth to its fins and skin. So you boys get gloved up when it's getting close, got me?"

"Got it, sir," Tavana said, and the others echoed it. "Sergeant?"

"Go ahead, Tavana."

"This cable, it is very thin, but it is carbonan, yes? So it should be extremely strong, strong enough to hold that thing's complete weight."

"I'd think so. Xander?"

"That's TaylerCord 5K. The 5K is its rated strength, so it's rated to five thousand kilograms. I don't think that thing's going to be even close to that."

"So we could just tie it to the landing strut and let it pull as hard as it wants, right?"

After a moment, the sergeant chuckled. "Might could at that."

"Won't work, if it's like most fish," Xander said. "Give it enough slack, it'll either find a way to pull the hook out, rip the hook straight out through its body, or peak at a high enough tension to snap even this line. I'll bet on the 'rip the hook out,' myself.

But that's why we have to keep fighting it this way; if it gets slack, it has a good chance of getting away."

"Then the choice is up to you, Captain Xander."

"I will do a properly Captain thing, then, and put off the decision until I see what shape we're in when it gets close to time to land it."

"Ha!"

Tavana turned his attention to the rod. The creature had once more paused in its struggles. Tavana lifted the rod, lowered it as he wound the line in, lifted again, and lowered while winding, dragging the creature towards them slowly but surely.

And then without warning it leapt away again through the water, dragging the line with it.

All of them became familiar with that dragging, tiring, yet still fascinating routine, pitting their timing and smaller muscles braced on the ground against the determination and vast power of the creature from the depths of the lake. After the first hour, Tavana started to wonder if the thing was going to beat them, simply because it was able to endure beyond anything they could manage. He muttered something about that as he took the rod for the third time.

"Don't you worry about that," the sergeant's voice said. "Tavana, human beings aren't the strongest animals on our planet. We aren't the fastest, and we aren't the toughest in a fight, either, but there *is* one thing we're just crazy-good at, and that's keepin' on keepin' on. Persistence hunting, that's our game. Sure, we can't outpower that monster out there, but you can bet your last dollar that we can out*last* him, if we don't just plain give up."

Tavana tried to keep those serenely certain words in

mind as the battle went to two hours, then three, then four, as Emerald's sluggish sun crawled across the sky.

The creature's runs were getting shorter and shorter. It was clearly getting closer and closer to shore. "Xander, I think we are winning."

Xander, who was eating some jerky that Francisco had brought from the lander, sat up straighter. "I think you're right."

The thing chose that moment to surge to the surface again, but even that powerful movement reinforced Tavana's impression. Unlike that first mighty breach, this was a lunge that broke the surface but did not come close to clearing the water. Barely a quarter of the armored fish-thing's length emerged before it sank back beneath the surface. "He's almost done, Sergeant!"

"Sure looks that way. Time for that decision, Captain."

Xander stood still, watching as Tavana dragged the thing closer to shore, now no more than ten meters away. Finally he nodded. "Let's do this. Francisco, go get the gloves. Boots back on, everyone. No chances, right?"

"Yes, Xander!" agreed Maddox.

"Understood," Tavana said. Having seen that nightmarish mouth, he had no desire at all to take any risks.

Tavana nodded to Maddox. "You're going to take the pole at the end. You hooked it, you get to bring it in."

The brilliant smile from the lighter-haired brother told Tavana he'd said the right thing. "Thank you, Tavana!"

"No problem. I'll stand right behind you just in case it pulls hard at the end."

Xander stood to the side now, sidearm drawn. As Maddox and Tavana slowly dragged the monster closer, Tavana saw Xander release the safety. His finger was still well clear of the trigger, laid along the axis of the gun across, but not through, the trigger guard. He held the muzzle of the gun pointed low and away from all of them. Francisco hung back as he had been instructed. The thing made one more lunge, showing two jaws filled with uncountable teeth, paired with ripping mandibles. The smallest of their crew shrank behind the landing strut.

"Keep bringing him in. Closer . . . closer . . . Tav, can you and Maddox drag him a little this way? Yeah, it looks flatter there, I think we can get him beached easier . . . yeah, that's it . . . *Whoa*, I think he knows something's up, that was a hard run."

Maddox pulled up, reeled in, pulled up, trusting to Tavana to keep him from falling. "Come . . . in . . . here, you stubborn little . . ."

"I would call it many things, but not little!"

Maddox growled a little, but focused his energy on pulling again. "Almost . . . there . . ."

The creature seemed to realize that it was the small animals up there, on the land, that were responsible for its torment. It swung about and charged towards the bank, throwing up twin bow waves in a startling rush of speed.

And then it came right up on the bank and started thrashing across the ground, straight for Tavana and Maddox.

Tavana didn't think. He just acted, literally *throwing* Maddox over his head and behind him. He ran to the side, waving his arms and shouting, keeping the attention of the hissing monstrosity.

Gunshots cracked out, one after another in rapid succession. The creature spasmed, jackknifed around towards Xander, and then caught three shots in the face for its trouble. The controlled charge turned into a writhing dance of agony that made everyone scramble back, waiting until the convulsions died down and the gigantic body was still.

Finally there were only a few dying tremors rippling down the creature's flanks. Tavana let himself sink down to the rough ground, shaking. "*Merde*, that was much more exciting than I was hoping for!"

"What did I tell you boys? Planets hold surprises. Back on Earth there are more than a few fish that could do that, though none of them were nearly that big. On the other hand, orcas do that kind of thing sometimes, and they're even bigger." The sergeant's voice was also a little shaky. "Good shooting. Good discipline there, Xander. And good reflexes, Tav. Everyone did good there. Just be careful approaching it."

"I remember why you are lying inside, Sergeant," Tavana said emphatically. "Believe me, a second lesson I do not need."

"Heh. I suppose not. So keep an eye on the others for me."

"That I can do."

They warily approached it. Now that it was still and fully out of the water, Tavana's omni could compute the exact dimensions: five point two meters long, and if the density was roughly that of water, massing something over a ton. "That *is* a monster."

Xander nodded. "Sure is. Stand back, everyone."

He put two more shots into the thing, but it only twitched sluggishly; there was no sign of the sudden, savage reanimation that had nearly cost the sergeant his life. Xander let out a long sigh. "Looks like he's *dead* dead."

"Doesn't mean it's safe," Campbell reminded them. "Approach with caution, and remember to be *very* careful touching anything."

"Sergeant?" Tavana said, as they closed in on the body. "Can you tell us now what the other thing was that was bothering you?"

"Sure," he said, and his tone was grim enough to get Xander to pause. "Take a look out there. What do you see?"

He wasn't sure what he was supposed to see, but he knew better than to question Sergeant Campbell. "Umm . . . well, I see the lake. Ripples on the lake. Then the other side of the lake, some of those tree things—"

"Right. How far do you think it is to the other side of the lake?"

"That's easy." His retinals sent the image to his omni along with the query. "Six hundred and fifteen meters."

"Little more than half a klick. And it's not much longer than that, if any. So tell me, how many fish or whatever do you think are in a lake that size, and how many does a monster like that need to eat every day?"

Light dawned. "You mean it shouldn't be in here."

"Damn straight. That means that it either somehow swam up that not-too-big stream running out of this lake, or there's some other way in that we can't see, because unless that lake's about three kilometers deep there's no way it's big enough to support things that size. It's like finding a great white shark in your local fishing pond." He paused. "Honestly, Xander, I'm glad you made the call you did. That beast's got a lot to tell us, and we need all the info we can get. Because I don't think we've even started to find out the surprises Emerald's hiding."

Chapter 24

"That's funny," Xander muttered to himself.

"In my experience," said a deeper, rougher voice behind him, "those words either mean a discovery, or trouble. Usually both. What's funny?"

Xander turned to face the sergeant, who was slowly and cautiously making his way over to one of the portable seats they had pulled from the shelter, hobbling with the help of one of the expandable crutches they'd found in the medical kit. "Well, you remember you told us to expand that app that Tavana had made?"

"You mean, I reminded you that burrows can often have *two* ends, and some of the ones near the edge of our little perimeter might have their other ends on the outside. You were the one who figured out that we should probably have something keep an eye on the ground outside all over, and look for things that changed."

Xander looked sharply at the older man, who just gave him an easy grin. "You would've made your 'advice' more clear if I hadn't caught it on the first try," Xander said.

"Probably. But part of being a commander is interpreting what people mean; it's my job to see how well you do that. But we're off the subject. What's funny?"

"The *ground*, Sergeant. Take a look at the feeds."

There was a pause, and then Campbell sat down in his seat with a grunt that was not all from pain. "I'll be damned."

He knew what the sergeant was seeing. If nothing had changed significantly over the last few days, the enhanced-reality view through the omni should look pretty much like it did to the naked eye. The app was tied into everyone's omnis, so it could even allow for things like the foot traffic back and forth across various parts of their clearing.

Instead, there were large blotches of blue shading to green all over the ground. To Xander's eye, they looked most prominent in the areas where the excavator seemed to have done a more thorough job.

"What does it mean, Sergeant?"

"Not a clue. Let's go take a closer look. If I read this right, it's saying that those areas are a little higher than they were after we graded 'em off. Right?"

"Yes. Not much—a millimeter or so, maybe—but ground doesn't grow."

"Not normally, no. And I'm not seeing any ground cover of the ordinary sort on those areas, which is what would *normally* be growing after you clear an area."

They reached the center of one of the largest areas and both of them knelt down. "I don't see anything different in ordinary images," Xander said after a moment.

"No more do I. Looks like the same white rock that's under most things here." Sergeant Campbell pursed his lips, then poked at the ground. "Hard. Damp, but that's no surprise. Hmmmm...Ah! Let's see what a magnified view has to say. What was that code...Got it!"

"Got what?"

"Modern retinals with a good omni hooked into them can do a damn sight better than regular eyes. Basically I can turn mine into pretty good microscopes. I don't know if I can give you the same app, but I'll bet Tavana could whip one up. By the way, where is he?"

"Tav's actually getting some alone time. He needs space once in a while. He's also working on coding some more Jewelbug adventures. I know that's not *survival* stuff, but we're waiting on a lot of things, and—"

"No worries, son. People need time to be people, not just working machines. This isn't a boot camp; I'm not here to drive you to find out if you'll break. If Tav needs a day to himself every couple weeks, and we need some games to make it tolerable to be here? Works for me, as long as it doesn't get in the way when an emergency comes up. Here, help me chip off a piece of this stuff."

Xander got out his Shapetool and quickly gouged out a small section of the whitish rock. "That good?"

"Perfect." The sergeant put the sample on his hand and brought it up close to his eyes. "Other kids busy?"

"Maddox and Francisco are cleaning clothes. I don't know how long the cleaners for the shelter and LS-88 are going to hold out, though."

"Yeah," the sergeant said in an abstracted tone, "we'll need new ways to clean clothes. And new ways to *make* clothes eventually, though that's at least not a major issue for today, thank God." He turned the little sample over. "I will be damned. Here, take a look at this stuff."

The sergeant opened up a data feed so Xander could look.

Under the magnification, the rock looked complex, a series of regular octagonal sections closely packed together. Some of those sections were empty, tiny pockmarks in the expanse of rock, but others...

"Is that *alive*?"

"Looks like it to me. Closest thing I've ever seen to that would be coral. Never came across anything like this on land." He sat back on his haunches. "Remember a discussion years back on Ulmo with a couple of big brain types on whether coral could grow on land; they both concluded it couldn't happen, mainly because coral like we know it lives off of stuff in the water. If we take it out of water, what's it going to eat?"

"So what's *this* stuff living on?"

Campbell stood up. "That *is* the question, isn't it? Makes me a little worried, actually. You know what coral normally lives on, right?"

"Um..." Xander thought for a moment, then decided there was no point in guessing and checked his omni's reference files to see if it had an answer. "Plankton. Tiny plants and animals in the water."

"Right. So if this stuff's anything like that, it'd mean we've got a lot of, well, air-plankton around. And we'd be breathing it."

"If there was something bad, though, our medical nanos would have noticed."

The sergeant's frown faded. "You know, you're right. Of course they would. Still... maybe this ecology goes down a ways. Normally soil on Earth builds from the top down, but maybe this place builds it from both directions and these guys are the source on the bottom, breaking down whatever the real base rock is." He shrugged. "I guess the main problem is that we're going to have to make sure it *stops* doing this once we build anything permanent. Something that grows a millimeter in a few weeks is the kind of thing that'll knock over anything you build on it, and not in all that long, either."

Xander didn't need to be told that; engineering experience showed what happened whenever things moved under structures. "How can we stop it, though?"

"My guess? We burn it. Heat it up enough and we'll get a dead layer that'll seal it, at least for a while. Might have to resurface every few months or years, but that's no big deal. 'Course, that depends on what happens when we try. I don't *think* this stuff would be flammable, but stranger things have happened."

"So a literal scorched-earth policy?" Xander looked askance at the sergeant.

Campbell shrugged. "Xander, that's pretty common in first camps, honestly. I bulldozed everything out of here. I think maybe I'm going to sterilize it with the lander's jets. Sounds heavy-handed, but my experience is that you really don't want any surprises waiting *under* you, and that's what this ground is. It's worth a try just to see what happens."

"So we have to take down the shelter?"

The older man chewed his lower lip thoughtfully. "Well . . . I can probably lift off and concentrate the heat on the other side of the clearing. But it *would* be a lot easier and safer if we take the shelter down."

Xander sighed. The idea of taking the shelter down— which meant moving all their stuff out of it first and packing it back into the lander—was not appealing.

But appealing wasn't the point here. "If you think we need to scorch the area, we scorch it. Which means we take the shelter down. Are we going to make more permanent shelters?"

"Sure, figure on it. The satellite grid's almost in place, so pretty soon we'll be able to set the excavators on automatic. If we can find us some reasonable building materials out there in the jungle, some quick digging for foundations, dragging in logs or what-have-you, I'll have us living in houses in jig time!"

"That easy?"

Campbell laughed. "*Easy* is a fuzzy concept. There'll be a lot of work involved, even with the excavators, but it won't take all that long if we find the stuff we need."

"That'll have to wait until you're well."

Campbell started to shake his head, then nodded. "I hate waiting that long...but you're right, Xander. That's an expedition you want me on. But one thing we can do: start shooting practice. Tavana and Maddox need to learn to shoot, how to take care of a weapon, all that stuff. Francisco's a little young compared to my usual recruit, but I was handling small arms before I was eight."

"You're okay with all of them learning?"

"What do *you* think...Captain?"

"Oh, cut it out. You—"

"—gave you command. Xander, you've got to let that sink in and *keep* it until I relieve you. I'm still a ways from being in shape to respond to any emergency. Hell, I'm a little ways from the diagnostics being willing to assume I'm getting better; there's bacteria here that just might cause an infection yet. And no guarantee that I won't get killed on the next expedition we have. You have to be ready to take the load."

Xander really didn't like that idea, but Campbell was right. "All right." He thought for a moment. "Tav's actually buckled down a lot more than I thought he would. He's not athletic in the least—which makes me wonder just how *insanely* strong he'd be if he was. Did you see how he managed to drag that monster fish's carcass around on his own?"

"Yeah. Some people're just born tough. Go on."

"So anyway, Tav's a no-brainer. He's got to be able to handle a gun—he's next in line from me. Maddox . . . well, he thinks guns are *cool*, which makes me a little nervous. On the other hand, he's always been a real good kid about listening. So yeah, him too. Francisco . . ."

"What about him?"

"I don't know. He's young. And he's got that artistic focus thing going on. I could see him getting all wrapped up in the beauty of a plant and not noticing something creeping up on him."

"True, but anyone can get bushwhacked. Do you think he's up to learning trigger discipline and proper weapon care?"

Xander hesitated, and then shrugged. It wasn't as though the sergeant wasn't there to second-guess him. "My guess? Yes, if we take our time and make sure he understands it all. Multiple times. He could use the structure of regular practice, too. Maybe we all could." He looked back at the sergeant. "Now . . . what do *you* think, Sergeant? Advise me."

Campbell grinned. "I think you're judging it reasonably, Captain. Maybe, back on Earth, I'd ask his parents to wait a couple years...but back on Earth, Francisco wouldn't be in danger of being eaten by some unknown whatsit. All of us need to be able to defend ourselves, and we've got to trust Francisco to be able to learn that trick too."

"All right then, Sergeant. I'm putting you in charge of that training. Set up a schedule and curriculum."

"Delegating responsibility already?" the sergeant said, still grinning. "*Now* you're starting to get the hang of things!"

Chapter 25

"We're up!" Campbell said to the little crew as he felt that faint *bob* sensation that happened when you were finally completely off the ground.

"How high are we going?" Francisco asked, nose pressed to one of the ports that were now uncovered.

"Not high at all at first. Going to focus all the jets under me and hover at, oh, a meter or so. Idea is to cook everything down there to boiling heat or higher to at least a few inches' depth. We've got a big ship, multiple high-powered jets, and a nuclear reactor. We can do that."

"How hot do the jets get?"

Tavana answered. "The temperature varies depending on the thrust. Hovering like this isn't maximum thrust, but it's pretty high. Within a meter of the ground? Well over a thousand degrees. It will melt the surface rock, I think. Maybe give us a parking lot."

"That *is* the idea, yes. You boys just sit back and relax. This will take a while, and even though I've got some rigged automatics to help, I'll still have to concentrate some."

"Isn't the GPS network up?" Tavana asked. "Couldn't you just have it run the whole pattern?"

"Not quite yet, Tavana. Fact is, a system like that isn't nearly as good on the vertical as it is on the horizontal. If we had all the ship's normal instrumentation, no problem; hell, I wouldn't need any GPS at all, the autopilot could do a pattern like this in its sleep. But with those satellites and missing the instrumentation? No, not taking that chance."

"Sir? You said 'at first' we weren't going high."

"Caught that, did you, Xander? Well, we're not going to want to just step out the door onto the fresh-roasted land anyway—and no telling if there's going to be some kind of poisonous fumes released. So I figure since we're already here, we'll do a little overflight survey, and take a better look at this island."

The boys looked happy about that. "Glad you like the idea. So settle back and be quiet for a bit."

Campbell was not taking chances. Hovering flight like this, on mostly-manual control, was a pain in the rear, but messing this up would be a lot bigger pain overall. Plus, he had to make sure he got the whole clearing. If he missed patches of the clearing, he just knew he'd regret it later.

It took two hours before he was really satisfied with things, and the view outside was filled with smoke, steam, and what appeared to be a lot of yellow-white powder. "Well, I'm seeing what looks like a lot of ash. We're not going to be quite so shiny when we land."

"Couldn't we wash *LS-88* off, sir?"

"You wanna haul that many buckets, Tavana? That's a job and a half."

"No, no. I was thinking, the ship, she is a lander,

yes? And for many different worlds. *LS-88* is water-tight, submersible to at least ten meters if I remember the specs right."

Campbell blinked. "Right you are, son, and I must be starting to go senile for forgetting that. Of course it is. Colony shuttles need to be able to handle a *lot*. And the nuclear jets can be reconfigured to be water jets. Not sure the current jury-rigged controls will handle that, but I'll bet you and Maddox can figure something out." He shifted the jets, raised the thrust a bit. "I'm going to take her up, set it on a circling loiter while I take a few minutes, hit the head, and get a drink. Then we'll do a little tour."

When he got back, he took the controls and eased out of the circular loiter. It looked as if they might have drifted a little. That wouldn't be all that sur-prising, though. There was no telling what the winds were like up here, and he wasn't using GPS control.

The first order of business was to survey their base camp. From a hundred meters, he could see the entire area had been seared to a uniform black-streaked yellow-white, with the dust all over pretty much everything. It was just as well they weren't coming back for a while. No one wanted to breathe ash, and there was no telling what else was in that stuff. He frowned. There were so many things to do that he was starting to do them half-assed, and that just wouldn't cut it. It could get them all killed.

Never thought about this situation; guess I thought I'd burn off the surface cover and mostly hit regular rock, but that coral-whatever-it-is seems to burn or something rather than just melt. Didn't figure on all that extra ash.

There was a brisk wind coming in, and he noticed some clouds to the west. Well, that might be for the best. Wind and rain would get rid of it—and clean off the *LS-88* in the bargain.

"Hey, Sergeant! Take a look at our lake!"

He rotated the ship around and tilted it so he could get a better look. "Well, well, well. I see what you mean."

In the slanting sunlight of the long Emerald afternoon, the little lake glittered a brilliant blue . . . a blue that was light around the edges, then suddenly became a deep, deep sapphire that shaded to black at the center. "That looks *damned* deep. I'm thinking that there might just be an underground cavern that connects to the sea."

Maddox shook his head. "But it can't, Sergeant! The water's fresh!"

He thought about that. "That *does* seem to be something of a stopper. But . . ."

What had been in the back of his mind, associating coral and that deep blue color and islands . . . *got it!* "But, on a lot of tropical islands, you can find fresh water floating on top of salt water. A lens, they call it. Been to a couple islands like that myself. This sure seems like the right kind of terrain and weather."

"So then you're saying there might be a connection to the sea after all?"

"Could be. Tides here are a lot weaker than Earth's." He paused. "If that thing's connected . . . a hell of a lot lower. I haven't noticed any regular variation of the water level; have any of you?"

The others shook their heads. "No, Sergeant," Francisco said positively. "It does not change like a tide. I have pictures. I was looking at them, and I would have seen it."

Remembering the boy's attention to detail, Campbell wasn't inclined to doubt him. "All right. But that's something of a puzzle, if that thing *is* connected to the sea. Tides shouldn't be near as high as on Earth, but they should still be noticeable."

Xander shrugged. "It's a mystery. The lake's not as round as I thought, either."

"Noticed that myself. More a rounded triangle, with almost little circular coves at the corners. Well, let's move on and see what else there is to see."

The next thing that struck him were what looked like lines—somewhat wobbly lines, but lines—through the forest. "Huh. What do you all make of that?"

Xander squinted down. "Well . . . looks like there's a sort of ridge running all the way across part of the island, in a kind of loop on one shoreline."

"It looks . . . jumbled in the middle. Heavy growth on each side, less in the middle," said Tavana.

"Fault line?" Maddox suggested.

Campbell felt himself sit up straighter. "You might just be on to something, Maddox. We've all been feeling those little quakes off and on. Makes a lot of sense if we're on a fault line. And that one big central lake I saw on overflight did have something of a volcanic look to it. Maybe we should take a closer look there."

"Hey, Sergeant! Can you drop us a little lower?"

"Sure, Tavana. What for?"

"Something I see. It looks a little funny, so I want to get a better look."

"Where?"

"Oh, right there," a dot appeared in his field of view, in the middle of some of the jungle below. "See?"

"On it."

A few minutes later, Tavana said, "Yes, it is very clear. Look, everyone. A lot of those things that look like tree trunks, they are hollow."

"You're kidding." But a close look showed that Tavana was right. Scattered through the forest were a large number of column-like *somethings* that showed dark, circular holes at their tops. He dropped *LS-88* even lower and zoomed in with his retinals as much as he could. "I will be damned. Looks for all the world like a giant concrete tower, all covered with vines and the top cut off. Maybe like a smokestack."

"Was this place *inhabited*?"

That had been his first thought, too, but . . . "I doubt it. There's no specific order to those things that I can see. Looks like they grow like the trees, or at least they're scattered about the same way. So I'm guessing it's some kind of natural formation."

"Neat. I wonder how deep those holes go."

"We'll have to check when we do our scouting expedition on the ground." His leg twinged as he adjusted the shuttle's level, but it was a lot milder than he'd been prepared for. It seemed as if it was really mending now.

"Hey, you see that?" Something like ants scurried far below. A number of some sort of creatures were moving through a clearing. "Looks like a herd of animals. Herbivores, I'd guess. Not far from our camp, either."

The *LS-88* vibrated slightly and the air darkened as the raincloud passed overhead. Rain spattered, and then poured onto the shuttle. "We're getting that rinse you wanted, Tav."

"*Oui*, I can see that. Are we landing?"

"No need to—this is just rain, not a storm, and we've got other things to see. Let's take a look at that mountain."

As before, he found himself reluctant to really call that oversized hill a "mountain," but it certainly was the highest elevation anywhere he could see. With some calibration based on the flight so far, he and his omni could now resolve the question of height: the peak measured two hundred ninety-one meters from the observed sea level. Still, it was fairly steep, part of another ridge that ran across the island with an average height of about fifty to eighty meters. It would be something of a challenge to climb.

Past that ridge lay the circular central lake, about ten kilometers across. A miniature island, less than a kilometer wide, was at the center of the lake.

"Are there underwater ridges between the shore and that island, Sergeant?" asked Tavana suddenly.

He looked more closely. The diffuse lighting from the cloudy sky made it harder to tell for sure, but it *did* look as though there were several lighter areas underwater that converged on the central island. "Looks like it."

"Volcanic?"

He consulted his omni. "Hard to say. One thing— that lake's about at sea level. Might even be a salt lake for all I know. Impact's starting to look more promising to me. Which, honestly, is what I'd prefer. If you've got an active fault *and* volcanic scenery, you've got problems just waiting to come knocking.

Not that I like having a fault nearby either, but the combo would be worse."

"There's one of those columns in the middle of the central island," Maddox observed.

"So there is." He checked his level and relative position again. "A big one, too. Seventy, eighty meters high and over ten wide. Interesting."

They were now on the far side of the island, and he could see the larger landmass, the one he thought was a continent, looming in the distance. That seemed closer than he remembered—but he'd been in a hurry when they landed and might have gauged the distance wrong. In any event, it didn't seem to matter. The other landmass was at least thirteen or fourteen kilometers away from the island.

"Any other observations?"

Xander pointed. "Harder to see in this lighting, but aren't those more ridges like the one near our camp?"

The darker lines in the forest did look similar to the ones near the camp. He took the *LS-88* down a little farther. "Sure does look it. Same kind of jumble—*whoa!*"

"I saw it too!"

Francisco looked suddenly scared, and Campbell couldn't blame him. Without any warning, something massive and tentacled lunged from the forest and grabbed up one of the grazing creatures they'd seen earlier. *Land predator. Big predator. Makes the centi-snakes look like garter snakes. Fast and mean.* Still . . .

"Classic ambush predator behavior, boys. That's one of the big reasons I wanted that perimeter; something like that isn't going to want to cross all that empty space on a hunt. Still, that's one big and ugly reminder that this place sure isn't safe."

"Look there," Maddox said. "Wonder what that is?"

That was a set of darker, disturbed patches in the greenery. There were three of them, maybe fifty meters across, apparently a little lower than the surrounding forest. Together they formed a triangle about four or five hundred meters across.

"No idea," Campbell said. "But . . . looks like there's another set over there."

They found three more of the sets of unknown marks, all near the jumbled ridge. "Now that's interesting," Campbell finally said. "All three of those look pretty similar to me." He frowned. This was reminding him of something . . .

"Our lake! It's just the same!" Francisco said suddenly.

Campbell stared. "I will be damned. You're right, Francisco. Those three little circular coves—just like these three marks. Spaced the same distance, too. Now I *really* wonder what that lake's story is."

"We don't have diving equipment, do we?"

"The heck we don't," Campbell retorted with a grin. "A spacesuit'll do just fine underwater. Might go check it out once I'm better, which won't be long now."

"Or one of us could—"

"Nothing doing, kids. First, I'm the only guy here certified for diving. And, second, after what we just hauled out of that lake, I am taking no chances with you having a run-in with a monster like that in its own habitat."

He turned *LS-88* around. "Well, it's been a while, and I'm getting tired of flying." His leg was really starting to ache, too. "Let's get back home and see if the rain's settled things enough that we can set back up!"

Chapter 26

Tavana finished checking the digging assembly and rolled out from under the excavator. "She's good to go, Sergeant!"

"All right! Everyone, get back—all the way to *LS-88*, please."

Tavana made sure that Francisco was headed back before he followed. Maddox and Xander emerged from the temporary shelter and also headed up the ramp of the lander. Sergeant Campbell came last.

"This isn't going to be too long a test, is it, Sergeant?" Maddox asked.

"Shouldn't be. I just want to check out the excavator's automation and performance under satellite guidance. We'll do the big excavations once we've found the right materials to build with. Why, you got something cooking?"

"We were working on designing some machetes," Xander said. "If we're going exploring in a couple of days, we should all have the right tools."

"That we should. Don't worry; I figure this'll take an hour or so, no more."

The satellite network had signaled full stability

during Emerald's last long night, so a test of its capabilities had seemed in order. Tavana had done a data demonstration by pushing his latest Jewelbug adventure up to the satellite, making it open for download so that Maddox could get it. That had worked perfectly.

But besides communication, the GPS and guidance capabilities were the major interest of the marooned group. In theory, it would allow their excavators to perform all sorts of tasks with minimal supervision.

"All right, everyone's clear. Cross your fingers—here we go!"

The excavator jolted to life with a lunge, digging savagely into the white coral-like rock, moving forward at several centimeters per second. Tavana noticed a frown on Campbell's face. "What's wrong, sir?"

"The way it started, Tav. Should be a smooth transition. Seems to be driving itself faster than it should."

They watched for a while, and Tavana felt the initial elation fading. "Something's wrong, Sergeant."

In their enhanced omni view, the ground had a clear green square drawn on it—the outline of the small foundation hole that the excavator was supposed to be digging. Instead, the excavator was carefully cutting its way along a line that slanted away from the planned direction.

"Damnation." The excavator stopped at Sergeant Campbell's signal. "What the devil's wrong with it? You checked out all the physical systems, so there shouldn't be anything mechanically wrong. And no one's tampered with the programming—right?" He looked around. Tavana shook his head, and so did the others.

"Any suggestions?"

Tavana raised his hand. "Let me paint a line on the actual ground, to see if it can follow just on optics. That will show, at least, whether it's something wrong with the internal guidance mechanisms."

"Makes sense."

Tavana ran into the ship, grabbed a can of marking paint. He jogged back out, down the ramp, and out to where the excavator sat. He had his omni project a line straight in front of the excavator. As carefully as he could, he sprayed the line onto the ground. "It is done!"

"Fine. Now get back up here where it's safe before I let 'er rip."

The excavator hummed back to life. This time it whirred smoothly to full speed and began a leisurely cut precisely down the middle of Tavana's line.

"Mechanics seem just fine, as do optical guidance systems. So what the heck...?"

"Can I access the excavator data stream, Sergeant?"

"Sure, here you go." An access ping updated his codes, and now Tavana could "see" directly into the rather limited interface code.

Tavana considered, then shrugged. Start with the most basic. Make sure that the GPS signals between himself and the excavator agreed. He moved over and sat on the excavator's seat, which was designated as the center of the excavator. *Let's see. GPS says...*

Que se passe-t-il? "They're not steadying down."

"*What* aren't?"

"The GPS readings," Tavana said, still watching. "It's like they're varying by a small amount all the time, like there's a whole lot of noise in the readings. No, wait. It's not noise."

Xander linked in. "Hmm. You're right. It's a pretty steady drift. Wonder what could cause that?"

"Maybe it's not perfectly synched with the rotation of the planet?" Campbell asked. "Day's different here, stands to reason the rotational speed would be different."

"No, I don't think so," Xander said. "The difference would be huge—hundreds of meters a second or something like that, I'd think. No reason for it to have accounted for all but a few centimeters per second of that, anyway."

One of the minor quakes shook the ground. Tavana frowned. "Yours is doing it too, Xander?"

"Yeah. So are Maddox's and Franky's."

"Then the problem must be with the satellites," Tavana said.

Sergeant Campbell shook his head. "One of them being off, I could believe. But if that happened, the others would just correct it, or lock it out of the network if that didn't work. I've seen these in use on four different worlds and never saw one go haywire yet. So there's no way I'm going to believe that all of them went wonky at once."

"But if that's true . . ." Tavana trailed off, feeling a strange sensation of unreality suddenly stealing over him. *No tides. Miniature quakes. No mountains. Stone like coral.* Feeling gooseflesh tingling its way across his arms, Tavana called up all the locations of his friends. *All of them varying the same way . . . but they're maintaining the same* separation. "Sergeant, it's got our relative distances dead-on. Within a millimeter or less."

"You mean . . . the difference between our locations stays the same, it's just the absolute numbers that change?" Campbell asked slowly.

"*Oui.*"

Xander's mouth dropped open, even as Sergeant Campbell's brow furrowed. "Holy mother of God. That means...we're moving."

"Yes," Tavana said, hardly able to believe what he was saying. "It means that *the whole island* is moving. At several centimeters per second. It is not, I think, an island at all. That is why there is no tide in our lake; when the tide comes, we rise *with* it. And that makes everything shift a little, so we have little quakes—"

"A *floating island*," breathed Maddox in awe.

Francisco's eyes were wide. "Wow."

"How the hell is that *possible?*" Xander said finally. "This thing's seventy kilometers long!"

Tavana hopped down from the excavator and grabbed a chunk of the rock. "Coral. Coral maybe with natural carbonan reinforcement? It repairs itself, yes? Doesn't have to endure flexing forever without reinforcement and rebuilding."

"I...guess. Still..." Xander shook his head in disbelief. "I can't grasp it."

"Oh, it gets better," Campbell said, though his grin and tone were subdued with the same incredulity. "Remember that I didn't detect anything much over three hundred meters on our whole flyover. Fifty to one that *everything* we thought was land is actually... whatever this place is."

"*Continent*-sized floating islands?"

"Something like, yeah." Without warning, the sergeant started laughing.

"What is it, sir?" Tavana found the sudden shift in mood worrisome.

"Sorry, son," Campbell said, still chuckling. "It's

just . . . I told you that Emerald had surprises waiting for us. Just didn't guess how *big* a surprise it was holding back!"

Maddox was looking thoughtful. "You know, that also makes it easier to understand those strange plant-animal things—the ones that look like plants, but weren't, that we found growing here. They were like underwater things."

"Explains a whole bunch of little things that were worrying me," Campbell said with a nod. "Have to think about what this might mean for our long-term survival. First things first, though; can we compensate for the motion so we can still use our GPS?"

"*Oui*, that will be no problem," Tavana said. "We will use nearby known locations as calibration points—the *LS-88* will be good—and this will tell the system our current motion. That motion will be subtracted from other systems' locations, such as the excavator, and should produce a stable set of coordinates to work from."

"Do it, then. Let's see if it works."

Tavana glanced towards Xander. "Could you help? Check my work, anyway."

"Sure."

It was a simple calculation; Tavana was reasonably confident he got it correct on the first try, but there was no point in taking chances. After a few minutes, they activated the compensation algorithm.

Instantly his location readings settled down, showing him unmoving near Xander, with Maddox standing nearby and the *LS-88* itself. "It works! We should be able to do the construction easily now, sir!"

"Good. Do a test run—not that I doubt you, but let's make sure."

The test run did not take long; the excavator smoothly and accurately cut its way along the designated path.

"Very good. Shut her down for now. I want to think on this a little before we keep going forward. First thing that comes to mind is to wonder just how far down I could cut before this giant boat springs a leak."

"If we are right, we are sitting right next to a hole in the 'boat,' so to speak. The whole thing floats." He looked around, grabbed up a chunk of rock from one of the furrows, and threw it as hard as he could up and out.

The white stone sailed high into the air and dropped on the other side of *LS-88* with an audible splash. Looking under the lander, he could make out something white floating on the water. "The rock's lighter than water. It must extend a long, long way below. There may be air chambers too, but if the stone itself floats..."

"...then they're a lot more stable than suspected," finished Campbell. "Still, let's think on the situation a bit. Get some other projects done before we continue with our construction projects." He grinned. "Our exploration trip's going to be even more interesting than we planned!"

Chapter 27

There was one matter Campbell knew they had to attend to before they went exploring. More precisely, a matter that *he* had to attend to, since it was something he couldn't delegate to any of the boys—and something he'd been avoiding for some time. His own injury and the need to recover from it had been the excuse he'd used to himself, but he couldn't use it any longer. If he was well enough to go on an exploring expedition, he was certainly well enough for the task at hand.

"All right, guys. It's time to give Lt. Haley a shower. She's overdue, and her suit and skinsuit will have to be cleaned also."

That last part was something he *could* delegate. "Xander, you and Tavana can take care of that chore."

Xander actually looked relieved. On the private omni channel, he said, *Sorry we put this off so long.*

It was my decision, after I woke up. It won't have hurt her, and saved us a little awkwardness. Don't worry about it.

Tavana made a face, but nodded. "It has to be done, yes. And we made the others help clean your

223

suit, so that is fair. Lieutenant Haley, are you going to wake her up, then?"

"No," Campbell said reluctantly. "It was necessary last time because of the treatment we had to give her, but right now? I'm not giving her body any more chances to speed up than I can help."

"So you have to clean her yourself?" Maddox's expression hovered between embarrassment and curiosity.

"Right. Maddox, you take Francisco into the cargo hold and . . . figure out something to do."

The thirteen-year-old opened his mouth as if to protest but then closed it again. He got up from his seat and headed toward the cargo hold. "C'mon, Francisco."

Looking a little confused, the younger boy trailed after him.

Once they were gone, Campbell went over to the seat where Pearce's unconscious form had been resting ever since they'd put her back into suspended animation. He released all of the restraints holding her in place and then, grunting a little from the effort, picked her up and headed for the sanitation facility.

"You wait out here," he said to Xander and Tavana. "This may take a while."

Tavana shrugged. "Like I said to Xander, your body-shyness is so ridiculous. But whatever you say, Sergeant."

Once he was in the chamber, Campbell tried to figure out the best way to proceed. The problem he faced was tricky as well as personally awkward. The shuttle's sanitation chamber was divided into two. The outer chamber contained the toilet facilities and was barely spacious enough for a person to turn around alone. Two people *could* fit into the area snugly, even when one of them was wearing a spacesuit, as Haley was at the moment. But they were so tightly pressed together that he didn't think it would be possible for him to get her out of the suit.

There was nothing he could do but back out of the facilities, still holding Haley, and return to the main cabin.

"You two get out of here," he told Xander and Tavana. "Wait in the cargo area until I call you in. I'll leave her stuff for you."

After they left, he got Haley out of the suit and then, adopting what he hoped was a good enough approximation of a nurse's clinical detachment, got the lieutenant out of the skinsuit. That proved to be difficult as well as embarrassing. The skinsuit, as the name suggested, fit a person's body very tightly. Getting it off a body that was completely limp was a lot harder than he'd realized it would be—and getting it back on was going to be a royal headache. *Last time Pearce was awake. Boy, that made a difference.*

The smell that filled the cabin as Haley came out of the garments she'd been wearing helped to concentrate his mind on the task at hand. Even with her metabolism running at a minimal level, the odor that weeks of immobility had generated was ... He decided to label it "ripe," that being preferable to any of the alternatives he could think of.

"Okay, guys!" he half-shouted. "Come get it in about fifteen seconds. I'll need the stuff as soon as possible."

Campbell carried Haley's now-nude form into the inner chamber of the sanitation facilities, which was often referred to as "a shower on steroids" or "the wash, rinse, repeat, and bake cubicle."

He immediately realized that he faced yet another problem—one he *also* should have foreseen.

Two, problems—no, three.

Problem one: Haley was completely limp, which meant there was no way she could stand unless someone—namely Chief Master Sergeant Samuel Morgan Campbell—held her up.

Problem two: Holding her up would require Campbell to be in the shower with her.

Problem three: The "shower" was actually a very sophisticated mechanism for recycling water as well as cleaning, which presupposed that anyone in the shower would stay there long enough for the water reclamation and drying process—the "bake" part of *wash, rinse, repeat, and bake*—was completed.

Which they couldn't do if they were wearing clothes, because the facility was designed to dry off a human body, *not* reclaim the water from wet clothing. That task was assigned to the machines in the shuttle's laundry facility, which were designed quite differently.

For a moment, the sergeant's combined exasperation and discomfiture was great enough that he contemplating doing so anyway—to hell with the water that would be lost from the shuttle's recycling process when he spilled it all over the floor of the outer chamber after exiting the shower in soaked clothes. What was the big deal, anyway? They'd landed on a planet with lots of water available.

But they still didn't know for sure if the water on Emerald was potable. It seemed to be, but there could be as-yet-unknown long-term problems. For instance, while they were sure the water itself was okay—their nanos would have detected any significant

toxins or impurities—there might be seasonal problems
they hadn't encountered yet. Those could be almost
anything. Seasonal migrations of fish or waterfowl (or
their analogs, more precisely), which carried parasites
that got loose in the water. Or if the seasonal varia-
tions were extreme enough, the fresh water sources
might simply dry up for long periods of time. They
might yet find that they had to rely completely on the
shuttle's recycling facilities at least for their drinking
water. Which meant he couldn't afford to lose any, as
much as he might personally prefer it.

He sighed, let Haley slump down in the shower until
she was more-or-less stable, and then took off all his
own clothes. Those he left in the outer chamber while
he went back to the shower, bent over, hoisted Haley
back onto her feet, and squeezed into the facility with
her. After fumbling for a moment to find the controls,
which were behind her back where he couldn't see
them, he got the cleaning cycle started.

That proved to be yet another headache, because
the cycle's design presupposed that the shower was
occupied by one person who was going about the
business of cleaning himself or herself in a conscious,
coherent, and rational manner—not two people, one
of whom was doing his best to clean the other, whose
unconscious mind and limp body seemed to be conspir-
ing to make the task as difficult and time-consuming
as possible.

Being a well-designed facility, the shower cut off the
water and began the drying and recycling process at
such a time as had seemed reasonable to the designers, back in their comfortable and spacious offices
somewhere on Earth. It was anything but reasonable to

one Chief Master Sergeant Samuel Morgan Campbell, who was trying to use the facilities in a way they'd never been designed for.

In the end, he had to cycle through the whole process five times before the task was finally completed. The second time, stoically; the third, not so stoically; the fourth, cursing silently those who had designed the facility; the fifth, cursing aloud pretty much the entire sidereal universe.

But eventually it was done—he realized in retrospect that the aggravation involved had at least had the benefit of overriding what would otherwise have been an extremely embarrassing and personally uncomfortable experience. Throughout, there had been some part of his mind—very carefully walled off from the rest—that kept reminding Campbell how much he would have enjoyed a similar activity under different circumstances.

There turned out to be another benefit as well. By the time Campbell was done, Xander and Tavana had finished the much more straightforward task of cleaning Lt. Haley's garments. So at least he didn't have to compound the awkwardness by having to remain with Pearce's still-nude body until her clothes were ready.

Putting the skinsuit back on proved to be just as tricky as Campbell had feared it would be. But he managed—by then he figured he could have corrected all the understatements and excessive optimism in the writings of Seneca and Epictetus. He'd once read them while stuck in a remote outpost whose tiny library, for reasons that were to this day mystifying to the sergeant, had consisted of nothing but classical philosophy.

Stoics, bah. Bunch of pikers.

By the time he re-emerged into the main cabin and put Pearce back in her seat, he was almost in a good mood. Allowing for Stoic values of "good mood," of course.

Chapter 28

"We're all ready, Sergeant!" Xander said.

"That we are," Campbell agreed, striding easily from the shelter. "Everyone clear on the ground rules? Francisco?"

The youngest of the boys straightened. "*Si*. Yes, Sergeant. We stay in a group. I stay in the middle because I am smallest." Xander could see that Francisco didn't like that requirement, but he wasn't arguing, which was good. "We follow your lead and I—I mean we—follow any order you give right away and ask questions later." He continued before Xander or the sergeant had to prompt him. "Oh, and the machetes are tools, not toys, and mine is to stay in my holster unless you say otherwise." There was a *definite* pout at that.

"Good," the sergeant said with a grin. "Now, our priorities are to get samples of a lot of things we haven't seen before. Everyone keep their eyes peeled for *anything* that looks different, but only Xander and I will be taking samples. We're also the only ones carrying guns today. You boys are making good progress in the training, but I'm still not quite comfortable with any of you carrying in a possible live-fire situation. Soon, though."

They checked each others' packs and supplies. "This is going to be a one-day expedition because we still don't know enough to camp outside our perimeter. As we learn more and figure out how to live here better, we'll expand our operations and do longer-range scouting on the ground. As you boys probably noticed, from above you can't see hardly anything except treetops."

"Where are we going?" Tavana asked.

"I figure first we'll follow that little seam or ridge we saw—the one we first thought was a fault line until we realized this wasn't even land." Campbell shook his head. "Still hard to believe. Anyway, we'll follow that for a ways and see if we learn anything useful, then head into the forest. Now that the GPS works, we'll be able to follow our progress pretty well and make sure we turn towards home at the right time to make it back at a reasonable hour."

The group climbed up the high wall of earth and coral-rock and paused on the top to survey the dense wall of greenery and other, brighter colors. "Whatever this floating whatsis is, it sure supports a lot of life. Wonder if that means there's an entirely different ecology way down underneath."

"Depends on how deep it goes," Xander answered, thinking about what he'd heard about other worlds. "If there's really no real land here, the oceans have to be *deep*. Like Europa, maybe—dozens of kilometers or more. It may have a top ecology, a middle one, and a bottom one, easy."

"I'd bet a biologist'd be able to figure out a lot about the world just looking at the lifeforms. Shame none of us have that background." Campbell pointed. "There's the ridge. Let's go."

They set off with Sergeant Campbell in the lead, Tavana second, Francisco third, Maddox fourth, and Xander bringing up the rear. As the rearguard, Xander focused most of his attention behind and to the sides. The greenery was dense on this side, but not so much close to the berm the earthmovers had pushed up. Now that they were on the ground heading into the wilderness, Xander found he could make out the funny ridge or seam; it was definitely two somewhat humped ridges, up to eight or ten meters high, with a depressed valley between them. The terrain was definitely less smooth, more jumbled, in this area, with weathered but still sharp boulders sticking up at frequent intervals. The valley was a little easier to walk through than the tops of the ridges, but not much.

After a hundred meters or so, the sergeant got out his machete and started chopping down larger growths—trying to avoid spattering himself in the process. They still didn't know how dangerous most of the stuff living here was; so cutting trees or brush could be really hazardous to their health. He remembered at least one dangerous weed that grew near their old home in Pennsylvania—the giant hogweed—that could burn or blind people with its sap. The sergeant was wearing goggles, but that wouldn't protect him if anything really virulent was in the plants' sap.

Looking back, he saw the way in which the greenery had closed in and gotten thicker. *That's odd.* "Hey, Sergeant," he called.

"Yes, Xander?"

"Maybe I'm wrong, but it looks like hardly anything's

growing down this seam until it gets a pretty good distance from our camp."

Campbell stopped and turned around, studying the area. "Hm. Looks that way, doesn't it?" He rubbed his chin. "Okay, a minor change in plan. Let's go back and check out this ridge on the other side."

A quick walk back and across the barrier to a vantage point overlooking the ridge confirmed it. "Same thing here. Closer it gets to camp, the less that's growing along it." Campbell frowned. "Looks like it doesn't get to the point of being like the rest of the surrounding forest until about a hundred fifty meters in or so." After another moment, he shrugged. "Well, I don't know what's causing it yet. We'll have to think on it and see if we can figure it out. Let's take a few samples of stuff along the way, where it's growing but stunted. Maybe we can compare the stuff with whatever its full-grown versions are like."

The expedition went back to their original exploration point and continued on into the jungle.

"This rock, it looks all broken up," Tavana said after they'd gone more than two hundred fifty meters deeper into the forest. "Like an old avalanche I saw on one of the islands when I was a kid."

"Huh. Does have something of that look about it," Campbell said. "Nowhere for an avalanche to have come from, though."

Xander found himself stiffening, straightening, and a chill raised goosebumps over his flesh, even though the air was hot and humid. "Not an avalanche," he said slowly. "Sergeant, not an avalanche; a *collision*."

The older man stopped suddenly, struck by the idea. "I'll be damned if you're not right. You *have* to be right. These islands can run into each other. Might break each other apart...or get stuck at the impact point." His head cocked sideways. "Or maybe in this case we're looking at an *impact*. Yeah. Remember our big lake in the middle? Imagine what might happen to one of these floating islands if a big meteor hit."

Xander's engineering training made it easy to visualize. "Wow. Yeah, Sergeant, that makes sense! It'd punch through, making a big hole, sending shockwaves through the island that probably break it up, or nearly break it up, and then the pieces bump back together and, I guess, try to repair all the damage."

"And *that* is why we saw those other ridges!" Maddox said. "They were all over the island because of that impact!"

"Makes sense to me, that's for sure," the sergeant agreed. "Island almost completely broke apart, then put itself back together."

"Need a sample of something, Sergeant!" Francisco called out. "Berries!"

They looked where Francisco pointed; sure enough, there were several colorful...*somethings* hanging from a nearby bush.

Xander joined the sergeant, holding a bag as Campbell clipped off a branch. "Look at those things; like multi-sided dice in colored glass, not berries. Wonder why they're growing in that shape?"

"Don't care what shape they are if it turns out we can eat 'em. Got the bag sealed? Good, let's move it." He surveyed the area. "Let's strike out a little deeper in the jungle."

Turning away from the jumbled seam in the earth, the little group soon found themselves on much flatter terrain. Tavana suddenly shouted a warning. "Sergeant! On your right!"

Following his gaze, Xander saw a circular hole, highlighted in his enhanced vision. "Is that a centi-snake burrow?"

"Looks like it," Campbell agreed. "Let's make sure we stay a good distance away. No reason to provoke one."

"Are any of those big columns nearby?" Maddox asked. "I wanted to get a good look at one from the ground!"

"Not too close; the nearest to us is a kilometer away. I looked over our flight record and they tend to be concentrated inland; the nearest one's an outlier, really. Don't see any of them on some sections. Still, I figure we should be able to reach that one, since it's over in the direction we're heading."

As they progressed, they came across other things that reminded them of the strangeness of the terrain: large plantlike things whose apparent "blossoms" were moving tentacles, probably venomous; one thing that looked like a flower and then retracted like an anemone folding into itself; even small flying animals similar to some of the fish they had caught, except with larger fins and a flattened profile. "It's like the seashore just came up on land for a while," Tavana said as they took yet another sample of what they hoped was a plant that looked something like an upright kelp.

"Something like, yeah." The sergeant froze suddenly. "Boys, look up and to the left."

At first Xander couldn't see anything of interest—just a lot of green leaves and brownish trunks or branches, with gray and black interspersed along with some brighter flowery colors.

Then, slowly, he started to notice little oddities about the coloration and shapes in one small area of the canopy. These abruptly resolved into the outline of something large, crouched high in the tree branches with arms or maybe tentacles curled beneath it. "What is it, Sergeant?"

"Damned if I know, exactly—but I think it's one of the same things we spotted hunting during our overflight. Looks about the right size."

"Then we *really* want to stay away from that."

"Exactly right."

They slowly made their way around the lurking monster, watching it carefully for any signs of aggression. It shifted a tiny bit at one point, but didn't seem inclined to chase.

"Why didn't we shoot it, Sergeant?" asked Francisco.

"Two reasons, son. First, we try not to go around killing things unless we have to. We don't know if the meat on that thing's good, and without a good justification it's just a waste to kill anything. Second, that's a pretty damn big animal. I don't know if what I'm carrying would kill it at long range. Sometimes if you just *wound* a big predator, they come at you with a vengeance. Why take the chance?"

That made plenty of sense to Xander, and apparently to Francisco too, because he didn't ask any more questions on the subject.

A grayish shape loomed up before them in the green-tinged light of the jungle. "The column!"

Seen from the ground, the huge column was awesome, a towering, massive form of solid stone that tapered very slowly as it rose tens of meters into the air. "It *does* look like an old-fashioned smokestack."

"But no smoke. And this isn't standard concrete or brick, either. It looks like the same rock, or something like, that makes up the bedrock we've seen." The sergeant looked pensively up. "I wonder what purpose these things serve?"

As they stood there staring, an unfamiliar voice spoke: *"Hello? Is anyone there?"*

PART III

ODYSSEY

Chapter 29

Laura stared at Sakura as her daughter ran up to her, white-faced, waving an uncomprehending Hitomi's omni at her. "What? What do you mean, Saki, someone else?"

"*Jewelbug*, Mom! It *updated*! Hitomi never turned off her omni's once-a-week update request, and the last time it went up, it found something to download!"

Laura found herself trembling. *What? Why?*

Almost instantly she answered herself: *Because I'd accepted we were here forever, and I don't know if I could stand to have this hope dashed again.*

She interfaced with the omni and immediately saw the update entry: less than two days ago. *But if that's the case...*

She activated a part of her own omni that had been shut down for months; in moments, she saw telltales that indicated a connection with a net—a long range net. A *satellite* net!

"Oh my God," she heard herself say, and sat down *hard*. "Akira, there's a satnet. I just connected."

"Is there anyone else *on* it?"

She took a tense breath, held it, let it out. "Only one way to know."

Laura told her omni to ignore the usual restrictions on broadcast messages and to transmit to any receivers outside of her local net—an emergency distress call, something colonists' omnis were expected, and in fact required, to be able to do. She felt Akira take her hand, saw the others gathering around with wide, hopeful eyes as she spoke into the omni: "Hello? Is anyone there?"

Seconds ticked away. She heard an audible *gulp* from Sakura. Just as she opened her mouth to transmit again, a voice responded, a deep, authoritative man's voice—albeit one with an overlay of stunned shock not unlike her own. "Yes, Ma'am, there is someone here. You just about scared us all out of a week's growth, though."

She started to respond, found her eyes going blurry, and a tear splashed down onto the omni. Laura looked up, and suddenly Sakura was shouting into her own omni. "Sergeant? *Sergeant Campbell?* Sergeant, is that you?"

"What the . . . *Sakura?* Then it's the Kimei family?" A laugh that Laura could now recognize burst from the omnis. "By *God* I thought you were goners back when old *Outward Initiative* started coming apart!"

All of a sudden there were other voices—a dozen voices, some on their end, some wherever the sergeant was—talking all at once, laughing, crying, cheering, all in a confused, impossible-to-understand babel of joy.

Laura saw her own tears mirrored in her husband's eyes. She reached out and hugged him so tightly that he grunted with pain. Then she put the omni back to her mouth again. "Quiet, please, quiet, everyone!"

"The lady said *QUIET!*" the sergeant shouted, and instantly everyone stopped talking. "Sorry, Ma'am."

She laughed, feeling an incredible relief just knowing there were other people out there. Maybe this wasn't a rescue . . . but it still *felt* like one. "No need to apologize, Sergeant. Who have you got with you? Other members of the security team?"

"No, Ma'am. I ended up in a civilian shuttle for the drill and, well, you know how *that* drill ended. Our little group of colonists landed here on Emerald just a few months back. Honestly, I'm surprised you—"

"Lincoln!" said Hitomi emphatically.

"Eh? Who's that, now?"

"Hitomi," the little girl said proudly. "The planet's name is *Lincoln*."

"No!" said an unfamiliar boy's voice with an obvious Spanish accent. "It's *Emerald*."

"Hold your horses, Francisco," said Campbell, a touch of humor in his voice. "Matter of precedence here. When did you people land here and name the planet?"

"Um . . ." Laura glanced to Mel, who always tracked things like that.

"We've been here a little more than a year," Melody said firmly.

"A *year?* I'll be damned. Sorry, Francisco, they beat us here by *months*. The privilege to name the place is theirs."

The obviously young boy made a very disappointed noise; Laura thought of a possible compromise. "Francisco, how about we call the whole *solar system* the Emerald system? Then we can name all the other planets after different shades of green or green things."

"Sounds like a great compromise to me. What do you say, Francisco?"

Francisco's voice was suddenly much more cheerful. "You mean it? *Gracias!* Yes!"

There were several chuckles over the link. "Well, now that this crisis is resolved, Ma'am, let me introduce everyone. You already know me, but now everyone introduce yourselves—in order, oldest to youngest."

A young man's voice, with the depth of someone just past the line of adulthood and an accent that sounded East-Coast American said, "Xander Bird."

The next voice had a different, lilting accent— French, yet not. "Tavana Arronax."

"Maddox Bird—I'm Xander's brother!" The younger brother's voice held an irrepressible energy that reminded Laura of Sakura.

"Francisco Alejandro Coronel," came the youngest voice from the other set of castaways.

"Very pleased to meet you all," Laura said. "Let's do the same. I'm Laura Kimei."

"Akira Kimei," said her husband.

"Caroline Kimei."

"Harratrer of Tallenal Pod—call me 'Whips,'" said their Bemmie companion.

"What?" came Campbell's startled voice. "You have a *Bemmius novus sapiens* with you? How the heck did that happen?"

"Same way you ended up in a civilian lifeboat, I'd bet," Xander Bird said. "Right?"

"Right," Whips said. "Alarm went off and I was nearest to the Kimei boat."

"*Any*way, let's go on! Sakura Kimei here!"

"Melody Kimei," Mel said, without a trace of her usual "bored with the world" act.

"Hitomi Kimei! Hi, everyone!"

"Well, now, hello to all of you, and we're pleased to meet you," Campbell said. "Being honest, I'm *most* pleased to hear your voice, Dr. Kimei."

"Do you have a medical emergency there?" she asked quickly.

"An ongoing one, Ma'am. It's not an acute problem but it's one I haven't been able to solve."

"Where *are* you?" Sakura asked. "I mean, if you're somewhere near us—"

"Afraid not, Sakura," Campbell said. "Checking the GPS markers, looks like you're about six thousand kilometers away. Satellite imagery tells me you're on what I'd picked as my tertiary landing site; shame it didn't come to that. Not that we can't get there, mind, but it'll take some time and prep. If we're lucky, my problem might be something that your mom can help with without having to make a house call. What shape is your boat in, anyway? *LS-5*, was it?"

Akira answered, "*LS-5* is gone, somewhere at the bottom of what's probably a hundred kilometers of water."

"You've been here for a *year* without even a shuttle?" Campbell's incredulous tone was echoed by murmurs of shock from the boys. "I take my hat off to you people. Had you unloaded the supplies, at least?"

"Not really," Melody said, with an obvious dawning pride in their accomplishments. "Our omnis, a shelter, a couple weeks' rations, and a winch were pretty much all we had."

"By God, that's something. You must've learned a *lot* about Emeral—beg your pardon, *Lincoln*—in that time."

"A lot indeed. Do you mean to say that *your* shuttle's

functional?" Laura felt a burning tension in her as she asked the question. *If it is . . .*

"Mostly," Xander answered. "*LS-88* got pretty badly fried by the Trapdoor Pulse and we had to jury-rig a lot of stuff. Main problem is we have to figure out a way to fix the Trapdoor coils. Our re-wind job wasn't perfect so we can't make the trip in reasonable time. But our cargo's all intact—except what we've used, of course."

"So you *could* get here."

"If we pack everything up, yes. It wouldn't take more than a few hours," Campbell answered. "You've solved the food problem, I take it? Because that's the thing we've been kinda butting our heads against; only so many things we dare try eating, and the packaged rations won't hold out forever."

Relief and hope welling up in her, Laura laughed. "We have *more* than solved that problem, Sergeant. If you can get here, I will honest-to-god bake a cake for you, just to prove it!"

"I may just hold you to that, Ma'am!"

"Go ahead. Now," she dropped into her serious mode, "tell me about your medical problem."

Chapter 30

Campbell offered a prayer of hope and thanks to whatever might be listening. Laura Kimei was a doctor, and a damn good one. If he'd planned on another group to land with them, he couldn't have picked a better one. There was something nagging at him about Akira Kimei—not his profession, but something to do with *Campbell's* profession. *Dammit, brain, I'm not that old yet. I think I've gotten too used to relying on the omni and ship-nets for info.*

But Laura was waiting for him. "I've got one other castaway who's been in suspension ever since the accident."

"Suspension? How in the world—"

"Military nanos and some real interesting code they gave us when we got deployed to hot zones. Fortunately, the victim was another member of the military: Pearce Haley."

"I remember Lieutenant Haley."

"Hold on, Sergeant," Xander broke in, sounding apologetic. "Um, Dr. Kimei, we're actually out in the bush right now. Maybe we should do this when we get back?"

"I would *strongly* suggest that, yes," came Akira

247

Kimei's voice. "Unless you've explored the area you're in thoroughly?"

"No, sir, this is our first expedition outside of the perimeter we set up when we landed. We would have done it earlier but..."

"...but that's a story and a half," Campbell said. Xander and Akira were right. *Don't let your emotions get ahead of you.* "We should turn around, get back to camp. I'll bet you have a lot of information on surviving here that we haven't even touched yet."

"Probably. But as these structures are stable on the order of a million years—hard though that may be to believe—there probably is considerable divergent evolution on them, so it may be that some of what we know will not apply there. Can you make a video connection?"

"Sorry, not with the current setup of the satnet. SC-178s are tough, small, reliable, and reasonably accurate, but they're kind of the bottom end of performance. We'll be able to set up video with a little work—after all, we don't have to reserve bandwidth for hundreds or even thousands of people—but not yet."

"A shame. I'd be able to tell you a lot about the area just by seeing it."

Campbell grinned. "Sure you could. But to be honest, the last thing I need is something distracting me or my boys out here by lighting up our omnis with something other than the forest we're in. I do have a question, though; the place we're about to leave has this big stone column like a chimney. You know anything about those? They seem to be all over the place here."

"Caroline here, Sergeant. We think those are part of the island's balance and flotation system. Maybe even breathing, literally, for whatever parts are alive inside. They equalize internal pressure for some really immense chambers."

"So there are flotation chambers in these things? It's not just the fact that the rock's light?"

"There are *some* kind of chambers here, yes. Although there are holes in other areas that seem to pierce the entire depth of the island, so it's not as though the whole thing is a floating balloon."

The little expedition began to make its way back. "Watch your step, boys. Unless we're following in our exact footsteps, there could still be a lot out here to get us in trouble, and that predator's probably still hiding in the trees."

"Tentacled creature? Ambush predator?" Akira asked.

"Yeah, and pretty darn big, too, about the size of a full-grown alligator."

"We call them 'tree krakens,' and they are very dangerous indeed."

"We saw one catch an animal during an overflight," Tavana said. "The danger, that is something we know already."

Rather than being offended at Tavana's comment—which could easily have been taken the wrong way—Akira Kimei chuckled. *Good. Of course, they've also got four kids; guess you learn not to take offense easily in those conditions.*

"Yes, I suppose you would," Akira said. "But what you may not know is that they often travel or hunt in loose groups. If you saw one, you are well advised to look around again even more carefully. There may be another, or even several others."

"Good to know. Boys, I'll keep a watch on high, you keep an eye on the ground, okay?"

"Yes, sir," the others chorused.

"Dr. Kimei," Francisco said after a few minutes, "we found some . . . well, we think they are berries. Do you know anything about them?"

"What do they look like?" Sakura's voice asked.

"They look like jewels, all faceted and everything!"

"Hedrals!" Hitomi said emphatically. "They're very good!"

"Hold on, Hitomi," Akira cautioned. "There may be many plants that produce similar berries. Until we get some more data I don't want them risking anything."

"Definitely not," Campbell said. "Last thing we need is to take risks, especially if we're going to be meeting up soon. Now in the interest of reducing said risk, we're going to sign off and call you back once we get to camp. Okay?"

After a moment, Laura's voice came back on. "Yes, that makes sense. We have things to finish up here, too."

"Oh my *GOD* I forgot about the furnace!" Sakura's panicked voice interrupted.

"Saki, cut out of the circuit please!"

"Did she just say *furnace*?" Campbell was trying to make sense of that. *What in the world . . . ?*

"Yes. We'll explain later. Call us when you're back at camp."

"You can count on it, Ma'am!"

The connection cut off, and Campbell looked up to the broad, almost unbelieving smiles of the others. "Well, boys, don't just stand there grinnin' like fools," he said, feeling his own ridiculous grin spreading wider. "Let's get a move on!"

The trip back took—by chronometer—considerably

less time than it had going out, as they weren't diverting or trying to evaluate every detail along the way. But it still seemed like it had taken six times as long. There had been good reason not to hurry anymore, though. Akira Kimei's warning had been dead-on-target: they'd spotted at least one more, possibly two more, of the tree krakens. *Damn dangerous things. Combined with the centisnakes, there are a lot of nasty animals around—more'n I'd expect, come to think of it.* They'd seen evidence of herbivores, true, but still, really large predators needed *space*.

Finally they clambered over the berm and looked down into their camp. "Here we are, boys. Getting late. Tav. Before I make that call, can you check the comm capabilities of our network and see if you can get it set up to allow full video? Sounds like we've only got a total of thirteen people to support. Make it twenty or so channels, if we include security feeds. Meanwhile, Xander and Maddox and Francisco can get dinner ready. I'll do a quick perimeter check and make sure we're all secure."

As he did a careful tour of the camp, he felt the ground quiver again. *Dunno if I feel more or less comfortable now that I know what's causing that.* The thought that the island could come apart around him was enough to make anyone nervous. On the other hand, they'd said the islands were stable on the order of a million years, so the chances of them coming apart *now* were awfully small, barring something causing it to happen.

As he was heading back, he got a ping and a sudden image of Tavana appeared in his retinal display. "I have it, Sergeant!"

"So you do. Good job. You think this will work for the satellite link?"

"This *is* a satellite link! I'm sending the stream to one of the satellites and back down. We're going to be pretty limited—2 or 3D imagery but no other sensory streams worth talking about."

"More than good enough. Do their omnis need to be taught how to do it?"

"No, the imagery, it is a standard format. They will recognize it when they get the transmit header."

"All right. Let's all get to dinner and we can sit down and make a call."

The Kimeis' channel responded instantly. Abruptly, seeming to hover in air across the room from the six castaways of *LS-88*, a group of people looked back, seated on various chunks of rock in what looked like a huge gouge carved out of the earth.

Campbell instantly recognized Laura Kimei. She was the tallest person there, over one hundred eighty centimeters, with long dark chestnut hair and matching eyes in a tanned face with a few lines that hadn't been there the last time he saw her.

Next to her, in the act of taking a bite of some kind of roast, was Sakura, whip-thin, with waves of night-black hair and the piercing blue eyes he remembered from his classes. Her father, Akira, was on his wife's other side, his hair the same black but pin-straight, far more delicate of build than Laura. He and Sakura shared the same slender strength.

In front of the two was the smallest member of the group, Hitomi, startlingly blond-haired and tiny—no more than a meter tall. She was perched atop the massive form of the *Bemmius* called "Whips," who was ripping into a huge chunk of meat with grip talons, shearing beak, and tearing tongue. Campbell thought he'd be leery of letting a kid of his sit on anything like that unless he was damn sure he could trust it. He then rebuked himself.

I can't let myself think of him as "it." No matter my own personal issues, this Whips is clearly one of their family now. If I ever, ever start to act like he isn't, they'll shut me down hard. And I'd deserve it, too. He made a mental note to have a talk to the boys about that. The last thing they needed was to offend the only other people within ten light-years, no matter what their reservations about Bemmies might be.

The smaller but older girl there, with the brown hair—that was Caroline. Which made the black-haired girl with her mother's build Melody.

"Nice to see you all!" he said and waved.

The seven other colonists waved back with excitement evident in every gesture. "After a year, you can't *imagine* how nice it is for us!" Laura said emphatically.

"Let me reintroduce you so you can put faces to voices, here." After he made sure everyone was properly introduced, the Kimeis did the same, confirming his guesses.

"I actually remember you, Tavana," Sakura said. "We were in that 'Control Design and Ergonomics' class on *Outward Initiative*, right?"

"*Oui,* that class, yes we were!" Tavana's accent seemed twice as thick, and the boy had straightened up as much as he could while at the table.

Ha! I thought I remembered something about that. He noticed Xander trying to hide a grin too. *Yep.* "Well, now, that's even better. I know *you*, Doctor, professionally, and I've talked to both you and your husband, but I admit that aside from Sakura I didn't know any more of your family."

"I am so happy you're alive, Sergeant!" Sakura said. "And you're *here*!"

"No more than I'm happy about your survival, Saki." It suddenly dawned on him... "Sakura—did *you* land LS-5?"

She blushed but drew herself up proudly. "Yes, I did." Then she slumped. "Well... I sorta crashed her at the end."

"Don't you feel bad about that. Tell me the whole story—a little later."

"Yes, Saki, we'll all tell our stories later. Sergeant, now that you're back at your shuttle, can you give me access to Lieutenant Haley's—"

"Coming right up, Ma'am." He pinged Haley's omni until it woke up, then directed it to allow an interface through the satnet. "Should be accessible to someone with your medical authorizations now."

Everyone was silent. Even the Kimeis, as they waited to see what their mother would say. Minutes ticked by. Campbell saw a frown on Laura's face that made his heart drop.

But then she looked up, and there was a tiny smile visible. "That's one of the worst cases of radiation sickness I've had to treat, Sergeant. But..."

"But?" He held his breath.

"But your suspension—and loading her up with so many nano-medical packs that you must have saturated her—gave her an excellent chance of survival. I'm going to have to start adjusting their programming and tailoring it to repair the damage suffered thus far, shut down some of the cascades that have already started, substitute for lost function . . ." She waved her hand as though dismissing a longer list. "Never mind. The important thing is, I think—I *think*—she will recover."

"Oh, thank God." He heard his voice quiver a little, the way it had after they'd landed. "How long will it take?"

"I'll do the reprogramming over the next few days. I don't have anything specialized for Trapdoor radiation flares since that's a pretty rare event. I'll have to tailor it myself. We've got other projects that can't wait, so I'll have to do it piecemeal. But she's in no immediate danger. Figure a week for the changes to fully propagate and begin execution, and then we can start bringing her out of suspension."

Spontaneous applause broke out around their table. Campbell grinned and joined in. "Ma'am, you've just made our day for the second time."

"It's my job," she said with an answering smile. "Now, can you make my day by telling me that you have more of those first-aid nano injectors?"

"About ninety of them, Ma'am."

Her smile fairly blazed. "Oh, Sergeant, you have made my *month*. With that many I can keep us with updated medical nanos for a long, long time. Maybe even upgrade us to military spec, with you and the lieutenant to help, if you don't mind."

"Ma'am—"

"Oh, please, call me Laura. We're all in the same boat here, so to speak."

"Laura, then. Laura, believe you me, if you can use anything I have, you're welcome to it." He leaned back in his chair, feeling relaxed for the first time in . . . maybe the first time since the alarm sounded, honestly. "We'll start packing up tomorrow and prepping to come join you, if that's all right."

"We'd like nothing better," Akira said promptly. "The more of us here, the more we can get done. And if your ship's intact, I'm guessing you have cargo we can use."

"We've got *excavators*!" Maddox said proudly.

"Excavators? You have *power tools?* Vehicles?"

"A whole lot of things perfect for a little colony, yes, sir."

Whips gave a buzzing sound that Campbell placed, after a moment, as a laugh. Several of the others joined in.

"What's so funny?" Tavana asked, puzzled.

"It's . . ." The alien got his laughter under control. "It's just . . . you would not *believe* the work we've had to do in order to accomplish things we could have done *overnight* with the right tools."

"Oh, I'd believe it," Campbell said firmly. "Been marooned on purpose a couple times for training. Strange how easy you think everything is until you suddenly realize you haven't the faintest idea how to do anything without the right tool." He leaned forward. "Now, why don't you all tell us the story we're all waiting to hear: how you got here . . . and how you *survived*."

Chapter 31

Mon Dieu, we have had it easy, Tavana thought as he listened incredulously to the Kimeis' tale of survival. They crash-landed on this planet, lost their entire lander, and then had to build everything from nothing but native materials and scraps of wreckage. They fought off monsters like the tree krakens with machetes . . .

He stared admiringly at Sakura. He'd known she wasn't afraid of much, but this was something else!

And it just got more incredible. Designing and building a house set in one of those columns, figuring out how to burn holes in them and set floors suspended above the nearly endless drop . . Tavana was an engineer and even he couldn't imagine how they did all that. Looking around he saw similar expressions of awe on the faces of his fellow castaways—except the sergeant's. Campbell looked simply relieved. *We must look like weekend campers compared to them.*

Laura passed lightly over another incident that sounded like it had been very dangerous with a warning that swamps on Lincoln could be very dangerous. "There is a sort of crocodile-like ambush predator that disguises itself as a small hillock of weeds, and an amphibious creature that combines the worst features of lampreys, jellyfish, and stingrays that is drawn to any kind of injured creature; we call them raylamps. They don't like quicklime, though."

Campbell chuckled. "I'll bet they don't. *Quicklime?* You've been doing some chemistry too, I see."

"I feel almost silly about all that effort," Laura admitted. "After all, now that you're here—"

"Ma'am, do *not* belittle what you've been accomplishing here," Campbell said flatly. "Maybe we'll be able to give you better tools, but we'll still be building on all the work you've done. Believe me, we'll be grateful for it every day."

"What about *your* group?" Sakura asked.

Did she look at me? Maybe she did!

"C'mon, you've got your story to tell, right?"

"*Oui*, I guess we have, but it won't be as exciting as yours," Tavana said.

"Don't be so sure," Campbell said with a grin; he seemed to glance at Xander as he said that. "But go on, Tavana, spin 'em a tale."

"Well . . ." He let his mind go back to that long-ago day. "Like yours, ours starts with the drill . . ."

Recounting their adventures took longer than Tavana had expected, even with the others helping. Little Hitomi fell asleep in the middle of it. Even Francisco was looking pretty tired. But to his surprise, Tavana saw the same expression of awe and intimidation on the Kimeis' faces as he'd seen on his friends.

"My God, Sergeant," said Sakura. "You guys had to *fix the drives?* In *space?* And then travel barely over *light-speed* to this place?"

"It is nothing compared to what you had to do!" Tavana said quickly. "Surviving without equipment?"

She waved that off. "Oh, that was just a *pain*. And depressing. But being stuck out there in the black with the *power* off? The drives *fried*? I'd have been totally freaked out!"

"All right, you two," Laura said with a smile that the sergeant shared. "Let's agree that both of our groups did some pretty awesome things. I'm proud of our family, and I think the sergeant's darn proud of you boys, too."

"That I am, no doubt about it. Together we just might make a real go of it here. Maybe even figure out a way to signal for help, with all the equipment we've got. But I can see you're all tired. I'll send you data summaries of everything we've gotten so far, and tomorrow we'll start packing everything up. Shouldn't take too long."

"You won't mind leaving your own camp?"

Xander laughed. "It's just a big cleared spot that we graded flat and scorched. Nothing fancy."

Tavana noticed an odd expression on Akira Kimei's face: a frown, down-drawn eyebrows and a moment where he opened his mouth as though to speak. But the expression faded and the older man didn't say anything.

"Well, then, we look forward to seeing you in a few days!"

"Count on it. We'll keep in touch, and let you know when we're lifting off. Shouldn't take more'n, oh, three hours or so once we're up. Be even less, but I don't want to push *LS-88* any more than we have to."

"Definitely not." Laura and her family waved. "Be seeing you!"

The images faded away, but the elation remained. "We're really going. We're really not alone!" Tavana heard himself saying, echoed by Francisco.

"That we are, kids!" Campbell said. "Time to do our perimeter check, Xander. The rest of you boys clean up and get ready for bed. We're going to make an early night of it, so we can get started loading everything tomorrow. We all want to get over there as soon as possible, right?"

"Right!" the entire group chorused, and a small tremor shook the shelter, as if even their island was adding emphasis.

The older two left, and Tavana, Maddox, and Francisco started cleaning up. "Remind me to pull out the waste containers and empty them before we collapse the shelter," Tavana said.

"We'll remind you," Maddox said, "But I'll bet that the sergeant will do it first."

"Probably, but better that all of us think about it. Don't want to try to collapse the whole thing with anything left inside."

Maddox nodded. He glanced over at the blank wall where the Kimei family had recently been. "Boy, they're incredible, aren't they?"

"*Oui* and then some."

"And you like her. Sakura, I mean."

Tavana felt as though someone had just set fire to his cheeks. "*Quoi*? I mean . . . Why?"

Francisco giggled. Maddox laughed. "You look like Xander did around a couple of girls back on Earth before we left, that's all."

Do I? Tavana tried to unscramble his thoughts. It was unusually hard to do. "Well, I *think* so," he said finally. "I don't really know her that well, but we were in the one class and . . . Hey, why am I talking about this with *you*?"

"Just wanted to ask." Maddox was quiet for a moment. "What about that Whips thing?"

"Do *not* use the word 'thing' about him. Ever," Tavana said sharply. "You heard their story. He's been with them all along and they rely on him. I don't feel comfortable around Bemmies either, but they think of him as part of their family. So before you say anything about him, think about what you say and if it's something you'd want to hear someone say about *your* family. *Compris*? Got it?"

The other two boys nodded quickly. For a minute Tavana wondered if he had to repeat it for Francisco, but the youngest boy's expression told him the advice had struck home. *Of course; family's a real big deal to him, so he gets it. Probably same for Maddox and Xander.*

The door opened and Campbell entered with Xander. "Perimeter's clear, nothing out there in our camp except us." He glanced around. "Good job. Xander, remind me to—"

"—make sure the waste containers are cleared?" Tavana and Maddox chorused.

"Ha! All right, everyone remind everyone of that. We'll want to make this place absolutely clean and empty. Remember, we'll probably be living in it for a while once we get there. Our hosts didn't build their house with guestrooms for six, I'll bet anything you like on that. So we want to make sure this one packs up in top shape."

"We *do* have another one, right, Sergeant?" Tavana asked.

"Yeah, but we don't want to have to *use* it, at least not now. No telling what the future holds, and we'd better hold a lot back for that future."

"Not arguing about that," Tavana said. "Just wanted to make sure, in case something went wrong."

"All right. Now everyone get ready for bed. We have a long day ahead of us tomorrow. I'm just going to transmit the data from our area of the world to them, and then get some rack time myself."

Tavana went to bed. But it was a long, long time before his eyes finally stayed closed. Even as he drifted off to sleep at last, one thought still ran through his brain:

We're not alone anymore!

Chapter 32

Sakura lay awake in her bed. She didn't know what had awakened her, but she couldn't force herself back to sleep. *And I need to go to the bathroom, too.*

As quietly as she could, Sakura eased out of her bed. She padded two floors down the stairs into the entrance hall where the bathroom was. It was still a little unnerving to think that when she sat down on the toilet that, aside from the grid that kept any possible nasties from getting in, there was nothing but air below her for at least a hundred meters.

On the other hand, that meant no one would ever have to worry about emptying this particular inside-outhouse.

She finished up by pouring water from the designated flush-can through the hole. While the entire grid got heavily cleaned during the weekly purges, it was a good habit to rinse it off after every use.

As she left the bathroom, she noticed light leaking out from under the kitchen door. Looking in, she saw her father sitting at the big table, staring into space with the faraway gaze that told her he was using his omni to display something.

"Dad? What are you doing up?"

"Saki. I'm the one who should be saying that." He rubbed his eyes and sighed. "Couldn't sleep, so I started looking over the data from Sergeant Campbell." His gaze shifted over her shoulder. "And hello to you also, Whips."

Her best friend gave a nonchalant wave with his top arm, multiple fingers spread wide. "Hi, Akira. Neither of you could sleep either?"

"No," they both agreed.

"You were frowning when I came in, Dad. Anything wrong?"

"Not entirely sure, Saki. Here, you and Whips look."

Their omnis suddenly came alive, projecting imagery from the other camp. "What are we looking for?" Whips asked.

"Well, take a look at this set of images. It was taken by their cameras as they did their overflight, the same day they did the burn-off they mentioned."

"Boy, they were lucky it rained that day," Sakura said.

"Lucky?" her father asked.

"Think about it, Dad. What happens to most of the rocks around here if you heat them up above a certain temperature?"

His eyes widened. "Oh, my, I hadn't thought of that. Quicklime all over."

"But the rain turned it to slaked lime," Whips said. "Which kinda put a floor on the whole thing. You're right, they *were* lucky. So what are we looking for?"

"See here? This is that fault or crack near their clearing. Notice that very near their clearing, the vegetation is sparse or missing entirely?"

"Yes," Sakura said. The line of the crack was fairly easy to see, a wrinkle in the jungle, a discontinuity. But near Sergeant Campbell's camp the green growths dwindled and eventually vanished, making the line starkly obvious.

"All right. Now look at these images from their ground scouting yesterday."

These pictures were very different. The riotous growth of the forest surrounded the viewer on all sides. Nearer the camera, however, the forest was reduced to scattered ground cover; the stunting continued onward for a considerable distance.

Sakura switched back and forth between the images. "Okay, Dad, I give up. The two views are so different I haven't got any idea what I'm looking for. Whips?"

"Ummm... Maybe? What is it, Akira?"

"That's it; I'm not sure. I'm not terribly good with measurements, and..."

"Oh. What do you want measured?"

"The extent of the area where the jungle growth is missing or severely depressed, in both sets of images."

"Hmm. Actually, you have tools that can do that in your omni, but I'll do it for you. I'm more used to this stuff than you are." An overlay from Whips' omni shaded the area in the first set of images, and then shaded regions in the other images. A few moments later he stiffened, all three arms going visibly rigid for a second. "There's a difference. A big difference."

A generated three-dimensional plot appeared, showing the other castaways' large clearing with the plowed berm around it and the long crevice of the fault not far away. "Here's the extent on the first set of images."

A purple streak reached out and became a sort of very elongated, somewhat irregular diamond. Sakura noticed that the fattest part of the diamond was adjacent to the camp.

"And here's the extent yesterday."

Red blossomed along the edges of the purple diamond, reaching far into the jungle in both directions.

Her father sat up. Tension suddenly rose in her. Akira Kimei's expression was grim. "That far, in that short a time? You're sure about the measurements?"

"Pretty sure. The camera specs for both sets of images are known, the aerial ones have metadata that identify all the orientation and altitude data associated with the image, and we've got the basic information on Sergeant Campbell and his omni's imaging suite combined with the GPS track of their scouting trip. I could be off by a few meters either way, but that wouldn't make any difference."

"No. No, it wouldn't." Akira shrugged. "Not the only anomaly, either. Here are some more images from the aerial survey."

As Sakura watched the landscape of the distant island stream by, something nagged at her subliminal sense of patterns. It took a few minutes—Melody probably would have gotten it right away—but suddenly it snapped into focus. "Those ridges . . . they're *all over* that island."

"Yes. That's part of it. Sergeant Campbell and his people clearly deduced the general reason. A very large meteoroid hit this island a while back—I would guess around a thousand years ago, maybe somewhat less—and nearly shattered it. *Did* shatter it, but not quite enough to get it to break up completely. It's knitting together slowly after centuries."

"But as you say, they mentioned that in their story," Whips said, puzzled. "So what's wrong?"

"It's not that in itself. It's that there's another mystery. Look closer."

Sakura started studying the highest, broadest images carefully. *Has to be a detail, something that doesn't quite make sense.* At first she couldn't see anything that looked worrisome, or even unusual. From that height, aside from the patchwork of lines, she saw the varied green of the forest, occasional dots of the columns that were visible from the air, blue dots of lakes or ponds, streams...

Wait a minute.

There were three dots of blue there, arranged in what seemed a near-perfect triangle. Then over here, another. And in this image, another. And in this image, right over their camp, she could see that the lake near Sergeant Campbell's camp seemed to be three similar dots joined together by a bigger lake. "There are these... groups of three ponds."

"Yes, I see it now," Whips said with rising interest. "Several of them. Hmm." He paused. "Here's something interesting; none of these are near any of the columns. They're all a considerable distance from any column. Not evenly distributed."

"That *is* another of the things that was bothering me, yes," Akira said. "I can't figure out a mechanism for them just forming by natural processes. There's no way these are regularly-occurring triads of meteorites or anything like that. Any other observations?"

"Well..." Sakura surveyed the images. "I'm not sure, but it looks to me like there's a lot of them on or near those seams. Whips?"

It didn't take long for her friend to run a statistical analysis. "You're right, Sakura. They've got a heavy bias towards those seams."

Sakura studied the images from Sergeant Campbell's

camp that actually showed the lake, broad and brilliant in the sun. *It's actually pretty big.*

"A sinkhole, perhaps? But why in threes? That's the problem."

"Maybe it's the way these things grow," Whips mused. "The chambers underneath might be those shapes collapsing when they get cut off?"

"I suppose it's possible, like a beehive, a symmetrical structure being constructed as part of the process. But we haven't seen anything vaguely like that here. Yes, we haven't covered nearly as much ground as they have, but statistically we should have encountered one or two."

"Maybe not," argued Sakura. "If they grow near the seams, well, there are no seams on our continent. At least, none we've found yet."

"True," Akira said with a nod. "Yet that would imply it has something to do with those seams, and right now I can't imagine what. The water filling them might indicate that they go all the way through, all of them."

"Maybe it has something to do with stabilizing the structure? Helps more water circulate to the interior better?" Whips was obviously just throwing out ideas.

Akira shrugged. "I suppose it'll have to wait until we can study it up close." He stood up, eclipsing the light, throwing Sakura into momentary shadow.

A chill ran down her spine as she remembered something else that had done the same thing. "Wait, Dad. I think I know what made those holes. It didn't come from above. It came from *below*."

Akira Kimei froze, staring at her. Images flickered in his omni as he reviewed them, checking, measuring...

Slowly he straightened. "I think I'd better make a call. Right now."

Chapter 33

Campbell came instantly awake at the buzz of his omni and the flashing from his retinal display. He didn't get to be a Chief Master Sergeant by being slow to get up. "Campbell."

"Sergeant, you mentioned you had felt occasional tremors on your island. How often?" Akira Kimei's voice was tense.

"Um . . . hold on." He thought a moment. "Once every three, four days, I guess?"

"Get out of there *now*, Sergeant!"

He didn't waste time arguing. He started yanking on his clothes. "Boys, get up. *Everyone up!* Move it move it, move it *now!*"

Everyone, he was glad to see, responded. They jumped out of bed and grabbed their clothes before asking questions. "What's wrong, Sergeant?"

"Don't know exactly, yet, but we have to get out of here *pronto*." He signaled for a private line to Kimei. "Do we have time to pack? I've got two excavators out, plus the shelter. Or do we hit the ship in our PJs, get into our suits, and lift off?"

There was a *tiny* hint of humor in Kimei's voice. As

his image manifested in a corner of Campbell's field of view, he could see a very, very small smile. "You might be able to wait until morning, but I'd much, much rather you didn't. I wouldn't leave anything behind, if you can get it done quickly."

"An hour, two at most."

"That should do, unless you're extraordinarily unlucky."

Campbell hesitated. *My gut says if he's that worried, we should already be lifting. But we're marooned on a world with no resupply. Leaving stuff like this behind could be a crucial mistake.*

Xander was already next to him. "What's happening, Sergeant?"

"I'll let you know in a few. Go on."

"Well, I know this is an emergency. So I am officially ordering *you* to take command."

Campbell grinned at that. "Acknowledged, Captain. I'm running the show now."

"Right, sir. So what do we do?"

"First," he said into the public channel, "everyone get their suits on *now*."

Francisco blinked. "Why do we need our spacesuits?"

"Because the sergeant says so," Xander answered sharply. Francisco jumped guiltily.

"This should be just a routine flight, but we don't take chances in a survival situation. I want everyone suited up." Campbell went and got his own and made sure every telltale showed green before locking down. Using his command authority he checked all the others'. "Maddox, re-seal your suit. You did it too fast and your seal's showing yellow."

Satisfied that everyone was properly suited up,

he turned to the group. "Xander, you and Maddox get the two excavators loaded back in and secure everything—and I mean *everything*—in the cargo bay. Tav, you and Francisco move absolutely everything out of this shelter. I'm going to yank the perimeter monitors. We lift in sixty minutes *no matter what*, so don't go slowly. Anything that's not on board in one hour stays here!"

The outside glowed with sunset colors—the slow rotation of Lincoln mocking the feeling that he'd been awakened in the middle of the night. "All right, Akira, talk to me. What's the urgency?"

"It's two things, Sergeant. You know that area of stunted growth near your camp?"

"Yeah. Up and down the seam near us. I was a little concerned about that."

"You were right to be," Akira said. "The extent of the dead area along that seam has more than doubled in the short time between your aerial survey of the island and today—well, yesterday, now, as you'd measure it."

Campbell blinked. *More than doubled? That's a fast die-off.* "You think you know why?"

"I'm afraid so. You understand that these floating continents and islands are basically massive colonies of coral-like creatures."

"Yes, sir. I understand that." He reached the first monitor unit. Pulling up the holdfasts for the monitor took a bit. He had to disassemble the unit and compact the mounting pole before he could pack them away. Clumsy rigs, but they worked.

"Well, it is my belief, based on very incomplete and preliminary information and my own knowledge of multiple ecologies on various worlds, that they are more than that. These masses are home to an immense variety of life, one that rivals that of Earth in overall diversity. A large proportion of lifeforms rely on the existence of these floating landmasses for their own survival. Many of them retain features appropriate for both land and water survival, which means that they are not absolutely dependent on being constantly above the water."

Campbell followed that, but he wasn't seeing the urgency. However Akira Kimei's decision to wake him from a sound sleep told him there was something he was missing. "Go on," he said, moving on to the next monitor.

"In short, I believe that these are large, symbiotic colonies. While there are undoubtedly many organisms that simply live and die on and around the floating landmasses, a very large number of them are connected to the landmass in a manner that causes them to respond to potential threats to the landmass." The other man's voice was grim now. "One of the most obvious ways to do that—especially if the threat manifests as something like an infection—is to find some way to remove that region, as we might excise infected tissue. That might be difficult in an otherwise completely healthy and intact landmass. Such a landmass might have different responses."

Oh, crap. Crap, crap, crap. "You're saying that by first bulldozing this whole camp area, and then sterilizing it when it started to grow back, we designated our area as infected, or otherwise too hurt to salvage."

"Yes. And your island was already severely damaged; it has spent perhaps a thousand years or more trying to repair earlier damage. That healing is not complete yet, or we would have a much harder time distinguishing the seams. So rather than fighting to keep your piece of the island together, it is allowing—*triggering*—a die-off of all species along the seam that borders your section of the island. In addition to the barren areas next to your camp there are already other dead, gray areas and many severely stunted ones along the entire seam."

He projected an image to Campbell's retinals, and the sergeant grunted. It looked like a damn dotted line all around the section they were on, practically labeled *tear here*. "Huh. And that'd extend below the living ground under us. The coral or whatever would also be dying off or withdrawing, right?"

"Yes."

"Still," Campbell said after a brief pause, "We planned on being out of here in a couple of days. Even if this process accelerates, there's no way it's going to reach the point of collapse in that time."

"Not by itself, no. But there's another aspect to a floating biosphere of this sort. There are—there must be—predatory species or colonies. They will consume the concentration of living biomass on, around, and inside these islands."

It was like a shot of cold water straight through his guts. "And they'll target weaker organisms—colonies that are already injured and sending out chemical signals that say *this part's hurt*."

Akira's voice had the warmth of a teacher who hears a student giving the right answer, although his face was still grim. "Exactly. That way they serve a positive evolutionary purpose, culling the injured and allowing the more intact and healthy to survive. But that means that you are on an island that has already been a prime target more than once."

"How do you know—" Campbell broke off, because suddenly he understood. He wasn't a biologist, but a soldier could survive a long time by making the right guesses at the right time. "Those three-hole lakes like the one we're next to. But if that's the case, these predators are..." He trailed off, trying to visualize just how huge something like that had to be.

"We saw one," Akira said. "The thing that took down *LS-5*. That circular lagoon that used to exist at the end of our continent—it was a hole punched through by a meteor. Undoubtedly there were cracks across the area nearby. The landmass was trying to repair it—had gotten a good deal of the repair started, even—when suddenly we crash-landed and *LS-5* dropped right into the hole, damaging the area again. So the distress chemicals started radiating through the structure and into the water, and eventually one of these things sensed it. We were incredibly lucky that it didn't strike until we were all out of the ship."

Campbell didn't need more explanation. With this area of the already-damaged island weakening, it would be a prime target for such gigantic predators—a large yet vulnerable section ripe for the taking. "Got you. You were right to call me. Yeah, this might not go critical in the next several days...or it might. We can't take the chance. We'll be lifting in forty-three minutes."

"I admit," Akira said, his face clearing, "that makes me feel much better. Thank you for taking this seriously, Sergeant."

"Thank *you* for figuring this out so fast. Now, I've got work to do. Talk later. Campbell out."

He switched to Xander's channel. "Okay, I've got the lowdown, and it's not good. Those lakes we saw—like ours—are the mark of something that preys on these floating colonies. What we've been doing here might just be attracting them."

"*Jesus*," muttered Xander. "Do we have *time* to load all this?"

"It's a calculated risk, but hell, if Kimei hadn't happened to figure it out so fast we'd still be sleeping. And we really don't want to leave this equipment behind. We're probably just fine for the next few days, but I'll be damned if we'll take any chances we don't have to. Keep me up to date. We've got thirty-eight minutes now."

By the time Campbell had gotten the last of the four monitors down and packed, Xander pinged him. "Excavators loaded and locked down. I *think* we've got all the other stuff in the cargo bay sealed back up, but I want you to do a walk-around and make sure. We're not doing anything as rough as the re-entry, but—"

"Right. No point in doing this half-assed, just in case. I'm bringing in these monitors, so I'll get them in the cargo area and do the walk-around. You two go double-check the shelter and make sure everything is out of it. If you're sure, collapse it so we can pack it away."

"Yessir."

Locking the improvised monitors into one of the hold-downs didn't take long, but doing a very careful survey of the cargo hold required more time. By the time he'd rounded up a couple of smaller items and satisfied himself that the place was otherwise clear, the four boys were dragging the shelter up the ramp.

He could tell from the compact shape that they had indeed emptied the shelter properly. "Good work, boys. We've done it with minutes to spare." He went down and started to help move the shelter up. "Xander, call Dr. Akira Kimei and let him know we'll be on our way very shortly."

"Yessir."

They got the shelter up the ramp. "Dog that down tight, boys, and then get in your seats and strap in. I'm doing one last check of the camp." As he walked out, he triggered the ramp to close behind him.

He was barely twenty meters from *LS-88* when a grumbling concussion knocked him off his feet, causing the trees to sway. Flying things took off in panic. He tried to regain his footing, but the shuddering vibration continued. In the distance he could hear cracking, groaning noises. He rolled several more meters and finally staggered up, needing sea-legs more than land-legs to keep on his feet.

Silhouetted against the red of the sunset sky, three immense pillars reared up like curved daggers, tearing through the deceptively solid earth as though it were barely there, towering over the landscape like edged mountains before sinking back down.

Chunks of stone and shreds of vegetation showered down around him. With a sickening lurch of his stomach he realized that some of the vibration continued—a long, drawn-out groaning, splintering noise, like a sheet of wood ten miles long being torn asunder. The ground was tilting!

"Sergeant!" Xander's voice was panicked.

The shout galvanized Campbell to action. He glanced to the shuttle and saw—racing across the campsite from one side to the other—a dark, dust-smoking crevasse. He looked from where he stood to where the airlock was, measuring distances and his steadiness. He knew he'd never make it, not in time.

Without hesitation, he triggered the overrides. The airlock of *LS-88* closed and sealed, all doors locked with a code that couldn't be overridden for two hours. He gave the autopilot the *liftoff* command. At the same time, he shut off his comm, knowing what Xander and the others would be saying—*screaming*—at him. None of it would make any difference now.

The tilt grew steeper. His piece was tilting *towards* the side that *LS-88* was on, while *LS-88* tipped in his direction. *Get off the* ground, *you lazy bird!*

Even as the wing jets' whine rose to full power, the ground he stood on began to crack. His omni blinked for attention—it looked like the Kimeis were trying to reach him, too. Below he heard a roaring, a thunderous sound of water surging, raging up while the pieces of the island rotated farther and farther towards the vertical. *Oh* hell, *this isn't good. Either I'm going to get smashed between these two pieces, or—*

LS-88 slid sideways and skidded drunkenly into the air, the simplistic autopilot trying with all its programmed skill to compensate for the impossible. *Go, go, dammit,* GO!

Samuel Campbell felt himself starting to slide down towards the crumbling intersection of the pieces of their camp, and looked up. He didn't really want to see how he was going to die. *I just want to know—*

The shuttle had stabilized. It was climbing, moving out from between the two gigantic slabs of island... when a shard broke off above and ahead, a shard a mere hundred meters or so long and fifty wide, falling, bouncing outward, plummeting down . . .

The autopilot couldn't avoid it.

Campbell heard himself curse as the white and green mass hammered *LS-88*'s starboard wing. It shattered, spinning the entire vessel completely around, twisting the other wing with the violence of the impact. "Xander! *Boys! HOLD ON!*"

Like a dying bird, *LS-88* plummeted from the sky, vanishing behind one of the huge slabs. The roaring from below told Campbell that it would not be earth, but water, that wrote his epitaph.

The impact was a sledgehammer as dark as the blackness that claimed him.

Chapter 34

Laura yawned as she walked into the kitchen. "I thought I heard voices. What's everyone doing up?"

"Hello, love." Akira gave her a quick kiss. "I couldn't quite get to sleep, so I started looking over the data our friends on the other side of the planet sent us."

She found herself a lot more awake as her husband—with some interjections by Whips and Sakura—summarized what they'd worked out. "So you've let them know?"

"Yes. As I had expected, Sergeant Campbell did not take this lightly. They are preparing to leave now. I must say, this makes me feel much better; it may not be likely that something would happen in the next few days, but best not to risk it."

"I certainly wouldn't want to, not with children on board. Good for him."

Her omni buzzed for attention. She could see from his reaction that Akira's had done the same. "Laura Kimei here."

An image of Xander Bird appeared in the air in front of her. She opened up the connection so that

Whips, Sakura, and Akira could see it too. Xander was in one of the acceleration chairs on board *LS-88*, and she could see the others moving to strap in nearby.

"Hi, Dr. . . . I mean, Laura. We're almost ready to lift off. The sergeant's doing a last outside check and then we're off."

"Good. I'm glad you took this seriously."

"So am I. And," he grinned, "it means we'll all get together a little earlier! We should be there in, what, three to four hours, I guess."

"Looking forward to it," she said with an answering smile, seeing Sakura's expression mirroring her own. "I'll make sure to have breakfast waiting for you, then—that will be our schedule's equivalent of morning, anyway."

"Great! I know that Tav will—"

The image shuddered. A rumbling noise echoed through the transmission. A spike of ice impaled Laura's heart as she saw Xander go white.

At almost the same moment, she heard a whirr-*chink!* sound.

"God *damn* him!" Xander said, anger and panic warring in his tones. "Sergeant! *Sergeant!*"

"What?"

"The sergeant! He just overrode my codes, shut the door, and locked it!"

"Oh, *merde*," Tavana said, his almost conversational tone laden with laconic dread.

The image stayed level from their point of view, but from the shift in the way the boys sat, Laura could tell that *LS-88* was tilting. There was an abrupt shift. Xander cut in the external camera of the shuttle and she could see, with a sick terror in her gut, a monolithic black shadow, three shadows. They rose against the sunset like swords, their outlines all too familiar.

"Oh, God, no..." she heard Sakura whisper.

Another sound—the rising whine of the turbines of *LS-88*. "What the..."

"The autopilot, it is engaged!" Tavana shouted. "Sergeant Campbell is making us take off without him!"

"Campbell!" she shouted, and her omni dutifully activated the connection. "Sergeant! Answer us!"

But there was no answer, even as the distant shuttle finally lifted off. With a swaying motion they could see the stabilized images Xander was sending. "We're... up!" Xander said with a combination of hope and horror. "The autopilot is getting things under control... Oh, no, the sergeant is—*Holy sh*—"

With a doomsday impact and a flash of spinning motion, the connection cut off and went blank.

Laura found herself—along with the others, which now included a bleary-eyed Caroline and Melody—staring at empty air.

"Tavana!" Sakura shouted. "Xander! *Sergeant Campbell!*"

There was no answer.

Akira sank into one of the kitchen chairs. "Too slow. Dammit, if I'd just been a few minutes faster!"

"Akira, it's not your fault—"

He clenched his fist and hammered the table with a violence she'd rarely seen. His long black hair hung in his face. "I...I know. But...if I'd seen the pattern just a few minutes earlier, they could have—"

"You don't know what *might* have happened," she said firmly. "Maybe you're right. Maybe you're not.

Who knows how long it would have taken Campbell to get back to the ship? How much more time would have to have passed for you to accept it wasn't your responsibility? Don't blame yourself."

Melody looked up at her with wide, tragic eyes. "They're gone?"

She put an arm around Melody. "I don't know. It doesn't look good."

"It's *unfair*," Whips burst out, a *crack!* of sound from one of his arms punctuated his frustration. "We just found out they were here a day ago!"

"Not even that," Caroline said dully. "Hasn't even been a day."

Laura closed her eyes and sat down, a wave of depression threatening to close over her. *To have found new people on Lincoln, to have found out they had so much we need, to be on the verge of meeting them, and losing it all so fast—*

Her omni lit up again. "Dr. Kimei?"

"*Xander!* Xander, are you and the boys all right?"

The face gazing at them was still pale as a ghost. Behind him Tavana dabbed at a small cut on Francisco's cheek, but they were obviously all there, and all alive. "Yes, Ma'am—Laura. We're okay. Got a little banged around, but no real injuries." He looked back at Francisco. "And *that* is why you should have kept your helmet deployed."

"The sergeant..." Sakura began.

Xander shook his head. "Last I saw he was starting to fall down into the canyon between the two pieces." His hands were shaking, Laura saw; he noticed her gaze and clamped the two together almost as though praying. "No response on his omni. Can't even get a command ping back, meaning the system doesn't even detect his suit or omni at all."

"Oh, no." Sakura's face crumpled. Akira put his arms around her.

Laura ruffled Sakura's hair gently. "What about LS-88?"

For several moments no one answered; the boys, like Sakura, were clearly trying to grasp the fact that the indomitable Sergeant Campbell was gone.

Finally Xander looked up, took a deep breath, and said, "Come on, kids. Gone or not, the sergeant would want us to keep going. He'd be happy we're still alive, and he'd want us to *stay* that way. Let's answer their questions."

"We're floating," Maddox answered, straightening a little and trying to keep the thick tone of someone who'd been crying out of his voice. "The hull seems all intact, the door seals are tight, and the reactor's online."

"Can you get her airborne again?"

The expression on the boys' faces gave her the answer. "No," Tavana said heavily. "The starboard wing, it is gone; the port wing is not gone, but it is badly damaged. I am not sure what we can salvage from it. The tail is not bad, but it will not give us the lift we need."

"Those shuttles can do a lot of shifting of configuration," Sakura said, pulling away from her father and rubbing her eyes furiously. "Couldn't you, I don't know, adapt some of that to give you a new set of wings?"

Tavana shrugged, but he didn't look optimistic. "I do not know the limits, exactly. We will do what we can, but I cannot say for sure."

"What about your island?"

Francisco answered, to Laura's surprise. "The camera is not pointing the right way. We see lots of waves and sometimes a little bit of what's under the waves." He shivered. "I hope we do not see that . . . monster."

Whips lowered and rose in his best equivalent of a nod. "I hope you don't, either. But I guess it will ignore you if you're floating by yourselves. To sonar— which my people use all the time, and I'd bet most animals here do too—a metal and composite boat like that looks very different from things you can eat. If they're still looking for food from the island, you're probably pretty safe."

"Might be other things that would try to nibble on *LS-88*, though," Xander said. "And even something a lot smaller than that . . . island-eater, I guess . . . would be way bigger than we can handle."

"All we can do is hope. Is there any way you can get moving?"

"I don't know. The one wing jet looks damaged, and the jets at the rear are mostly underwater."

"Jets . . . *jets!*" Tavana suddenly sat straight up. "Yes! Remember when we did our survey, Xander? The sergeant, he said these jets can be reconfigured to be water jets!"

"That's right, he did. If we can get working water jets, we can *drive* our way across the water! It won't be as fast as flying, but it should work!"

"But the wing," Maddox said, "That would get in the way."

"We could remove it, or maybe if we can fix it, reconfigure it—"

"—the tail, it could perhaps configure down, make a rudder—"

"Slow down, boys," Laura said, their sudden enthusiasm starting to lighten the leaden weight in her chest. "You're saying that the *LS-88* can be a watercraft?"

"Colony shuttles are designed to dive some distance underwater, Dr. Kimei," Tavana said. "That's probably part of what saved us; we must have hit a depth of at least five meters when we crashed, but nothing leaked. Normally the jets would probably reconfigure on their own, but with the AI automation all out that's not working. Still, the specifications for that shift should still be in the systems. Between Xander, Maddox, and me, I think we can do that, yes!"

"None of us are engineers—Whips is the closest we have—but you let us know if there's anything we can do to help you," Akira said.

"We mean it. Even if it's something very simple and silly," Laura agreed emphatically. "We want to see you here, safe and sound."

"Um, Laura," Xander said hesitantly, "Can you, um . . . still work on Lieutenant Haley?"

She smiled naturally at the young man. "Yes, I can do that. The connections are all still there. She'll be up and ready to help us in no time!"

"Great!" Then his face fell. "I don't look forward to telling her about the sergeant."

"No," Laura agreed quietly. "That's always a terrible thing to have to do. With current medicine, I haven't had to give that speech often, thank all the gods that are, but as a doctor I have given it more than once. All you can do is try to be as straightforward and sympathetic as possible."

"Yeah." He looked up, a determined smile fixed on his face. "But at least we're still alive."

"Yes, you are," she said, "and we want you to stay that way."

"Then we'd better get to work!"

The kitchen looked darker once the display faded. The others' sad faces echoed her own worry and loss.

But as Xander had reminded her, there was still much to be grateful for. "All right, everyone. That was a terrible accident, but most of our new friends are safe. Let's get breakfast, and then start figuring out what we're going to do with them when they get here!"

Chapter 35

"The timing, it is beyond belief," Tavana said, half to himself.

"What do you mean?" asked Xander. He held the cover plate for the drive control subsystem while Tavana did diagnostics.

"I mean," Tavana said, squinting uselessly at the images being projected to his retinal display from the miniature probe, "here I am, again, trying to get a half-wrecked ship running well enough to get us somewhere. And all because some stupid predator couldn't wait, what, ten minutes? We were there for a few months, and just as we're going to leave everything has to happen?"

He consulted the data from the probes, compared it to the manual, and found himself cursing again.

The other three looked worried. "Don't tell me it won't work," Xander said.

"Work?" Tavana blinked. "Oh, *non*, that is not the problem. The jets themselves, they have to be reconfigured physically. It's not just a matter of reprogramming, and I can't trigger it here. I'm going to have to go outside to do it."

Maddox and Francisco looked at him wide-eyed. "But Tav, the jets are *underwater* most of the time now."

"I know." He tried to say it with an air of nonchalance, but instead it came out flat and heavy with fear. If the jets were underwater, and they had to be reconfigured manually, he'd have to go out onto the hull, that rocked and swayed with the ocean waves, and interface with each jet . . . hoping that nothing out there would decide he was worth a nibble.

He wouldn't even worry about it if this had been the familiar blue sea off his native Tahiti. Despite many land-dwellers' fears of the ocean, the chances of sharks or anything else attacking a human were ridiculously low, especially if you were just working on part of a floating craft. But this wasn't his home sea. It was an alien ocean, one where something the size of a small mountain had just shattered part of a floating island. There were pieces of coral all over, they could see that much from the front port. It might be the equivalent of blood in the water, signaling a feast. No telling what other creatures lived in these waters, or what they might do.

But what choice did he have? He was the propulsion engineer here, and even if he could tell Xander or Maddox how to do it, someone was still going to have to go outside to do the work.

"I know," he repeated, a little less leadenly. "But it shouldn't take too long. I shouldn't be in much danger if I'm quick about it."

"Can we do anything to help?" Xander asked.

"Just belay me with a rope and haul me in quick if I fall off."

He climbed up into the airlock along with Xander.

It was a tight fit but they both managed, along with the carbonan-reinforced cable. Lincoln's morning sunshine slanted in as the door opened. It had been over eighteen hours since the disaster.

Then again, there was no way he would have tried this at night, so if it hadn't taken them that much time to recover, rest up, and figure out what to do, he'd have had to wait anyway.

They tied the line to one of the handholds at the edge of the lock; Xander then looped it loosely around Tavana. "Okay, you go up first. I'll climb up after you and brace myself in the lock. This won't take too long, right?"

"If it works at all it should be quick, yes." Tavana heaved himself up onto the top of *LS-88*. For the first time, he could see back to the floating island they had left. The main mass was still there, forests waving green and solid; but a great chunk had been carved out of it in the shoreline facing them, leaving white cliffs of broken coral-stone. One area rose up into a curved, dark opening, showing that—as the Kimeis had said—part of the island was indeed hollow. Massive fragments still drifted nearby, looking tiny next to the main island but still towering, skyscraper-sized masses. Trees clung precariously to their sideways bulk, exposing mats of algae and other sea life drying in the sun.

Xander poked his head up. "From this distance it doesn't even look like much damage, does it? I—*whoa!*"

A mile or so off, one of the floating fragments had shuddered. It shattered to pieces in slow-motion as the incomprehensible immensity of the island-eater drove straight through the drifting rock. Tavana caught a glimpse of a cavernous mouth between the three curved-blade projections before the thing sank back.

"Most of the interesting things will be going on there, then," he said confidently. It fit the pattern at home: when the big predators ate, the smaller ones would be circling nearby, trying to catch what the bigger one missed. A little anomalous fragment like theirs should be mostly ignored.

Cautiously, Tavana advanced towards the tail section. A flash of scarlet caught his eye. "Look at that. One of the tree-anemone things decided to hook onto us."

"Don't touch it."

"I'm not an idiot. Besides, I'm wearing my suit. It can't sting through that. Even a shark couldn't bite through this." He realized that was true, and that cheered him immensely. Anything large enough to really threaten the active-controlled carbonan suit would be too large to likely notice something his size.

The jets were mostly underwater, as he expected, but he could reach them by crawling onto the tail, and then edging along the pylons that supported them. Fortunately the control signals passed through optical junctions; seawater would completely disrupt electronics.

Not for the first time, he wished the sergeant was there. He might know a way to trick them to work from inside. And he would certainly know how to deal with any trouble that might show up.

With great difficulty he eased out onto the slowly rocking pylon. He managed to disengage the access panel. It slid aside—fortunately, like many such panels, it was designed to stay attached unless specifically and carefully removed, so he didn't need to worry about it falling into the water. There was the access port!

He took a careful look around, then had his suit helmet deploy and seal. Dunking his head under the water, he looked out into the blue-green depths.

There were a few very distant, faint shadows visible for a moment, and some small creatures like fish darted here and there, but he saw no immediate threat. Tavana slid fully onto the pylon, legs gripping it as tightly as possible, and slid the TechTool improvised probe into the port. His omni immediately lit up. *Yes! Systems are all connected!*

Now he had to find the reconfiguring code. If you were going to be using the nuclear reactor's heat to drive a jet of water over seven hundred and eighty times the density of air, you needed different intake, heat transfer, and exhaust geometry to make the jet reasonably efficient. But calculating exactly what those changes were? That'd be really hard, even with the tools in his omni; this wasn't the kind of problem he'd expected to run into in his studies. *Maybe I should have. This is the kind of problem colonies have to deal with all the time. They'll have a piece of equipment that's almost what they need and have to adapt it.*

If the sergeant was right, the reconfiguration for that kind of operation was already in the system somewhere.

He glanced through the augmented reality display again, surveying the water around him. Again there were some distant shadows in the clear water but nothing close. *Good, stay that way.*

He paged through the various control codes for the jets—there were more than he'd expected. But if the AIs and other systems were running, they'd know where everything was.

Suddenly it was there, in front of him. The code was even labeled *Water Jet Transition* and displayed a diagram of the mode shift. "Got it! Xander, I've found the code!"

"Great! Can you activate it?"

"Of course I can. It will just take a moment. I want to be sure to do this right."

Let's see . . . transition activated in that *sequence . . . Oh, ouch, I do* not *want to be near this when it shifts, so I need a delay. Thirty seconds should be plenty . . . There!*

Even as he sent the command a flicker of motion out of the corner of his eye made him throw himself backwards, scrabbling for purchase on the side of *LS-88.*

Something gray-black, broad and streamlined like a stingray, shot just over him. In the same instant, the line went taut and Xander yanked him hard onto the upper hull of the shuttle.

The gray thing landed with a wet *thud* on the metal and composite, then slewed around with surprising speed. It had no obvious eyes, but clearly sensed his motion. Writhing tentacular appendages stretched out from the creature towards him as he scrambled backwards.

Xander's pistol fired three times, each shot a flat, authoritative *crack!* The creature was blown apart, pulped by the concussion and ripped by the slugs. "You okay, Tav?"

"Fine, *oui*, fine," Tavana said, feeling his whole body shaking. *That is stupid; that thing, there is no way it could have gotten through the suit. But I was scared all the same.* "Yes, I am all right. It didn't even touch me." He looked down and saw that he was still gripping the TechTool in his glove. "The real question is, did it work?"

A hum vibrated the hull beneath him. The starboard jet shape shifted, broadened, parts sliding back, morphing and stretching to match the phantom image still displayed in his omni's retinals. "*Yes!* That's the way it should look!"

"So you can get the port jet to shift too?"

"Much faster—I won't be there long enough to attract anything." His legs did not completely believe him, but he forced his still-trembling body to obey. He couldn't think about that much, or he'd get too scared to do the work.

He slid out on the pylon, connected with the port, sent the same code he'd transmitted to the first jet, and backed off. Seconds later, the port jet transformed into a water-jet.

"Done! Let's get back inside!"

Xander helped him stand, and the two made their way back to the hatch. "So are we ready to go?"

"Not quite. We should test the jets and make sure they work and we need to get the remaining portside wing off, or find a way to configure it into something useful. And the tail—it will have to be changed to a water rudder. I still have to figure out how to do that."

He retracted his helmet and grinned at Xander. "But now? I think we can do this. The sergeant," his grin faded, but did not completely disappear. "The sergeant, his last act will not have been in vain. We will *sail* this shuttle all the way to the Kimeis!"

Chapter 36

Why the hell is it so dark?

The question was the first thing that occurred to Sergeant Campbell when he opened his eyes. If it weren't for the fact that he could feel his eyelids moving, he'd have thought his eyes were still shut.

There was also the sensation of floating, but not null-g; he was drifting, twisting in something that resisted motion. *That's right. I fell into the water.*

Augmented-reality controls lit up at his mental command. *Suit's intact. No surprise there, really—if it wasn't, I'd probably be long dead. Pressure...damnation, I'm at a depth of a hundred and six meters.*

That also explained some of the resistance. The suit was providing pressure protection and had to adjust geometry in real-time to allow him to move while not giving way to the tremendous water pressure—over ten times that at the surface. *Damn, but Tayler-Hussie builds these things well*, he thought, not for the first time in his career.

Then he remembered the last glimpse he'd had of *LS-88*: wing shredded, plummeting to an unknown fate. *I have to get moving, dammit!*

He reached up and his hand brushed something hard and unyielding. He noticed a faint flicker of light somewhere in the gloom. *Bioluminescence? Probably. Doesn't look like daylight.*

Campbell activated the lowlight imaging capabilities, crossing his suit's fingers as he did so.

Instantly the pure black shimmered to a deep, enigmatic blue, with sparks of brilliance scattered throughout, and many moving shapes that flickered with a faint luminance.

Some of those shapes were uncomfortably nearby and looked like they were circling.

The telltales told him his gun was still secured on his hip. It would fire underwater, though he wouldn't want to shoot a thousand rounds that way. The range would only be a few meters, though, so he really didn't want to get in a scrap if he could avoid it.

Fortunately, there were plenty of tactics for scenarios like this. It wasn't like he was the first soldier ever stranded in water—though, admittedly, no ocean he'd ever heard of was quite like this one. *First, just show I'm alive. Start moving and they might decide I'm nothing worth eating. My suit probably doesn't smell right anyway. Too bad it's not primarily meant as a dive suit; I'd have sonar.*

As soon as he straightened and began moving along the overhang that lay above him—and that had probably been keeping him from floating to whatever surface might be above—the circling creatures scattered, fleeing far enough away that they were barely detectable through the fog of underwater distance.

A check of the telltales verified what he was already certain of. There was no sign of contact with the satellite network, not even GIS pings. Of course, he was a hundred meters under water and only God knew how many meters of coral-rock. He couldn't have driven a signal through this much stuff with a megawatt transmitter and a fifty-foot antenna.

He'd also been out for hours. If it weren't for his nanos he'd have probably been dead. As it was he felt vaguely nauseated: his nanos kept him from puking in his suit. The suit records showed multiple impacts and accelerations. He'd been sucked down with the sinking end of the island shard and bashed against random pieces. Then he'd finally floated back up inside the damn thing.

A vague, flickering shape moved towards him again. This one was amorphous, but the movement and fact that he could only really see it due to a very faint phosphorescence on its surface made it impossible to distinguish.

On the one hand, this *was* a military-issue suit. He didn't believe any creature on any planet could breach the suit easily, if at all. On the other hand, there was no reason to test that. If he'd learned anything on Emerald—Lincoln—he'd learned it would surprise you whenever it got the chance.

He continued moving along the outcrop, but made a sharp gesture towards the unknown approaching him. It balked, hovering about fifteen, twenty meters away. "Good, stay there," he muttered. He didn't mind company, as long as it didn't get too intrusive.

Suddenly his hand met empty water. His instincts, as well as the pressure indicators, showed that he was starting to rise through the water. His unknown observer was rising with him, but—so far—not closing the distance.

With a *thud* he bumped into another outcropping and sighed. "Yeah, I figured it wouldn't be that easy."

He considered whether it would be wise to try to use some high-intensity light pulses to image the area around him. Some surfaces had faint bioluminescent coatings. Others didn't. Without some idea of what this whole cave was like, how'd he know he was going in the right direction? On the other hand, even with advanced image processing, how far out into the distance could he expect to see, and what would the reaction of local lifeforms be to such a display?

"Hell with it, I need to at least *try.*"

Light detonated from his suit in a synchronized imaging sequence. To save his dark-adapted eyes, the helmet went opaque momentarily.

Instantly an outline of the cavernous space around him appeared.

At the same time, his follower darted away to a much greater distance. The captured images, however, showed him a creature that he'd never seen before, about three meters long, with rippling fins along all four symmetrically-placed ridges. Those fins had been the reason his prior dim impression was of something without fixed shape. The mouth was only slightly open, but he couldn't see what passed for dentition, even in an enhanced version of the image. It had large, clearly functional eyes and a strong, semi-cylindrical body that ended in a four-vaned tail. The body was covered by what looked like fur, something he hadn't noticed in the few native creatures he'd seen thus far. The head had things that might have been spikes, tendrils, or manipulators—hard to tell.

It looked fast and maneuverable.

Other creatures in range had also jumped or otherwise showed their startlement. Of more immediate interest was the fact that he could see far below him—the light and multiple-exposure, multispectral processing by his suit gave him useful data out to around four hundred meters. Ultraviolet was the best waveband underwater, and that's how he was getting a lot of this.

Below him, much of the cavern vanished into haze, but he could see walls on two sides; he was in a volume of uncertain height but about four hundred fifty meters across in total, stretching into unguessable distance ahead and behind him. More importantly, the outcropping above him only extended another twenty meters. *Maybe I can get clear after all. And I can't take all day about it, either!*

He wasn't in a terrible hurry for himself. The suit had been fully charged when everything fell apart, and the superconductor coil batteries would last a long time. As he was actually breathing air at surface pressure rather than hundred-meter pressure, there should be no nitrogen narcosis, the bends, or other depth-related issues. Air was being reprocessed, and he even had a couple days' rations from the in-suit reservoir—not tasty at all, but it'd keep him alive.

But Xander, Tavana, Maddox, and Francisco? Who knew what they might be going through now? The boys were either just fine, or far beyond his help. It had been quite a few hours. But Sergeant Samuel Morgan Campbell wasn't going to rest until he knew, one way or the other.

Moving with more certainty now, he pushed well out past the end of this outcropping, making his suit morph slightly to give him fins and broader hands for swimming. The imaging system sent out another brilliant survey flash.

This time he could make out high walls rearing up several dozen meters above him, ending with a peculiar shimmering wall that *had* to be an interface between water and air. There were also several large creatures in the water between him and the surface, but he wasn't planning on swimming between them anyway. He would stick near the walls and keep an eye out for holes that the underwater equivalent of the centisnakes—or, as the Kimeis called them, minimaws—might pop out of.

Something about the wall bothered him; as he rose steadily upwards, he studied it more carefully. Occasional cross-structures spanned the gap from side to side, spaced along the wall. As he passed one, he could see that it was an outgrowth *of* the wall, stretching all the way across.

Such a growth made sense as a support column. "Well, I'll be damned. I'm inside part of the floating island, but it's floating on its *side* right now."

A flicker of motion caught his eye. His odd companion was back, once more hovering fifteen to twenty meters away. Campbell watched the thing narrowly, but it maintained that distance, making no attempt to close the gap. "Well, if all you want to do is watch, you're welcome to," he muttered.

The wall quivered under his hand; one of the large creatures had struck the wall and was clinging to it. In a moment, it pulled away, moved to an area a little way off, and did the same thing. The motion reminded him of an algae-eater in his old aquarium back home. Maybe it was eating all this stuff growing on the walls— anemone-type creatures and whatnot. That made it less likely to come after him, although that wouldn't protect him from being accidentally ingested.

Another of the big things swam down past him, its back like a ridged, chitin-covered whale. It disappeared beyond the reach of another light pulse. The passage of the huge creature distracted him. Just as he turned his attention back to the coral-rock wall, something lunged out at him.

The slow-motion feeling of adrenaline took over. In the enhanced view he saw a mouth like a hundred-toothed grinder, tendrils stretching out like a net about him. The serpentine, segmented body was wider than his own. He didn't have a chance of dodging it, couldn't even finish putting up his hands—

A blur of motion and a whipsawing current, a shockwave through the water, and the attacking creature was *gone*. Campbell glanced around, trying to grasp what had just happened, when he saw his enigmatic companion with a four-meter long wormlike thing twitching in its now-open jaws.

"Well, I'll be damned. You nailed it before it could get me. Why, I wonder?"

The ever-hopeful, and anthropomorphizing, part of himself wanted to assume that this was a gesture of friendliness, a creature that might even be sapient as humans and Bemmies measured such things, protecting a unique and interesting visitor to their realm. The more realistic and cynical part noted the way in which his companion tore into the body and let some parts drop while dragging the others upward, chewing briskly. He suspected that it had simply been curious, and then taken advantage when Campbell's movement had drawn out one of its preferred meals.

"Well, either way, I'm obliged. Thank you very much, my finny friend," Campbell said with a grin. He bobbed slightly in the creature's direction and flashed dimly at it. If it *was* intelligent, it might even recognize potential gratitude.

Still, he'd gotten hellishly lucky. He couldn't let himself get distracted like that again. He couldn't be sure these things couldn't pierce his suit. Whatever made those islands able to support themselves had to be something like carbonan reinforcement, so what if that thing's teeth had something like that?

In a little while, the dim lighting showed the dancing reflections of air above. His head broke the surface, and he immediately looked back down; a lot of predators on Earth would often choose the moment their prey was on the surface to attack. However, his strange companion still floated about fifteen meters off, and nothing else seemed interested in him.

"Well, my friend, this is where I say goodbye. Thanks for the escort, even if you didn't mean it."

Without water to interfere, he could easily make out the fact that he was in a vast, cavernous space that stretched upwards at least a kilometer. The wall was almost vertical, but very rough, with numerous ripples, creases, and other defects that afforded a reasonable grip. About a hundred meters above him was a large hole, maybe fifteen meters across. Could it be the base of one of those columns they'd seen on the surface? That seemed his best bet.

It was going to be a hell of a climb. Sergeant Campbell dug in his hands and his feet and started moving up, one step at a time. There were people out there who needed him. There was no way he was going to stop.

Chapter 37

"That's the solution, Tav!" Xander grinned across at the younger boy, waiting to see if he understood what he'd said.

Tavana scratched his head. "What? I was just mentioning our traditional canoes back—" he broke off, and a grin spread across his face. "How stupid can I be? *Oui*, of course, the canoes. The *outrigger* canoes!"

"What are you both talking about?" demanded Maddox.

"What to do with the port wing. We were able to retract the pieces remaining of the starboard wing, but the port wing's damaged. It's still mostly there—we don't want to retract it all, we'd probably have to dump what's left of the port wing jet, and I think that might be able to be salvaged if I can get the time to work on it. What to do with the wing, that was the question," Tavana said. "But now we know. We will make it an outrigger. That will make *LS-88* much more stable in the water. Reconfiguring that much will let us keep the port jet, even though that won't be working."

Xander was already hooked into the systems, checking the configuration that would be needed. Weight, center of gravity, balance . . . He felt his spirits rising. "Yeah, I think we can extend it out far enough fore and aft to make a reasonable float support. Here are the specs."

Tavana nodded as he received the information and started interfacing directly with the controls. After a few minutes, however, he rolled his eyes. "Make a guess."

It wasn't a difficult guess for Xander. "The rear jets and the tail. We'll have to go outside and use the service and test interfaces to force the shifts."

"You are correct. And more. The jet casing, it is damaged and some pieces are in the way of the shift. They will need to be pulled in enough to let the morph proceed."

"And?"

"And that has to happen *when* I start the morph, at least at the beginning—enough to make sure it stays clear for the complete reconfiguration."

A diagram of the situation blinked up on his omni. The external casing of the jet was peeled back, with two long spikes of metallic composite projecting directly into the morph path. "Oh. We'll *all* have to go out there."

"I can't figure it any other way. I have to trigger and direct the shift—this is a custom job, never done before—and those stupid pieces of casing will be *hard* to move. You can probably move one yourself—"

"But," Francisco finished, "Maddox can't. He'll need me to help."

And even that might not be enough. "Couldn't we just pull them out of the way one at a time?"

"No, the whole pathway has to be clear, at least to start. Once they start moving, the notched areas those shards are resting in will be out of the way and possibly we can let go."

Xander studied the diagram and came to the conclusion that Tavana was right. They couldn't spend days and days trying to figure a way around this. They had a long journey ahead of them and didn't even know how fast *LS-88* would go in the water.

"All right, everyone. Suit up. Let's get this done and get moving!"

Before he stepped out, he looked in on the lieutenant. The telltales showed that Dr. Kimei's therapy coding had taken hold, and reconstructive operations were underway. At a best guess, in three or four days they'd be able to finally let Pearce Haley out of her suit.

And then I'll have to tell her about the sergeant. A few scattered blips last night had given him a momentary hope, but they'd been intermittent and finally ended. Probably the sergeant's suit, or pieces of it, floating to the surface and running out of power. No, Campbell was gone, and Xander would have to tell Lieutenant Pearce Haley that the man who'd done everything to keep them all alive wasn't here to see that he'd succeeded.

But at least she'd be alive and on the way to recovery, he reminded himself. The sergeant would've been ecstatic.

"Maddox, check the outside."

"I can't see anything outside the top lock except sky, bro," Maddox said. "Problem with it being straight up. We should probably put a camera on the top somewhere."

"Let's do that now. Who knows how often we're going to have to go outside on this trip? Break out the perimeter monitors we made and we'll put a couple of them on the upper hull. Don't need the supports, just the camera units."

Francisco ran back into the cargo area and came back dragging two of the monitor cases. "This is what you meant, right?"

"Good work, Francisco." It only took a few minutes to remove the camera heads. "We can probably gecko-tape these things onto the hull. What do you think?"

"Should work," Tavana agreed. "Maddox, the optics— can they be adjusted to a wider field of view? I seem to remember—"

"Yeah, that's no problem. I'll give them about a one-ninety each. They'll have a few degrees overlap on each side and that'll give us full coverage."

By the time all the preparations were done, Xander realized it was lunchtime. It would be another hour before they were once more assembled at the lock. "All right, everyone. I'm going first, since we don't have the monitors out there yet."

Not entirely to his surprise, there was a faint hiss and sound of motion as he pushed the airlock door open. Cautiously sticking his helmeted head out, he saw two of the flat, gray, slick ray-like creatures. "A couple of those 'raylamps,' as the Kimeis called them," he reported. "Wonder what they're doing here? It's not like LS-88 is bleeding or anything." He climbed out on the upper hull. The raylamps slid farther away, so he gestured for the others to come up.

"Who knows?" Tavana said. "They may be eating the tree-anemones that seem to like our hull as an anchor. We're still in the debris field of our island, so the water all around may smell like a dinner. Maybe the hull material combined with the water and our electrical field makes them think this is edible. I don't know. Just keep the nasty little things away from me."

Xander grinned sympathetically. Tavana hadn't forgiven the creatures for the scare he'd gotten, and Xander couldn't blame him. With the worst features of manta ray, squid, and lamprey, the raylamps really didn't have much to recommend them to anyone. "I'll go kick these guys off before we start work."

"Why not just shoot them?" Tavana asked.

Xander shook his head. "Two reasons. First, even though *LS-88* is tough, I really don't like shooting firearms near her hull. Second, that'd just scatter pieces of dead things near us. No point in chumming the water, right?"

Tavana grunted. "*Oui*, you are correct. I should have thought of that. Two or three of those things are no problem, but from what the Kimeis said they can swarm."

Using prybars to adjust the broken engine casing, Xander and Maddox shoved the two raylamps— with some lashing, ineffectual protesting from the creatures—off the deck. They slid down the curve of the hull, struck the edge of the port wing, and then fell into the water. "Good, now let's get the monitors on and get to work!"

The camera heads were secured with gecko-tape—a generic term for adhesive materials that used Van Der Waals forces to achieve adhesion on virtually any surface without damage or marring of the original surface. After a couple of strong tugs to make sure the monitors were secure, and after verifying operation, the four boys finally made their way down onto the port wing.

"Too bad we don't have gecko *boots*," Tavana said, as the entire vehicle rocked gently in the swell.

Xander nodded. The wind was gentle, the sun shone, the sky and sea were blue and green, and the waves were small and regular, but Xander agreed with the sentiment. He'd *really* have liked to be sure that he couldn't lose his footing, and there were a lot of areas his adjustable magnetics couldn't grip well on the wing. "Well, we don't, so everyone just be careful."

Tavana found the control interface and locked his TechTool into place. Augmented-reality imagery materialized in Xander's retinal display.

"All right! I see good responses from the control network!" Tavana's voice was cheerful, and Xander saw answering smiles all around. "Now, the engine should have parts of it marked in your displays, yes?"

The damaged jet, in a generally upright "liftoff" configuration, glowed with various red, blue, and green lines. "Yes," he said, and heard Maddox and Francisco echo it.

"Good. Xander, you have the area farthest from me, near the damaged edge. Francisco, Maddox, you are closer to the main hull."

As Xander approached, he could see an area clearly highlighted with arrows, showing where to put his prybar. He slid the bar down and hooked the curved elements into the indicated slot between one part of the jet's casing and the remainder of the configurable wing. On the other side, Maddox and Francisco did the same. "Got it."

"Yes, good. Now, when you see red arrows in your retinals, push *hard* in the direction the arrows point, understand?"

"Got it!" Francisco said.

"Okay, we will do a little practice, just to get ready. Don't push too hard in these practice runs, though."

With a few tests, Xander found that the three of them could easily synchronize the push-and-pry motion. "I think we're ready."

Tavana's brilliant grin flashed out. "This time, the pushes will have to be full strength, yes? Especially for you and Francisco, Maddox."

"No problem!"

"If this works," Xander reminded them, "this whole wing is going to morph. The far end there will bend down and stretch out. Parts of this will be shifting in and out. It's not dangerous for us directly, but keeping our balance is not going to be easy. Move to the center of the wing as soon as that starts happening, understand?"

Francisco nodded vigorously, dark hair emphasizing the motion. "We understand."

"All right." Tavana squatted down next to the Tech-Tool, making sure it was in position. "Here we go!"

The red arrows came on, blinking insistently. Xander threw his weight against the prybar, saw the casing yield just a tiny bit and pushed harder. Nearby, Maddox and Francisco strained against their own bar.

A sudden *click-whirr* vibrated through the prybar, and the entire wing started to shift. "That's done it!" Tavana shouted triumphantly.

The four boys were suddenly forced to dance towards the center as the material of the wing *flowed*, parts of it narrowing, others lengthening. The tip swelled and bent down, stretching out as it touched the water, turning into a float. *LS-88* tilted upwards, leveling out from its prior slight portside list.

At that moment, a wave, slightly higher than the others, passed directly under the float. Francisco lost his balance and started to fall.

Xander didn't think. He dove forward and caught the boy, pushing him back towards the center of the wing. Just as he saw Francisco rolling safely to rest near the base of the wing, Xander felt his body pitch outward into empty space. He grabbed desperately for the wing, but the still-in-progress morph made it impossible to get a grip, and he dropped straight into the green sea.

It was only a drop of about two meters, so the impact wasn't much. The water closed above his head, but with the helmet sealed, Xander didn't have to worry about getting wet.

The gray-black shadow that turned towards him as he started to float back to the surface, however, *did* worry him. A *raylamp*.

He began stroking swiftly towards the deployed float; if he could get onto that, climbing back onto the wing would be pretty easy. "I'm okay!" he shouted back in answer to the concerned babel of voices from his friends. "Just got to get to—*whoa!*"

Something caught his foot and pulled back, dragging him underwater again. He looked down to see the slick tendrils of the raylamp entwining his boot. A faint pressure and grinding sensation told him the thing was trying to bite him. He kicked, hard, twice, and the creature was forced to let go. Then another dark shadow crossed the sun and tendrils spread across his helmet, tendrils with a sucking, crystal-toothed circular orifice in the center, gnawing and biting right in front of his face.

His own cry of horror and disgust rang in his ears, amplified by the helmet. *It can't get through*, he told himself, *it can't get through*, but there was a visceral revulsion to seeing that hungry, pulsating maw mere centimeters from his eyes. He brought up his arms and beat at the raylamp, his blows slowed by the water but still pushing hard, and it released its grip for an instant.

Immediately Xander shoved hard again, getting the creature clear of him. He turned towards the float, but now something had hold of his boot again. Adrenaline sent a shock of terror straight through him as a *third* gray-black form rippled up through the water. *I'm a struggling object on the surface. I'm sending the signals of a distressed creature!*

But it was too late to change his behavior; two of the things were already on him, the third on its way, with maybe more homing in. The damaged, dying island nearby must have drawn scavengers and opportunistic predators from hundreds of kilometers around, and he was just one more morsel for them to sample.

With a supreme effort he kicked, lunged, and managed three more strokes, his fingers actually brushing the float before two sets of tendrils hooked his legs and yanked him back down. Xander tried to get his gun out. He wasn't even sure it would work properly underwater, and one set of tentacles was spread across the holster. He tugged desperately at it, got the gun partially out, and then another creature seized his arm, twisting it, sending the weapon spinning uselessly into the water to dangle, out of reach, at the end of its lanyard.

Oh, God, no, they're mobbing me. Even if they can't get through the suit, they'll drag me down until it's too deep for the suit to take, and then—

He fought. The heavy, slick bodies were easy targets, but the tendrils and gripping, grinding mouths slowed him, dragging him farther down.

His fist, driven by the strength of panic and desperation, finally drove *through* one of the raylamps. He instantly felt a shift, a movement, as the creatures turned on one of their own. With a twist and a leap off of the back of one, he sprang towards the surface, only twenty meters above him. *Please, please let them be distracted, please—*

But a glance down showed a swarm rising, as though they knew things that made for the surface were vulnerable. Other shapes moved in the dim green, but all he could think of was to swim, swim, *swim as fast as you can—*

He wasn't fast enough.

Black slick hunger wrapped around him, and he screamed. There were streaks on the helmet—he didn't know if that was just drool or if the thing was scratching its way through.

Without warning there was a thudding concussion, a shockwave that Xander felt throughout his entire body and echoed through the water. Another followed. He felt something else seize him and darkness was rent into brilliant sunshine. He was hurled from the water, skidding full-length onto the now fully-formed outrigger float; instinctively he reached out and wrapped his arms tightly around one of the float's two supports. *What the...*

The water seethed nearby, and three more shock-waves echoed from beneath. A large creature, streamlined, four-finned, over three meters long, streaked from the depths and leapt into the air, a raylamp caught in its mouth.

And then another shape burst from the water and heaved itself up onto the outrigger. "Can't you boys stay out of trouble for a couple days?" demanded a grinning Sergeant Campbell.

Chapter 38

"Whoa, whoa, boys, let a man catch a breath," Campbell said. Despite his words, he couldn't wipe the grin from his face, and he didn't make any attempt to pull either Francisco or Maddox from their tight grips on his suit and Xander's. He could feel Xander shaking and couldn't blame him. That had been a hell of a horror show. If he'd gotten there a few minutes later...

Finally he pushed away. "If you're done out here, let's get inside and I'll tell you about it. After I get out of my damn suit and get cleaned up, that is."

"*Si! Si!*" Francisco had lapsed into Spanish, something he almost never did anymore. "*Estoy tan contenta de que estés vivo!*"

"So am I, believe me, son. Now let me get somewhere I can clean up and sit down."

By the time he managed to use the shower and get dressed again, the others had set up the table, turned the seats to face it, and there was an honest-to-god Buckley dinner waiting. "Guess you figured I hadn't eaten much the last couple days."

"Nothing worth eating anyway," Tavana said. "The helmet rations, I have tried them, and maybe they will keep you alive. Maybe you will not *want* to be alive after a while."

"Amen to that, son. Thank you all kindly."

"Should we call the Kimeis? They'll want to know."

"I was about to suggest it myself. No point in doing this twice, right?" He suited actions to words. "Dr. Kimei and family, this is Sergeant Campbell calling. Got a few minutes?"

"*Sergeant Campbell?!*" It was Sakura's disbelieving voice. "Oh, thank God! Dad, did you—"

"We heard, Saki." Akira Kimei's face, sweaty and covered with soot, appeared. "Sergeant, as you can hear, my daughter—and the rest of us—are tremendously relieved to hear that you are all right."

"I was about to bring the boys up to date on that. If you're at a point where you could pause whatever you're doing, I'd be happy to have you all in on it."

"Give us . . . fifteen, twenty minutes? I have to make sure the fire's well-stoked. Everyone has to make their way here, so that we can keep the furnace going."

"I can wait. Just a clarification . . . what exactly are you *doing*?"

"We're smelting iron," Caroline answered, her face materializing near her father's.

"Iron?" Xander repeated disbelievingly. "How . . . this isn't land! I mean, not really. How in the world—worlds—can you—"

"Limonite," she said proudly.

Xander looked puzzled for a moment, and then his face cleared. "Bog iron. The swamps last long enough to accumulate bog iron!"

Caroline's expression was pleased. "Oh, you're quick! It never even occurred to me, not until after we found it. There must be a lot of species of the floatcoral that concentrate iron—maybe it's an important nutritional component for various symbiotes, I don't know yet—but that means when the streams run down—"

"—they dissolve or wear away particles containing iron, then they precipitate out in the bog or get eaten and concentrated by bacterial action. Yes."

Campbell let the two—with the other Kimeis arriving and adding their own comments—continue the technical discussions as he ate. Once more, he found himself incredibly impressed by the Kimeis' achievements. They started with almost nothing and had lived here for a year, even built themselves a home. Of course, they also had the right people for the job. Still . . . it was impressive.

"We're ready, Sergeant."

He was just finishing off the peach cobbler, savoring every startlingly fresh-tasting bite. "You probably saw me falling down the rabbit hole—"

Sakura shuddered. "Yes. You disappeared into the crack between pieces."

"Wasn't any fun, either. The water surged and then it sucked me down, *way* down, bashed me all over the place until I lost consciousness. I would've been dead without my nanos."

He narrated what had come next: awakening in darkness and the realization that he was somehow stuck underwater inside an island fragment.

"Of course," Whips murmured. "That's why we couldn't detect you. That much water and rock—"

"Perfect shielding. Heck, even a few feet of water'll do it." He detailed his slow exploration of that underwater realm of darkness and ghost-lights and his near-disaster with the worm-thing and his strange companion. "So then I started climbing. Took a while; my leg's not really up to snuff yet, so I had to stop every so often, lock the suit, rest, and keep going.

"Finally, I reached a darker-than-dark patch and found, sure enough, it was the base of one of those forest columns. The island piece I was inside of must have been tilted. I made my way down that after resting for a bit, and I could see light ahead of me, blocked by something that moved. Whatever it was, though, I didn't find out. It moved away from me and disappeared, dropped off the end I'd guess.

"So I got to the opening and looked out. *Damnation* but the setting sun looked good to a guy stuck in that pit for all that time, but I was mostly worried about finding out what'd happened to the boys."

He remembered the worry as he scanned the waters over and over again. "I stretched as far out of that hole as I dared. Even with the tilt I'd followed, the end was pretty high up—must've been thirty, forty meters easy. At first, I didn't see anything—just pieces of island, little tiny rocks, bigger blocks the size of houses, waterborne hills, all the way to things that were small floating mountains.

"My biggest fear—other than that you boys had all crashed and been killed, of course—was that you were on the other side of the chunk I was on. I'd have to climb onto the outside of that column, make my way back to the fragment's main body, and then somehow go around it or up on top where I could make a full three-sixty survey. Didn't like those odds, or the amount of time it'd take."

He took a drink of water. "Still wasn't getting reception, either. That rock was interfering. I don't know what else was going on there. Maybe the iron content you mentioned, who knows. Anyway, after a while, I figured I'd climb out of the column, see if I could get some reception and get through to someone.

"Turned out that someone upstairs has a sense of humor. After managing to swim more than a hundred meters through a black sea, climb another hundred, and then walk down that slime-slick column, it was the top edge of the column that decided to let me down. Broke right off in my hand."

"But you were forty meters up!" Sakura said.

"And aware of that all the way down, yeah. But this is a military suit. Dropping like that has some options your average suit doesn't have to order. I straightened out and let it go to drop-dive configuration. Bit of a slam when I hit, but that didn't bother me—as I was falling, I saw a glint that I knew wasn't coral, and if it wasn't coral, it pretty much had to be *LS-88*."

"So why didn't you surface and call?"

"Tried to once. Didn't work, surrounded by all that shattered crap. Anyway, I didn't know if you boys were alive, and the Kimeis were too far away to give anything other than moral support. If *LS 88* was floating on the ocean, either you were waiting for me . . . or you were wrecked. Since I hadn't been able to contact you, I was pretty sure that you had given up on me. I know *I* would have, given what happened. So that meant that the ship was down. I'd have made my way there anyway, even if I did get hold of you boys. You couldn't bring that beast safely into those waters, not with all the wreckage around . . . and then I saw that monster out there eat another piece of island, and I was *sure* I didn't want you even thinking about trying."

Sakura and the boys were staring at him. "So you *swam* back here...with all those things in the water?"

He grinned. "Like I said, this is a military suit. It's got great swimming morphs—I can move a *lot* better in the water than any ordinary human—and I have a military-issue sidearm that works fine underwater."

"I wasn't sure mine would," Xander said, paling a bit as he recalled his recent ordeal.

"Probably would," the sergeant said, "but yours isn't made for that. Mine is, if I don't do it too often. Pressure differential isn't good for it in the long run. Anyway, survival on a planet's one of my specialties. I traveled far enough under that I didn't look like debris, and I used my imaging suite to see a lot farther than you boys could have managed."

He stepped to the door and tossed a few scraps out into the water. Something rose up, snapped, and rolled back, exposing a brilliant scarlet fin. "And then there was *him*. About nightfall, when I was trying to decide what rock I was going to go rest on, I saw something following me. I can't prove it, but when I got a look, I was sure that it was my old friend from inside the island. Why he'd come all the way out and come after me, I had no idea. But he was there, and he watched as I finally climbed up on one of the medium-sized rocks that still had a lot of vegetation on it."

Akira leaned forward in his projected image. "Fascinating. You're sure it was the same creature?"

"Like I said, I can't *prove* it. But Finny there had followed me all the way up to the top of the water, so it was either him or his twin brother."

"Very interesting." Akira vanished off-screen,

presumably putting more charcoal into the fire, but Campbell knew he was still listening.

"I didn't want to go on if it was dark, and I was pretty sure that the boys weren't going to launch in the dark either, even if they *could* launch. The fact the ship was still there didn't speak well for their chances—though by the looks of things I was being way too pessimistic." He smiled broadly at the boys.

"Anyway, once it was light, I grabbed a quick bite from my dispenser and dove back in. Sure enough, there was Finny. He moved to about fifteen meters off and followed, just like he had before. I had a feeling he wanted to see where I was going." Campbell grinned. "Of course, I keep saying 'he,' but for all I know Finny's a girl. Or a member of some other sex that we don't have a good word for.

"Now where was I? Oh, that's right. I'd taken a good look around from atop my little boulder, and I'd been able to make out *LS-88* about eight kilometers off. That's quite a paddle, but I wasn't worried about making it—as long as the ship didn't take off, or sink, while I was *en route*. Swimming, I'd be underwater and incommunicado, and I'd already decided that there was no way I'd want you coming after me in that mess anyway."

He looked into the distance, remembering. "I got a glimpse of the island-eater that made me sure I'd made the right choice. Thought I saw *land* underneath me at first, a wide, wide ridge like a submerged mountain. And then I realized it was *moving*. Honest to God, I've never felt so damn small in all my life. It cruised on beneath me, kept going, going, *going* like it was never going to end, and really it didn't. As it got narrower the part I could see just got deeper until I couldn't see it anymore.

"Finny had the same reaction. The two of us just froze in the water, hanging there as still as could be as that monster went by. When I thought it was finally past, I took a look around, and that's when I saw it—two 'its,' really. Nasty gray-black things. They'd been drifting up on Finny from behind. Now, I knew Finny could take care of himself, but still, I didn't like the looks of those things. Then I saw a bunch more. Maybe they're like scavengers following the big predator around? Anyway, I moved quickly towards Finny. He swam toward one of them and it flowed out of the way.

"'There,' I said, 'guess we're even for that worm-thing you saved me from.' He didn't say anything, but he did keep following me.

"We were about three hundred fifty meters away from *LS-88* when Finny suddenly darted a little ahead of me. He seemed to be startled or excited about something, so I swam faster to keep up. Sure enough, when I got close I saw someone—you, Xander—being attacked by the same gray-black things, and, well, you know the rest."

Xander went and waved to where the creature might be; "Finny" wasn't visible at the moment. "Thanks to him, then."

"That's a remarkable tale," Akira said. "Do you think your 'Finny' actually has sapience?"

"Akira, I could name two species that people swore up and down were fully sapient and turned out to be nothing of the sort, and you could name at least one that people thought the opposite of, and were wrong. Whatever he is, I'm grateful for his help and the company."

"Fair enough. We'll have to keep an eye out for his species around here. Perhaps I'll have a chance to make a real evaluation one of these days."

"Let's hope so. But for now, I want to get ready to head out. Thanks for listening."

"Thanks? You couldn't have *stopped* us from listening!" Sakura said emphatically, and the other girls—including Laura—nodded. "And we're so happy you're back!"

"Well, thank you kindly, Saki, and all the rest of you. Now, if you'll excuse us, I need my boys to bring me up to date on what they've done, so that—not too long from now—we can all sit down together for real!"

He turned to the others as the Kimeis, and Whips, waved and vanished. "All right, boys; tell me what we've got!"

Chapter 39

"Okay, here's where we find out if all that work you did pays off," Campbell said from the pilot's seat.

"Hold on," Tavana said. Everyone looked at him, and he felt his face going hot.

"What's up, Tav?" Xander asked.

"Well...it is tradition to have a name for a ship, yes? And I do not think *LS-88* is really a good name. We will be going a long ways in this ship. Shouldn't we name it?"

The others were quiet, and Tavana looked down. "Sorry, I...let's just go."

"No, no, son, I'm sorry. You're perfectly right. We should've named her months ago when we were living in her. Now, sailing the poor thing halfway around the world—"

"More like a sixth of the way," Maddox said.

"Don't get all technical with me, son. It's all the same if you had to swim it," Campbell retorted. "You got any names in mind, Tav?"

"Well...I was thinking of something from home. At least partly."

"You mean Tahitian?"

"It's an outrigger, like our old canoes, so I was thinking the name should have *Maui* as part of it—Maui is like the biggest hero-god figure in all of Polynesian mythology, and—"

Campbell grinned. "Don't need to explain, Tavana. I've heard some of those legends. Fisherman, trickster, catcher of the sun, and lifter of the heavens. A good name to travel with."

"But it should be a name for here, too," Francisco said.

"Right," agreed Xander. "So it should be something-Maui, or Maui-something."

"How about *Emerald Maui*?" Maddox suggested. "Our name for the planet, and for the system, and your hero-god's name?"

Tavana felt a sudden glow of *rightness*. "I like that!"

"So do I!" Francisco said—not surprising, of course.

"It's settled, then," Campbell said. "Here, let me go get something..."

He came back from the cargo area with one of the emergency water bottles. "Not much of this left, but we don't need it anymore," he said. "Genuine water from Earth. C'mon, kids, let's go topside for a minute."

Tavana went up first with a prybar just in case, but the cameras showed that for once there weren't any raylamps or anything else on the hull. They'd been drifting slowly away from their island, and the activity was dying down. The five of them gathered in a circle around the airlock and Campbell handed Tavana the water bottle. "Your idea, your show."

"Oh, okay." He hadn't thought much about any ritual, but he'd seen a few ships christened. "Ummm... We are about to embark on a long voyage across an unknown sea, as my ancestors did between the great islands thousands of years ago. We travel to meet new friends and start a new life. Let us survive the perils of *moana*, the sea, and be guided by the spirit of Maui. So in his honor we name this ship, *Emerald Maui*, christened with the water of Earth on the seas of Lincoln!"

The bottle was unbreakable, so he just poured the sparkling-clear water across the hull, polishing it to a mirror-gloss in the warm orange glow of the rising sun.

"That was a damn good speech for off-the-cuff, Tavana. Got some poet in you?"

He grinned, feeling a bit embarrassed but proud at the same time. "In my family, there are some who were good at that. Maybe I have inherited it, a little."

"I'll make a picture of this!" Francisco announced.

"That's a great idea," Xander agreed, as they began to go back down. "Wait until we're underway and we're sure everything's working."

"I have a good feeling about that," Campbell said. "Everyone strap in and we'll find out!"

Tavana made sure he was locked down securely, and then linked into *Emerald Maui*'s systems. "The name is now recorded in the ship's records. We are now officially *Emerald Maui*, formerly *LS-88*. Rear jets fully converted to waterjet configuration. Reactor showing all green. Outrigger showing stable. Ready whenever you are, Sergeant."

"Captain?"

Xander gave the somewhat sheepish yet proud grin he still wore whenever Campbell referred to him that way. "Start us on our way, Sergeant, at your discretion."

"Yes, sir!"

A low, throbbing hum echoed from the rear, the jets taking in seawater and then expelling it at high temperature and speed behind. Tavana felt *Emerald Maui* begin moving forward.

"Well, she's working so far. Tail-rudder configuration testing as we get up to speed."

The rocking of the vessel, so noticeable when still, diminished, fading to almost nothing. *Emerald Maui*, the former *LS-88*, had major advantages over the old-style canoes, and the largest was sheer size—it was well over thirty meters long and made of the most advanced materials available to human ship engineering. *Emerald Maui* was an iron, plowing over the waves that it dwarfed in this currently calm sea. *So far so good . . .*

"And we're now over ten knots, almost twenty kilometers per hour!" Campbell said cheerfully. "Let's try this rudder out!"

Emerald Maui began a slow, majestic turn. As it did, Tavana heard several thuds below.

"What was that?" Xander demanded.

Tavana was already scanning the sensor records. "Looks to me like minor hull impacts. We're running over the debris left in the water around us. We might also sometimes have—"

The ship's smooth engine sound paused, like a giant with hiccups, making the whole cabin vibrate.

"—temporary interruptions in the jets as they deal with stuff coming through or getting stuck," Tavana finished.

"Is this going to be a problem?" Campbell asked; he'd straightened out the ship and decreased speed as they talked. "I mean, in the sense of endangering *LS*, er, *Emerald Maui*?"

Tavana looked at the records. "Not really. If we ended up going too fast or ran through too much of this stuff and it couldn't get passed through or removed from the jets, yes, but we aren't even close to the limits. The jets are really tough and designed as minimum-moving-component units. The hull's even tougher—layered microstructured foamed metals integrated with linked-carbon composites."

"You agree with him, Captain?"

Xander's focus was on mechanical engineering, not propulsive, and things like *can this take a beating?* were a little more in the older Bird's line than Tavana's. And as long as Xander was the captain, he had to be the one making the decision.

Xander didn't answer immediately. Instead, Tavana saw him link to the same databases Tavana had, and run his own simulation query. If it had been in a classroom setting, Tavana might've been a little annoyed. But if their desperate adventure to survive had taught him anything, it was that there was nothing stupid about checking things two, three, or four times if you had to.

Xander sat back and nodded. "He's right. The only theoretically weak area on *LS-88* is that point where it got a little overheated on re-entry, and even that won't matter unless we try pushing her to hypersonic."

"Okay, then, we'll run her up and ignore the little noises unless you boys say otherwise."

This time the rumble of the engines increased to a low thunder. The cameras showed a beautiful arrow-straight double wake following them, one broad and coming from the main ship, another narrow from the outrigger cutting through the green sea. *Emerald Maui* turned smoothly to port, staying level. The outrigger showed minimal strain in Tavana's display; the turn to starboard was smooth and stable.

"I *like* this ship!" Campbell announced. "Solid, this is. You boys did some fine design work. What're we looking at for best speed, Tav?"

"Based on what I'm seeing? I think that if weather is good, we can cruise her at about fifty kilometers per hour!"

"Over twenty-five knots? Damn impressive."

Tavana grinned, proud of the performance. "Well, the ship, it has a nuclear reactor for power. It is not small, and we have a good stable outrigger. We could probably double that speed and hold together pretty well."

"Well, let's test your cruise speed."

The droning thunder rose another notch and *Emerald Maui* responded, lunging forward. The strain telltales barely twitched; even damaged as parts of the wings had been, the materials had vast reserves of strength. There was vibration through the hull, occasional *thunk!* sounds as pieces of floatcoral struck the hull. Once in a while one jet or the other hiccupped, but overall the motion was smooth, continuous, and powerful. Tavana let out a whoop of triumph.

"It works *great!*" Maddox said. "So how long until we get there? We'll have to drive only in the day, right?"

Campbell wrinkled his face. "Technically, no. No reason we can't have the GPS run things pretty much all the time. But there are only five of us, and honestly—sorry, Maddox, Francisco—only three of those can stand watch and take over if something goes wrong. Watchstanding's boring duty, too, so you need frequent reliefs. We can do a lot of automated stuff based on what the topside cameras see, but the fact is we still don't have sonar or radar, and even enhanced-spectrum cameras aren't as good for obstacle detection. So, practically speaking, we'll be doing this only during daylight hours, about eight hours' cruise out of every twenty-four average, because that's about all the time I think we can manage with a good alert lookout crew here. Once Pearce wakes up, we might be able to stretch that a bit. Doc Kimei thinks that'll happen pretty soon."

"What if something tries to catch us?"

Campbell shrugged. "Depends on the 'something,' Tav. There's nothing we can do about a creature the size of that island-eater except hope it misses, or that we sense it coming and get the hell out of the way. Something like that isn't really a pursuit creature, though. It gets moving and rams upward, but it isn't going to keep up with us on a surface chase.

"Smaller things? Well, like Tav said, this is a pretty tough ship, and it'll take something big and nasty to break it. So we've got to trust *Emerald Maui* can take whatever Lincoln throws at her."

He scratched his head. "Now, to get back to your question, Maddox. We've got about six thousand kilometers to go as the four-winged crow flies, but actually we're going to have to go around a large part of the Kimeis' island continent to reach them. Either course looks to me like it comes to about seventy-five hundred kilometers total. So figuring we keep to Tav's cruising speed and eight hours a day"—he squinted at apparently empty air—"I make it eighteen, nineteen days. A little less than three weeks."

"Well, then," Xander said, sitting straighter in his seat, "Let's not waste any more time. Like my uncle used to say, make it so!"

"Aye aye, Captain!"

With a rumble and a cheerful fountain of white foam, *Emerald Maui* turned and charged towards the sunrise.

Chapter 40

"We've got work to do," Whips announced at the breakfast table.

"And that's different from, like, every other day?" Sakura said.

He gave a buzzing snort in her direction. "I mean *new* work."

Laura looked up from spreading hedral jam on her driftseed bread. "You mean besides trying to figure out where our new friends should set up camp and getting things ready for them?"

"More of that, actually. And something we should probably figure out first." He triggered his omni, showing an outline of *Emerald Maui* based on the information Campbell's party had sent. "I'd almost forgotten how big a landing shuttle like *LS-88* is, and that's going to be something of a problem." He glanced around the table with his topside eye, but the others were just looking at him.

Akira shrugged apologetically. "Sorry, Whips, but I guess none of us are quite getting the point."

"*Emerald Maui* can't fly anymore. So when they

arrive, how are they going to get onto shore, back and forth, and unload cargo and all?"

Sakura hit her forehead with the heel of her hand. "*Duh!* We don't have a dock or anything like it!"

Laura frowned, nodding. "A very good point, Harratrer," she said, using his real name as she often did to emphasize how seriously she took something. "Sergeant Campbell and the boys could swim to shore, and perhaps the simple automation could do station-keeping, but unloading the cargo will need a loading ramp on a solid foundation."

"And we *want* that cargo unloaded," Whips said. All the heads around the table nodded. "Akira, we should be able to make use of a lot of that equipment without triggering anything, right?"

"I would think so. We know better than to just do huge clear-cut areas. Unlike their island, our floating continent seems to be in mostly good shape." He looked around, smiling at Hitomi as she took another slice of smoked capy. "So . . . you usually don't bring up a problem unless you have an idea, Whips. What do we do?"

Whips triggered the next set of commands. As the others studied the image, he let one of his multifingered hand-arms pull a large chunk of roast to his mouth. Beak and ripping tongue busied themselves for a few moments.

"So here you see the map we've managed to make of our continent—well, all of it we've been on, which isn't much. I'm overlaying the satellite views we can get now.

"The only really decent candidate for a harbor is at Broken Point, where the lagoon we landed in broke off. It's still got some pieces that curve around to make some protection from storms and such, and the 'skirt' that often grows out underwater from the shore hasn't regrown all that much. *Emerald Maui* should be able to get pretty close."

Melody shook her head. "It still can't get too close, though."

"Close enough," Whips said. "We just need to be able to get a line over to the ship from the shore. It'll be easy to do that—if we can't throw the line, I could swim it out there in seconds."

"There is no way even all of us together can pull that beast up on shore," Caroline said emphatically. "Especially if we have to get it up far enough that we can do unloading operations."

"The winch could do it!" Hitomi said unexpectedly.

"Exactly my thought, Hitomi. Plus we can add mechanical advantage with the block and tackle. If you remember, we were planning to try to do that with *LS-5*," Whips said.

"So we were. But *LS-5* was grounded right up against the shore; we would have needed to tip it down and drag it a few meters inland. Plus...well, *LS-5* was pretty much a wreck, much worse off than *Emerald Maui* is now. Dragging it across stone wasn't going to make it worse. We don't want to do much more damage to *their* ship."

"And *that* is where the work comes in. Old-fashioned solutions always involve lots of work." The next image was so self-explanatory that Akira started to laugh.

"Work indeed!" he said. "Float logs under *Emerald Maui*, and put more in front—rollers strong enough to support it, but still softer than the hull."

Hitomi looked worried. "But their ship is really, really big and heavy. Won't it just break the logs?"

Sakura smiled and shook her head. "Not if we pick good logs. Plenty of ancient peoples moved stones weighing tens of tons or more like this. And if we do it right, we might be able to set it up so that it's a sort of launch ramp, in case we need to get *Emerald Maui*—I really love that name, gotta remember to tell Tav—back into the water again. We don't really want to strand her."

"Good thinking," Laura said. "But you're right, this will not be easy. Those won't be small logs, and we'll have to drag or roll them down to the docking area."

Whips gave the arm-gesture and flickering pattern that meant *no*. "Not drag or roll. *Float*. We'll cut trees along the south shore and drop them in the water. We can guide them along the shore and down to the harbor. I'll swim on one side, and a few of you will walk along shore and pull with me. It won't be very fast, but it'll be a lot easier than trying to get all that lumber overland."

"You've really thought this through," Akira said. "All right, we'll do it. We can't stop everything else, though. Still have to stock up for our newcomers—even if they're going to get food along the way, we have to expand our facilities a bit—and there are still other projects. I think we can wait on the ironworks. The equipment they're bringing is a total game changer for that."

More than you could believe. Whips was proud of everything they'd done with essentially nothing, but with the equipment on *Emerald Maui*? They'd leap-frog *centuries* of technological progress. "Completely."

As usual, everyone looked to Laura to make the final call. She thought a moment while she finished her breakfast. "This is a good plan. Akira, you're the only one who can make halfway educated guesses about how much we can harvest without damaging our ecology here, so I want you and Whips and... ummm... Hitomi, I think, to go and start picking out the trees for this project. Take the SurvivalShot, just in case. The rest of the girls and I will keep the other projects going: some hunting, getting food prepared and preserved. I want to do a large smoking again soon. Once we've picked out the trees we can figure out a work roster for getting the logs to the harbor once they've been cut and trimmed."

"Sounds like a plan," Akira said, standing. "Let's wash up and get started!"

Chapter 41

The young woman's eyes flickered open with a flash of brilliant green, and then closed. They snapped open again suddenly, staring up at them. With difficulty, Pearce Haley's mouth opened. "S . . . Sergeant . . . ?"

Xander could barely make out the word, but Campbell was grinning so widely it looked like his cheeks might split. "Yeah, Lieutenant, you're awake again. And this time," his voice wavered just a touch, "this time, Pearce, it's for good."

Her lips managed a smile. "Still . . . feel half dead."

"You've been on ice even longer than last time, Pearce. Let your nanos bring you the rest of the way up before you move. There's no hurry, now." He gestured to Xander, who moved up and put the end of a narrow straw in Lieutenant Haley's mouth. "Take a tiny sip of that. You have to get moisture going down your throat and start the muscles working again."

She choked slightly on the first sip, waited a moment, and tried another. That one seemed to go down all right. She looked around. "We're still . . . on *LS-88*? But I feel gravity . . . movement. Are we . . . at Orado?"

Campbell sighed. "Sorry, Pearce. We couldn't get

there. We're on the god-damned strangest planet I've ever landed on, but it's a livable world, and that's the important part."

"A new planet? I mean . . . a planet not on the charts?"

"Completely off the charts. We're good and marooned, Pearce."

"But if that's true . . ." She stared at him. "How . . . did you do it? Fix me, I mean? I saw the data"—she took another sip—"before I went back under. Samuel, I was *dead*."

Campbell took her hand and squeezed it. "No one knew that better than me, Pearce. But we got luckier than we thought. *LS-5* survived the wreck, too."

"*LS-5* . . . the Kimei family! The doctor!" Pearce managed a real smile now. "A trained frontier doctor."

"Plus you remember all those nanomedical emergency supplements I pumped in you. That kept you going long enough for Dr. Kimei to put you back together via remote control."

"Remote?" Pearce gritted her teeth and levered herself up. Her freckles stood out on her pasty-white skin. She kept moving until she was sitting. Seeing the pain on her face made Xander wince in sympathy, but she said nothing about it, just sat breathing hard for a few moments. "Why didn't she come here? Or we go there?"

"Long story short, their shuttle's gone and ours isn't ever flying again, not without one hell of a lot of work. We're on our way to meet up with them. We've got about six thousand kilometers to go."

Emerald Maui chose that moment to hit something hard enough to make a bump ripple through the ship. Lieutenant Haley's eyes narrowed, and then widened. "Then . . . we're on water. We're a *boat*?"

"Yes, Ma'am!" Tavana said. "Welcome aboard *Emerald Maui*, Lieutenant Haley!"

She chuckled, a noise that turned to a cough that doubled her over with agony. She let the sergeant lay her back down. "God, everything hurts."

"I told you to take it easy. Coming out of months of suspension *and* having your body just about nano-rebuilt from scratch? You're lucky you can move at all right now. If Doc Kimei wasn't just that good, you'd be in that suit until next Christmas. Whenever that is around here."

It took another two hours before Lieutenant Pearce Haley was able to stand and finally take—with the sergeant's assistance—her first steps since they'd put her back into the suit. Once she started moving, though, Xander was astounded how quickly she adjusted. It was clear that she wasn't *nearly* back to her original self, but Pearce Haley wasn't wasting time on excuses or pain. "I am taking a real shower now," she said. "Or the best this shuttle can manage. And then I want to *eat*."

"We'll get you something," Campbell said. "But it won't be much."

He helped her over to the shower and turned his back while she stripped off her suit and got into the facility. "Your stomach's completely empty and hasn't been processing much of anything since you were suspended. You get a light broth and that's it until we see how you hold it down. Also do not lock that door. If you fall down I don't want to have to try a security override to get in."

"Yes, Sergeant," her voice answered from inside the tiny shower area.

"While she's doing that," Campbell said loudly, "Xander, go back and get an outfit for her. Small adult."

The clothes they'd found on board weren't terribly stylish—basically a variant of the heavy T-shirt and jean pants that had been a common working clothing style since the 1800s—but they were tough and easy to wear. Xander quickly found an outfit, and then realized he didn't know if there was appropriate underwear. A quick check of the crate revealed several packages of underwear on the side they hadn't dug into yet. He folded the clothes into a little pile and brought them up front. "Here, Sergeant."

"How you doin', Pearce?"

Her voice was exhausted, in pain but still cheerful. "Oh, getting there. Haven't fallen. But that skintight suit, um . . ."

"I'll grab it. We've got some other duds for you, don't worry."

Campbell snaked the now-empty suit out of the bathroom. "Tavana, I hate to do this to you again . . ."

"*Oui*, someone has to. Francisco, you will be helping me. Maddox and Xander are on forward watch right now."

"Ugh," said Francisco, but he followed after the older boy.

Tavana's words had reminded Xander that he had other things to do. He gave the clothes to the sergeant and left him to take care of Pearce.

Once they were alone, Pearce gave Campbell a look he couldn't quite interpret. It definitely made him uneasy. He busied himself with the environmental controls on a nearby instrument panel.

The lieutenant chuckled softly. "Nice try, Sam," she said. "But it's not going to work. While I was taking my shower, it dawned on me that although

I was pretty grungy I wasn't nearly as grungy as I should have been—unless someone gave me a cleaning somewhere along the way."

Campbell grunted noncommittally.

Haley chuckled again. "That someone would have been you, of course. It's not the sort of thing you would have delegated to one of the boys."

"Um," he said.

"You've now pushed the same button four times, and that panel's offline. I'd like an actual response, Sam."

"Okay. I . . . Um."

"What a conversationalist. All right, since it seems I have to do all the heavy lifting here, let me start by saying that one of these days I'd very much like to do a repeat of that process—well, more-or-less—while conscious."

That finally tore the sergeant's intent gaze from the control panel. His eyes widened as he turned to look at her.

"For Pete's sake, Sam," she said, with a bit of exasperation. "You can't be *that* clueless. I'm very attracted to you and I'm pretty sure the reverse is true."

He swallowed. "Well . . . Yes, it is. But I'm old enough to be—"

"My father? Not hardly. I'm twenty-eight and you're . . . what? Forty? Forty-one?"

"Forty-three," he said.

"That's a fifteen-year spread. Big deal. The average lifespan these days is around one hundred and thirty years. I know one couple where the woman is thirty-nine years older than her husband. They seem to be doing fine."

She held up her hand. "And don't bother prattling

to me about military regulations against fraternization between officers and enlisted personnel. I'm an officer in the regular UN military and you're employed by Colonial Security. Technically speaking, you're not in the military at all. You're a civilian contractor."

Seeing the scowl on his face, she laughed aloud. "Yes, sure—I know and you know and the man in the moon knows that almost all personnel hired by Colonial Security are ex-military and when push comes to shove Colonial Security does a lot more in the way of what you might loosely call 'combat' than any regular military does nowadays."

Campbell managed a crooked smile. "It's mostly thumping on belligerent wildlife, not what you could really call 'military action.' Still, we do see a lot more action than you regulars usually do. That's the main reason I resigned from the U.S. Army to take a job with CS. The extra money was nice, but mostly I was just bored. Earth is a pretty peaceful planet these days."

She nodded. "What I figured. But the relevant point insofar as you and I are concerned is that, first, we are not in the same chain of command. Secondly, the issue of 'fraternization' is a moot point. As far as military rules and regulations are concerned—even those of the Uniform Code of Military Justice that you uptight Americans favor—you are legally no different from a bartender that I might decide to hit on." A bit primly, she added, "Not that I would ever do such a crude and unladylike thing."

By now, Sam had managed to bring his embarrassment under control. "Lieutenant Haley, are you asking me out on a date?"

"Yes, Sergeant Campbell. I am."

He looked out the viewscreen at the ocean they were sailing across. "Dinner and a movie is out. Maybe a swim by moonlight?" Something very large and covered with spines and tentacles surfaced for a moment before sinking back under the waves. "Well, maybe not."

As it turned out, they just spent some time quietly talking and holding hands.

In the control cabin, all the boys were back in their seats. Xander was smiling slightly. Tavana had an expression on his face that was way more sophisticated than a sixteen-year-old's should have been. Maddox was obviously trying not to smirk. Francisco looked confused again.

Emerald Maui's forward camera showed mostly a boiling mass of white foam, occasionally punctuated by either a momentary glimpse of the sea and sky, or a green and empty flicker of underwater.

The topside cameras, rigged from the monitoring units they'd made back on the island, gave a much better view. *Emerald Maui* cruised swiftly through the water, still heading mostly to the east. The sky above was clear. In the distance there were wispy white clouds on the horizon.

"Anything, Maddox?" Xander asked.

"Actually . . . yes. Watch there, in front of the outrigger."

Several minutes went by. All he saw was the outrigger cutting its way cleanly through the water. "I don't see any—*WHOA!*"

Something leapt out of the sea in front of the

outrigger and fell back, surfing the wave front. *Four-finned profile* . . . "Is that the sergeant's 'Finny'?"

"Looks like him! But more than *just* him—watch in front of us!"

The long expanse of *Emerald Maui* got in the way of a view directly ahead, and the remaining built-in camera was still seeing mostly foam. But Xander caught a few glimpses of *something*, or maybe more than one something, leaping high enough for the monitor cameras to catch. "A . . . school or pod of Finnys?"

"Seem to be riding our wake like dolphins on Earth."

"I'll be darned. That's . . . interesting. Really interesting. I wonder if it really is the same one."

"If I could get a better picture we could probably tell. The sergeant's suit recorded a lot of video of Finny; he's got to have unique patterns or scars or something on him."

Xander thought a moment. "Might be able to do that, actually. Everything's clear ahead for as far as we can see, so I think I can cut the monitor for a few minutes. I'll revise its field of view so it's focused ahead of the outrigger only. That'll give it effectively much better resolution. We'll get a few pics that way, and then go back to the monitor configuration."

The software they'd already put into the monitor cameras made it an easy switch, and Finny—if that's who it was—made several good jumps in fairly quick succession. Xander got excellent photos of the alien creature.

The sergeant came up front, guiding Lieutenant Haley to one of the shuttle seats. "Okay, Pearce, here we are," he said. "And here's your soup. Drink it slow. If you keep it all down for a couple of hours, we'll be able to step it up a bit." He looked up. "How's it going, boys?"

"We might have friends, Sergeant." Quickly, Xander explained what Maddox had seen.

"Well, now, that's downright neighborly. Here, open up your omni interface. Okay, there you go. Those are the best shots of Finny I managed to get."

Xander ran the images through a comparator program, and the comparator lit up. "It's a match, Sergeant! Look, it's showing me these markings here, and the fin configuration, and—"

"Hold your horses, son. Yes, those do look pretty much like the kind of thing you'd expect to use to differentiate individuals, but we don't *have* footage of multiple individuals yet. Could be those are all characteristics of this lifeform that are really, really similar. I admit I think you're right, for the record, but let's not make assumptions about identifying an individual of another species when we aren't even sure we've seen a second of his type." He glanced at the display as Finny, or his twin, jumped again. "But it's fascinating either way."

Xander called up the map and satellite images; he added a transmit code for Pearce Haley, so her omni could decode it as well. "In two or three days we'll turn north, skirt the edge of the continent, and then run alongside it."

"Right. Stay *well* out to sea, mind; remember what Akira told us. These big, well-established colonies have shelves that extend around them for miles. We don't want to run aground."

"Then we . . ." Xander trailed off.

The satellite view showed land, sea, and clouds.

That wasn't unusual. But there was a huge swath of cloud ahead of their path. Even to Xander's untrained eye, there was something obviously threatening about it. It wasn't an undefined shape, but circular and almost spinning.

He reached out and triggered his omni to magnify the image. The circle of cloud swelled, showing a tiny dark spot at the center. Xander looked over and saw Campbell's mouth already tightening.

"Next," Campbell said in a deceptively cheerful voice, "we are going to find out how well *Emerald Maui* can survive a storm at sea."

Not just a "storm," Xander thought, but didn't say. *A hurricane.*

Chapter 42

Tavana gripped the armrests of his seat even tighter. The forward camera momentarily cleared as *Emerald Maui* reached the crest of one of the immense waves. He could see the gray-green, white-streaked masses of heaving water that surrounded them, the trough twenty meters below. Some of the waves looked as though they might be higher than *Emerald Maui* was tall. *"Hold on!"*

The shuttle tipped, plummeted down into empty space, and impacted with the water. *We tried to evade this storm*, he thought grimly, *but—like hurricanes across known space—it didn't follow our predictions. Took a sudden north turn and caught us full-on.*

Another rise, another sliding, crashing fall. The forward camera went dark, looking only into deep water roiled by the storm. Suddenly the topside monitor view rolled crazily and spun away. Half the display glitched— for a moment he could see two views: one looking over the rear of *Emerald Maui*, the menacing waves towering up all around, and a sideways view of the outrigger lander plowing its way doggedly through the impossible surf. The display glitched again, and then went black.

"We just lost the front topside camera," he announced.

"Damn. Thought we had them secured well enough."

Xander's exhausted voice answered. "Not much holds up to being hammered with water like this over and over again."

Maddox shook his head. "Can't we dive below ... *aaaaaaauuuugh!*" *Emerald Maui* hit another wave and slewed around, so this time the sickening drop happened both front and sideways. "... dive *below* these waves?" he finished.

"I'd like to, believe me, Maddox. But I don't know if we can manage it with the systems we don't really have." Campbell looked grim. "On the positive side, our nanos keep us from getting seasick, which would be a real big problem for me right about now."

Francisco nodded emphatically. "Me too, Sergeant."

Tavana thought about the diving idea. They might be able to reconfigure the remaining smart material on the starboard side to make a usable diving plane. It'd be easy to do on the port side, though he'd have to be careful to keep the engine from jamming the morph again.

"Sergeant? I think we might be able to. And it'd be a lot easier on us, I think."

The older man glanced at Tavana from his seat, then over at Xander, who nodded. "Let us see it."

Tavana transmitted the morph parameters. "See, make diving planes here. We can use the jets at high power—I am thinking about seventy percent—to drive us forward and down. At fifteen to twenty meters we level out. I can automate the controls of the jets and planes to keep us down." *Emerald Maui* normally floated, of course; it would take force to put her underwater. A good thing overall, but for diving it was a major impediment.

"Dive rating takes us to thirty, right?"

Campbell nodded. "Specs say thirty meters depth rated."

"I hate to be a killjoy," Haley said from her seat next to Campbell, "But I'd like to point out that if you're twenty meters down and one of those big waves goes by overhead, you're at least momentarily *fifty* meters underwater."

She's right. "Um. Then I don't know..."

"Let's not abandon the idea yet," Xander said. "There's got to be safety margin in this. Let's see if we can dig it out. We're seeing a lot of strain in the outrigger in this storm, so right now we've already got a situation that might end up breaking *Emerald Maui.*"

"Difference being that losing the outrigger will be a pain in the...rear, son, but having our hull integrity breached underwater will relieve us of any pain ever again," Campbell pointed out.

Two waves came together almost under *Emerald Maui*, a concussion of foam and ocean that heeled the improvised ship over by almost seventy degrees. Tavana heard his own shout of shock echoed by the others. *Emerald Maui* came back down with a shuddering crash and was momentarily buried in foaming water. The second topside camera went black.

"On the other hand," Campbell continued calmly, "if that's the kind of thing we might expect, the risk's worth taking. None of us are getting any sleep, and we haven't hit the worst yet."

Tavana started digging into the manual and maintenance data for *Emerald Maui*. "The information we need, it has to be in here somewhere."

"I'm setting up a simulation using the known specs,"

Xander said. "I know we'd rather have the real data, but this could at least let us know if the idea's crazy or not."

Tavana nodded. He dove deeper into the manuals, trying to ignore the rises, sudden falls, and thundering impacts as *Emerald Maui* continued its battle with the storm and sea. *Hull material strength ... seal designs ... Allowances for peak loading ...*

"It will work," Haley said abruptly into the middle of the storm-roaring silence.

"What?" Even Campbell, who had made clear how much he respected Pearce Haley's capabilities, looked startled. "Lieutenant, you're not an engineer—"

She grinned. "But I can do a search on databases like nobody's business. A *Newton*-class Landing Shuttle—same class as *Emerald Maui*—dove eighty-two meters underwater on Cambria, a planet with surface gravity 1.03, during a rescue operation to recover stranded divers. It made three trips and showed no sign of damage." Tavana's retinal display lit up, showing the link to the data Haley was talking about.

Xander looked impressed. "That's sure good evidence that there's a large safety margin on this thing."

"The main hull and seals still show all green," Tavana said. "We've put *Emerald Maui* through a lot, but her main body's still sound."

Xander and Campbell exchanged glances. From what Tavana could tell, they also had a short private exchange via their omnis. Finally, Xander sat back. "All right, Tav, we'll try it. If you can get the reconfigure to work."

"I think I can." *I hope I can. The port morph is going to be the tricky one, and if that goes wrong, it might be* really *bad. No one's going outside to fix it this time!*

Tavana modeled the port morph sequence six times; the others were clearly going to work within two or three tries. The jet was always the difficult part. But maybe he could simply accept a little inefficiency... he didn't need nearly all of the material...

Finally he nodded, heart beating fast. "Okay... here goes."

His omni displayed the progress for everyone as he began; no point in keeping anything secret. First the starboard wing remnants came together, forming a not terribly long but still functional diving plane. The rear rudder was next, forming into a set of diving and rudder planes for three-dimensional movement.

Then the port outrigger. "Hold on, it's going to get really rough for a few minutes."

The outrigger began to retract and reform. As it shrank and moved, the stability it had provided began to diminish, and *Emerald Maui* began to roll more and more. "God, even *with* my nanos I'm not sure I'll be able to keep lunch down," Haley muttered.

Francisco looked paler than usual. "Tavana, make it stop spinning! I don't like it!"

"Just a little longer!"

The entire middle section—containing the damaged but still-hopefully-salvageable engine—suddenly folded inward, coming to rest against the main hull. The morph continued, binding and reinforcing that section. It left a simple diving plane sticking out to the port side, a little broader to make up for the slightly asymmetric shape that *Emerald Maui* now presented to the water.

"Diving!"

As a massive wave loomed up before them, *Emerald Maui's* diving planes angled down and the rear jets' song rose to a vibrating roar that rivaled the storm. The shuttle lunged forward, digging into the side of the wave like a dagger, tunneling inward and downward.

The wave passed overhead and the trough approached, but *Emerald Maui* drove hard down, down, and then leveled out.

It was suddenly quiet in the shuttle. Only the droning of the jets—less intense now that they weren't sucking in air as well—made its way into the cabin. There was a sense of rising and falling, but vastly smaller, far less intrusive, and without the impact and violence of the intersection between air and water.

"At a depth of . . . twenty-three meters. Peak pressure indicates waves between fifteen and thirty meters, mostly around twenty," Tavana said after a moment. "No leaks, no alerts aside from a depth warning."

"Can we maintain this depth?" Campbell asked.

"I think so. That's something we can automate. We won't have GPS guidance, but I think we can keep roughly on course."

"What's our headway?"

"You mean, how fast are we moving?" Tavana ran a quick model. "Hard to say for sure, but I think we're probably doing about ten kilometers per hour."

"Then let's not worry about it too much. This storm isn't going to last more'n a day or two at the outside, and in that time we won't have gone far even if we go in a straight line. We were pretty far out to sea, so we shouldn't hit anything. And we're close enough to the surface that we shouldn't be getting into—whoa, what was *that*?"

Something flashed past the forward camera.

Tavana took the controls and turned in the direction the thing had gone, heart beating fast again. *So many things down here we probably don't ever want to see . . .*

This far down it was very dark, but the nose camera was multispectral and ultra-high sensitivity with a huge dynamic range. It adjusted to the conditions and sent back a bright adjusted image. A long, almost torpedo shape with four fins spaced around its body materialized.

A short, startled laugh exploded from Sergeant Campbell. "Well I will be damned. Finny."

"And there's another one. Two, maybe more that we can't see."

Xander looked a little uncomfortable.

"What's wrong?" Tavana asked him over a private channel. "I think this is good news. If they're hanging around, there are probably no big predators nearby, at least now."

"No, you're right there." Xander hesitated. "It's . . . the mouths. Surrounded by tendrils and stuff, and that biting, ripping . . ." He shuddered. "I've been having nightmares about the raylamps. That mouth in front of my face. Right now anything that reminds me of that creeps me out."

Tavana remembered watching Xander going down under a mob of the things and shivered. "*Oui*, I can't blame you. But remember that *that* mouth showed up to help you."

"I know. And really, I'm glad they're there. I just don't want to look at the business end much."

Tavana nodded; at least now he understood what

was going on. He focused on the control loops and conditionals he would need for this operation, ignoring the now less worried, and certainly much less shouted, dialogue around him.

Finally he looked up. "It's set. Automatic pressure peak and valley tracking, depth verification, and alerts for anything non-Finny that shows up in the camera field of view. We can finally get some real rest." He grinned and patted the control console. "*Emerald Maui* will take care of us!"

Chapter 43

"Cast off," Whips said, his voice burbling slightly in the water.

Sakura hesitated. This would be the third trip today, and Whips was doing much of the work. "Are you *sure* you're okay to go, Whips?"

"I'm fine!" The flickering of color on his flanks brightened, but also showed some of the herringbone shimmer she associated with her friend trying to fib.

Still . . . *she* was tired too. Everyone was. Whips wasn't going to stop unless she did, and she really did want to get this done, even with the gray rain now starting to sheet down. "Okay. Just let me know if it's too much, right?"

"Right."

She shoved hard, and the raft of logs—eleven of them—grated slightly, moving away from shore. Next to her, Caroline pushed as well, using a pole like Sakura's. The grating noise increased, and then suddenly ceased. At the same time, the raft's motion smoothed out, and Sakura felt a slow, steady acceleration as Whips began pulling the raft along.

It had been Melody who pointed out that making rafts was a much better idea.

"Who wants to stumble along the shoreline a hundred times back and forth? If we put a couple of people on a raft, we can help pole it along as long as we keep to the shallows, and Whips can pull. A *lot* better than some silly . . . I mean, better than trying to drag one log at a time between ropes or something. Sorry, Whips."

Whips—true to his normal temperament—hadn't been offended. Instead, he'd been very happy to see there was a far better way to accomplish the basic goal.

But even with two humans poling the raft along, the majority of the work was on Whips' nonexistent shoulders. Sakura could see him now, a little underwater and ahead of the raft. Twin ropes from the forward part of the raft stretched taut as bowstrings as the *Bemmius novus sapiens* used his internal jet and undulating fins to drive forward as hard as possible. A gentle wake formed behind the raft.

She looked over at Caroline. "You think he can make it?"

Caroline's brown eyes narrowed in concern. "I really hope so, Saki. But he does drive himself hard." She pushed with her pole, shoving the raft forward, and Sakura mirrored her.

"Not like the rest of us don't sometimes," Sakura said after a moment, and wiped the dripping water out of her eyes. *Maybe it's time to tie my hair back.*

"Most of us do, yes. But Whips always is afraid he'll fall short. Even now. You *do* know that, don't—"

"He's my best friend. Of course I know it. Why do you think I'm worried? All that crap about his people being unstable or maybe a failed experiment—he's got to try to prove he's twice as stable, twice as reliable, twice as tough as he needs to be. Stupid."

Her older sister laughed; the sound was sympathetic. "Not stupid. So very normal. For any person, Bemmie or otherwise. You know how...unusual our family is. I hate to say it, but anywhere else, Whips' attitude would probably be the right one."

Sakura didn't answer right away. Caroline was right— of course she was—but that still made Sakura's gut churn with anger. She shoved harder with the pole, felt it grate on stone below, yanked it up, and shoved again. It wasn't fair to Whips or his family, but a lot of people thought that way. They were just scared of Bemmies because they were big and funny-looking.

"Hey, Caroline," she said slowly.

Her sister looked up, raising an eyebrow.

"Do you...well, I never really asked Sergeant Campbell and I don't know most of the others...Do you think they'll have, you know, trouble with Whips?"

Caroline pursed her lips, pushing and balancing as a larger wave than usual lifted and dropped the raft. "Honestly, Saki...probably. We're the odd ones. We've lived around Bemmies so much that we don't even jump when we run into one unexpectedly. Dad's been working with them since before I was born. Chances are that at least a couple of people on *Emerald Maui* aren't going to be comfortable with Whips."

"Well, they'd darn well better *get* comfortable with him!"

"Let's not borrow trouble. Maybe I'll be wrong. So far they seem like perfectly nice and polite people. They'll be our guests, at least to start, and Sergeant Campbell will certainly make sure they show manners."

Sakura had to laugh at that. "Yeah, I guess he will! I remember..." She suddenly noticed that the wake was decreasing.

Immediately she whirled, stepped to the front. The ropes were still stretched out, but Whips' fins were undulating much more slowly. He weaved slightly, no longer pulling in an absolute straight line, and his movements were erratic.

That's not good. In Europan *and* Earthly oceans, erratic movements were signals of wounded or weakened animals, and Sakura was sure it was the same here.

Unfortunately, with Whips underwater, she couldn't contact him through the omni. He was still doggedly pulling, maybe not even aware of how tired he really was.

"Pull on the ropes? Might signal him," Caroline suggested.

Sakura grabbed the portside rope and yanked hard, three times. Then three times more, carefully timed. Then again, three times.

The rhythmic repetition seemed to penetrate. Slowly, Whips came to the surface. "Sakura? Are you trying to tell me something?" he asked through his omni. His colors were definitely muted, and the patterns were flickering.

"You're wiped, Whips. I know you want to get this done, but there's no way we're making it now. We've got four kilometers left to go and you're almost dead in the water. Head into shore and we'll tie up for the night."

"But—"

Laura's authoritative voice cut in. "Listen to Sakura, Whips. Telemetry tells me you *have* pushed it much too far today. In fact, I want you on the raft now. Let the girls pole it into shore."

"Yes, Mom," Whips said with exhausted humor. "Saki, Caroline, back up to counterweight me when I come on—"

Without warning, Whips disappeared below the surface as though yanked under by an invisible hand. A momentary whirlpool marked the place. At the same time, a tremendous yank on both ropes pulled the bow of the raft down, the aft portion heaving up.

Sakura windmilled her arms, desperately trying to maintain her balance, but it was too late. She plunged overboard into the rain-spattered gray-green sea of Lincoln.

The good thing about retinal implants and displays was that they compensated for underwater distortion. Opening her eyes, Sakura could see as far as the water would allow. *Whips! Where's Whips?*

She followed the ropes and saw him, trailing purplish blood.

Something moved, something the color and texture of the bottom, something that seemed to be settling back like a deflating balloon. Sakura became aware that she was drifting directly towards it. *Oh, no, I don't want that.*

The thing moved slowly along the bottom, in her general direction. Its outline was difficult to discern, but she had the impression of a broad, flat body and a bloated, flattened round head. Sakura swam up, seeing the dark linear shapes of the raft logs overhead, and practically catapulted herself onto the raft.

Whips was trying to drag himself onto the raft too, as was Caroline. Sakura stumbled towards Whips and let him grab hold of her arm.

Another tremendous tug came, a sucking, dragging

pulse, and through the rippling water she could see
it—a gargantuan mouth had opened, creating a massive suction to drag anything in range into the fanged
vortex. Whips had a grip on Sakura, and one of his
arms locked to the logs with all grip talons extended.
The *Bemmius* gave a honking grunt of pain and stress,
but his arm held fast. As soon as the pull subsided,
he yanked himself onboard.

"*Vents*, that was close."

"What the heck was it?" Sakura said, her heart still
hammering in her chest.

"Something new," Whips said. "Never... seen anything like it... before."

"Well, it'd better go away for now," Caroline said,
shaking and furious as well as dripping. She seized
her pole and jabbed downward several times. One
of the blows connected, and there was an explosion
of mud from below. A massive, broad form fled into
deeper water.

"Are you all right?" Akira Kimei's voice demanded.
"I heard shouts!"

"I'm okay, Dad," Sakura said, hearing her voice shake
a little. "Met a new predator. Whips, you're bleeding!"

"Some of its teeth caught me before I pulled free,"
Whips said. "Dr. Kimei...?"

Her mother's voice responded. "Mostly surface lac-
erations. A few punctures, and you severely strained
some of your anchor plates holding on. But nothing
serious, if you get real rest. You're taking tomorrow
off, Whips."

"But—"

"I did not say you could *argue* this with me,
Harratrer."

Whips closed his mouth immediately. No one argued with Laura Kimei when she took *that* tone.

"You girls pole in and tie off," Laura Kimei continued. "Since there's no good way to get Whips home tonight, he'll have to sleep on the raft. I'll come down with food in a little bit."

Sakura poled in with Caroline. Now that the emergency was over, she was furious at Whips. "Next time, *you tell me the truth!*" she said in a low, angry undertone. "You nearly got us killed because you wouldn't tell me how tired you were!"

Whips' color was almost white. "I know. I know. I'm sorry."

"*Sorry* isn't the point, Harratrer," Laura said over the omnis. "The point is whether you *learn* from this. Will you? Because Sakura is right. This was a very bad misjudgment on your part, and even though it didn't end in complete disaster, it's going to cost us several hours of time just to make sure you're safe and comfortable on that raft for the next day or so." Her voice warmed with a touch of sympathy. "Whips, you don't have *anything* to prove to us. Don't do this to yourself."

A jagged pattern of embarrassment ripped across the *Bemmius*' hide. "I . . . I know. I'm sorry, and it won't happen again. I promise."

"All right. We all make mistakes. We'll say no more about it. Sakura, Caroline, I've got his nanos to stop the bleeding; make sure they're done by the time you get tied up, please. If not, use some of the greenweed from the shore to bind him up."

"Yes, Mom."

They found some good strong rocks and tied the

raft to them with three separate ropes. Sakura looked Whips over carefully, but there was no sign of continued bleeding. "Looks like the nanos have it under control."

"I won't forget how stupid this was," Whips said to her. "Now we'll lose at least a day."

"Don't worry about it," she said, her anger gone. She hugged her friend, stretching her arms around him as far as they could go. "We've still got plenty of time. You'll be back on the job in no time. And then," she grinned at him, "we'll surprise our guests with a genuine loading dock!"

Chapter 44

"Sherwood Column," Campbell said, using the name the Kimeis had given their home, "This is *Emerald Maui*. Come in, please."

Laura Kimei's face appeared in the augmented reality of his retinal display. "Sherwood Column here, Sergeant. Go ahead."

He could see she was busy mixing something in a bowl as he replied. "Our GPS and images show us approaching what you called Broken Point Harbor. We will be entering the harbor in about an hour or so, if any of you want to be there when we arrive."

Her smile was brilliant. "Sergeant, you could not possibly keep us from being there. We can't wait to see you all."

"Likewise, Ma'am. We'll focus on getting there safely. I'd like to avoid sinking our ship with only a few kilometers to go."

"Yes, avoid that, please. We really don't have much capability to stage a rescue."

"Don't worry. See you all in a little while. *Emerald Maui* out."

The boys had all sat up straighter. "We're *that* close?" Maddox said, almost bouncing in his seat.

"That close. The shoreline we're seeing there"—he pointed to the land with its dense jungle-like profusion of trees—"the Kimeis may even have walked on. That's how close we're getting. Everyone stay strapped in, though. Now that we're in close, I'm watching for any sign of shallows."

After the hurricane had passed, Xander and Tavana had put new topside cameras up—securing them with far more reinforcement this time. That gave Campbell the ability to watch the water ahead, to the side, and behind for the signs of shallower water: changes in color or more breaking waves. The satellite images gave him a good idea of the shallows, but the fact that the islands weren't really land made it harder to be sure that a variation in color was a change in depth and not the underwater "skirt" itself.

Finny, or one of his friends, leapt from the water ahead of the outrigger, spraying diamond-sparkling drops of water over the front of the ship. *Why the hell have you followed me all the way across the ocean?* Based on images they'd gotten of the other Finny-species individuals, he was now about as certain as he could be that one of the creatures playing in the bow wave of *Emerald Maui* was indeed the same Finny that had watched him climb through the blackness of the shattered island.

Well, whatever your reason, it's been good having you along. The sea was never empty with the little school or pod following them, and he suspected their presence also kept some other creatures at bay.

The forest on the shore slowly petered out, replaced

by shorter growths and meadow-like fields. *I think I can see traces of . . . yes, I'm sure of it.* "Take a look *there*, boys. Part of the crash scar from *LS-5*."

"*Ouch*," Xander said. "That must've been nasty."

"But they survived the landing. Remember, that was the first time little Sakura ever tried landing *anything*. She took 'em from orbit all the way down and only lost it in a storm at the very end." He didn't even try to keep the note of pride out of his voice.

"So she did well, yes?" Tavana asked.

"*Damn* well. Her mother sent me the recordings of the landing. She only bobbled it with the conversion to hover, which is the hardest damn transition in the whole book."

"I see the end!" Francisco sang out. "Up there, that must be the harbor!"

"Good eyes, Francisco," Campbell said. The boy was right; they were only a few kilometers from the entrance to the harbor now. "Remember, stay strapped in until I tell you otherwise."

"Yes, Sergeant," the others chorused.

Pearce smiled at that and sent him a private message. *You've got them well-trained.*

He smiled back. *They're good kids; I didn't need to do much training.*

Aloud, Pearce said, "So how are we supposed to anchor in the harbor? From their story, the 'floor' of that bay's probably gone."

"I don't know exactly, but they've obviously got some kind of answer. I thought about cheating and zooming in on the harbor, but if they've got a surprise for us, why ruin it? Speaking of that, though," he said, turning to Tavana, "Have you got the reconfiguration set?"

"Yes, Sergeant. The outrigger, that will be retracted for...whatever they have in mind. I used the port and starboard smart material to make a couple of anchor points as they described—lower down, so they're actually a little ways underwater, and as far back as I can get them, which is pretty close to the tail. The design of the wings—even reconfigurable—wasn't meant to be used that way, but I don't think there's going to be any problem with them. Flight at high speed still puts the material through compression, tension, and shear stresses, so they should be okay even with quite a bit of pull."

"Good. Well, I look forward to seeing what their whole plan is."

The point of the harbor was finally passing them on the starboard side, so he began the slow turn to enter. Everyone leaned forward, trying to catch the first glimpse of the others. Campbell was doing it himself—they were all just staring into the same camera feed!

Something was coming into view, but it wasn't people, not yet. Something long and dark. Several somethings, lined up. "What the heck is..." Then he suddenly understood. "Well, I will be damned. That might just work."

Xander squinted at it. "I don't...ohhhh. Logs. *Big* logs."

"Supports and rollers," Campbell agreed.

"There they are!" Maddox shouted.

Standing on the shore, waving madly at *Emerald Maui* were seven figures: six human and one *Bemmius*. The general conversation band suddenly went active. "Welcome to Broken Point Harbor, *Emerald Maui!*"

"Thank—" Campbell's reply was temporarily drowned out by cheers from his entire crew. "Ow, boys, don't deafen me! Thank you, Dr. Kimei, and all your family there. I see you've been very busy getting ready for our arrival."

"That's Whips' doing, mostly," Sakura said. "If we can get the logs underneath *Emerald Maui*—"

"I get the picture perfectly, Sakura. It's a good idea, if you've got something that can pull us up the skidway."

The buzzing voice of the alien replied. "We have a Cyclical Technologies self-contained winch, model SCW-15000, and a lot of carbonan reinforced cable with a block-and-tackle for mechanical advantage."

Campbell glanced at Xander. "Will that do the trick?"

"An SCW-15000? Um . . ." Xander's eyes went blank as he consulted his databases. "I think so. That's a powerful little machine, and the carbonan cable won't break. Block and tackle had better be tough, though."

"They've set this stuff up, I figure they know what they're doing."

As they got closer, Campbell nodded. *Someone, probably Whips, did think this through.* The logs meant to lift them up onto land were strung together with bumpers on the side to keep them from being able to just slide away or under. Campbell thought he saw other lines, too, probably part of the plan to help get them up the slipway. "Tavana, time to retract the outrigger and reconfigure."

"Are you ready to try this?" Whips asked.

"We don't have much choice. We need to get her up on land again so we can unload."

"Okay, I'm on my way."

On the screen, Campbell saw Whips dive into the

water. Of course, he'd be helping maneuver the logs as they tried to drive over them. That was going to be a bitch and a half to—

The water suddenly exploded with motion. Water churned to foam in front of *Emerald Maui*, and multiple streaks tore through the water.

Finny and his friends were charging straight for Whips.

Chapter 45

Whips was barely in the water when he suddenly heard strange, sharp noises: *Pong! Bing! Pong!* They vibrated through the water, echoing around. Even though he'd never heard these exact noises before, he recognized them instantly. *Sonar pings!*

He gave one of his own scanning pings to see if he could visualize the source; the unknown ones would take some time to adapt to visualization, although he could already tell there were multiple sources.

Four, five, maybe more forms arrowed through the water directly for him. *Spirits and Ancestors!*

Instantly he reversed his course, jetting backwards as fast as he could. The three-meter attackers closed in, spike-fanged heads driving towards him. *Up! Up the ramp!*

At maximum speed he hit the ramp and felt it skid painfully by, scraping his belly pad, but at the same time guiding him up, bursting from the water and sliding to a halt eight meters up the dry portion of the ramp. A beached fish with fourfold symmetry ran up the ramp itself, but made it only two meters up and then struggled to flop back into the sea.

"What in the *Vents'* name was *that*?" Whips said, his voice vibrating uncontrollably.

"Didn't expect that," Campbell answered. "I mentioned we had some company along the way. Looks like Finny and his friends thought you were a threat."

"Not entirely surprising. Perhaps I should have expected it," Akira said, laying a comforting hand on Whips' topside ridge. "You look pretty frighteningly alien to anything living here, you know."

Now that he was able to relax, Whips gave a sigh of assent. "Yes. I'm three-sided, not four, and I *am* a predatory design."

"And stockier than Finny," Campbell said. "He might be a little longer than you, but I'll bet you outweigh him. I don't know why they latched on to us and followed all the way here, but they've obviously decided to keep anything that looks dangerous away."

Sakura frowned. "But you'll *need* Whips—and maybe a couple more of us—to help you dock."

"No doubt about that, Sakura. Give me a minute and I'll come out."

"Is that safe?" Laura Kimei asked. "They seem agitated enough now. Tough as you are, Sergeant, I'm not sure you're a match for—"

"Ma'am, I appreciate your concern, but I think it's just fine. Finny got to know me first while I was swimming around in my suit, so I'm pretty sure he'll recognize me."

A moment later the airlock opened. Whips could see the sergeant wave to them on shore before making a clean dive straight into the water.

Even from shore they could see the faint movements as Finny and his group darted towards the sergeant. They followed at a short distance as Sergeant Campbell swam swiftly towards the ramp. In a few minutes, Campbell clambered out of the water and strode up to the group.

Sakura immediately ran to hug him, despite the hard military suit. "Sergeant, it's *great* to see you!"

"And you too, Sakura. Now let's solve our little problem."

"You're going to introduce me to your fish friends, right?" Whips asked.

"You got it, Whips. I figure if I go down and you follow me, I can get across that I don't think you're a threat."

Akira nodded. "That should work. Certainly makes sense, given their prior behavior."

"Still, won't hurt for you to try to look as non-threatening as possible," Campbell said as he started down the ramp again.

"I'll do my best," Whips said, trying to keep nervousness out of his voice. He had to stay calm; a lot of creatures could sense nervousness. He curled up his arms, furled them as much as possible, hid the griphooks, and closed his mouth

The sergeant entered the water at an unhurried walk. Whips followed a couple of meters behind, trying to ignore the stings of pain from his abraded belly pad. The nanos were working on it, but it'd still be a while before it wasn't tender.

Finny—Whips guessed that it must be him—immediately darted towards them. Campbell spread his arms wide, blocking any direct route to Whips. He then turned around, stepped towards Whips, and put a hand on him. Whips felt a gentle forward pressure and followed the older human's guidance, drifting slowly to float beside Campbell.

Finny and his group backed up a meter or two and hovered there. Then Finny cautiously moved forward again, finally stopping a meter and a half from the sergeant and Whips.

From this distance, Whips evaluated Finny as a possible ally or enemy. The four-finned body was definitely sleeker than his own, but had similar vents on each side. Whips presumed they were water-jets like his, explaining the creature's great speed. Four spikes protruded from near Finny's mouth, spikes that moved in and out. These ramming or impaling spikes had enough maneuverability to be easily disengaged after impact. His mouth was four-jawed, like a lot of others on this world, with backward-pointing teeth to hold things, what looked like cutting planes, and maybe a ripping tongue like Whips' own. He didn't want to fight this thing if he could avoid it. Finny also had some tendrils around the head for grasping and manipulating, but they didn't look nearly as complex or capable as Whips' own arms—more like orekath or Earth squids.

Finny rocked slightly in the water. With a slow ripple of his fins, he drifted closer. Whips stayed unmoving.

Without warning, the creature darted away, rejoining the rest of its pack. Now Whips could see six of the creatures, all of whom now hovered in the distance, watching.

Campbell leaned closer to allow the near-field link to work between their omnis. "Looks pretty good, Whips. I'm going to head back to *Emerald Maui* and see if everyone stays friendly."

"Go ahead. I'm okay here."

A few minutes later, the water vibrated with the burbling hum of *Emerald Maui*'s engines and the shuttle turned towards the mass of logs. To Whips' relief, Finny and his group seemed no longer concerned about his presence. Still, he kept watch on them with his skinsense as he prepared for the tricky part of this maneuver.

The key was to get logs underneath *Emerald Maui*'s bow, and, eventually, farther back. The shuttle was too solid and massive, and the jury-rigged floating dock too fragile, for them to just hook the winch to the front and drag it up. Whips figured he needed to have at least half the length of *Emerald Maui* already supported by logs, with some roller logs between the support logs towards the front, before they dared brute-force it. That meant working the logs down under the ship as it very slowly moved forward. The landing skids wouldn't help since they'd put too much of its weight on three points.

Emerald Maui's nose was now over the first log. Whips stayed on the outside of the ramp and gripped the external rope to stabilize the ramp as much as possible. If they had more cable, he could've anchored the ends to parts of the harbor, and forced it underwater. But they'd been slowly using up parts of the cable they had over the past year. If this didn't work, they'd have to see if there was cable in *Emerald Maui* that they could use.

The first log slid back under the forward pressure, exactly the way Whips had hoped. Whips pulled down and back, moving it backwards as *Emerald Maui* rumbled its way ahead.

The second log also slid backwards as intended, but the third balked, pushed up by the pressure of the second log ahead of it. It caught on the nose and started to push on the ramp. Whips lunged forward, dragged down as hard as he could on the second, and yanked it farther under. That caused one side of the third log to drop a bit. He darted underneath the ramp, grabbed and pulled on the other side, and jetted down at full strength. The third log hesitated, and then slid backwards.

Three down, he thought. *Emerald Maui* was thirty meters long—he needed at least fifteen of those on the logs. Even with the massive logs they'd selected, that meant almost thirty, plus five of the spaced roller logs starting at about ten meters.

But Whips had something prepared to make that a little easier. Now that there were three logs under the bow, he popped up from underwater to transmit. "*Emerald Maui*, go to station-keeping. Try *not* to slide back."

"What're you planning, Whips?" Sergeant Campbell asked.

"You know those anchor points you've deployed on the sides? I'm running ropes from the end of the dock up through those points. They come together at a crossbar in front of *Emerald Maui*. That will let the rest of my family pull on them to keep the logs from sliding back, and help the next ones go under your nose smoothly."

"I see what you are doing," Tavana said, "but would it not be better to use the winch instead of people?"

"The SCW-15000 is pretty good at control," Whips admitted, "but it doesn't do feedback and reaction nearly as well as humans or Bemmies do. Remember, the Trapdoor Pulse fried all of our effective AIs; we were lucky the omnis kept working. So hands, eyes, and brains with some block-and-tackle to amplify the pull, that's what we're using for this stage. The winch will be used when we get enough of *Emerald Maui* up to make it reasonable to pull you up on shore."

"Got you. I see what you're doing; you'll at least keep it from sliding back and you'll help guide the other logs down that way. Go ahead—we're now on station-keeping, as best we can manage. But you'd better be *real* careful back there."

The danger, of course, was that even station-keeping meant that the water-jets were active, with a twin threat of either sucking an unwary Bemmie straight into the intakes, or of parboiling him if he got too close to the exhaust.

"I know, trust me. Now when I get the lines on and my family has started pulling, you should be able to detect that tension, right?"

"Let me check." A momentary pause. "Yes, that should be detectable pretty easily. The smart material's basically instrumented everywhere—has to be, to make the reconfigurations work."

"Okay. When you see that tension—*not before* — go back to the slow-forward drive. If this works, we should be able to get the rest of the logs to move down and under."

"Got it," said Campbell. "You be careful, now."

"I will."

This was going to be tricky. Still, living on Lincoln was filled with risks. He dove back underwater, found the first line, grabbed it, and swam back. As he approached the rear, the rumble of the station-keeping jets rippled his skin. He could see the heat-wave shimmer of the jet exhaust behind. After all, it wasn't much different from the thermal vents that dotted much of the Europan seafloor, which his people had evolved to detect.

Whips caught the portside anchor loop with his topside arm and used the other arms to carefully feed the line through. He kept one eye on the logs, rocking and with a tendency to slide or roll back up, while *Emerald Maui*'s station-keeping attempted to maintain its attitude and position.

The young Bemmie jetted forward now, the first line feeding smoothly up through the wide anchor point. *Watch it; the moving logs could really do a number on me, as Akira might say. There! There's the crossbar!*

He slid the line into the slot on the port side of the crossbar, the large knot on the end serving as an anchor, and then slid the latch on the end shut; he felt the *snap* as the latch went firmly home. He popped up above the water for a moment. "I've got the portside line attached and locked," he said through his omni to anyone listening—probably everyone. "Going to do the starboard side now!"

He snatched up the second rope and jetted swiftly for the other anchor point. *Grab the anchor with my topside arm, feed the rope through—*

Emerald Maui twitched suddenly, adjusting to a shift in current and position. That—combined with an unexpected tug on the line from behind—caused Whips to fumble the line.

He whirled around, instantly understanding what was

happening. The line headed for the water-jet intake. He lunged forward, and caught the line, feeling the sucking inrush of water pulling on him. He turned, jetting as hard as he could to the side.

Whips evaded the intake, pulling in the line as fast as he could to keep the rest of it from going in. But there was no way to completely avoid the jet exhaust plume. A blast of steam and water screamed through the sea, ripping in scalding agony over Whips. He closed his eyes and kept going, ignoring the tight, pin-tingling pain on his skin and mantles as one of them drew some of the overheated liquid through. He forced himself out, around, forward, then opened his eyes. *There, the anchor point, grab hold, don't lose the line... it's through!*

He caught the end of the line with one arm and fed the extra line through with the other. Trying to ignore the increasing hot pain of the burns, he jetted forward, keeping a gentle tension on the line as he let the excess feed out. *There will be a little slack when I lock it into the crossbar, but not enough to let it get caught up in the jets. Vents and Sky, that burn* hurts! His medical nanos were trying to tend to it, but that would be far from instant. He had no choice but to ignore it.

There was the crossbar. The first line was still fixed! He completed the maneuver, locking in the second line, and then popped up from the water. "Locked! Everyone, *pull!*"

The pain faded to the background for an instant as he saw the lines going taut, pulling on the anchor points. *My family's got it! Tavana and the sergeant* have *to be able to sense that!*

Even as he thought that, *Emerald Maui*'s jets shifted their song, and the floating shuttle slowly, majestically began to nudge forward.

Yes! The pain meant little compared to the fact that this half-crazy plan seemed to be working. Whips threw himself against the crossbar connecting both ropes and pushed as hard as he could, adding his own strength to the pull. With a distant clang and thump, another log slid under the nose of the craft. Then another.

His nanos were trying to report on the severity of his injuries. Whips didn't listen. *Have to get this done.*

Now that the logs were moving back under the combined forward movement of *Emerald Maui* and the pull of the Kimei family, he could dart up to the logs, yank them sideways and down, adjust their angles. *Emerald Maui* started to tilt upward. The buoyancy of the logs was lifting her!

Another log slid under the water, and it was clear. The front of the massive shuttle was indeed riding higher in the water. This was the tricky part. If it tilted up too high, no one was going to be strong enough to keep the logs in place; it would roll or slide back. If that happened, it would mean probably weeks of work to get more cable, anchor it underwater, find a way to pull a large section of the floating dock underwater, and try again.

Under the relentless pull of the Kimeis, augmented by part of the block and tackle, more logs slid under. It was getting close to halfway. But that tilt, Whips really didn't like. The ship looked unstable, even as the second of the roller logs passed under the bow.

That's it. I'm going to take the chance. The insistent

pain from both his skin and his top-right mantle threatened to distract him; he instructed the nanos to numb the pain, overriding their advice for treatment. *Laura will deal with that later.* He jetted up; the shock of air hitting the raw burn sent sparkling pain through the anesthetic, but he only allowed himself a grunt. *Where? It's supposed to be right up here!*

The logs moved and shifted under him. He inchwormed his way up, desperately trying to keep his tail grippers and arms up so they couldn't drop into any of the gaps that opened and closed beneath. *There it is!*

It was another carbonan-reinforced cable with a red flag at the end. He grabbed it with his topside arm and flung himself backward. *The nose of the ship . . . there, there's the ring!*

With a supreme effort, he reared most of his length up and *shoved* with his tail. It was, by human standards, a pathetic jump, barely clearing eight inches of air between his tail and the log, but it was—just barely—enough. His topside arm caught the large anchor ring just beneath *Emerald Maui*'s nose and slammed the locking hook through it. Dropping back into the shallow water below, he shouted, "*Start the winch!*" and transmitted it for good measure through the general omni band.

Sakura released her grip on the central cable and leapt to the winch, which was anchored to the rear of a huge exposed block of the coral-like bedrock of the continent. Her hands flipped back the safety lock and hammered the power button.

The winch hummed to life, spooling in the slack; its hum deepened and increased in volume as tension rose. There was a faint *creak* as the full tension transmitted itself to the massive stone support, but it remained solidly in place. *Emerald Maui* swung about a couple of degrees and then began to creep up the ramp.

"Reconfigure the tail," Whips said, forcing himself to crawl rapidly up the ramp. "You don't need the rudder anymore. Open up and then retract the anchors on the side—let my family pull the ropes there back up."

"On it," Xander said. "It's getting rocky in here!"

"Hold on," Laura said. "Only a few more minutes."

The tension on the center line suddenly dropped. The Kimeis were hauling quickly on it now, dragging it as fast as they could away from the still-running jets. "Kill the jets now," Whips said, trying to ignore the tension in his voice that came at least in part from reaction to pain. "The winch has you."

"Shutting down," Campbell said. "I can feel the lift under most of the ship now. Whoa! Moving forward with a bump . . . I think the rollers are rolling!"

Without warning, *Emerald Maui* lunged forward, the winch whining at the sudden increase in speed, and rumbled upward. Whips rolled off the ramp and the huge shuttle thundered past him, its underside crunching and spraying woodchips and bark from the logs beneath it.

"Shut the winch down!"

The winch went abruptly silent. *Emerald Maui* coasted grindingly to a halt—now a full twenty meters inland from the shore.

"*Emerald Maui,*" Whips said, pride and relief momentarily eclipsing any pain, "you have made landfall."

Chapter 46

The cheers nearly deafened Xander, but he didn't care. He yelled joyously too, at the relief and exhilaration that the Kimeis' ridiculous improvisation had somehow worked. Once more, they'd made a long and dangerous journey and gotten where they were headed safely. All of them.

"Are we stable?" Pearce Haley asked.

Whips' voice replied. "You could deploy your landing skids now if you want to be sure, but honestly, *Emerald Maui*'s crushed the center of the logs down pretty well. You should be perfectly fine."

"We'll leave her as she is," Campbell said. "Skids would put too much pressure on the ramp, probably break one or more of the logs. We might want to put her out to sea again. No reason to wreck our ramp."

"No 'might' about it, Sergeant," Akira said. "A vessel that size will have many uses for our little colony. The real job will be to make a loading dock large enough and permanent enough for real use. But if the equipment you've brought is anything like you've described . . ."

"It's *everything* we've described, and a lot more. We didn't lose our cargo, and this crate was jam-packed,

379

no wasted space." Campbell unstrapped and stood. "But my kids are getting antsy—let's finally get together!"

The airlock doors opened, and Xander restrained his impatience as the two older adults went out first. Then it was his turn to scramble down the ladder. He waited at the bottom to watch the others. *They* would be in a hurry too, and that could lead to someone slipping.

Soon all six were on the dock, facing the Kimeis.

The first thing that struck him was that Laura Kimei was the tallest of their group, about a hundred-eighty to a hundred eighty-five centimeters—still considerably shorter than he was, and almost twenty centimeters below Sergeant Campbell's nearly two meter height. Her husband was significantly shorter and more slender than his wife, with pure, arrow-straight black hair and delicate features. Caroline, their oldest, was a good ten centimeters shorter than her father but built almost identically—although her straight hair was the same chestnut-brown as her mother's.

Next to her, Sakura bounced with irrepressible energy, towering over her older sister and even topping her father by a few centimeters, wavy ebony hair going past her shoulders and setting off eyes so bright blue the color was visible from where Xander was standing. Then Melody, far smaller, similar to Caroline, but with even sharper eyes that studied their group with an analytical expression far more suited for someone two or three times her age. She restrained the youngest, Hitomi, from running to the newcomers. This didn't seem hard, even for Melody, because Hitomi was tiny—Xander guessed her at barely over a hundred centimeters. Her hair was a startling golden blond, shining in stark contrast to the blacks and browns of the rest of her family.

Whips was just dragging himself out of the water; Xander averted his gaze and tried to repress a shudder as the arms splayed wide and the tripartite mouth with its shearing planes and ripping tongue gave a grunt. *Got to focus on something else.*

"Let us officially welcome you all to Lincoln, and especially to the little part of it we've explored," Laura said.

That signal broke the ice. Campbell stepped forward and gripped Laura's hand in his own. As the others came forward it was suddenly a whirl of "Hello, so glad you made it!" and "Wow, you're taller than you looked in person!" and "Oh my god, *new people finally!*" and handshakes, and quick, impulsive hugs.

Xander found himself crying, grinning so broadly his cheeks hurt. Caroline had the same tears of happiness on her face, the essence of *we really aren't alone!* and the relief that they'd all survived so many things. He couldn't help but laugh at that, at tears and smiles united, and all of a sudden everyone was laughing, a laugh that said so many things that they couldn't put into words. All the relief, joy, and triumph of both groups concentrated into a single, unified sound of victory and exultation beyond any language to convey.

Finally, the laughter died down. Laura, still smiling, said, "All right, everyone, come on. It'll be a bit of a hike, but we've got a special welcome for all of you back at Sherwood Tower."

"You don't have room for us to stay there though, right?" Maddox asked.

"No, but we can get your shelter set up nearby, if you like. Let's worry about that later; there's plenty of time now."

Campbell nodded. "But first, I have two things to do. Don't worry, they're quick."

He turned to Sakura. "Sakura Kimei, I understand you're responsible for this." He gestured at the long scar ripped into the very bedrock of the floating continent.

The black-haired girl looked embarrassed and guilty. "Um, yeah. I kind of lost it at the end..."

"You landed an orbital shuttle on an unknown world with no beacons, no nav aids, no AI support on board. You used the manual controls, and even though you crashed, every single person on board lived without serious injury," Campbell said emphatically. "Saki, you've done me proud. You never finished your courses. You never even flew a single actual kilometer. But you did something trained pilots have been known to screw up." He put both hands on her shoulders, and Xander grinned again at her wide-eyed expression. "By the authority vested in me by the Colonial Initiative Corporation and the Captain of *Outward Initiative*, I hereby certify you as a fully-qualified pilot for *Newton*-class orbital shuttles and all similar vessels."

Sakura gaped at him. "I'm...you're not...*qualified pilot?*"

"You did a hell of a solo flight, kid. If I'd been told beforehand what was going to happen, I'd have bet you wouldn't survive re-entry, let alone landing. You passed a tougher final exam than I've *ever* given. If that didn't qualify you as a pilot, nothing does. Sure, you've got plenty of studying to do, but I still study, too. Welcome to the brotherhood, Pilot Sakura Kimei."

"Congratulations, Saki!" Whips said, with real happiness in his buzzing voice. All Sakura's family crowded around her, adding their own congratulations and hugs.

"And the second thing," Campbell said, though it was obvious that the Kimeis weren't paying attention. Campbell clambered back up inside *Emerald Maui* and emerged with a large bundle—it looked to Xander like most of the meat they'd brought with them.

"Need a hand, Sergeant?"

"Here, catch." Xander caught the bundle, and then followed the older man down the ramp.

Campbell took the bundle, and then dove into the water. Xander saw Finny and his group move closer, darting in and out as the sergeant began handing out strips of meat. *Saying "thank you" in the best way we can.*

"Wonder if they'll stick around now that we're back on land?" Tavana said from next to him.

"I don't know. They might. They must have had *some* reason they followed us seven thousand kilometers across the ocean. I sort of hope they do. I don't know if they're intelligent like us, but they're sure smart for animals, and for whatever reason they seem to like the sergeant."

Campbell emerged from the water a few moments later. "There, that's done. Sorry about the delay, Ma'am," he said to Laura, "but—"

"No need to apologize, Sergeant Campbell. You were doing your duty—in both cases. And you've just made my daughter the happiest I've ever seen her, so believe me, I have no objections."

"Thank you, Laura," he said, with a smile. "Then lead on, Kimeis—we look forward to seeing what you've built here!"

Chapter 47

Sakura saw the newcomers' eyes widen as they finally got a good look at Sherwood Tower.

"My *God*," Sergeant Campbell said after a moment. "Looks a hell of a lot more impressive in person."

"You did all this by *hand*?" Xander said.

"Well, mostly," Sakura said, feeling a thrill of pride. "The winch let us pull off a few tricks we might not have managed without it, but . . . yeah, almost everything was done by hand."

Pearce Haley ran her hand along the column's surface. "That's tough stuff. How thick is it?"

"The thickness varies along the height," Melody answered. "At the very top it can be about two hundred fifty millimeters thick, while it'll be more than two meters thick towards the bottom. Well, the bottom we can *see*—it actually goes through to the interior of the continent."

"The latter bit I know from experience," the sergeant said. He looked with admiration at the column, with the ramp leading to the interior and windows visible higher up. "Had to walk out of one from the inside."

Sakura couldn't imagine what that must have been

like—waking up trapped in blackness, within an almost limitless cavern filled with who-knew-what. Then, suddenly, she *could*... because she remembered her own desperate run through the jungle to get help for her family, and what it was like to lose her omni and be lost in the dark. Except Campbell'd had to be in the dark a lot longer than she did—a dark he'd never been through, while Sakura had known where she was going.

The group began to head up the ramp. Campbell's crew made remarks of respect and surprise as they noticed new features of their home, but Sakura looked at them with a clearer understanding. They were impressed by the Kimeis... but they'd been stranded in the real dark, out between the stars, for months. They'd had to fix their shuttle and find a way here with a lot more trouble than the Kimeis had had.

The kitchen was a little more cramped-looking today. The table had been modified and designed to be expandable—there were several more "leafs," as Whips called them, inserted to make the table big enough for everyone.

Campbell stopped and surveyed everything. "Well, now, this is downright *home*, isn't it? I'll be damned. And what in the world is that incredible smell?"

Sakura ran over and opened the oven, which had been damped to a slow-cook temperature. *Perfect! We judged it perfect!* "This is a capy roast with a barbeque glaze. The block-crab and quadbird appetizers will be ready in a few minutes. We have filegrass pickles, and—"

"Tomatoes! I smell tomatoes!" Francisco said excitedly.

Akira laughed. "Not quite. We have these tubers we call totatoes, which have a very tomato-like flavor, and the juice is useful for flavoring things like that barbeque sauce."

"That roast, I think I could eat it all by myself," Tavana said. He stared at the gloriously red-brown meat as Sakura and Laura hoisted it—with difficulty, because it was quite heavy—to the counter to rest a bit before carving.

"You're welcome to try," Laura said with a smile, "I think there's more than enough for all of us." She suddenly stopped smiling, and her eyes narrowed. "Akira, Caroline, Sakura, take care of things for a bit. *WHIPS!*"

Sakura flipped to their private channel. *What did you do?*

Um...I've been on anesthetic induction. For a while.

You're hurt? *And you didn't* say *anything?*

Her mother moved Whips into the lower room for examination. *Well, I couldn't while I was working, and then between the anesthetic and all the excitement...*

Even from the other room they could hear Laura's low, infuriated tones. "You can't ignore injuries like this! Whips, I know how important it is for you to not be a burden, but..."

"Here, everyone, let's choose our seats and I'll start getting the appetizers ready," Akira said. He shut the door tightly, cutting off most of the sound.

Sakura couldn't blame her mother for being angry, but now that Mom knew, Sakura was sure Whips would be okay. Just scolded a lot. Dad was doing the best he could to keep that from being much of a damper on things.

Tavana took a seat across from her. She'd already noticed that Xander—the really tall young man who was clearly the oldest of the boys—had chosen to sit near Caroline. And the way the sergeant was talking to the redheaded woman, Pearce? She wondered if they were dating.

"So," Tavana said, "the cooking, do you do some of it, or is that your father?"

"We all do, some. Well, Hitomi's not old enough to cook much yet, but she tries to help. Still, Dad's really the gourmet in the family. Here, try these pickles. They're kinda crunchy, almost like pickled green beans."

Tavana did. "That . . . is very good! You made these here?"

"*Everything*. The base is opal vinegar, with some hedral sugar plus salt we've been making from drying setups. It takes some work to get out the grit, and we're trying to figure out how to separate out some of the other minerals, too. Then there's a little Lincoln pepper for a bit of a bite, and—"

"I know the hedrals, you mentioned those before, but what are opals and Lincoln pepper?"

The discussion continued like that. Tavana was clearly interested in everything they'd found, and how they'd gone beyond merely surviving to actually *living*. Most of the other conversations around the table were similar, exchanging personal experiences, observations, talking about the new inventions—or, really, re-invention of old ideas—that had made Sherwood Tower and the rest of their little piece of Lincoln habitable.

By the time the appetizers were passed around, Sakura's mother came back in, looking less like a thundercloud than when she'd left. *Is he all right, Mom?* she sent via private channel.

He will be. But he was much worse than he let us suspect. Emerald Maui's jet-wash scalded him across a large part of his body. *It would have been more obvious on a human, but even on a Bemmie that's a serious injury. I've set the nanorepairs and treated him, but he's going to rest downstairs for a bit before coming back up to eat. I had to debride some areas and prep them for regrowing.*

That meant that large parts of Whips wouldn't be expressive for a while; the chromatophores that made Bemmies able to shift color and pattern at will were near the surface. *Poor Whips!*

Yes. But he should have told us right away. Enough. Let's enjoy this meal.

With Laura present, the roast was carved and distributed.

Pearce was the first to speak after taking a bite. "Dr. Kimei—"

"—Laura, please."

"Laura, I've tasted fine barbeque before, and maybe it's just been a long time...but this ranks up there with the best I've ever had."

"Thank you, but the credit goes mostly to Akira; he devised the glaze and sauce. I tend to stay out of his way when he's creating."

"Then, Akira, this is amazing. Once we're settled in, could you possibly show me how you make this?"

Sakura liked seeing her father get that gratified smile. "I would be honored. The real challenge is making everything that you need to make everything else, if you understand what I mean."

Pearce nodded. "Too well, I think. My grandmother used to make her own cider vinegar, and to do that she first had to make a bunch of hard cider—not that that was bad, mind you! So you've got two processes and a fair amount of time—I think a month or so?—just to get your vinegar."

"You've got the right idea. And of course there's gathering all the opals, or hedrals, or whatever fruit you'll use beforehand..."

The food discussion continued, mingled with other technology, invention, and exploration discussions. Sakura, while still talking with Tavana, focused more on her roast. *Because we don't make things* this *fancy very often, and I really appreciate it when we do!*

"...how you landed?"

"What?" She looked up at Tavana. "Sorry, I was... well, concentrating on the roast. What'd you say?"

"It is all right, this is a roast worth concentrating on! Much better than centisnake. What you call minimaw."

She grinned at him, a smile he returned. His rich brown complexion and black hair contrasted startlingly with the emphatically gray eyes. "Minimaw isn't bad, but capy's a *much* better meat for most things. We haven't even gotten near to trying everything. I'll bet there's better stuff out there."

"That might be true, yes, but then maybe that would be a bad thing. You see, normally it's hard for me to keep my weight down."

She shook her head. "You won't end up overweight, Tav, just not tall and skinny like me and my family. Anyway, what was it you asked?"

"Can you tell me the story of how you landed? The sergeant may have read it all, but that he did not share with us."

She managed not to blush. "Sure, I'd be happy to."

Sakura cast her mind back to that terrifying, exhilarating day. "Well, we'd gotten into orbit around Lincoln . . ."

Maddox and Francisco drifted over as she told the story—the approach, the determination of how she would have to enter the atmosphere, the beginnings of the descent. Dinner seemed to be finally slowing down, and it wasn't really time for dessert yet.

Out of the corner of her eye, she noticed Caroline and Xander heading for the door, with Hitomi tagging along. She looked back at Tavana. "So anyway, we finally came in sight of the continent I'd chosen, but the correspondence started blinking yellow, which made no—"

Xander gave a shout of shock and fear. He stumbled back, fell to the floor and continued to scoot back, face pale.

Whips stood in the doorway, frozen in mid-motion. He had obviously been in the act of trying to open the door, lower arms splayed as props, upper arm stretched up and reaching for the latch.

"What's wrong?" Hitomi asked. "It's just Whips, see?"

Xander looked down and away, refusing to glance back.

He . . . he can't look *at Whips?* Sakura felt a slow, burning anger rise. *That's right, he seemed to be walking farther away from Whips, not ever looking at him, when we came back. Never from in front, anyway,* she added to herself with an effort at fairness. *Still, how dare he act like that?*

She could see Caroline's face frowning in annoyance too.

"Whips is our *family*," Hitomi said. She stamped her foot for emphasis. "If you don't like him . . . I don't like *you!*"

Tavana was up from his chair. "Wait, wait, *pardon!*" he shouted, and everyone turned towards him; the Polynesian boy's voice was startlingly loud. "Understand, please, yes, we are not used to Bemmies. And we know that is not your problem, but ours. But Xander, his problem is not that."

Campbell nodded. "Thanks, Tav. Sorry, Xander, we'll have to face this right here and now." Xander looked around the assembly of faces. Sakura knew he could see her suspicious glare. "You heard that I got there in time to save Xander from attack by those raylamp things, right?"

Sakura nodded. The movement was echoed by the rest of the family.

"They were trying to eat their way into his suit. One was fastened right in front of his face, tentacles, lamprey-mouth and all. Seems that image burned its way into Xander's head."

"I'm sorry," Xander said finally. "It's . . . anything built like that freaks me out now. Finny's head and mouth did it too. Whips," he said, still not quite looking at the Bemmie, "I . . . it's not your fault. I should've thought of that problem. I just . . . if I'd known you were right there I could've been prepared."

Whips had sagged down to a flatter posture, but he rose a little at that. "I did not mean to—"

"I *know*." Xander hammered a fist against the solid floor so hard that the sound echoed. "My problem. Not yours."

Sakura looked over to her mother. Laura closed

her eyes, took a breath, and nodded, her face relaxing. *Mom believes him. That's good enough for me.*

"You've developed a new phobia," Laura said. "That will have to be treated. The good news is that since it's new, it should be a little easier to cure. It hasn't become ingrained habit of thought."

"I'll try to stay out of your way," Whips said. "Unless Laura says otherwise."

"We will figure out a desensitization approach," Laura said. "But I want to emphasize that what Hitomi said is absolutely true. We know what a lot of people think about Bemmies, but we also know it isn't true. Whips has been one of our *foundations*. He's saved our lives more than once. He's the one who figured out how to land your ship, and he got himself almost killed just *building* that thing, and then again today—as I just discovered—he got himself burned badly in one of the jets, and never said a word while he kept working. He is our friend. He is our *family*. If any of you have a problem with him, you have a *real* problem with us."

"Understood completely, Ma'am," Sergeant Campbell said instantly. "We had a discussion about that back on our own ship."

"Then let's say no more of it," Akira said emphatically. "You all understand that we're all one united family, and that's that. Xander has a problem, and we'll all work to help him through it. Now, Whips, you can go down to your usual place—mind you don't scrape off those dressings that Laura put on you—and I'll get you served. Then," he said, with a more natural smile, "I'll get out the desserts!"

Slowly, Sakura let herself relax. The nervously apologetic expression on Tavana's face, made her smile. "It's okay. And . . . thanks for getting everyone talking right away. Before we had, you know, a fight or anything."

Tavana's smile was brilliant with relief. "I . . . it was just what had to be done. But thank you." He sat back down, as did Francisco and Maddox. "So you were just coming over the horizon to see this continent, yes?"

"Right! So, anyway, it starts blinking yellow . . ." Tension melted away as she saw the honestly fascinated expressions, Tavana's clear, gray eyes, eyes unwaveringly fixed upon hers.

Chapter 48

"It's been one hell of a day," Campbell said. He raised a small glass of the peach-tinted liquid to his lips. "Not a bad finish, I have to say. I mean, I've tasted a lot better, but I've also tasted a hell of a lot worse. That's drinkable wine. From the stuff you call opals?"

Akira nodded, taking a sip himself. "A blend of opal and pearberry, fermented. Makes a fairly decent wine. But, as you say, it still can use some work."

"Don't worry about it," Pearce said emphatically. "You've accomplished wonders here. The more I think about it, the more my mind boggles. Having any kind of a drink for after-dinner discussion is an accomplishment."

"Shows we're adults," Laura said with a grin. "If we were all, say, Xander's age, we'd have been more interested in just distilling it to make it as strong as possible and damn the taste."

"Truth there, Ma'am," Campbell agreed, returning the grin. "Sure is what most of my old recruits would've planned."

"All right, Sergeant, you made it clear you wanted to talk to us in private, and we've finally managed it," Laura said. "Let's cut to the chase; we're pretty tired. I can't believe you aren't."

She's the no-nonsense boss of this colony, no doubt about it. And she's right. "As you say." He looked over to Akira. "Took me a little bit, but I finally remembered something about you, Dr. Akira Kimei. You're one of the reps for Project Triton."

He could see by the way the smaller man had stiffened and almost spilled his glass that this was something Akira wasn't prepared for. *Too bad. This is important.*

Laura looked with surprise at her husband. "Project Triton?"

"He didn't tell you, Ma'am?"

Laura frowned. "I have never heard that phrase before, no."

"Neither have I," Pearce said.

Well, now. I guess he took his oath very *seriously. Which is good—means I really can count on him.* "Sorry, then, Ma'am. It would've been something he wasn't supposed to talk about." He looked to Pearce. "And I couldn't talk about it either; you weren't on the need-to-know list. But in the present circumstances I don't think there's any more point in secrecy, and since I was head of security..."

"I'm sorry, Laura," Akira said, with trepidation clear in his voice. "It was a direct order by the Board. Only I and the other representatives were allowed to discuss it."

"The *Colonization* Board?" Her brows came together. "Oh. That bastard Yermolov, yes?"

"Laura, he was doing his job."

She rolled her eyes. "All right. What is—or was—Project Triton?"

Campbell answered. "An ethological study of *Bemmius novus sapiens*—a long-term study to find out if the current crop of *Bemmius* were really stable in all areas as they were supposed to be, stable enough to trust as full partners with human beings in the extremely dangerous and challenging conditions of colonizing new worlds."

Laura Kimei was still frowning, but her forehead smoothed slightly. "So *that* was what you were doing those times I found you writing something and you closed it up, saying you'd just finished."

He looked down. "Yes."

She stared at him for a few moments and then sighed. "It's all right, Akira. Yes, I'm rather unreasonably annoyed at you right now, but you had a clear commitment, and if you weren't the kind of man to keep his word through everything . . . well, you wouldn't be the man I married." She drained the rest of her wine. "So, Sergeant, why are you bringing this up now?"

"I can guess," Pearce Haley said. "That confrontation downstairs."

"Partly," Campbell conceded. "That was more excuse than anything else, though. The real point is . . . I know Whips has been a great help to you, but I don't know all the details. I don't know if your stories are one hundred percent of the truth, or if there are parts you left out. So I need to know, Doctor Akira Kimei—have you completed your *professional* evaluation?"

"Months ago," he said promptly. "If I had any way of filing the report, I'd have done so. I suppose I can file a copy with you—you'd be one of the ones getting it, after all." A large report document suddenly was transmitted to Campbell's headware.

"I'll read the whole thing later. What's your professional conclusion?"

Akira Kimei suddenly laughed, reached out and poured himself another glass, refilled his wife's. "My conclusion? What was *your* conclusion about my daughter Sakura and her piloting? Sergeant, you've all talked about how impressed you are with what we've accomplished here. Well, that's in great part due to Whips' intelligence, drive, and stubborn ability to endure whatever he had to to get the job done. The Board's tests would have been child's play compared to what Lincoln's been throwing at us." He took another drink. "Are *all* Bemmies stable and suited for colonization? Of course not. Neither are all humans. But there are at least as many of Whips' people suited to be colonists as there are humans, in my professional opinion."

He gestured outward, towards the dark windows. "This just shows how much we need them, to be honest. We are creatures of the land; they are creatures of water. We both function to some extent in the other's domain, although Bemmies are much better at it than we are. Together we can do things that are difficult, or perhaps impossible. Human divers, especially amateurs like us, could not have accomplished what Whips did today with shepherding *Emerald Maui* safely onto land. We can't swim that fast, that well, or that long while expending such effort. Similarly there are many things he could not accomplish that we do almost without effort. We are perfect complements to each other in colonization, at least where there is land and water in abundance—and there really is no world humans want to colonize that lacks in water.

"The fears and prejudices from the prior failures must

be eradicated, Sergeant, because today's Bemmies—as Harratrer of Tallenal Pod proves—are our full and rightful equals."

By the end of his speech, Laura was smiling at her husband again. Campbell was impressed. There was genuine passion in that recital and, he could tell, an immense amount of thought behind it. "All right, then. I'll take that as settled. I've got some remaining doubts to eradicate, and probably so do my boys, but we'll sort that out. I just really needed to make sure there weren't any signs of instability that you hadn't mentioned."

Laura shook her head. "The only time Whips ever really showed signs of breaking down was at the same time our entire family was on the verge of collapse. And it took him no longer to recover after that than anyone else in the family. So, no. He's exactly what he's shown himself to be—a young man not much different from us two-legged types, always trying to prove he can do things two steps better and faster than we can so that we won't doubt him."

"All right, Ma'am. If the boys ever ask me, I'll set them straight—though Hitomi already did most of that herself, I think."

Pearce laughed. "She certainly did. That was one of the most heartwarmingly adorable things I've ever seen."

"The way she defended Whips? Yes, no doubt of it," Campbell said with an answering grin.

"So, Sergeant, can I ask *you* for a status report on something?" Akira said.

"Fire away."

"*Emerald Maui* seems mostly intact. Is there any

chance that we can somehow escape Lincoln in her? Or some way that we can call for rescue?"

"That question's not one with a straightforward answer, really. We might be able to get her airborne again, with the right tweaking of wings and such, especially if we can get the damaged engine running again. But that's a great big *maybe*. I would guess that it'll stay that way for quite a while.

"As for calling, well, the satellites we put up are transmitting a distress call constantly. That's not going to reach another colony for at least ten years, but anyone coming in-system will pick it up pretty quick, I think."

He finished his own little glass. "Xander and Tavana have been playing around with a possible design. It takes some of the reconfigurable portside wing and incorporates the old engine in a modified form to make an orbital probe that could boost itself into orbit, for a one-way Trapdoor journey to Orado. I'm skeptical about that, since I don't think even with a damn good set of superconductor coils it'll be able to store enough power to hypersonic its way into orbit and then make it to Orado, but I could be wrong."

"So we're stuck here until someone else comes along?" Laura asked quietly.

"Well . . . yes. But that doesn't necessarily mean forever. All it'll really take is someone noticing this star where the Earth maps say there isn't one. Any decent modern orbital telescope would show them that there's at least one habitable world around this anomalous star, and I'll guarantee that combination will get some kind of probe sent here. I don't know why Earth hasn't seen us—seems to me the explanation of 'miniature nebula' doesn't hold water—but that's more than strange enough to get people to come look."

"In the meantime, though," Pearce said, leaning back in her chair, "we've got plenty to do for our little colony." She looked over to Laura. "But I have to wonder, what if we are stranded here for decades or more?"

Laura straightened. "We'll have plenty of things to do, that's for sure. But if you mean 'can we survive as a group,' I think so. If we're talking a literal *colony* we have a very limited gene pool, but I do have a lot of genetic analysis and therapy capability and education, so it may not be quite as bad as it looks." She gave a wry smile. "I noticed your Tavana looking cow-eyes at Sakura already, and I think Caroline finds Xander rather handsome, aside from his recent phobic incident, so there will certainly be some interpersonal . . . events to consider.

"Individual survival, well, everyone here has had the basic longevity treatments. You have a fairly large supply of first aid nanos that I can reprogram and use to help clean out and update our existing medical nanos far more efficiently than my prior plan of trying to distill them out temporarily and recycle them. Depending on what we can do with all your cargo, there may be other things I can do. In any event, we should be able to survive for many decades here, maybe longer. Our long-term problems will likely be power generation—the nuclear reactors won't run forever."

"No," agreed Campbell, "but they'll last for a good long while. We'll work on finding new solutions for that problem before it ever becomes one. We can't keep from backsliding a little, but we can do our best to keep the brakes on."

"And keep the lights burning," Laura agreed. "All right, Sergeant Campbell. Welcome, all of you, to Lincoln Colony." She stretched out her hand.

Campbell took it, felt the strength of her grip. "Pleased to be a part of it, Ma'am."

Pearce's hand covered theirs, followed by Akira's. All four hands held together briefly before letting go.

Then Akira stood and poured out a tiny bit more of the wine. "A toast—to Lincoln Colony!"

Campbell laughed and rose to his feet, raising his cup as the others did the same.

"To Lincoln Colony!"

1636: The Kremlin Games   HC: 978-1-4516-3776-2 ◆ $25.00
    (with Gorg Huff & Paula Goodlett)   PB: 978-1-4516-3890-5 ◆ $7.99

1636: The Devil's Opera   HC: 978-1-4516-3928-5 ◆ $25.00
    (with David Carrico)   PB: 978-1-4767-3700-3 ◆ $7.99

1636: Commander Cantrell in the West Indies
    (with Charles E. Gannon)   978-1-4767-8060-3 ◆ $8.99

1636: The Viennese Waltz
    (with Gorg Huff & Paula Goodlett)   HC: 978-1-4767-3687-7 ◆ $25.00
    PB: 978-1-4767-8101-3 ◆ $7.99

RING OF FIRE ANTHOLOGIES
Edited by Eric Flint

Ring of Fire   978-1-4165-0908-0 ◆ $7.99

Ring of Fire II   HC: 978-1-4165-7387-6 ◆ $25.00
    PB: 978-1-4165-9144-3 ◆ $7.99

Ring of Fire III   HC: 978-1-4391-3448-1 ◆ $25.00
    PB: 978-1-4516-3827-1 ◆ $7.99

Grantville Gazette   978-0-7434-8860-0 ◆ $7.99

Grantville Gazette II   978-1-4165-5510-0◆ $7.99

Grantville Gazette III   HC: 978-1-4165-0941-7 ◆ $25.00
    PB: 978-1-41655565-0 ◆ $7.99

Grantville Gazette IV   HC:978-1-41655554-4 ◆ $25.00
    PB: 978-1-4391-3311-8 ◆ $7.99

Grantville Gazette V   HC: 978-1-4391-3279-1 ◆ $25.00
    PB: 978-1-4391-3422-1 ◆ $7.99

Grantville Gazette VI   HC: 978-1-4516-3768-7 ◆ $25.00
    PB: 978-1-4516-3853-0 ◆ $7.99

Grantville Gazette VII   HC: 978-1-4767-8029-0 ◆ $25.00
    PB: 978-1-4767-8139-6 ◆ $7.99

MORE . . .
ERIC FLINT

MORE . . .
ERIC FLINT

THE CROWN OF SLAVES SERIES with David Weber

Crown of Slaves   978-0-7434-9899-9 ◆ $7.99

Torch of Freedom   HC: 978-1-4391-3305-7 ◆ $26.00
                                     PB: 978-1-4391-3408-5 ◆ $8.99

Cauldron of Ghosts   HC: 978-1-4767-3633-4 ◆ $25.00
                                     TPB: 978-1476780382 ◆ $15.00

_____

THE JOE'S WORLD SERIES

The Philosophical Strangler   978-0-7434-3541-3 ◆ $7.99

Forward the Mage   978-0-7434-7146-6 ◆ $7.99
(with Richard Roach)

_____

THE HEIRS OF ALEXANDRIA SERIES

The Shadow of the Lion   978-0-7434-7147-3 ◆ $7.99
(with Mercedes Lackey & Dave Freer)

This Rough Magic   978-0-7434-9909-5 ◆ $7.99
(with Mercedes Lackey & Dave Freer)

Much Fall of Blood   HC: 978-1-4391-3351-4 ◆ $27.00
(with Mercedes Lackey & Dave Freer) PB: 978-1-4391-3416-0 ◆ $7.99

Burdens of the Dead   HC: 978-1-4516-3874-5 ◆ $25.00
(with Mercedes Lackey & Dave Freer) PB: 978-1-4767-3668-6 ◆ $7.99

_____

The Wizard of Karres   978-1-4165-0926-4 ◆ $7.99
(with Mercedes Lackey & Dave Freer)

The Sorceress of Karres   HC: 978-1-4391-3307-1 ◆ $24.00
(with Dave Freer)   PB: 978-1-4391-3446-7 ◆ $7.99

The Best of Jim Baen's Universe   1-4165-5558-7 ◆ $7.99